This Nearly Was Ours

ELIZABETH GUIDER

Foundations Book Publishing
4209 Lakeland Drive, #398, Flowood, MS 39232
www.FoundationsBooks.net

This Nearly Was Ours
By
Elizabeth Guider

ISBN: 978-1-64583-142-6

Published in the United States of America
Worldwide Electronic & Digital Rights
Worldwide English Language Print Rights

Dedication

Kenith George Trodd

For opening windows on the past, and imbuing those times with such rich music, video, and narrative that they resonate anew.

Contents

Part One

1939

A courtyard in the French Quarter 1939

Chapter One
NO ORDINARY TIME

At twenty-one, Claire Endicott believed things could only get better. The pall that lay over New Orleans would soon lift, like the fog did on damp winter mornings. Soup kitchens, boarded-up shops, and hobos huddled at street corners would give way to bright lights and big dreams.

The drab Thirties would dissipate; the fun-filled Forties would follow.

It would be their time. She and her classmates were told so by their esteemed professors at Sophie Newcomb, the city's foremost college for young women like themselves. Adventure awaited around the corner.

The only person who rolled her eyes at these pronouncements was Claire's best friend, Myra Kaminsky, who, as the smartest girl in the class, tended toward the skeptical. Plus, she was twenty-two and knew a thing or two more about life. Or so her classmates assumed.

"You must seize the day," their French professor oft proclaimed, gesticulating with a wide arc of her arm, as they plowed through Flaubert and Stendhal, whose heroines did not, be it duly noted, come out well in the end.

3

For us, it will be different, Claire believed. Fervently. With energy and ingenuity, she, and presumably Myra too, would be able to side-step what most parents wished for their daughters: marriage, children, a house to run.

Claire's made no bones about their preferences. She had heard her father sum it up to her mother barely a month before. "The ancients were rarely wrong, my dear. They believed marriage was for women what war was for men: the fulfillment of their true nature."

As usual, Mrs. Endicott had inclined her head in agreement. Her husband was steeped in the classics, boasted a law degree, and proudly displayed his medals for bravery. He was also pompous. How could she demur?

Making matters worse for Claire, they even had a suitor for her ready-to-hand.

Because of that looming prospect, she would have to deftly wrest her independence.

That's when serendipity stepped in.

She was performing household chores—admittedly not onerous ones—but to make them less tiresome, she switched on the wireless and danced around, dust cloth in hand. The most evocative song came on. She did not recognize the lyrics. She could not place the voice. It was like a silver bell. The words were of Paris: the rooftops, the cafes, the romance of the place.

Humming the refrain, Claire settled on a plan. An adventure in Paris.

Was she, as some who met her surmised, a spoiled, frivolous young woman? She refused to accept that. As for her blond hair, blue eyes, and pale skin, she did not object, but neither did she obsess.

What she did know was that if she did not move quickly after graduation, events would overtake her. She would find an engagement ring on her finger. Life would be over.

That's where Myra came in. Level-headed and resourceful, she had worked her way to where she was, encouraged by her parents. Her father ran a music store upriver in Alexandria; her mother taught at the local high school and ran the public library. Myra was accomplished before she ever got to college. She could name all the presidents, play the violin, and, like her parents, speak three languages.

Myra was, after all, Jewish, her people more worldly, more intellectual than her own, Claire had come to believe.

What did it matter that the two girls were a study in contrasts?

"There go the pretty one and the pensive one," more than one of their classmates quipped as the two crossed the campus arm-in-arm.

Claire did not care. She and Myra were bonded. They would conspire.

And, with her friend's help, Claire would convince her parents that nothing was more fitting than allowing her to spend the upcoming summer abroad.

For one thing, Myra herself would be there, albeit not specifically in Paris. She and her father would be in Germany on what she hinted was "a high-stakes mission." Something about an aunt trying to escape from some unpronounceable place and uncertain fate. If that adventure sounded dramatic, it probably was. Things abroad for the Kaminskys' people had become "tricky." Myra took Contemporary European History. She excelled; Claire muddled through World History. She learned a little about a lot of places.

If Mr. Endicott thought Myra was overly opinionated, forever fretting about the state of the world—"something of a Cassandra," he had once dismissed her—that should not be a hindrance to their traveling together.

Even if Claire was not the most studious in her class, she was a prospective holder of a degree, a feat achieved by only a select few young women in New Orleans.

"But enough of all this," she heard her father mutter to himself more than once. Higher education achieved, he expected his daughter to marry and get on with things. Her mother may not have agreed, but she deferred.

After all, they had their man in mind.

From their perspective, Richard Carrollton could not be more

5

suitable. Aside from his upright family and his own irreproachable manners, he emulated everything Claire's older brother Addison did, and managed to like Claire almost as well. Also, as her father saw it, Richard had "propitious prospects" within the Carrollton shipping business.

Childhood chums were one thing. Once Claire met Myra, all she wanted to do was be more like her. The challenges of being Jewish hardly registered with her.

If, in her view, Myra was destined to do something with her life, why shouldn't she too have ambitions? Simply put, Claire did not want life to pass her by, with no way to grab on to it.

That same winter afternoon she heard the song, Claire mingled with her parents' friends, which included the Carrolltons and two other couples, before the grown-ups sat down for supper and two tables of bridge. Card-playing at home had had something of a resurgence since the Crash of '29.

Part of the chit-chat pertained to her. "We hear you're soon to be awarded a degree," Richard's father, Harold, threw out, a hint of challenge in his voice. Claire nodded politely. "And then what?"

"This and that. Travel abroad. Europe and such." Her father's face twitched.

"If the world can hold itself together and other enticing things don't emerge closer to home." This last comment was tossed out by Richard's mother, Helen, a reproving expression on her face.

As soon as she could, Claire bowed out of the room, grabbed her satchel, and hopped on the first streetcar along St Charles Avenue. Impatient, she jumped off at Broadway, skirting the campus and winding her way down familiar cross streets.

Despite not having the presence of mind to change out of high heels, she picked up the pace down Pine Street to a rather rundown three-story where Myra had resided since her sophomore year. Along with a cat she found bedraggled during a rainstorm. There was a downpour threatening now, the kind that can turn sidewalks into rivers, ruining shoes, and turning ringlets into incorrigible corkscrew curls. A drizzle began right on cue.

When no one responded to the doorbell, Claire plopped down on the porch swing to await the arrival of any one of the tenants with a key. Ferns hung from the rafters, obscuring chipped paint. She rehearsed what she would say to convince Myra to intercede with her parents. Closing her eyes, she repeated, in her best French accent, "*Paris, Paris, j'arrive.*"

Ten minutes later, she heard footsteps on the wet pavement.

"Sorry," Myra said, bounding onto the porch with her book satchel and a shopping bag. There was a lilt in her step. "My tutorial dragged on," she said, making a circle with her free arm to suggest it wasn't her fault or that Professor Daniel Calhoun, the chair of the European Studies department, had much to impart.

"Since you are his favorite student, you may as well take advantage," Claire replied matter of fact. Myra quickly fished for her house key.

As soon as she switched on the light in the third-floor apartment, the cat, now known as Katzenjammer, leapt off the sofa and dashed to the tiny kitchen. The two young women followed, Myra immediately beating up an egg for the cat, Claire filling the tea kettle and scanning the counter for a match.

"Forget the tea. We need to celebrate," Myra suggested, flicking her hand toward the shelf where several wine bottles were poised.

"I should have brought over a bag of my mother's *hors d'oeuvres.* Silly me."

Soon they settled in the other room at what served as both a dining table and a study desk. The cat trailed behind, contenting himself at Myra's feet. The two friends clinked glasses. Claire took a deep breath ready to lay out her plan when she was abruptly cut off.

"No one else can know," Myra began, conspiratorial. "He told me today he plans to leave his wife."

Claire's nose twitched. She was flummoxed.

7

"As you'll remember, she is practically an invalid, and never goes out."

Whatever is she going on about? Claire wondered, exasperated.

Myra took a swig of the wine and tilted her torso back so as to gain a beat, or to backtrack. "After all these months, you really don't know?" she asked rhetorically, her tone disappointed.

Claire summoned the faces of the most handsome and popular seniors at Tulane University, a few of whom they'd gone to dances with uptown, or to the movies downtown, or merely to the campus library. If any were married, it would be news to her. Taking a sip of the wine, she tried to rearrange her clueless face into something more knowing.

"The thing is," Myra plowed on, "we are in love, and we want to be together, openly and freely."

Claire nodded, as though to indicate the sentiment made perfect sense, even if she had no clue who the object of her friend's affections was. She tried to accommodate the revelation that Myra had harbored, unbeknownst to her, a bonafide love affair. For an instant, an image of Addison flitted past, he having once or twice commented on her friend's poise or some such. But not enough to be... Besides, the man in question is married.

"Actually, Claire, I'm relieved it isn't obvious what is going on *entre nous*," Myra went on in a prim kind of way. "You will though recall last semester. All the extra work I did on the Weimar Republic. Not for the course itself but to edit essays for some anthology he is overseeing. Many long evenings, many things to share."

Myra's dark, depthless eyes seemed to focus on a faraway place as she confided this last detail. Not beautiful in the conventional sense, she did have an arresting face, Claire thought, the eyes enough to stop men in their tracks. At least one for certain.

Finally, it dawned on Claire that the affair was with Dr. Daniel Calhoun, whom she had by definition regarded as inexorably removed from his students, as formal in his role and aloof in his interactions as any Prussian general might have been. In class, he cut an unfailingly formal figure, (in mostly thread-bare three-piece suits), holding forth in stentorian fashion, and capping off his lectures by pulling out his pocket watch to check how much longer he must endure the company of clueless students.

Claire recalled the flash of a gold wedding band. Did Myra not notice or not care?

"But he is so much older, I mean, really old. Surely—" Claire blurted out.

"Well," Myra snapped, snootily, "he has much experience of life, if that's what you mean." She wiped her mouth with a dinner napkin and drew in another breath, before letting it out. Peeved. "Besides, I'm twenty-two and counting."

Ignoring this, that Myra was only a year older than she, (as if that justified anything), Claire came back with a new objection, asking what her parents thought of this, uh, dangerous liaison.

"In due course we shall tell them," Myra replied, ignoring the implied critique. She poured them both more wine. Is she actually sleeping with this man, and how ever long does it take to get out of a three-piece suit? Claire wondered but dared not inquire) "Right now, however, they have a lot on their minds, what with my Aunt Lena and all that."

Which reminded Claire why she had come over in the first place. But would Myra be venturing abroad now that she is, whatever she is: engaged, entangled, or more likely, out of her depth?

Whether from the wine or this bombshell revelation, Claire felt queasy. Enough to down the entire glass of water in front of her. "I know there's more to say about Professor Calhoun, I mean Daniel, but you said so yourself, time is of the essence."

Myra looked up, puzzled.

"I have something to announce as well." Claire's voice sounded less assured than she would like. "I am aiming to go to France for the summer and thought it would be splendid if we traveled together, for the first part of the journey. Then you could take care of getting your aunt out, or on to Paris, or whatever you'd have to do."

Myra's face slowly darkened. Claire rushed to finish. "I'm sure I can get recommendations or introductions, from Professor Truard and others, so I won't be wandering around the *Champs Elysées* aimlessly." She made this self-deprecating aside to lighten the atmosphere. To little avail. "There's the Sorbonne and all, but my parents would be immensely reassured if you and your parents were on the continent as well. At the same time, in contact. Things being so shaky over there."

Swirling the last of her wine, Myra appeared to parse this peroration. Claire did not intend for it to sound portentous or be so disjointed. But she had not bargained on the complication of an inopportune lover, an inappropriate one at that. However it came to be, her friend's liaison mirrored that old French play they had read in Professor Truard's class—: as in *dangerous*, Claire thought. If discovered, that liaison could jeopardize Myra's standing at the college as well as her personal reputation.

Myra upended the wine bottle, pouring the last drops into Claire's glass and setting it back on the table. She took a deep breath, a resigned one, before responding.

"You do know that Europe is in upheaval, that things could worsen if Hitler gets his way. For us—my father and me—this trip has nothing to do with pleasure, Claire." Her tone came across as patronizing. Claire resisted a retort. "It may even be dangerous. Subterfuge, even bribes, may be involved. But it is Aunt Lena's last chance to get out, we being her only living relatives. In theory, her paperwork should allow her to emigrate, especially if we are there to facilitate. However, it could be that—"

Claire cut her off. "You needn't be concerned, Myra. I would not dream of being in your way unless I could be helpful. I have my own money to spend, and, if we do get around to that Racine play this evening, I may come away with good marks in French class—(here Myra managed a smile, though more condescending than sympathetic)—and a convenient place to stay, on the Left Bank, walking distance of..." She trailed off, seeing that her argument landed like water off a duck's back.

Abruptly, Myra pushed back her chair. "How about fresh pears? They're at their juiciest and won't last. They go well with cheese."

While her friend fussed around in the kitchen, Claire rapped her fingers on the table in exasperation for being inept in getting her point across and superficial in arguing the point at all. Still, she could not help but think Myra exaggerated the severity of the situation in Europe, turning the process of getting a stamp on a passport into a drama of international intrigue. Perhaps her father was right: her friend was something of a Cassandra.

Re-entering, her jaw set, Myra positioned the bowl of slightly bruised pears at the center of the table. Without a word, she peeled her own fruit in one long golden ribbon, laying the skin deftly on one side of her plate. Claire fumbled with hers and had to wipe the juice off her fingers.

As they ate in silence, Claire suspected that, in Myra's eyes, she had been revealed to be a shallow young woman, bent on a pleasure trip to Paris while the whole world goes to hell. Still, she wanted to be charitable. Across from her sat a fascinating young woman, who had enthralled a man of means, and position, the two of them unashamed of breaking whatever bourgeois barriers stand in the way of their happiness.

Far be it from me to be petty or judgmental, Claire chided herself. She looked her friend's way, inviting her to elaborate.

Myra picked up one of the previous snipped threads. "Far be it from me to dissuade you, Claire. We each deserve to make our own way. But keep in mind that Papa and I plan to set sail from New York to Hamburg, cutting the time abroad as close as possible. The trip would be costly even in ordinary times. But these are no ordinary times."

"But that's how I too feel, Myra, and why I brought up Paris. Because these are no ordinary times, I do not want to waste them."

Chapter Two

DANGEROUS LIAISONS

Myra must have been dreaming to think Claire would grasp the import of her love affair. How could she, coming from such a strait-laced family? Their Uptown New Orleans home suggested the Endicotts were still living in the age of Queen Victoria or even the time of the Puritans! It wasn't only the gloomy furniture; to discourage vanity, there were no mirrors that she could spot in their home, not even in the bathroom.

The last time she was invited over for dinner, Claire's father made a performance out of carving the roast duck at table, while everyone sat around in rapt silence. Even Addison—graduate of Annapolis, a law degree to boot—remained ramrod-straight, as though in church. Eventually, with the bird bereft of meat on its bones, Mr. Endicott put down the knife with a flourish, nodding to his wife that the dishes could be served.

Myra half-expected them all to break into applause.

Once a blessing was recited, Mrs. Endicott inquired how her studies were progressing, to which Myra replied politely. She could have elaborated, but Claire's father interrupted, changing the subject to the governor's latest misdeeds in Baton Rouge. For an entire half-hour, he engaged only his son and Richard Carrollton, ignoring everyone else. If Addison were embarrassed by the rudeness, he did not let on: his father was clearly oblivious to his own condescension.

Like so many men are, Myra reckoned.

For her part, Claire seemed unperturbed, and unaware of the unfairness of it all. Clearly, the Endicotts never allowed their daughter to have much freedom. No male friends except for their sad-sack chum Richard, no strenuous sports, and regular churchgoing.

It was a wonder her parents allowed Claire to go to college, Myra concluded. Addison, meanwhile, had enjoyed more leeway in his life, likely to be assigned a high-level military command post in Washington.

Later in the parlor, Myra proceeded to ask Mrs. Endicott where she and her husband first met. The elder woman blushed, her hands fluttering, as she whispered it was at a dance, "Actually a ball, in Richmond, but so many years ago."

"How romantic," Myra replied, eager for details. But overhearing, Mr. Endicott stopped what he was saying to the young men across the room to shoot them a glance of disapproval. The women sipped their sherry. He flicked on the radio. Everyone sat attentively.

As was often the case, the news that evening was all Hitler, Churchill and Roosevelt: Hitler rattling his saber, the British prime minister warning of a gathering storm, and Roosevelt trying to calm the country's nerves.

Claire's mother lowered her head in dismay, her father rolled his eyes, and Addison and Richard looked distracted but said nothing.

"Serious people who know what they're about," Mr. Endicott declared, inclined apparently to give Germany the benefit of the doubt. No one dared object. He poured the two young men more Cointreau.

Myra wondered if he remembered that she was Jewish.

And yet, she had to sympathize with her friend. To her mind,

Claire viewed the world through rose-colored glasses, while she, on the other hand, prided herself on having her eyes wide open.

Better not to be harsh or churlish. If unlikely friends, better than none at all.

Thus, Myra had let Claire wax on about Paris that evening in her apartment. Something about a song she heard, which she swore crystallized what had been in her head—"for eons." Tears had pooled in her friend's eyes.

Eventually they turned to Racine, where they discussed the illicit love affair in *Phèdre* and the heroine's tragic fate at the hands of her husband. Myra read aloud a couple of the famous passages, advising Claire to memorize the verses. "Citing them with your best accent will impress old Truard," she said.

Finally, Claire circled back to ask how the *liaison*—she had fixated on that word—had begun. Myra obliged, at first with the intention of providing an abridged version but soon losing herself in juicy details, as though she were speaking about someone else.

Claire's eyes widened as the account progressed.

"I had agreed to drop over to their home, right off Broadway. You know, the street lined with chestnut trees, the potted plants on the porches."

She went on. Daniel suggested, almost casually, that they might get more done to ready her final thesis if they did so in his study, rather than in his poorly heated office. "Only a few suggestions I have, really, but better to hear them over a roaring fire, if that works for you, Miss Kaminsky."

Claire looked bemused. Myra hastened to defend her actions.

"I did so want to get the degree out of the way, and then audit a couple of graduate courses until time for the trip. Because of the way he said my name, with a hint of irony or intimacy or something, I decided to go over."

"What happened when you got there?"

15

He met her at the front door, a book in hand, and shook Myra's with his other, a beat longer than necessary. They walked through a well-appointed living room, with oil paintings in gilt frames, hard to know at a glance, if they were ancestors or historical figures. Gesturing for her to proceed him, they entered a study with bookcases lining every wall, a capacious oak desk in front of the only window, sofa and chairs in a grouping.

"I stood uncertain, Claire, but forced myself not to be so impressed as to exclaim over his books. He is an academic. What else would be in his room?"

Claire smiled inquiringly.

The professor asked Myra to sit at his desk and go over his comments. He went to get them something to drink along with a platter of cheeses. She nodded, not wanting to object to his offer.

"My wife, you know," he added, resignedly. He gestured with his hand to indicate upstairs.

"I did what he asked. In one place, he indicated I should spell out the rational for Germany's claims on the Gdansk region; in another, that I had overstated the animosity between the Polish government and the Jewish intelligentsia since the end of the Great War. Things like that are easy enough to fix or finesse."

Claire nodded, though she did not know where the Gdansk region even was. Myra had selected Modern European Politics for her final history unit; Claire had settled for a more general world history overview.

Within a few minutes, Daniel re-entered with a lacquered tray, a wine bottle and the platter of cheeses, which he brought not to the desk but to the coffee table in front of the sofa. Without a word, he retrieved two crystal goblets from a small cabinet and then bent down in front of the grate to slide another log on the fire. A few sparks landed on the hearth. When he straightened up, he turned and eyed her.

Flustered, Myra felt the need to say something. "These all look like reasonable requests, astute requests, I mean," she babbled, squirming in his leather chair. "I may need the library for a day or so to flesh them out, but by next week I should be able to turn it over to the department."

He responded with the slightest nod, as though used to having his professorial notes accepted graciously. Picking up the wine bottle, he studied the label and then expertly uncorked it. "Well then, that's that. I thought you might enjoy a hearty red. New Orleans is surprisingly cold in winter, wouldn't you agree?"

"Indeed," she managed, though she was trembling, but whether from the cold or the situation at hand was unclear.

"It's decidedly more comfortable over here," he said, keening his head to invite her to move to the sofa, feet away from the fire. And from him.

Things went from there.

Myra drank, mainly to steady her nerves, and he, for whatever his reason.

"I tried to think of something interesting to say, Claire—what opera was playing at the Saenger, what Roosevelt was saying about Lend Lease, things like that—but nothing came to mind."

In the silence, she strained to make out book titles in the nearby cases, hoping she might alight on something clever there to comment on. The light was too dim and her eyes too weak. Eventually, the professor turned halfway toward her.

"You do realize, Myra," he pronounced her name with studied emphasis, "that you are the most gifted student I have had the pleasure of coming across." His expression appeared wistful as he gazed into the fire, apparently scrolling through all his years at the university—how many she had no idea, but there were etched lines on his forehead—only to pause, perhaps, on some other, smarter young woman than she. Running his hand through his still thick but gray-speckled hair, he shook his head as though the effort to conjure anyone else were fruitless.

Her mind a blank, she stuttered a response to his compliment. "Not really," she blubbered. "There must be many who—"

"No, no," he countered, as he offhandedly traced his index finger along her arm. "You are the one, the only one who..."

Wiggling free, she made an effort to stand up. He rose too and herded her toward the door, backing her up against it. She could smell his breath, a woody scent. Then, without another word, he kissed her, his tongue insistent in her mouth, his body hard against her pleated skirt. She would have fallen over if he had not held her upright.

At that very moment, a voice from on high rang out. It was his wife, likely at the top of the staircase. "Don't forget, Daniel, cold chicken and fruit salad in the inbox. When you wish to take a break." Her voice was not feeble. Solicitous, yes, but not noticeably sickly.

For an instant, the professor and Myra both froze. But then, the sound of footsteps padding the floor above them only made Daniel more amorous. His left hand fumbled up her thigh, while his other searched under her sweater for her breast.

"Thinking it over, I should have resisted, Claire, or I should have fainted, but his ardor was contagious. I had never done anything remotely like this."

Bewildered, Claire could not think what to say at this recitation. She was breathing as hard as Myra was. Both of their faces were flushed.

Both too had been in that English Literature class several semesters back. That poem by Yeats, Myra suddenly recalled. She saw herself as Leda and Daniel as a god-like swan. She had swooned, he had his way with her. And things would never be quite the same.

She did not share that image with her friend.

Chapter Three

THE LAST VICTORIANS

"Perhaps we are too strict with her," Esther tossed out, letting the comment hang in the air. It was late, their bridge friends had departed, and husband and wife were both in the kitchen, she putting away the china and the wine glasses, he finishing up the butter-scotch pudding.

For a long minute, Edward did not respond. He rarely spoke abruptly, preferring to weigh whatever question his wife put to him before committing himself. He did not relish arguments, especially with his spouse. They spoiled his digestion and interfered with his sleep. Further, he was, he believed, rightly in charge of the household, as he had been in charge of his Brigade, however ragtag, during the Spanish-American War. At the time, he was only twenty-three, and, like the conscripts he commanded, had no idea what the struggle was all about. Useless to dwell upon it. He did find, however, that the fewer words he uttered, the more powerful their effect on his subordinates.

Silence in short could be a powerful weapon and obviate the need to take a stand one way or the other.

When the conflict with Spain was over, now Lieutenant Endicott had continued the practice, choosing his words sparingly, allowing each of them to carry a weight they might not otherwise have justified. Such a habit stood him in good stead throughout a twenty-year law career in Virginia, where he was known for his probity. And his good looks. His sexual dalliances up until then had been just that, brief encounters: he coming across as aloof to the young ladies in question, they as frivolous or gormless to him.

He was forty-four when everything changed. At the annual ball given by the Virginia Bar Association, his eyes snagged on one young woman. She was fairer than most of the others and moved more gracefully on the dance floor. He asked her to waltz. Although they barely exchanged three words over the violins, he registered the feel of her hand in his. Later, he got her particulars from the elderly cousin who chaperoned her—: "highly reputable family, nicely educated, exquisite manners, and, as you noticed, a beautiful dancer."

Three months later, he took the train to New Orleans and proposed, as custom dictated, to her father.

Edward looked over at his wife, who was now counting the silver before returning the pieces to their chest. Her movements were still graceful. As far as Edward knew, no piece had ever gone missing. Still, she remained absorbed in her ritual.

"Or perhaps we are not strict enough," he responded, their conversations cryptic with the passage of years.

A cloud flitted across Esther's face. She noted the clock on the wall. It was 10:15. Claire was presumably still out at her friend Myra's place, a fifteen-minute walk in the dark.

"She needs to start thinking about the future—Richard Carrollton could, you know, have his pick of the hens—and then what coop would our daughter alight in?"

Stiffening, Esther wanted to counter that life might consist of more than a hasty marriage to her childhood friend, but arguing, especially about such a ticklish subject as a daughter's future, seemed futile. She rarely won arguments with her husband. At best, they ended in a stalemate, like in chess.

If it had not been late and she tired, Esther might have opined that Claire rarely did anything to provoke their criticism or to make them worry. She was doing well in her classes at Sophie Newcomb and helped out at home without a murmur. If anything, it might be that she needed to make more friends or live on the campus so that she had more of a social life.

These thoughts too she kept to herself. Instead, she turned attention to their son.

"I forgot to tell you. Addison phoned this morning. Seems the Navy is gearing up for military maneuvers. Out in the Atlantic. He may be given command of something or other, but he couldn't say much on the phone. Likely won't get down here until the spring."

Edward took a final sip of the Cointreau the men had drunk with their cigars and set the glass down on the kitchen table. "All this, despite what Roosevelt pledged. Not to get embroiled in Europe's troubles. After all, Hitler has a point."

Ignoring this last comment, Esther went on. "By the way, he did sound wistful for home. Even asked after Claire's friend. You know. Myra, the one she studies with. Now and again." She instantly regretted this remark.

As if on cue, Edward sighed audibly. "You'd think our daughter could come up with..."

At that moment, they heard a key turn in the front door, followed by approaching footsteps.

When Claire entered the kitchen, her father still looked peeved, her mother disconcerted.

"Anything wrong?" she asked, looking from one to the other.

Both the Endicotts hesitated, Esther casting Edward a quick glance and then suggesting with her upturned palm that he had the floor. He snuffed out the last of his cigar—at sixty-four, he only ever smoked two, and only when they had guests—and cleared his throat.

"Your mother and I are concerned about your comings and goings. Late into the night, unaccompanied. Isn't that correct, Esther?"

"It would be better if—" she replied, meekly. Her shoulders were now hunched over, as though apologetic of her own height or weight in the world.

"I did tell you I was going over to Myra's, where I've been a hundred times. And where we're studying for mid-terms. She has to pass the algebra exam. I have to do well in French." Both parents looked unconvinced. Claire rolled her eyes. "As I've said before. Uptown New Orleans is hardly a den of iniquity," she wound up, with a touch of sarcasm.

"In case you haven't noticed, young lady, there's still a Depression, and it has thrown up riffraff..." Edward gestured to indicate his disgust with the down-and-outs roaming the streets.

"I have noticed, Father. Mother has been supplying the train hoppers with table scraps for years, right here on the back stoop."

When did my daughter become so rebellious a person, when Esther had over the years become so docile, Edward suddenly wondered. It occurred to him that college might not be the best thing for young ladies, so many aberrant views being put into their heads. Communism, women's rights, free love. Especially since he also had to pay for the privilege of letting his offspring be indoctrinated.

Edward closed his eyes and gathered in excess air, a prelude to delivering his final summation.

Claire shot a glance at her mother but received no visible sign of support from her. She braced herself.

"From now on, you will need to let us know your plans for the evening, and by whom you will be accompanied to and fro." He paused for a moment to let his decision sink in, then turned to his wife for back-up.

"As we were discussing earlier this evening, dear, with the Carrolltons, Richard is perfectly capable of, indeed amenable to..." Esther broke off, bewildered by the fuzziness of her thought, or the overall turn things had taken.

"That's ridiculous, Mother. Richard has his own life to think about. Figuring out what his father wants him to do in the shipping business. And besides—here she stopped, not sure what more she wished to share with her parents—besides, Richard is more amenable, as you put it, when Addison is around. The two of them... Oh, never mind."

"I'm sure the Carrolltons would be delighted to have Richard drive you around, when necessary," Edward stepped in to counter.

"Actually, I don't see why I can't drive Addison's car around town. He taught me how, and he isn't here. And I'd be able to avoid encounters with all the riffraff apparently wandering around," Claire threw out.

Sensing they were losing ground, and that their daughter had more ammunition for the argument than they themselves, they ignored this last salvo and suggested they all sleep on it. Tacitly proposing a truce, as it were.

In bed that rainy night in February, Esther tossed and turned, puzzled not so much by her daughter's newfound assertiveness, which she admired, and regretted that she herself could no longer lay claim to any, but more by her off-the-cuff comments about Richard. Presumed by all to be Claire's likely betrothed, and incontestably a respectable person, things about the young man nagged her. Things that she could not put her finger on, but that their son, perhaps their daughter too, may also have sensed. Or grown accustomed to and ignored.

Like, for instance, an afternoon back in '29—she recalled the year because the stock market had recently crashed, Edward had lost his civil service job, and the children were more underfoot than usual. No more violin lessons for Addison; no more ballet classes for Claire. At fifteen, her son fiddled around with ham radios and walkie-talkies; her daughter, at eleven, went back to her baby dolls. Living only blocks away, Richard often came over to play.

Before supper, she went upstairs to check on them, only to find both brother and sister in Addison's room, busily working on a new device. A Quaker oatmeal box was being fitted with wires. Across the hall in Claire's room, she found Richard, then thirteen, seated cross-legged on the floor. Several dolls formed a half-circle in front of him. He was dressing the smallest with booties and a frilly smock. She shut the door and stole away.

Do boys outgrow such predilections? Esther pondered this idea, staring at the ceiling. Next to her, Edward breathed rhythmically, with manly assurance. How on earth could she bring up such a memory to him, or to anyone else? So long ago it was. She wanted to believe that all boys are at some interval of time interested in girlish things, but a glance at her husband's face in the winter moonlight disabused her.

Rather, she counseled herself, she would cling to the notion that Richard Carrollton, cowed by his overbearing father and his imperious mother, was unusually sensitive and empathetic. Moreover, he was devoted to both her son and her daughter. Since forever. What could be wrong with that? she asked herself as she drifted off.

Chapter Four

THESE FOOLISH THINGS

Myra waited to take the bus home until late April, having told her parents that her courses had become so demanding she needed to study extra hard, ensconce herself in the library, and keep distractions to a minimum. She mentioned nothing about a man in her life.

Missing her as they did, the Kaminskys were disappointed but did their best not to let it weigh on their daughter.

"We will cook something special when you arrive. So many people have been asking after you—Mrs. Murkowski, the Wallensteins, and, naturally, Frederick," her mother said before she passed the phone to her husband.

He shifted gears. "You'll see it all from the bus, Myra, when you come. They're bulldozing the fields, setting up barracks. The entire county is being transformed in front of our eyes." Silence at the other end. He plowed on. "They know something we don't, which is all the more reason we'll need to get things underway as soon as we can."

She had no idea what they were talking about—Alexandria had always been a quiet town where nothing much happened—but it was getting late, and Dr. Calhoun had left her a note (unsigned for safety's sake) in the mailroom cubbyhole that he'd "drop over" this evening. He had never done that before, stuffing a note into her student's box, because it could be construed adversely. She had retrieved it an hour later and crumbled it immediately after reading the one line.

Interrupting her father, Myra repeated that a short visit home would not be a problem and rang off.

Had she lied? Arguably, she had misled them. From now until May 30 she would be coasting toward her degree. She had excelled at her mid-terms, excepting a modest grade in math. For his part, Dr. Calhoun had seen prudent to award her only an *A-* on her term paper, so as "not to raise any eyebrows," he told her.

As far as Myra could tell, their affair had remained secret, though they had made love more than once in his office on campus and even more daringly behind a row of carrels in the library. Taking risks excited him, and that in turn excited her. She was his chosen one, he would murmur during their lovemaking, and that excited her even more.

Still, Myra mused as the bus labored on into the Louisiana countryside, she would have relished being out and about, with Daniel by her side, showing him off at dinner in the French Quarter or during intermission at the Saenger Theater. Perhaps while enjoying a champagne toast, their eyes locked on each other, as other patrons looked on, curious.

The bus lurched to a stop. Several passengers disembarked. An old man, carrying a crate of chickens, got on and plopped down in the row in front of her.

Myra closed her eyes to revisit the ups and downs in the affair. Especially the down parts.

During a class discussion about the political crosscurrents in the country, Dr. Calhoun let slip that he and his wife had recently attended the opera, a performance of Wagner's *Siegfried*, where, he explained, a few folks had booed the supposedly Nazi-like plot overtones.

Why ever did you take her? Myra wanted to ask aloud in class but bit her tongue. She did, however, begin to wonder how much of an invalid Margaret Calhoun really was.

Then there was his recent visit to her place.

Myra had waved him inside the unlocked apartment door as she was finishing up the conversation with her parents. "Don't worry. I'll be on the 6:30 Greyhound, and if you're not there by 7, Papa, I'll take a cab. Tell Mother not to go to any trouble."

"Ah, I'm sure your parents will be delighted to have you home for a spell," Daniel said, matter of fact, as he hung his hat and briefcase on the rack near the door. He placed a heavy wicker basket on her dining room table, pulled out a bottle of cabernet, a loaf of French bread, a wedge of brie, and a tin of pâté.

After hanging up the phone, Myra turned and smiled, wetting her lips as she approached the table. She had not seen the professor all week. Barely looking up, he busied himself with the gifts.

"This will become hard to come by," he pointed out, his tone conspiratorial. He twisted the tiny key attached to the top of the tin of pâté. Deftly, he rolled the lid back. In response, Myra began to unwrap the cheese.

"Hard to come by?"

"If there's a war, many things will be in short supply. Most assuredly, luxury items from France or Italy. Wines too."

"But if we're not in it, how bad can it be?"

"That will depend. For one thing, on which side we come down."

The thought of a recent rally at Madison Square Garden, where newspapers said 20,000 Americans chanted *Heil Hitler,* flitted across her mind.

Up until then, Myra had not mentioned to the professor her family's plan to travel abroad to bring her aunt to the States. Having been designated his chosen one was surely enough to indicate where his political sympathies (as well as his personal affections) lay. In short, her absence for a few weeks abroad should, she kept telling herself, not only deepen his desire for her but also his sorrow for the plight of her people across Europe.

No need to spell all this out.

At the way station in Opelousas, Myra got off to stretch her legs and down a cup of coffee. It was acrid. Just as it had been when she had brought Claire home a year ago to meet her parents. The two young women had stopped in the same dreary depot and drank the same bitter brew.

Hard to admit but she missed Claire more than she had bargained for. Seeing her scampering to class a couple of times, she could not bring herself to call out. (The wariness between them had not entirely dissipated since she had confessed her affair and thrown cold water on her friend's Paris plan.)

About Daniel, Myra volunteered little when they did meet up, other than that he was working to free himself from his marriage. Claire had nodded, whether convinced or not it was impossible to tell. Once or twice, the two friends hopped a streetcar to take in a movie. Both of them had different reasons to need the diversion. They had laughed at *Ninotchka* and cried at *Dark Victory*. About the newsreels that came on before each feature—Nazi goose-steppers, tanks rolling into villages, refugees clamoring to board ships—neither knew what to say.

Myra's mind was wandering.

Fifteen minutes had passed. The bus driver was still flirting with the sallow-cheeked station clerk. She went back outside and got onboard. Whatever was going on with her friend and her proposed trip to Paris, she had not made enough of an effort to inquire. As soon as she got back from Alexandria, she would reach out. The thing with Daniel had become more complicated. She needed a sounding board.

The bus set off again but at a slower speed. It was growing dark. The roadway had narrowed, and ruts were everywhere. A lot of things out in the countryside seemed to be still in disrepair. The caged chickens on the seat in front of her began to cluck their displeasure. She closed her eyes and once again thought about Daniel's last visit to her lodgings.

While he uncorked the wine, Myra retrieved goblets from the credenza. The professor poured them each an ample glass. Rather than propose a toast, he motioned for her to sit down.

"There is something I need to tell you," the professor began, picking up the serrated knife she kept handy on the table.

Myra looked across at him, but his eyes were fixed on the French bread.

"It won't be possible," he announced, holding the knife aloft. He cleared his throat to elaborate.

"Not possible, that is, for us to spend the last weekend in May to celebrate your graduation," he hurried on.

"I don't understand. Why ever not? I have already—" she countered, flustered.

He cut her off. "Because things had slipped my mind—: a birthday celebration for Margaret's mother. It's an elaborate affair in the Garden District. Many distinguished guests. I would be missed."

Here he paused to catch his breath and downed more of the cabernet. His cheeks reddened but his lips kept moving silently, more words apparently struggling to get out.

As if she had been slapped, Myra tried to right herself after this blow and to martial her own defense.

So much time and effort had been spent on planning a weekend with her lover away from the college. Taking time from her studies, she had gone downtown to make reservations for a late-night dinner at the Roosevelt Hotel. She had booked a room, paid upfront, endured the smirk of a hotel clerk.

To Myra's mind, the tryst would be the most romantic thing they had done together, a harbinger of what she envisioned would be their life together. Meaning as soon as the professor extricated himself from his burdensome wife. From whom, she had intuited, he received so little, whom he no longer loved, who would be better off with proper caregivers—or, now that Myra knew more, back at home with her own mother. In the Garden District, behind a high wrought-iron fence where she could look out on banana trees and luxuriant ferns.

There were more reasons to be despondent. Only a week ago, Myra had spent a Saturday afternoon at Maison Blanche trying on gowns, settling on a blue satin affair, with an empire waist, better to enhance her breasts, and a flounce at the hem, in case they took to the hotel's dance floor. Surely, her lover would not have denied her a waltz.

Raising her eyes to Daniel's face, she searched for a sign of his disappointment, on a par with her own, but he was now slathering paté and brie on slices of bread. Her stomach churned. She would need—nay, demand—an adequate explanation.

Since he is preparing to leave his wife, why must he put in an appearance at his mother-in-law's when his young lover has her own milestone to celebrate? Surely, his presence there would be disruptive, even unkind. Surely, it was more civilized to make a clean break and not delay the inevitable.

Did she say all this aloud? As the bus to Alexandria jerked along, she could not remember.

The professor passed a plate with the heavily laden bread across the table and then refilled their glasses. Faint music crackled on the radio in the corner, a sad tune she could not identify. She did make out the words "*easy come, easy go.*"

Devastated though she was, Myra allowed Daniel to make love to her that evening, if for no other reason than that the act would take place in a bed rather than across a desk or up against a bookcase.

How had she—the smartest one in the Class of '39—let things come to this? she asked herself, as the bus threaded its way among equipment trucks and construction signs a few miles out from its destination.

Yet another blow fell after Daniel hurried to dress and depart that terrible evening. He forgot his briefcase.

Noticing it on the hat rack minutes later, Myra rushed down the stairs to catch him. She tripped on the last step. The contents of the briefcase spilled out. Among the scattered papers was a pamphlet. Not university material but rather something from a group called *Americans for Germany*. She sat down on the bottom rung, rubbed her swollen ankle, and read the first page. If he subscribed to this propaganda, she concluded then and there, the professor might well be described as antisemitic.

It occurred to Myra now that she might not be that different from the clucking hens in their cage: clueless. When the bus pulled in, she followed the old man off, wiping away a tear or two. Relieved that her father was nowhere in sight, she composed herself, and took a cab to the house.

Ilona Kaminsky did go to some trouble, having spent Saturday morning to make her Polish specialties, *pierogi* and *golabki*. In the afternoon, she baked apple strudel. She considered inviting Frederick, her daughter's most assiduous high school boyfriend, over for the dessert, but decided against it. She had recently grown leery of trying to mastermind a love life for Myra. Besides, from comments her daughter let drop of late, she suspected that another young man, likely a fellow Tulane student, had entered the picture. She would try to tease out more during this visit.

Visibly tired from the tedious bus trip, Myra ate ravenously, quick to say how much she had missed her mother's cooking. Po-boys and gumbo bought from shops around campus only went so far.

Throughout the meal, she bore up as best she could under the barrage of questions fired at her, dodging or deflecting where and when she could.

"Yes," when asked, she was grateful for that history professor who had taken her under his wing, having benefitted under his tutelage. "Perhaps he'll see fit to write a recommendation, if you should require it," her father interjected.

Reddening despite herself, Myra tried to remember what she had ever said on the phone about Dr. Calhoun, but could recall nothing that suggested anything out of the ordinary. Even so, thinking they had become unusually inquisitive, she tried to divert her parents' attention.

"So, dear, about your plans for graduation. Will there be a party or a dance? And a young man to take you?" her mother asked. "What about that, that protestant friend—Claire, it is, *yah*?" Mr. Kaminsky piled on. "Will she too be getting a diploma?"

"Yes, she will be there. With her parents, and likely her brother," Myra explained between bites of the cabbage rolls and sips of the Riesling her father had bought for the occasion. "Neither of us need bother with the party afterwards," she added, more vehemently than she intended.

Her parents exchanged a glance.

"It's not every day a daughter graduates from college, a prestigious one at that, and having done so with such excellent grades," her father went on, raising his glass, undisguised pride in his voice. "Of all the other families—the Wallensteins, the Edelmanns, the Bauers—correct me, Ilona, if I err: none can boast such a feat. For a daughter, that is."

"You are gifted, Myra—a chosen one," her mother chimed in.

This last remark rattled her. She had been bamboozled by Daniel's designation of her as "the chosen one," when clearly the designation meant only one thing to him. She strained to squelch the niggling thought of the professor toasting his mother-in-law in the Garden District, his wife by his side, both sipping champagne.

Myra drained the last of her wine and shook her head in an attempt to refocus.

"Like you said, Papa, I did see all those trucks south of town—Army vehicles, tractors too. What do you reckon they are up to?"

"The papers say they'll be training troops around here because it's far from population centers. There'll be plenty of jobs for local folks. God knows we all need that."

"Already they've made a difference. Bauer Dry Goods is adding a wing, enlarging their stock. Frederick is spearheading it; his father is taking a step back," Mrs. Kaminsky hastened to add, darting a glance at her husband.

"Your mother over-dramatizes. Heinrich Bauer will be back to man the cash register in no time. Still, Frederick is a good son. Came back home and stepped right up. Helping his parents, learning the business, going to synagogue..."

Myra emptied her water glass but did not comment. Frederick? She had not thought of him in ages. But parents, especially Jewish parents, never relent, she mused.

In the silence that followed, the Kaminskys could make out the sound of a car backfiring and the barking of dogs in its wake.

I have not become the kind of daughter they would have preferred, Myra suddenly imagined, the memory of making love to Daniel in the college library obtruding. She dabbed her lips with her mother's linen napkin, and thanked her, yet again, for the dinner.

As was their custom, the three retired to the living room for coffee and second, albeit smaller, portions of strudel. Myra inquired about business around town. Fortunately, things were picking up, the music shop was selling out of albums for the piano, wind instruments, even violins. The local high school where her mother taught would sponsor a prom this year.

Those subjects exhausted, Mr. Kaminsky switched on the radio, tuning it to a classical station. At that hour the signal came on strong.

Myra recognized the strains of a Brandenburg Concerto. She glanced at the front-page headlines in the newspaper on the coffee table. It was the German-American weekly that was printed in Shreveport. Mr. Kaminsky lit his pipe, propped his left leg up on a gout stool, and sat back in his armchair.

"Hard to fathom how the homeland of Bach could fall prey to a madman like Hitler," he said aloud. "And that our people are bearing the brunt..." he trailed off. And blew a couple of smoke rings.

In a few minutes, as the music wound down, Mrs. Kaminsky announced it was time. "No need to wait any further, Konrad. I'll retrieve it from your desk now."

Myra looked up, attentive.

"A letter from your aunt. Arrived last week, after a month in transit," her father leaned forward to confide. "The mail is a disaster over there."

"Ah," Myra replied, her enthusiasm for this European expedition having recently faltered, and now wondering if her father, with a foot that bothered him, was up to such a journey. She said nothing.

"It's partly in Polish, partly in German. In a jittery hand," her father continued *sotto voce* while his wife could be heard opening a drawer in the adjoining study.

Mrs. Kaminsky re-entered with the letter in hand. "You can pour over it yourself tomorrow, Myra, but best I read or translate bits," she said, pulling out two cream-colored sheets from a crumpled envelope with strange-looking stamps.

Myra nodded her assent, motioning her mother to sit next to her on the sofa and switching on the nearby lamp.

"Lena's handwriting is not what it once was—so cramped. And yet, such beautiful fingers, such a gifted pianist," she lamented, shaking her head as she stared at the pages.

"A miracle the thing got to us," Mr. Kaminsky added, tapping his pipe into an ashtray.

"*Daß ist richtig*," his wife agreed, using German when she wished to drive home a point. She fished her spectacles out of her smock.

Dear Ilona und Konrad,

I remain hopeful that this letter arrives to you there in Alexandria, a place I often dream of. I also pray that we will be together again, as things here in Germany are more difficult by the day.

If I were not beset by health issues, I might have made it onto the latest ship sailing with refugees—like me, those who qualified have no relatives here—to America. Sometime in May that ocean liner embarked from Hamburg. But alas, not with me aboard. I remain among acquaintances in the countryside, but even here...Still, I give lessons for my keep, and for my own sanity. Best I say no more.

If you are still able to make the voyage over and vouch for my acceptance in your country, this summer were ideal. Some whom I know are being sent to work camps—even from this out-of-the-way place, not far from Lübeck. One such camp is called Neuengamme, another is Sachsenhausen. Even the very young, and the very old.

Prefer you respond in Polish. Only essential information. To the persons and address on this envelope. They can be trusted. God speed.

Lena

Mrs. Kaminsky shook her head and placed the two sheets of vellum back in their envelope. "Breaks my heart, breaks my heart. My own sister," she murmured, wiping away a tear and handing the envelope over to her daughter.

"Perhaps it won't be so bad or get any worse," Myra said softly, patting her mother's arm. For an instant, she thought of Claire, who, for all she knew, was still planning to embark for Paris. Before long, it might not be safe for anyone, anywhere in Europe. "Whatever we need to do for Aunt Lena, I am ready to help. You can count on me," she said, before kissing her parents and tip-toeing upstairs. She slept fitfully, ominous images from the newsreels flitting through her head.

The next day Myra walked around town, noticing a lot more hustle and bustle, and more men milling about, none of whom she recognized. Although she found herself at one instance in front of Bauer Dry Goods, she did not go in.

To cap off her visit, she insisted that they all dine out at one of the town's Italian restaurants. "You always say how much you enjoy hearing laughter," she reminded her father, so they settled on Antonio's, one of the oldest eateries in central Louisiana, likely to be crowded, and noisy.

Myra wasn't wrong about the place. Men in military uniform occupied several tables. The Bauers, Wallensteins and Edelmanns sat at one of the round tables, nodding when the Kaminskys entered. None of them came over to speak.

After a couple of glasses of Chianti, her mother asked the obvious. "So, my dear, after the situation with Lena is resolved, what are you planning to do?"

"To translate from your mother, is there a young man in the picture? Must be many to choose from in New Orleans, as well as from here," her father added, redirecting the conversation.

Myra bristled. There was no way on earth she'd ever be able to justify this thing with Daniel. If it were still a thing. Still, their presumptions irked her.

"I did not go to Sophie Newcomb for four years to find a husband, Mother. I will look for a job—teaching or whatever," she retorted, waving her hand in the air to suggest myriad options, even if she could not conjure any. Daniel Calhoun had taken up too much of her mental space.

"That makes eminent sense," her mother said sweetly, stealing a glance over at the Bauer table. Frederick was gesturing animatedly to a young woman seated across the table from him.

Chapter Five

RITES OF PASSAGE

The two friends met up at the fitting for cap and gown on a bright spring morning in May.

Claire thought Myra looked puffy, no doubt attributable to her mother's Polish pastries; she required a size larger than usual. Myra thought Claire had shed a pound or two, probably from fretting over French and German exams; she went down a size.

Like the three-dozen other graduating seniors in their Newcomb class, they presumed they would do well enough to pass, if not excel, at their finals. What most of these young women would do in the aftermath of college was not fuzzy. A good portion had become betrothed in the last few months, and it was obligatory to ooh and ah over the diamond rings flashed about.

Ever polite, Claire did so. Myra pretended to be adjusting her cap to sit correctly now that she was putting her hair up in a bun.

If anyone noticed her lack of enthusiasm for the good fortune of the affianced, no one said a word. By all accounts, Myra was different, and, of late, decidedly distracted. Besides, she was Jewish, and, inarguably, the smartest one in the class of 1939.

No one knew that better than Claire, but she had concluded that even the smartest of women could behave like a fool, and over a tweedy professor who appeared more attached to his pocket watch (and to his long-suffering wife) than he was to her friend. She had largely kept her opinion to herself.

In the final sprint to a diploma, the two friends recommenced to study together in earnest. Only a couple of exams remained for Claire —the advanced math course would be a cinch; French drama of the seventeenth century and German literature of the nineteenth century were different matters. She needed her friend's familiarity with the texts and the likely questions she'd have to answer in the respective languages, no dictionaries allowed. For Myra, the only remaining hurdle was to come away with a decent score in algebra, and for that she needed Claire's expertise with equations.

They did not discuss their respective history courses: Myra's advanced seminar on Contemporary Europe, Claire's generic course on World History. Neither brought up Dr. Calhoun's name, even though he taught both subjects. Rather, the two huddled together in the library several times a week, remaining so late one evening that Claire felt obligated to call home.

"They've decided there's too much riffraff on the streets, so I'm now obliged to have an escort at night. Can you believe it?" she told her friend, her tone defensive.

Twenty minutes later, Addison, who had recently flown in from Washington, showed up in his Ford Tudor. To their surprise, he got out with alacrity and helped both his sister and Myra into the car. Once inside the vehicle, the two girls could smell his cologne. It was 10:45 at night.

"No, no, I don't mind at all, Myra, giving you a lift. Too dangerous for damsels to be out walking at this hour. So Mother tells me." He had a way with banter, she remembered. "Plus, we have to pay you back for helping my sister actually get a degree," he went on, jokingly.

In the back seat, Claire rolled her eyes; in the passenger seat, Myra laughed.

"If you must know, Addison, we trade off. Claire tutors me with algebra; I help her with French and German. We muddle through the rest on our own."

After they drove a few blocks down St Charles Avenue and missing, (oddly or on purpose), the right turn onto Broadway, Myra eyed her friend's brother more closely. In profile, he shared Claire's good looks. His jaw line though suggested a confidence his younger sister lacked. That French expression, *bien dans sa peau*, fit him, she decided. She wondered how much older he was and what his job with the Navy entailed.

"So, Addison, is there going to be full-fledged war in Europe?"

He appeared to weigh the query until he pulled up in front of the boarding house on Pine Street. Killing the motor, he swiveled in his seat to face her. Such a deliberate person, she thought.

"It does look that way. Hitler seems bent on taking over whatever territories he can, and no one seems up to stopping him." He hesitated, then added, "Your people, in particular, need to do whatever they can to get out of there. From what we've learned—"

"I know," she interjected. "My aunt, among them. We're trying to help her. If we can locate her in time."

"Hmmm," he replied, not wanting presumably to say anything further to upset her.

Myra gathered up her satchel and fiddled with the car door. "Call me tomorrow, Claire. We'll go over our notes one more time," she said, her tone brisker.

Brother and sister watched as Myra climbed the steps to the front door and, once inside, flicked off the porch light. Neither sibling spoke on the way home until the car was parked at the curb.

"Looks like you made a worthwhile friend, Claire, whatever Mother and Father think," he remarked, his tone more sober than usual. She did not know what to make of it.

Graduation went off with the obligatory pomp and circumstance on a balmy Saturday morning in late May. Two women received a *cum laude* designation with their degrees; Myra was the sole student to attain a *summa cum laude* commendation.

The Kaminskys, careful to contain their excitement over their daughter's achievement, were introduced, briefly, by Claire to the Endicotts, and to the Carrolltons. Several of the professors, including Dr. Truard and the math instructor, Dr. Penley, congratulated both young women and chatted with their families. Dr. Calhoun milled about, consulting his pocket watch nervously. Myra made no signal for him to approach. If anything, Claire thought, she snubbed him.

Over the luncheon buffet for graduates and guests, Mr. Endicott found himself seated next to Myra. "So, Miss Kaminsky, we understand there's a graduation dance tonight on campus. Richard Carrollton, whom I believe you have met, is squiring Claire. Who might be the lucky man escorting you?"

Myra flubbed a reply, "No one actually. I'm returning with my parents to Alexandria. I haven't seen them, really, often enough, you know, these four years," she soldiered on, "while dances, well, I've been to quite a number of them."

For once, Edward Endicott was at a loss for words, wondering if the young woman's race meant no Tulane man would deign to take her out. Or, if she were simply too smart for her own good. He turned to his eggplant *étouffée;* she picked at her shrimp salad.

In the car going home that afternoon, however, he circled back to the subject, Claire, Addison and Richard chattering in the back seat, and Esther next to him flipping through the program with the pictures of the graduates.

"Turns out, Myra Kaminsky, *summa cum laude* notwithstanding, has failed to entice any young man to take her to the dance this evening," he trotted out, trying to keep his tone neutral.

Claire took the bait. "That's not what happened, Father. It's more complicated than that."

"College is a fine institution," he further opined, ignoring her retort, "but for women it can create more problems than they can easily—"

"Really, Edward. Newcomb is providing rare opportunities for these women. Dates to dances are not the only thing they can now aspire to," his wife jumped in, indignant.

"Actually, that was the very place that I met you, dearest. In that Virginia ballroom. Something to be said for keeping to the proper steps, so to speak."

Esther shook her head but let the remark pass. The three young people exchanged looks, as if to say those two are woefully out-of-step, even with each other. It was useless to correct them.

Late that afternoon, while he could hear Claire starting her preparations for the dance, Addison marched to the upstairs hall phone and rang Myra. No, she had not, in the end, traveled back home with her parents. But yes, she would be happy to go to the dance with him. She would even wear the blue satin gown that could not be returned to Maison Blanche.

By the middle of June, Claire wrapped up her first week at a job on the Rue Royale, neither of her parents enthusiastic, but neither outright opposed. What could be wrong, she had argued, with working the cash register at the city's most prominent antiques store? "She wants to be independent? Let her find out how hard that might be," Mr. Endicott had commented to his wife, not his daughter. Besides, Richard, her supposed fiancé, would be traveling all summer, Addison was barely around, and her college classmates had scattered.

It being a glorious afternoon, and missing the camaraderie of college, Claire was eager to join Myra at Café du Monde to catch up, and though she would not confess to it, to impress her friend with her newly confident self.

The place was half-empty. Several work-a-day couples, a group of elderly ladies in straw hats, and a solitary young man with a news-paper spread in front of him were the only other customers seated outdoors. He looked their way when the waiter approached to take their order.

"My goodness, so business-like. The linen suit, matching heels, nail polish," Myra immediately commented.

Claire beamed. "It's not life-changing," she said in self-depreca-tion. "But it's a job. They pay me. Not much, but it keeps me from twiddling my thumbs, or being moody all the time."

Myra nodded, seemingly familiar with the sentiment. But soon her face fell. She closed her eyes and puffed on a Lucky Strike.

"Why the cigs all of a sudden?" Claire soon asked, as Myra blew a smoke ring. An ashtray already held a couple of stubs. "You, of all people. Miss *summa cum laude*," she teased, giving her friend a side-ways glance.

"You didn't do badly yourself. Your parents must be pleased." Claire nodded noncommittal. "In case you didn't know, Addison takes your side. Thinks it's high time your parents gave you leeway, even if the Paris thing—(here she faltered, not knowing if she should broach such a sore subject)—is no longer an option."

Claire nodded her assent. "Yes, forget Paris. Dr. Truard—I'm supposed to call her Lucille now—came over shortly after graduation and waxed lyrical about the charms of the place. She overplayed her hand."

"What do you mean?"

"My father scowled as she went on, extolling the virtues of a Parisian summer and the personages that she would contact on my behalf."

Claire shook her head at the memory of the scene in their dining room, the spinster in full Gallic gesticulation after a single glass of sherry, her mother and father exchanging dubious glances. "If that performance didn't dissuade them, there was that recent Fireside Chat. Unwittingly, Roosevelt convinced Mother that Europe is on the verge of catastrophe."

The two friends paused while the waiter brought their coffee and beignets, along with the bill. Handing him two dollars, Myra told him to keep the change.

The young man with the newspaper signaled the same waiter and placed a second order.

"*Mais, ça suffit*," Claire said, thinking it best to change the subject. "At least they let me take this job at Rothmann's. The wealthy still have money, and they love antiques. Besides, it's something to do until I figure out what comes next..." She faltered, staring off at the horse-drawn carriages with sightseers atop.

In the pause that followed, they both stirred sugar in their cups and took a few sips. Myra maneuvered the warm beignets out of the bag and placed one on each plate.

"Way too much powdered sugar on these things, don't you think?" Claire said off-handedly.

Out of nowhere, Myra teared up.

Claire's jaw dropped. "What's wrong, Myra? Did I say something?"

"No, silly." She sniffled, reaching into her pocketbook for a handkerchief. She blew her nose, dabbed at her eyes. "I did not want to bring this up. It's too awful..." She averted her friend's puzzled gaze and gulped more coffee.

"What are you talking about, Myra?"

"You can't tell?" She darted her eyes around, then leaned across the table. Lowering her voice, she whispered, "As my mother would say, it's about 'the curse.'" Even more flummoxed, Claire gestured with her hand to elicit more. "I now know, menstrual periods are not a curse: the curse is *not* having one's period."

"What—are—you—saying?" Claire asked, it slowly dawning on her what the mystery must be.

"I'm pregnant—and I have to figure out what to do. Before I have to go to Germany with my father, who would surely die, after killing me, if he found out." At this point, Myra broke down, her sobs audible.

Claire looked around for the waiter. Not spotting him, she hurried inside the shop for a glass of water. The young man at the nearby table glanced her way as she passed.

"Drink this," Claire ordered, handing the water to Myra before sitting back down.

In a few minutes, the rest of the story spilled out. Including that Daniel, when informed of his lover's predicament, insisted that he wanted none of it.

"He said to my face that he is ill-prepared to leave his wife or to bring up what he had the audacity, or obtuseness, to refer to as a foundling." Myra spit out this last detail with unaccustomed bitterness.

Claire's mind began to race. If the professor washed his hands of the problem, the two of them would need to connect with the health services at the university. Myra simply could not be the first young woman who had gotten herself into such a mess. She had heard, but never paid mind to, hushed conversations about unmarked door fronts in Storyville or across the river in Algiers. If the college health services could not legally be called upon to assist, they might be willing to provide some addresses.

"Don't worry, Myra. We'll figure this out. There are people; there are places." Claire swirled her wrist as though to suggest she knew all about what it took to obtain an illegal abortion in the only officially Catholic state in the country.

"You do understand, right, Claire? Not only can Daniel not be counted on, but I can't let my parents down—and this problem is not going away. The clock is ticking."

Claire reached over to squeeze her friend's arm.

Eyes soon dried, beignets only half-eaten, the two got up to leave. As they weaved their way among the now crowded tables, Claire's eyes fell on the young man still seated alone. Glancing down at his table she saw not only the *Times-Picayune* but, tucked inside, another newspaper, headlines in German. Fleetingly, she took in his angular face—he looked drained, if not wary.

Without thinking, she paused to address him in German. "*Guten abend*," she blurted out before Myra tugged at her sleeve. They needed to get uptown to Sophie Newcomb before the offices closed.

Chapter Six
VOYAGE TO NOWHERE

Between cigarettes, Tomas noticed the two attractive young women deep in conversation at the coffee shop. If it had been a different time and he not so disoriented by recent events, he would have smiled their way. Perhaps spoken. After three years in the States, he was fluent in English, though a slight Teutonic accent was detectable to those with a good ear.

Still, to watch two young women mull mundane things in their lives was a salve.

He decided to linger that June afternoon, and to make an effort to revel in his surroundings. After all, he had been on something of a roller-coaster. Even now, he barely had the wherewithal to do anything but go through the motions: wake up, get dressed, go to work, and somehow keep it together. He had no one with whom to share his fears on the subject that obsessed him.

When one of the other workmen at the cabinetry shop on Esplanade Avenue asked him, "Why ever go to Havana, man?" Tomas could summon only the barest of explanations. "I went to meet an old family friend who was to arrive there, but it didn't work out." He left it at that. No one inquired further.

He did not say that his trip to Cuba left his stomach clenched, his heart broken, his hopes dashed.

But every day since he returned to New Orleans, he scoured the papers for news that the snags that prevented a thousand Jewish refugees from reaching safety in the New World had been ironed out.

Nights were worse. Images of the ship docked in Havana bobbed in his head. All those people, hanging on the rails, waving, or shouting, or, in a few cases, trying to hurl themselves overboard. To freedom, or, if not, to drown trying, it was said.

Among the desperate passengers was presumably his childhood friend and first love, who—thanks in large measure to a mutual childhood friend back in Germany—had gotten onto that coveted list.

Having read of the ship's proposed route across the Atlantic, Tomas had scrambled to get himself to its port of call. It was in Havana, the papers said, that passengers could disembark to meet friends or family before eventual transfer to the United States. There, if their documents were in order, they would be allowed safe haven.

Instead, nightmarish scenes unfolded as soon as the vessel docked at Havana Harbor.

Tomas and others found themselves paddling in rowboats out to the moored ship, kept at bay by armed security guards on the ocean liner, no one onboard allowed to disembark. They circled the ship even through the night, searchlights on the vessel probing the waters to curtail any intrusions.

Still, Tomas and others were bent on doing whatever they could to signal their loved ones. And, to mime signs of hope that somehow, whatever snafu had been thrown in the refugees' way by the Cubans or by the Americans, they would soon be able to touch *terra firma*, and embrace their loved ones. The refugees' costly letters of transit would be duly stamped; they would then set sail to their final destination in New York harbor.

On his second day in Havana, Tomas was lent binoculars to scan the rows of passengers. Around noon, he thought he had spotted his friend among the crowd on the top deck. In any case, a young woman with flowing blond hair, pressed against the railings, peered anxiously at the crowd on the dock and at the people in skiffs.

Standing precariously in his own little rowboat, Tomas held up a welcome sign he had concocted in his hotel room the night before. In big letters: *KATRIN: Ich bin Tomas Steinberg. Wilkommen aus Amerika!*

Eventually, the fair-headed young woman began to jump up and down. She cupped her hands around her mouth and shouted, but the deck was too high up, the ship too far away from him to make out her words.

Still, it must have been she; and she must have realized it was he.

Tomas went into Havana proper that evening and drank himself silly.

More days passed. No person from onshore was allowed to embark; no passenger to disembark, except, rumor had it, one man aboard who was deathly ill. Another, it was bruited, had jumped overboard and drowned.

Despite his scant Spanish, Tomas soon grasped enough to know that blandishments of all kinds, and bribes of ever greater amounts between government officials, had become futile. Too much corruption among the Cubans; too much dithering by the U.S. State Department.

The captain of the *St Louis,* one Gustav Schröder, Tomas learned, had himself been spotted at the rails a few times, his face lined with fatigue, his expression stoic. He was reportedly doing all he could to keep order on the ocean liner, and the passengers from despairing.

But after a week of frantic but fruitless negotiations, Tomas read the outsized headline in the Cuban press: "Setting Sail!" In short, the *St Louis* would not be allowed to disgorge its human cargo. On the contrary, it would be obliged to return to Hamburg, its original port of embarkation.

Not everyone around him grasped the import of that decision, but Tomas did. Jews across Germany were being rounded up and sent to work camps. Others simply disappeared. His own parents—if sporadic reports could be believed—were still living surreptitiously in the countryside not far from the Baltic Sea.

For the first time, Tomas realized his own good fortune. He had been blessed with parents who insisted when they did that he abandon his homeland and make his way in America. "While it is still feasible for us Jews, my boy," his father, a professor of engineering, had urged him. His mother, through tears, had seconded the plan.

Tomas was twenty-three at the time, a newly minted architect, but, like his father who had been ousted from his academic post, with no prospects at home. He had sailed for New York in 1936, soon making his way to a German enclave in Texas called Fredericksburg. There, he found work, but when the desolate expanse and the dust in his throat became too much to bear, he hopped a train headed east. Along with some hobos, he jumped off at New Orleans.

That balmy city surrounded by water reminded him of the seductive European seaports that his family frequented in summers long past. He was determined to stake a claim there.

And for the brief time that he stood on that pier in Havana, he hoped to share that new home in Louisiana with a girl named Katrin.

During those final hours in Cuba, Tomas and others rowed in the wake of the departing liner as far as the Cuban authorities would allow. Of all things, a last-minute rumor flew. Passengers would be released onto a nearby atoll once used as a penal colony. Cheers went up from the makeshift fleet of tiny rowboats. Tomas wiped away tears of joy.

Hours passed, but then to general dismay, the ship skirted the isle, picked up steam, and receded toward the horizon. Several hard-bitten reporters on the story cursed in anger as the ill-fated vessel vanished from sight. Others bowed their heads in despair, Tomas among them.

Distraught and benumbed, he somehow made his own way to the Florida Keys and on back to New Orleans.

The trials of the *St Louis* did not end there. Whatever Captain Schröder's orders were from back in Germany, he idled the vessel offshore of Miami for several days, Tomas learned from the papers, until, that is, the U.S. government washed its hands of the matter. Definitively.

The day-old *Picayune* in front of him that June afternoon at the Café du Monde reported that the ocean liner had set course toward home. The German-American paper Tomas bought that same morning on Canal Street supplied additional details. Feverish negotiations were underway abroad to convince European countries to accept a quota of the desperate passengers upon their return. Four nations raised their hands.

Tomas tried to envision Katrin safe in Holland, Belgium, or France—or even better, in England. His coffee now cold, he ordered another, along with a beignet. When had he last eaten a proper meal? He could not recall.

One of the young women at the table nearby, the one with dark hair, was suddenly sobbing. Her blond friend was trying to console her. Whatever could two pretty girls enjoying the afternoon sunshine have to cry about, he wondered.

Averting his gaze, he focused on the paper once again. Apparently, once apportioned to the three willing European countries, the refugees would be out of harm's way. Unless Hitler continued to... Tomas did not want to dwell on that.

As for Katrin, the only way to find out anything more about her fate, he surmised, would be through their childhood friend. That would not be easy, or arguably advisable. To Tomas's chagrin, Hans Durst had parlayed his degree in engineering or aeronautics (he wasn't sure which) into a career in the military. Did that mean Hans was a Nazi? He had no idea.

His friend's last correspondence, indicating Katrin's inclusion in the ship's manifest—and extolling his own efforts on her behalf, "despite risks to my own standing"—was written on German Navy letterhead.

Chapter Seven

QUITE A PICKLE

The visit that same June evening to Sophie Newcomb's health services unnerved both Myra and Claire, starting with the sour nightshift nurse.

"Seems you've gotten yourself into a real jam," the woman offered, eyeing Myra from head to toe, especially her middle portion. "What does the young man have to say for himself?"

"He's, he's not involved in this," Myra stammered, eyes lowered.

"Surely was at some point..." the nurse countered, "*involved.*" There was a hint of glee in her voice.

Unaccustomed to being shamed, neither of the two young women could think what to respond.

In the interval, the nurse shuffled through papers on her nearby desk, then wiped her glasses and slid them back on her nose. She shook her head as though to indicate that the standards at the college had sunk to a new low.

It was left to Claire to ferret out what she could on behalf of her friend. Perhaps the woman was disagreeable because she had to work the night shift, as the college had largely closed down for the summer. Few students left to help, or to excoriate. *Portia Pepper, RN*, the nurse's name tag read.

"What would you suggest we do, Nurse Pepper, since time is of the essence?" Claire asked, aiming for an unemotional tone. Briefly, she considered mentioning that Myra was alone in the class of 1939 to have attained *summa cum laude* status, but something told her such a revelation might be counterproductive.

Sighing audibly, the nurse appeared to consider the question. A clock on the wall ticked loudly. Myra began to squirm.

"Given your years here, you should be aware that the college does not condone and could not legally help any of our, mostly proper, young ladies—a category into which neither of the two standing before her presumably belonged—terminate an unwanted pregnancy," she divulged, her tone condescending.

Myra's lower lip quivered.

Nurse Pepper then clucked her tongue and crossed herself as though in disgust that the world was sinking ever further into a morass of immorality.

Anger, however, was rising in Claire's chest. "My friend is not the first person in this college to be in this position," she retorted. "In our four years here, several of our companions have—. Surely, you could advise us."

"Well." Nurse Pepper sniffed. "It is no secret that there are places in and around the Quarter. A few dare put their shingles out. I suspect, since you're both so smart now, you'll be able to—"

"Yes, I suspect we will be," Claire snipped, pulling at Myra's arm, and walking her out. Without another word. She did not regret her tone or her exaggeration. She felt invigorated.

In the end, the two found themselves on an unprepossessing street in Storyville, a rundown section of the city adjacent to the French Quarter in which neither had ever set foot. Although a cloudless

Saturday afternoon in late June, Myra was shivering, her head lowered, a floppy hat pulled down over her bun.

To compensate, Claire marched clear-eyed and purposeful, scouring for "an unmarked door with chipped paint and a door knocker shaped like a gargoyle."

That's what Bernice, one of the other young women who lodged in the same house on Pine Street as Myra, had told them. Vividly. Seems one of her roommates had suffered the same trouble not a year before—Myra had sensed a crisis unfolding on the apartment floor below but had not considered it her business. Fortunately, she remembered the episode and went downstairs in desperation several days after the visit to the college health services.

Willing to help, Bernice would have gone on to describe the medical ordeal itself, but Myra shushed her. "I don't need to know the details; I simply need to have it done. That's all there is to it. Besides, I'll have Claire with me, like your friend had you," she replied.

"Take cash," Bernice wound up. "Plenty of it. Dr. Spindle is his name."

The walk through the questionable streets to find the doctor's office was unnerving enough. The rusted shingle hanging lopsided outside read:

Dr R Spindle
Obstetriks & Ginecology

The spelling did not instill much confidence in either young woman.

After glancing around, Claire pressed the bell. When no one responded, they pushed the creaky door open and entered a dank-smelling hallway. Exactly what one would expect, Claire thought. She squeezed Myra's hand. It was clammy.

An assistant of sorts—graying hair gathered up and held precariously with bobby-pins—jotted down Myra's particulars, which were limited to her age, her last period, and any recently ingested pills. After glancing at the responses, she jerked open a drawer and pulled out a tattered cigar box.

"That will be $115 upfront—for the operation. Any complications will be extra." Neither asked what those latter might be.

Gesturing for Myra to sit back down, Claire unsnapped her pocketbook and handed over a hundred-dollar bill and a twenty. And stood there waiting, expectant.

"We don't make out receipts for this service, miss, and we don't make change no how," the woman said in a tone that suggested weariness with such requests. She stuffed the bills into the box and slipped it back in the drawer.

"I see. But..." Claire trailed off, unsure what else might be relevant or knowable in the circumstances.

The woman raised her eyes to Claire's face. "You too might want to sit back down. The doctor will see your friend as soon as he's available."

Before long, the woman hoisted herself out of her squeaky chair, she was more overweight than her gaunt face suggested, and waddled into a back room with the scribbled notes she had taken.

A clock with a pendulum ticked away on the wall opposite the two young women. It was already a few minutes past four. Voices could be heard coming from the adjoining room, but the words were muffled. Something about anesthesia running long—or low.

To steady her nerves, Myra took deep breaths. Claire picked up a days-old *Picayune* from the coffee table in front of them and made an effort to concentrate on the news.

The governor was preparing to speak at a farmers' rally in Baton Rouge; a streetcar on Claiborne Avenue struck a pedestrian and his dog on the tracks; a ship with Jewish refugees was barred from docking at U.S. ports and was headed back to Germany. Claire thought better of mentioning this last item to Myra. It was too distressing, especially with the aunt still stuck over there.

She flipped to the society pages, stopping on a squib about the Carrolltons. Seems Richard Carrollton would be shadowing his father on a tour of facilities upriver, as far north as Cincinnati. "As a new executive in our legal department, my son needs a first-hand look at our different locales, especially since business is newly brisk," Harold Carrollton was quoted as saying.

Had Richard mentioned the promotion at the graduation dance? If so, it had not registered.

"Anything interesting?" Myra inquired, her breathing again shallow, her left leg restless.

"Nothing much. A streetcar ran over a man trying to get his dog off the tracks. The man died. His dog survived. But only with three legs."

Myra winced but said nothing. The clock ticked on. A faint smell of antiseptic wafted into the room. Then out of the blue, she turned to her friend. "You do think this is the best thing, the only thing to do, right? Otherwise, my parents, my life. And Daniel was so horrible about it. I mean—"

For the first time since their meeting at the Café du Monde, Myra began to tear up.

Claire handed her a handkerchief. "Everything is going to work out," she offered as convincingly as she could. She had vowed not to bring up Professor Calhoun's name or to badmouth him, leaving that solely to Myra, if she so chose.

More important would be what to do to avoid anything like this happening again. Ending up in a place this sordid was not something to be wished on anyone. Claire could not fathom revealing this incident to Richard. What would he say? Probably blubber and change the subject. After all, he and she had never even... Or discussed children. (Did he even want them? Do I?) Perhaps he'd encourage her to give Myra short shrift.

"Is something wrong, Claire? You look worried. More than me," Myra asked, her face all angles.

"No, no. I was thinking how brave you are—to be making this trip abroad. And how clueless I have been, about Paris and all."

Myra sighed, shaking her head in sympathy. "It'll be for another time. Paris, that is. After things get sorted out. Hitler and all."

In the silence that followed, Claire tried to envision herself arm-in-arm with Richard on the *Champs Élysées* but soon abandoned the effort. Not the time or the place.

Myra meanwhile pictured herself arm-in-arm with her father, compensating for his shaky gait as they scanned doorways in a German town called Lübeck. She imagined marigolds in neat picture windows in neat houses, a delicatessen at every corner.

But how could she and her father pull off such an unlikely coup, like finding a needle in a haystack?

"Those poor Jews on that doomed ship," Mrs. Kaminsky had mentioned when they spoke days ago. "Sent back to Germany, to what terrible fate. And Lena, my own sister..." she had gone on.

"Now, now, Ilona. *Daß ist genüg*," she heard her father cajole. "Enough of that." He took the phone from his wife to let Myra know that Frederick's father had suffered a fatal heart attack. "You might want to phone or send a card, sweetheart."

Too distracted by her own troubles, Myra had yet to send condolences.

While the two friends were still caught up in their own thoughts, the old woman shuffled back in, this time with a nurse's cap atop her head. It sat there like an afterthought.

"The doctor will see you now, Miss, Miss Kamin—whatever. Please leave any valuables with your friend and come this way."

Chapter Eight

INTO THE UNKNOWN

T hree weeks later, Myra and her father boarded the Crescent City for New York, with Claire coming to Union Station to see them off on a sunlit morning. Brief showers had cooled things off during the night. Father and daughter were traveling light, a suitcase apiece, though Ilona Kaminsky had added a last-minute woolen dress for her sister "in case she is cold on the ship over or otherwise...," she explained, faltering at the end, not knowing what condition Lena would be in, if indeed they did manage to locate her twin's whereabouts and hustle her out of the country.

"By hook or by crook," Konrad had averred, patting his wife's arm. "We'll do whatever it takes."

At the sound of the conductor's whistle, Claire shook hands with Mr. Kaminsky and handed Myra a basket of sandwiches and fruit for the two travelers. She stopped herself from commenting directly on her friend's newly bobbed hair or the apparent application of light-toned powder. A disguise perhaps to make her appear less overtly Jewish, it occurred to her.

"You look so stylish—as though you're going on a trip some place exotic," she blurted out, immediately regretting the word *exotic*.

"I ironed it," Myra volunteered, affixing a stray strand behind her ear.

While Claire fumbled for something neutral to say, Addison came into view, dashing along the platform. He too shook hands with Mr. Kaminsky and then helped with the luggage. Inside the compartment, he handed Myra a wrapped package.

"Something to pass the time and bring you up to date on things over there. A great writer, I'm told," he said, blood suffusing his cheeks. Quickly, he turned toward Mr. Kaminsky. "I believe they say *Gute Reise*, so travel safely and let us all know something. When it's feasible," he wound up, jumping off as the engine clanked into gear.

He was met by a quizzical look from Claire on the platform.

"What?" he asked, knowing full well what his sister was thinking.

By the time they pulled into Grand Central station the next afternoon, Myra had finished Thomas Mann's *Mario and the Magician* but decided against handing the novella over to her father. There was a reason the author had fled Germany, taking refuge in the U.S., where he could write and speak out freely against Hitler. When asked, she described Addison's gift as interesting, not wanting to alarm her father. They would find out how things stood abroad soon enough.

After a good night's sleep, the two spent the next day wandering the city, admiring the skyscrapers, the fast-walking people, Horn & Hardart, and Central Park, Myra careful though not to overtax her father. By sheer luck on their last evening, they secured tickets to Carnegie Hall, and heard a program of Beethoven and Brahms.

"Too bad your mother could not be here. We must save the program for her."

"And for Aunt Lena. She will want to know such sublime music is still performed."

Mr. Kaminsky nodded, his eyes bright, his expression pained. "Yes, for both of them, God willing."

Upon leaving the Commodore Hotel for Pier 36 along the Hudson River, Myra scribbled a postcard of the Manhattan skyline to the Endicotts. All four of them.

The transatlantic crossing went smoothly, leaving both father and daughter none the worse. Once they disembarked at the port of Hamburg, they braced themselves for the ordeal of customs. As forewarned, they were grilled separately and at length. Steeling themselves, they painstakingly went through several bureaucratic hoops to explain their mission, meeting skeptical if not suspicious reactions followed by more pointed questions.

At one point, two officials in the room with Myra exchanged snickers, which she did not catch, other than the expression "Jewish slut" or some such. She smiled politely and pretended not to understand.

Still, as they had bargained on, the fact of being American citizens in the end trumped the fact of their race. And if one fewer Jew living in Deutschland could be gotten rid of without the state's intervention, so much the better. That seemed to them the gist of the authorities' attitude to their intervention on Lena Walenska's behalf.

Relieved and exhilarated, father and daughter walked to a quaint hotel near the port. They ate a soup of potato and leeks and shared a bottle of Riesling in the dining room, without venturing out. And slept like logs.

The next morning, map in hand and stamped passports in pocket, they took an exploratory walk. Despite the fresh air and brilliant sunshine, they were aghast at what they saw: broken glass or boarded-up shops, other buildings with huge *J*s scrawled on their façades, or simply abandoned, seemingly haphazardly, with no indication of their owners' fate. People scurried about with their heads down, a few with yellow armbands, not daring to lift their eyes unless accosted by the *polizei* in uniform, or by truculent young men, who apparently wished to be in uniform.

To Myra, these thugs seemed to be ubiquitous, and to swagger.

Once Mr. Kaminsky began to tire, Myra accosted a couple of

middle-aged women to ask for a restaurant recommendation. The two locals exchanged a furtive glance, pointed down the street, and hurried off.

It was as though everyone was expecting the skies to crack open and unleash a storm upon them.

Over plates of bratwurst and boiled cabbage, father and daughter conversed in hushed tones. As did the handful of other customers in the place. A radio crackled behind the bar; dance music wafted through the air. A picture of Hitler hung on the wall next to a row of whiskey bottles.

"We'll head to Lübeck as soon as we're rested, Myra. I asked the concierge to book us train tickets for tomorrow. In daylight hours so we can enjoy the landscape."

Although not a demonstrative person, Konrad patted his daughter's arm, feeling restored by the hot food and the sound of voices in conversation. "If things were normal," he went on, glancing around to make sure no one was listening to them, "we'd linger a day or two. After all, it's your first ever..."

"Never mind, Papa. I have seen enough already," Myra replied, her tone controlled but telling.

"And further," he added in barely a whisper, "we don't want the *Gestapo* to locate Lena first, or to follow us while we go about our business."

Myra nodded in agreement. She had glanced at the day's headlines that morning in the hotel lobby. Hitler had authorized a sweep through western Poland, rounding up Jews to be sent to work camps further east. She did not mention that to her father.

In the afternoon, they strolled through a small park and then over to see the *Rathaus*, or city hall. "Such beauty, such a symbol of imperial power," Mr. Kaminsky muttered, arguably both awe-struck and aghast by its significance. Only a handful of tourists were about, clicking photos or pouring over guidebooks.

They bought ice cream cones, licking them as they meandered back toward their hotel, hoping to project a sense of normality. Yet every noise—a car backfiring, a voice raised, a door slammed—jolted them. So too did seeing the occasional yellow *J* sewn onto someone's clothing. Ironing her own hair, Myra reckoned, was not enough to obscure the obvious.

Back at the hotel, a helpful concierge gave them directions to the train station.

After dinner, they sat in the lobby and wrote letters home.

Konrad was too skittish to spell out the changes in the country he and his wife had lived in all those years ago, before the Great War. *Worse than you will remember of 1914, Ilona, but hopefully we are here in time to aid your sister.*

Writing to Claire, Myra kept her observations cryptic. *I would have been even more adamantly against your trip over, had I seen what I'm seeing now. I will have much to tell you once our mission is over. Trust you are enjoying things. Love to you*—and here, thinking of Addison, she paused before adding—*and to your family.*

During a nerve-racking journey, the train stopped in the middle of nowhere to allow military convoys to pass or lingered at local stations to allow for passenger searches. Finally, the two got off at Lübeck and made their way to a hotel the concierge in Hamburg had recommended. Father and daughter had to share the last available room.

Despite their exhaustion, they went out for a walkabout in the old city. From what they could tell from the adjacent side streets, several shops had been ransacked. People did not scurry past as quickly as in Hamburg, but their glances were as furtive. At one point, Myra sensed they were being followed. Again, she said nothing.

Back in the hotel that evening, they phoned the number Lena had provided in her last letter. Various attempts, no answer. It occurred to Myra that her aunt might have been one of those unfortunate souls recently collared and sent to a camp in Poland. She did not sleep well that night.

But the next day, they set about on their search. After multiple inquiries, a couple of dead ends, and then a plausible lead, they found themselves on a horse-drawn cart headed south into the countryside. The driver was affable enough, and provided a non-stop patter peculiar to that part of the country, and barely comprehensible to Myra. But, as they soon realized, he was familiar with all the surrounding villages.

"*Ya, ya*, decent folks in these parts—*Jüden* too for that matter— even if..." Shaking his head as though trying to throw off some distasteful recollection, he giddy-upped the horses.

"Even if?" Konrad persisted.

The old man scrunched his face. "Even if some have been taken away." He jerked his head this way and that to make sure nothing he said could be heard.

Father and daughter exchanged glances. Not a person in sight on what had become a rutted, dirt road.

They clattered along in silence until signs heralded the spa town of Bad Oldesloe up ahead.

Farmhouses soon dotted the landscape. A few pastured sheep stood in the sunshine, passing the time.

Bucolic, peaceful, Myra thought, wondering what it would take to make folks want to flee such a place. She did not voice this thought to her father. Along with his swollen foot, he was now nursing a head cold. She did not want to make it worse. Instead, she patted his arm, overcome by her affection for him.

Mr. Kaminsky smiled and straightened his back.

"Back to my sister-in-law, Herr Brockmeyer. Her name is Lena Walenska," he specified, aiming to refocus the old man's attention.

"She gave piano lessons to folks in this area," Myra chimed in, gesticulating at the houses that were now numerous. "She mentioned the town up ahead and a few families—the Vögels, the Kleindorfs, the Goldsteins," she persevered, pronouncing each surname with care, hoping to spark a memory.

The driver swerved to avoid a gaping ditch. Then he slowed his horses.

"The Kleindorfs had a grown daughter, and you could hear her playing when the windows were open. Lessons from a Polish lady, they say."

Myra's mouth dropped open. "Can you take us straight there?"

The hunch was right, though the family itself could not be located. After persistent questioning, nearby residents confirmed that a Polish pianist, "of some renown," they said, had given lessons to several townspeople, including the Kleindorf daughter. However, the young woman had recently obtained passage to America. Her parents? People shrugged; none knew or would say.

Herr Brockmeyer waited patiently while the Kaminskys took all this in and then drove them around the tiny spa town. At what looked like the busiest intersection was an *Apotheke des Volkes*, as in a people's drugstore. They went in to pick up Bayer aspirin. With no one else in the shop, Konrad took a chance.

"She came in often, until recently," the druggist volunteered. "Needed pills—for this and that."

Konrad raised his eyebrows to encourage him to go on.

Madame Walenska, as he called her in a slightly exalted tone, was now residing in a converted barn on the outskirts of the town, he confided under his breath.

Father and daughter brightened, thanked him, and bought two tins of aspirin.

"Take some food with you. She doesn't go out much. Not since —." The druggist shook his head and shrugged, a gesture from the locals the Kaminskys were becoming accustomed to.

At a nearby delicatessen, they loaded up on pumpernickel, salami, cheese, a bottle of wine and what they were told were locally grown strawberries.

Their driver had not deserted them. Herr Brockmeyer drove

them out to a seemingly abandoned structure bordered by overgrown spruce. And waited.

The first thing they noticed in the dimly lit interior were Lena's eyes. Enormous but sunken. Once she focused them, a smile broke out, followed by a few tears. "You came, you came. It is really you, *n'est-ce pas?*"

Konrad nodded, overcome. They embraced, tentatively, yet somehow familiarly.

Myra stood apart, struck not so much by how gaunt her aunt was but by her still striking resemblance to her own mother. Expressive hands, wise eyes. Twins indeed.

Other thoughts too, including what her father had revealed on the ocean voyage over. That he had first been enchanted by Lena before he had even glimpsed Ilona. All those years ago in Warsaw. But Lena left to study at the Conservatory in Paris. Ilona remained in Poland, as did he.

Her father pulled her over to be introduced. "And this is our daughter Myra."

Lena beckoned her to come close to her rocker. "So young, so beautiful, so brave of her to come all this way..." she trailed off, a faraway look in her eyes.

"You'll be pleased. Your niece speaks some Polish as well as good German." He waited for this explanation to register. "And, naturally, our daughter speaks perfect English."

"Ah, would that I did so as well," Lena responded, fumbling around on the table next to her rocker. She picked up a well-worn copy of Dickens' *Hard Times* and held it up to them. "I have been plowing my way through it, with the help of a German dictionary, hoping that I will have need to use the tongue, if ever I make it to your country."

"Don't worry, Aunt Lena. That's why we're here," Myra said, she too tearing up.

"First things first," Konrad said, collecting himself. "You must eat. We all must," he continued, opening their packages, and bringing out the wine and bread. Myra located a few chipped plates and divided up the salami and cheese. She left the strawberries in the dilapidated icebox, which seemed barely colder than the barn itself.

"And then Myra and I shall return tomorrow, and we'll go from there."

Somehow, perhaps by flashing so many stamped papers in the face of bureaucrats, and parting with the remainder of their Deutsch marks, Konrad and Myra finagled an extra berth for Lena on the *Europa* out of Hamburg and on to New York City.

For Lena, leaving the continent was upsetting, but she had seen enough of what had already befallen friends to know that she was among the fortunate few. Hard times ahead? "Come what may," she told herself.

As for father and daughter, they too did not do a lot of talking during the crossing, their feelings too raw, or too complicated, to express.

Chapter Nine

NEW BEGINNINGS

S ummer in New Orleans unfolded to a new beat, everyone moved more briskly, as though they needed to get things sorted out before—well, it wasn't clear what.

Sensing something ominous in the air, Claire wanted to talk about it with Myra, who was more astute than she, but her friend was still away. The Endicott family had received a postcard from New York City, but there was little to pick apart. Several weeks later an actual letter, postmarked Hamburg and addressed solely to Claire, arrived. It was not very revealing, as though written with the thought that someone else, like one of those Nazis, might be in a position to intercept it.

Nonetheless, it wasn't hard for Claire to read between the lines. Things in Germany were fraught, and tense on the rest of the Continent as well.

Paris included. She had already banished the notion of a trip there. When Dr. Truard—"please do call me Lucille"—rang up unexpectedly one evening to ask about her travel plans, Claire responded that she had attained a summer job in the Quarter, and was finding her French much in demand by the clientele. Besides, talk of war had heated up, and spread throughout the Continent.

"Quite so," Lucille replied. After an awkward interval, the professor turned elsewhere. "Still, you've got a degree now. More ambitious plans afoot?"

"Not at the moment, but I will keep you abreast," Claire went on, not as loudly.

"*Bien*," the professor lobbed back. "But I do remember there was a young man. Unless I err."

Claire bristled. And in reaction put a new routine for herself in place. To begin with, she awoke early on weekdays, dressed more meticulously than she had done in college—tailored suits and high heels—prepared the coffee pot and drank her own before either of her parents came downstairs. She left the house at 8:15 sharp, grabbed a streetcar to Canal Street, and entered the shop on Royal Street minutes before the stroke of 9.

Even so, she quickly figured out that Otto Rothmann lived somewhere within the dust-ridden bowels of the building, likely sleeping on some high-canopied, but lumpy bed. As of mid-July, she had never managed to arrive before him. Whether he was bustling about or not, she set about arranging the most attractive pieces in the store window or going over the previous day's accounts.

The owner had little to complain about with his new hire. Claire was easy on the eye, attentive to customers, knowledgeable enough about the furniture, and excellent with the accounts. In fact, she was better than his own wife, who could not be bothered with the cash register, preferring to spend her time polishing the most expensive items on display—Louis Philippe desks, Chippendale chairs, Italian credenzas.

With well-heeled customers from old families in the Garden District, it was Claire who began to close the sales. Often engaging them fluently in French, or less well in Spanish, whichever the clients seemed more comfortable with.

Mr. Rothmann noticed. Unfailingly, he addressed her by her last name, often held the door when she exited to take her lunch in front of the cathedral and complimented her when she convinced a formidable client to splurge on a *chaise longue* he had despaired of ever off-loading.

"You have done, Miss Endicott, what neither of us believed possible. Not to mention that Lady Marie Monceau left with a smile on her face."

"I told her that we had a similar, though not nearly as beautiful a piece in our own home, and that our Coco had taken a shine to it. I had noticed cat hairs on her black skirt, so I thought that might entice her to take a look. Besides, what I said is all true."

He gave her a curiously crooked smile but added nothing. She turned her attention back to the cash register.

There was something off about the exchange, she thought, but could not put her finger on it. Likely her fault. She should not have mentioned the family cat.

Weekends at home were uneventful, bordering on boring, especially after Addison returned to DC to take up his hush-hush post with Naval Intelligence. To do her part, she helped her mother prepare leftovers for vagrants who still found their way to her back porch; in the late afternoons, she dutifully played chess with her father, allowing him to checkmate her more often than not. Occasionally, she went with her parents to a concert or a play. Otherwise, she scanned the newspaper, trying to stay abreast of European affairs, or, having lost interest, she opened one or another of the foreign novels she had never gotten around to in her college courses. Or she daydreamed.

At the dinner table, conversation flagged more than it should, or became divisive when politics were touched on. Her mother plumbed for President Roosevelt and wanted the country to support the British; her father was reluctant to see the country drawn into what he called a squabble among feckless Europeans.

Claire knew better than to throw the plight of the Jews into the mix.

71

Eventually, she reconnected with Myra, figuring that things would have settled down now that the beleaguered aunt had been rescued.

When she rang the Kaminsky home, Myra began *in media res,* rushing through a description unlike anything Claire had intuited.

Beginning with the tense train trip from Lübeck to the port at Hamburg, she recounted the countless intrusions of the conductor calling out for their passports, "*Karte, bitte,*" in every compartment. "Everyone froze, every time, except my aunt. She always managed a smile and handed her exit papers over with a flourish."

The extraordinary details did not end there. It turned out that Lena Walenska had taken another risk. She had sewn a pouch with her jewels into her undergarments. And once through the ordeal of emigration and safe in the Waldorf Astoria, Myra went on, her aunt pulled out a packet of Deutsch marks from behind a flap in her luggage.

"A bank haul," Myra said. "Papa's eyes were as big as saucers."

"I'd say she's a person not to be tangled with," Claire responded. "And a born survivor."

Her friend went on: "We call it *chutzpah.* And she is indefatigable. After her first hot bath in ages, she emerged dressed to the nines, insisting we go to Carnegie Hall. 'Somehow, there are always tickets,' she claimed. And she was right. Dinner afterwards was in a fancy place she had heard of years ago. A Russian tearoom. We had blintzes and caviar."

"I guess she had missed all those things, what with—"

There was silence on the phone except for the sound of a piano. Someone running scales, deftly.

"Must be jolting to end up in little ole Alexandria," Claire mused.

"If so, she hides it. Swanning around as though she owns the place, you might say. It's we that are having to make the adjustments."

The two friends agreed that Claire would come up on Saturday for the long Labor Day weekend. "Mother insists we invite my high school chum Frederick as well. And a few of their friends. Other people for my aunt to overwhelm."

Claire chuckled, though she wasn't sure if Myra was joking.

"One other thing. You'll have to share my bedroom. Aunt Lena has the guest room until whenever.

Not wishing to waste time on the train, Claire drove Addison's car to Alexandria. Along the way, Army trucks passed her left and right; tanks rolled by; makeshift barracks appeared to be going up. She wondered what all that forbade.

Upon meeting Lena Walenska, Claire held out her hand, which was grasped with a languid gesture. If she had expected to find a frail remnant of a human who had barely managed to slip through the Gestapo's dragnet, she was disabused.

In a mere six weeks in the U.S., the woman had arguably regained not only her footing but her flair.

Still pale, still boney around the hips, she wore that Saturday evening a silk sheath that, though visibly thread-bare, still looked expensive. She stood erect, seemingly an inch or two taller than her twin sister, who hovered behind her, apron-clad.

"You will pardon my *lamentable* English," Lena said, putting the accent evenly on all four syllables of the adjective, "but I am pleased to meet the *amie de coeur* of my niece."

What they call stage presence, Claire thought. In fact, the newcomer reminded her of Greta Garbo, not the character she played in *Ninotchka* but the aging ballerina in *Grand Hotel*, accustomed to being waited on and fawned over.

As the dinner unfolded, Claire got a closer look at the new dynamics in the Kaminsky household.

Ilona Kaminsky spent half the time doing the waiting on, rushing to and from the kitchen for the bone broth she had distilled for her undernourished sister and doctoring the roast chicken with newly plucked herbs from her garden.

Konrad did the fawning, going on to the Edelmanns and the Wallensteins about how Lena had charmed the ship's captain into upgrading her room onboard and then stolen into the ship's dining room to perform an impromptu concert for unsuspecting guests.

Myra kept unusually quiet, rising once to help her mother but otherwise focused on her meal, cutting her meat into tiny bites, chewing them overlong.

Sometimes the conversation drifted into Polish—the glory days in Warsaw)—or into German—(the worsening present—which left Frederick and Claire to converse on their own. Quite a contrast to the fussy, (or was it fustian?) Daniel Calhoun, she thought. Well-mannered and deferential to the elder Kaminskys, Frederick jumped up twice to help Ilona from her chair. To her, he spoke enthusiastically about the latest shipments of men's shirts and ladies' dresses into the dry goods store, and revealed, proudly it seemed, that leather prices were about to soar.

"If you wear heels, Miss Claire, buy them now. It's going to get worse," he leaned over to confide.

Finally, Ilona rose to retrieve the strudel from the oven. "And who would like a scoop of ice cream on top?" she asked the table.

The guests ate dessert in silence. Lena too, who accepted two scoops on her pastry.

"Better than what we were served at the hotel in Hamburg, right, sweetheart?" Mr. Kaminsky piped up to break the tension. Her mouth full, Myra nodded in assent.

Eventually, Frederick spoke up.

"If you'll permit, Madame Walenska, I was wondering, my mother Mrs. Bauer too, what it was like for you—what it is like in general terms—for our people in Germany. The last year or two."

Eyes were raised from their plates as Lena slowly put down her fork. She dabbed at her lips with her sister's starched linen napkin. Myra, who was sitting next to her, noted a tremor in her hand.

"I have learnt that in English you say *bad, worse, worst*. It is now *worst*. First, professors at the university were dismissed, including *mein Freund*, my special friend Stefan," she said with an emphasis that left little doubt what she implied. "He disappeared to we know not where." She paused for effect.

"So sorry," Frederick murmured.

"Then renowned artists, you may know of them—Kurt Weill, Artur Schnabel, Thomas Mann—were forced to flee." She clicked her fingers to suggest their suddenly forced departures, then scoured the assembled faces to make sure their attention had not flagged. "Finally, my own pupils—lovely young people for whom music was —how do you say?—a solace. All scattered, into hiding: Johan, Ursula, Katrin."

Claire stole a glance at Myra, but her friend was staring at her plate.

Her breathing audible now, Lena appeared to have lost her train of thought. For the first time that evening, she looked disoriented.

"You have described things vividly, Lena," Konrad slipped in, trying to reassure her. "Myra and I saw it too, right, dear?"

"Yes. People in the streets were frightened when we stopped to ask for directions. Even the skinny cows we saw from the train. They looked stunned. It was so eerie."

Myra paused for a beat, something more immediate coming into her mind. She turned toward Frederick down the table. "I never told you I was sorry about your dad. I know he followed the news closely —all those German newspapers at the store. Left there for any and all. He was such an engaging person."

"Appreciate that," Frederick mumbled, his eyes lowered. "We miss him. But glad too, because no one wants to see what happens next. Over there, that is."

Most everyone drained their drinks after that exchange. No one dared offer up a toast.

"Nowhere is safe anymore," Konrad said, more to himself than

to the table at large, "and being Jewish is hugely problematic wherever one is."

Stealing a glance at Lena, Claire reckoned the woman was a more
confounding presence than anyone initially imagined. A couple of
tears had streaked the woman's thickly powdered face.

"If everyone's had enough, we can all adjourn to the parlor,"
Ilona finally announced, reclaiming her hostess voice. "I'm sure we
could all use coffee."

The group decamped to the adjoining room where Lena was
accommodated in Konrad's armchair. He reached over her to turn
on the radio.

With static on the classical station out of Shreveport, he tuned to
a stronger one out of New Orleans. A Louis Armstrong number was
winding down. It was followed by breaking news. The German
Wehrmacht had just invaded Poland.

Later that night, Claire and Myra lay wide awake in bed, a late
summer breeze wafting through the lace curtains.

"So, what do you make of things?" Myra asked, shadows dancing
across the ceiling.

"With your aunt or with Germany?"

"Either. Actually, both."

Chapter Ten

THE HERE AND NOW

One evening in late September, Claire accompanied her parents to the Saenger theater for the opera *Die Zauberflöte*. During intermission, they sipped champagne in the foyer, her parents nodding here and there to acquaintances. Looking around, Claire recognized no one until she spotted Lady Monceau, she of the *chaise longue*.

As she prepared to make her way over to the old lady, a young man materialized out of nowhere right in her path. Oddly familiar, he was wearing an old-fashioned suit, she noticed, something not many young men of her acquaintance would have done. But he was not unattractive.

"The girl from the café! Back in the spring. You said good afternoon—in German." He sounded excited by the recollection.

Returning her mind to that fraught afternoon, Claire blushed. Had he overheard her conversation with Myra that day?

Before she could respond, her father cleared his throat and took her arm, as though to signal they should move on through the crowd. But the young man's gaze, piercing gray-green eyes, remained fixed on her. Since he did not budge, she felt obliged to introduce him to her parents. "Oh, this is..."

"Tom Stone," he volunteered with a trace of an accent and thrust out his hand.

Mercifully, the chandeliers dimmed, indicating the last act about to begin. Tom inclined his head and stepped aside to let the threesome return to their box, and soon made his way to his seat up in the balcony.

What he blurted out to the young woman's parents, he reckoned while waiting for the music to begin, was about as innocuous an American name as he could wish for. And given how the world was now wobbling, an Anglicized version of Tomas Steinberg might spare him problems he did not need.

The conductor returned to the pit and raised his baton. The curtain went up. Newly minted Tom Stone opened his program and let the familiar strains of *The Magic Flute* wash over him.

After the encores, he lingered out front on Canal Street, keyed up but not daring to light a cigarette. The fall air was bracing, the scent of salt air perceptible. He felt more invigorated than he had in months. Accidentally on purpose, he soon found himself walking in the same direction as the young woman who had piqued his interest.

"I say—Tom, is it?—what did you make of the opera? Could you make heads or tails of all that?" Mr. Endicott asked.

Heads, tails? Tom hesitated, stymied by the question.

Claire jumped in. "Tom is fluent in German, Father. I imagine he had less trouble with the plot twists than we did."

"Lovely arias, and sung well enough, especially Papageno," he offered, diplomatic, hoping that would end the discussion.

Mrs. Endicott eyed him sidelong. The young man was taller than her husband, but, like him, had a bearing.

Tom slowed his pace to walk beside Claire, trying to formulate an invitation. But how in such a circumstance? He had not caught her name. And now it was too late to ask.

The parents stopped in front of an Oldsmobile sedan parked on Iberville Street.

"This is us," Claire's father pointed out. Needlessly.

Several other opera goers skirted the foursome, one or two inclining their heads at the Endicotts. Lady Monceau herself nodded to Claire as a uniformed servant hustled her to a waiting car and driver nearby. Tom showed no sign of moving on.

Claire's mother intervened. "May we give you a lift somewhere, Mr. Stone?"

"Oh, no. But thank you. I work not far from here. Caxton's Cabinetry. Repairs to antiques. Musical instruments too, on Esplanade." He felt ridiculous.

Claire's father scrutinized him more critically but added nothing.

"I'm there, most every day," he further burbled, turning red in the face. Fortunately, the lights were not so bright on the side streets.

Hurriedly, he helped the mother into the passenger side, and stood aside as the car clanged into gear and drove off, turning toward Canal Street and disappearing out of view.

If he had failed to learn the young woman's name, Tom tried to reassure himself that she at least knew where he spent his time.

However disapprovingly the father might have surveyed him (and his prospects), he considered himself lucky to have landed the job he held. Nothing to sneer at, given the times. In short, flaunting an architect's degree from a German university no longer seemed a good idea in America.

With only a couple of generic character references from former bosses in west Texas, he had simply wandered into the nondescript building on the edge of the French Quarter, enticed by the sound of carpentry tools and a radio blaring Beethoven. The owner, a pipe-smoker with an open face, put him to work fixing table legs, and then the most dilapidated of credenzas and curio cases—pieces that were likely not salvageable to begin with. It did not take long for the owner to realize that the young man could saw and plane and chisel and varnish and retrofit knobs and club feet as well as anyone he'd ever hired.

An odd sort, formal even, but the young man was willing enough. Old Mr. Caxton did not overdo the questions.

Neither did the landlady, a beady-eyed matron who showed Tom a top-floor apartment of her nearby boardinghouse—the sights, sounds and smells of the French Quarter bringing back fond memories of home: the spires of Lübeck, the promenade along the Trave River, the seagulls from the Baltic, the pleasant people he grew up with.

He handed over three months' rent in advance and bought ferns for the narrow balcony outside his single window. From there, if he craned his neck, he could see the towers of the cathedral and a sliver of the Mississippi.

After almost nine months, he had yet to have a single visitor to admire the view—or to do anything else. If it were never to be poor Katrin in his bed, then why not, he fantasized, the young woman from the café?

In the meantime, he spent his free time sketching. He wanted to build houses—not for the fancy people, like those in the Garden District, but for the dispossessed who needed something more than hovels over their heads. In America, he could not help but see, it was mostly black people who lived from hand to mouth.

He had mentioned the barebones of such a project back in Texas but only got stares from overseers who liked him, and snickers from those who didn't. "You be barking up the wrong tree, son," one of them had told him. He had gotten the gist, even if he did not understand the colloquialism.

However, now that the Depression appeared to be lifting, he might have a chance to make a mark. If he could not do anything to help Katrin, not to mention his own parents, he might make a difference in this new place.

Perhaps Mr. Caxton would warm to his ideas. He determined to banish the unclean thoughts that intruded on his evenings, pull out his drawings from under the bed, and get to work.

A few weeks later, while pouring over diagrams, someone knocked on his door.

"Mr. Steinberg. A letter for you. From overseas. Official looking."

The scratchy voice was his landlady's, who had not been in his rooms since he first moved in, at least that he knew of. He needed to be polite.

Putting down his implements, he called out, "A minute, please." Hurriedly, he stashed his half-eaten plate of red beans and rice in the sink. From the back of his chair, he grabbed his jacket.

Mrs. Jennings trundled in. She scoured the furniture, including a half-built bookcase, and the makeshift kitchen. She sniffed, wriggling her nose, but said nothing. Tom was relieved to have already unplugged the hotplate.

"So," he began, "thank you for coming all the way upstairs with this." He took a step toward her and held out his hand.

She stared once more at the envelope, and smacked her lips together, disapprovingly. He took the letter, trying not to appear anxious, as though it were normal for him to be receiving correspondence on German government letterhead.

Mrs. Jennings turned her attention to her tenant's worktable. "All these squiggles," she said, wiggling her fingers in imitation of the lines. "A young man like you, working day and night, for Philip Caxton." She shook her head, as though something in the scheme of things was amiss.

"It's a project I'm working on in my spare time. Mr. Caxton is a good boss. No complaints there."

She nodded absently and ran her finger along the edge of the table. "I'll be sending up a cleaning woman on Wednesdays, presuming you are at your regular job then," she said.

"Absolutely. And thank you for bringing up the letter," he repeated.

The landlady shot him a final glance, lingering a beat too long. Sighing audibly, she turned and left the room. He could hear her heavy tread on the stairs.

Now to the letter. The stamps themselves made an impression but so did the return address in the corner, in Gothic script:

Leitender Ingenieur Hans Durst
   Kriegsmarine der Ostsee
   Bismarck Straße 367
   Port of Kiel
   Deutschland

If Tom had held out hope that his childhood friend would become disenchanted with the German military, especially as war was now what Hitler had in mind, the envelope itself was enough to disabuse him of such a fantasy. He suspected that his friend was using the envelope to signal where he now stood in terms of his allegiance. If Hans had gone out of his way, months earlier, to help their mutual childhood friend escape the fate that awaited Jews in Germany, he likely now was in no position—nor had any desire— to do so now.

Grabbing the last can of Lone Star from his icebox, Tom sat down to read what his friend—now an officer in the German Navy —had to say.

Tomas,

   As will be clear from the envelope, I have been promoted and trans-ferred to the Baltic, and await further orders, dependent on what the Navy has in store. I cannot discuss specifics, even if I were privy to them. As you know, I am first and foremost an engineer and secondly a mili-tary man. If and when we are called upon to defend the homeland, or

take back territory historically part of greater Germany, then that is
what I shall be called to do.

You will doubtless want to know of more familial things. Sadly, of
those I have scant knowledge. Your mother and father vanished a year
ago, and I heard conflicting reports. As for Katrin's whereabouts, you
likely already know that the St Louis *returned to Antwerp, where*
passengers were sorted for transfer to one of four countries. I had occa-
sion to see the lists: her name appeared on one as relocated to the Nether-
lands; on another, bound for England. I have heard nothing further,
though, resourceful as she is, she would be able to contact me, if desired.
At one time, (a year after you sailed for America), she and I were
romantically involved. Like all good things, it ended.

I trust you are well and making a good life there. New Orleans is
near the sea, so perhaps it reminds you of home. I would be glad to
know it were so.

Hans

That night Tom could not sleep. He tried to reconcile the empathetic
boyhood friend he knew growing up and the harder-edged man—the
military man, the Nazi-beholden man—he had become.

Per the latest reports, Hitler's troops were in the midst of over-
running Poland, rounding up innocent civilians, specifically those
who were Jewish, and sending them to work camps, whatever those
entailed. It was unlikely the German chancellor would stop there.

Those thoughts led him to question why he himself had not
made greater efforts to trace his own parents—: were they nestled in
the German countryside or had friends whisked them away to the
Netherlands or France—and why did Hans sound so cavalier about
it all?

Switching on the night light, he got up to drink the last of his
beer and close the shade on his window. A full moon shone on the
spire of the cathedral and cut a swathe across his bed. Of all the
saints, he whispered, this church would have to be named for a

Louis, whatever he did to deserve the honor. He could not entirely shake the image of that ill-fated ship of the same name, and of Katrin. So stricken her face as the vessel pulled anchor and set sail back to Germany. He called out to her, as did others in the rowboat, but none of the passengers on the liner could hear.

And now there was this other girl. He took a final swig and went over that evening at the theater. Probably bespoke she was, he reasoned, which might explain why her parents looked askance at him. Or they sensed he was German, or Jewish, or simply foreign. "From away," is how he had heard the locals refer to those not from the region.

He shook his head, berating himself for his negligence, for his selfishness, for his lack of commitment to things spiritual. Do I even know where the nearest synagogue is around here? Do I know what I will become?

Snatching the tassel, Tom pulled down the shade and returned to bed. Eventually sleep came, but it was fitful, and he was beset by dreams.

In a vivid one, he, Katrin and Hans were gathered at the piano. In her nearby home in Lübeck was a highly polished Bösendorfer, and it was she who usually played. Both boys could carry a tune, but Hans was broad-chested, and less timid. His voice carried, and Katrin's fingers followed his phrasing. Tomas turned the pages for her, humming along if he did not know the words to pieces by Schubert or Schuman.

They even played songs to improve their English. Simple lyrics, limpid melodies. One such threaded its way through Tomas's dream: *Flow gently, sweet Afton* and so on. The two older children had laughed at him when he asked what *Afton* was.

"A river, silly. Somewhere in Scotland."

Had he not noticed the looks of admiration that Katrin darted toward his best friend? The two of them always rode ahead on their bicycles, he pedaling hard to keep up with them. His eyes would train on the back of Katrin's head, her blonde braids, her white shoulders.

Her mother was Swedish and steadfastly Lutheran; her father was German and staunchly Jewish.

Sometimes, she let go of the handlebars to point at something in the distance. Which, being behind them, Tomas could not see but which Hans ostensibly did.

But then when his friend went off to that military academy in Cologne and on to the university in Berlin, he and Katrin were left to do what they did.

"Totally besotted I was," he murmured, knotting the bedsheet, remembering what it was like to fuck, and fret about nothing.

Toward morning, light suffused his room in the boarding house. Tom returned to the letter. Why was it that Hans felt the need to tell him—*By the way, I screwed the one girl you were ever in love with.*

And yet now? That very girl who had crossed the ocean in one direction and then forcedly in the other remains a refugee without certain refuge. And Hans, all decked out in his starched uniform, no longer cares.

"I care," he mumbled to himself, "but there is nothing I can do."

Once the sun had taken hold of the day, Tom brewed a cup of strong coffee and drank it black. On his way to Caxton's place, he resolved to throw off what of the past he could not change and focus on what he could become.

"*Im Hier und Jetzt, im Hier und Jetzt leben,*" he repeated as he walked. Determinedly. "Live in the here and now."

Chapter Eleven

MONKEY WRENCHES

Bertha's Beauty Parlor was across the street from Kaminsky's music store and was arguably where the best gossip in Alexandria could be picked up. Locals quipped that idle talk was much cheaper than hair spray, though more detrimental to women's health.

What customers were talking about under the dryers or in their swivel chairs in the fall of 1939 was all the men who were pouring into town now that the U.S. Army had set up shop on the outskirts of town.

The younger women were getting bobs and manicures in order to show themselves off; the older women were discussing how long the newcomers would be hanging around, and to what purpose.

Myra too had culled her college wardrobe, having discarded tired or shapeless outfits and acquired more colorful dresses—new arrivals at Bauer's Dry Goods, where she waved at Frederick but went about her business.

And she did have business now, having insisted upon filling in for her father three days a week at the music store. His health had not improved since their trip abroad, the Vick's Vapor Rub by which he swore smelled up the house but did little to stymie his cough. He paid his daughter slightly more than the going rate, relieved that she had volunteered to help.

Her friend Claire had persevered in her job in the French Quarter, even announcing last time they spoke that from her savings she would soon be able to rent a small place of her own.

"My parents will be astounded and opposed, but I'm relying on Addison to lean on them," she had confided.

Surely, I can do as well, Myra told herself, squelching a twinge of jealousy. The world is supposed to be our oyster, she recalled one of their professors proclaiming to the eager young women in the classroom.

But now she wasn't so sure: the world was a scary place and opportunities seemed to be slipping past her. She felt constricted but did not know how to break free.

Even home itself had become cramped. Although not openly discussed, the tension between her mother and her aunt rattled her.

Konrad Kaminsky, benighted as most men were about the female psyche, exacerbated the situation between the reunited twin sisters, sometimes inadvertently, other times with what Myra thought was mischievous (if not malicious) glee.

Whenever he switched his attentions to Lena, praising her prowess at the keyboard or admiring her elegant (if woefully out-of-date) attire, Ilona would retreat into her shell. Other times, when he lavished praise upon his wife, for her baking, or bridge-playing, or flower-arranging, Lena would feign disinterest, or retire to her room.

Myra had no idea how to deal with this irksome, if not ridiculous, *ménage à trois*. Her father was inching sixty; her mother and aunt would turn fifty in November. What could they possibly be thinking? Myra asked herself.

Part of her hoped her aunt—who had for decades basked in the bright lights of Warsaw, Paris and Berlin—would soon tire of Alexandria. As her English improved, Lena had latched onto the adjective *quaint*, which she invoked when referring to the customs, the people or even the architecture of the tiny town.

Such comments made Ilona roll her eyes, Konrad, lower his in embarrassment. Myra squirmed but eventually came up with a plan.

Why not introduce her aunt to New Orleans—to the music department at Sophie Newcomb? Surely, piano instruction from a renowned European pianist would be a welcome addition to the staff. A couple of local high schoolers had come over to the house for lessons already, including Frederick's younger sister. After a month the girl was tickling the ivories with flair.

Lena did have a gift.

One day, her aunt came into the store and began to thumb through the bins. Myra finished dusting the cabinets that housed the violins and repositioned herself behind the counter.

After a couple of minutes, she said, "Let me know if you don't find what you're looking for, Aunt Lena. We have oodles of sheet music in the storage room."

Before long, her aunt had selected several books of advanced exercises as well as albums of Chopin études and Liszt rhapsodies. Myra looked impressed.

"We all need to work on fingering and I, unfortunately, have lost dexterity. As you may have observed, dear."

A wave of sympathy swept over Myra, remembering their first encounter in that drafty barn.

"If I am ever to perform again, Chopin would be *de rigueur*. We must never betray our roots," the older woman trailed off. She began to fumble with her pocketbook.

"Don't be silly, Aunt Lena. I'm not ringing these up. To hear you play at home is sufficient reward," Myra responded, and quickly slipped the albums into a shopping bag.

The older woman seemed touched by the gesture, averting her gaze to compose herself. She cleared her throat. "I walked all the way, but if you like, we can take the bus back home together, once you close up shop."

Myra checked her watch. "I have another hour. What will you do meantime?"

"Look around. That expression you have in English: window shop. It should be fun."

Later on the bus, the two sat quietly, side by side. Several kids sucked lollipops nearby. A couple of men in business suits flipped through the local paper. Myra could make out the main headline "German troops overrun Polish villages." She decided not to point it out.

"I'd like to confide something, Myra, as I'm unsure how to proceed with your parents," Lena began, her voice lowered so as not to attract attention.

Myra inclined her head, anxious but in assent.

"I'm thinking I should try my luck in, say, New Orleans. You do understand, do you not? Music is my life as well as my profession. And cities of a certain size, and allure, are where my life has flourished."

Stunned though she was to hear this, it did make sense to Myra. And would solve other issues as well.

"I see," she replied. "I loved it there. So much to do, and you're right: music is everywhere. You might even enjoy the jazz."

"Hitler has banned such music in Germany, which is all the more reason to pay attention to it," Lena replied.

As they turned off Main Street, several older passengers with shopping bags got on and took their time to get seated. The driver waited until they were all situated. Once they set off again, Lena leaned in closer to her niece to confide something else. She had spent an hour at the Hibernia to exchange her German marks for dollars.

"The bank manager said the dollars should 'tidy me over' for quite a while," Lena revealed, beaming at the thought of her good fortune. "Apparently, it was a good exchange rate. When the time comes, we shall splurge!"

"Then we must have a first meal in the Vieux Carré."

"And afterwards, I shall depend on you to take me on my first New Orleans streetcar."

The bus approached their stop. On the short walk to the house, they agreed that nothing would be said until Lena had assessed her finances and updated her résumé.

"I do not know what you plan to do with your life, Myra dear, but you have observed many things already. Been through difficulties yourself, I suspect."

Myra wondered if her aunt had an inkling she had gone through an illicit love affair, and an illegal abortion only a few months before. She could not think what to respond.

Her aunt went on. "It's harder for women on their own. Mistakes are going to be made. And for us Jews, in particular, there is discrimination."

Myra nodded her head without countering this opinion, the memory of that brochure in Daniel's briefcase flitting through her mind. She took her aunt's arm as they maneuvered the uneven sidewalk.

"Still," Lena wound up on a brighter note, "the rewards of independence are great, especially if one dedicates oneself to something— or to someone."

At that moment, Myra regretted having judged her aunt so harshly. The woman had lived quite a life—and apparently was prepared to keep doing so in her own florid way.

"It's going to get rowdier," Frederick opined, as Myra gazed out the window at the passers-by. They were having lunch at the diner across the street from Bauer's Dry Goods. It was a blustery day in December though Alexandria's holiday shoppers were undeterred. So too were clumps of young men, several in front of the pool hall at the corner, others milling about.

While he studied the menu, she took note of three young men in dress uniform, Negroes, apparently exchanging pleasantries with a couple of girls. White girls. They all appeared to be laughing. Out of nowhere, a couple of locals in work overalls materialized. White men. One grabbed the arm of the shortest black soldier and pulled him into the street.

"Uh, oh," Myra said.

Looking up, Frederick followed her gaze.

One of the other white men threw a punch. A scuffle broke out until the other Negro soldiers managed to free their comrade-in-arms and hustle him off. Name-calling followed in their wake. The girls had skedaddled in the opposite direction.

Frederick shook his head. "They're treated worse than we are. It doesn't take much for things to get out of hand."

"They're probably from away and don't realize"—she hesitated, before completing her thought—"that this is the Deep South."

"They'll find out soon enough. Camp Claiborne is preparing for several hundred thousand soldiers. From all over the country. Whatever Roosevelt says about not going to war."

Myra looked unconvinced. Frederick made efforts to be informed, but his horizons were limited and did not extend to the government's plans. Claire's brother would know more; she would ask after Addison next time they spoke.

When the pork chops and grits arrived, they ate in silence.

Myra sensed there was something on Frederick's mind but no longer read him as well as she did in high school. She had changed. In her view, he had not.

He began, chatty enough, "You know they're looking to hire locals, right? Young women especially. Typists, secretaries, things like that. To assist the top brass. The pay is said to be good."

Myra could feel his eyes boring in on her. She continued to cut her meat, chewing each bite carefully, sipping a coke to wash things down. All the while she kept her face neutral.

"Unless you're going to take over the music shop, or teach at the high school..." She arched her brow offhandedly, no hint of an intention.

Frustrated, he passed her the breadbasket. She broke off a piece from the warm loaf and took two pats of butter. "Or, like Ruby Tate—remember her?—get a job at the Hibernia. Work yourself up through the ranks."

"I was thinking of moving back to New Orleans," Myra declared. Her lunch companion looked crestfallen. Ignoring his disappointment, she fixed on the butter, largely unmelted atop her grits. She stirred it in and finished off what remained on her plate.

The waiter came and made a clatter removing their plates. He then poured hot coffee into their cups. They ignored him.

"My best friend Claire is there and she—" Myra gesticulated with her free hand; Frederick tightened his jaw. "She has a job in the French Quarter. And taking graduate courses."

He looked dismayed. Decidedly so. "But you already have a degree, *summa cum laude*, to boot. Do you really need to...?" Reddening, he spooned sugar into his coffee and drank it down.

She cut back in. "I don't *need* to, but I want to. And then, there is my aunt. She expects me to—" Myra twirled her wrist the way Lena did to finish off a sentence when words failed her.

"I don't understand you, Myra. Not like before. I mean, with everything happening, and me now in charge of the store. I was of the impression..."

She pulled her head back. Defiant.

Swallowing hard, Frederick picked up his water glass and upended it. Then he glanced around to see if other customers were watching them. No one was. He straightened his back. "I was hoping that you could see your way to getting married."

Myra blanched, not having expected anything so absurd from her childhood friend, especially since they'd barely been together alone since twelfth grade. And all he had ever done was kiss her, sloppily at that, at the end of the senior prom. On her family doorstep, mushing her corsage. Whatever was he thinking, and why reveal it in the Main Street diner?

Seeing her dumbstruck, Frederick took another tack. "Unless

there's someone else. I could imagine such, but your mother indicated not."

Myra looked irritated at the thought of a conspiracy.

The same inopportune waiter returned with their check, turning from one to the other customer.

"Now I remember. From high school. You were a couple of years ahead, and very smart," the waiter interjected, looking toward Myra. "Both of you, actually." Blushing, he handed the check to Frederick. "Skeezix is the name. Like the comic strip character."

Since the two diners remained stone-faced, he slunk away.

With his line of thought severed, Frederick reversed course. "Perhaps you need time, Myra. Things are in flux," he declared. "As it were," he added, his voice rising at the end.

Neither knew what that aside meant.

Chapter Twelve

ELECTRIC DREAMS

C laire could not get Tom Stone out of her mind. She continued to work at the antiques store and to avoid undue interactions with her boss. About some things, Otto Rothmann was accommodating. He allowed her to take off early on Tuesdays and Thursdays for her graduate classes, one in advanced calculus and the other in contemporary history.

She was stunned when one of the rotating lecturers in charge of the latter course turned out to be Dr. Calhoun. She did not mention that to Myra. What she did miss was a steady study partner and a confidant. The other girls persevering with graduate studies appeared as frazzled or preoccupied as she was, though none of them took to sharing their concerns with her. She needed her old friend. Getting older meant having more questions about life and love than she had bargained for.

About sex too.

To be sure, Claire's mind, when not focused on equations, wandered to that subject more than she was comfortable with. And to the young man who knew so much about *The Magic Flute*. How German was this young man—and what difference would that make, she wondered. And was he, as her parents insinuated that night in the car, Jewish? And what difference would that make?

One evening after her parents had gone up to bed, she looked up Caxton's Cabinetry in the phone book and memorized the address.

On a warm but windy Saturday afternoon in mid-December, she went downtown to Christmas shop. Browsing through several floors of Maison Blanche, she eventually settled on silk scarves for the Kaminsky ladies, and something, as her mother had suggested, "manly and purposeful" for Richard.

That task accomplished, she exited, eyeing the clock across Canal Street in front of Adler's. She could get something for her mother there, Depression be damned, but decided to put that off. Instead, she walked briskly through the French Quarter toward Esplanade. If memory served, Caxton's would be tucked between Dauphine and Burgundy.

Once there, she took a deep breath and peered through the window.

Tom was visible, bent over what looked to be the innards of a grand piano. In the late afternoon sun, his lower arms were bare, muscular. In profile, his brow appeared furrowed in concentration. She stiffened, about to leave unnoticed when he suddenly righted himself. As he caught sight of her, a smile crossed his face. He wiped a smudge off his cheek with the back of his hand. Claire managed a tentative wave but did not dare enter the place. Tom soon placed his tools on shelves behind him and ambled to the door. He gave her a questioning look.

"I was in the neighborhood, buying gifts, and then spotted your shop," Claire said, holding out her Maison Blanche-emblazoned bag. "I thought we could take a walk, together, since I have to walk anyway, at some point." The sides of his lips curled; she blushed further.

"Give me five minutes to close up and change out of these," Tom replied, running his hands along his overalls. She lowered her eyes to his clothes. "I'd ask you in but there's sawdust everywhere."

She nodded, he went back in, unhurried, and disappeared. She wondered where the owner was but decided not to inquire.

As the two meandered through the Quarter, they were careful not to touch, though Claire could smell the scent of Lifebuoy, which her father also used whenever he did odd jobs around the house. It was not an unpleasant odor. She regretted not having worn perfume, but on second thought that might have been too forward.

To lessen her awkwardness, she pointed out this or that landmark —Lafitte's blacksmith shop, the Old Absinthe House, figuring he likely had not read up on southern history or had bothered to take a tour. Without being asked, she mentioned that she worked on Royal Street, to make extra money and afford a place to rent.

"You will understand what I mean, having met my parents," she confided, though in a more affectionate than irritated tone.

Tom remained guarded, nodding politely, keeping his comments neutral.

At a certain point, they paused in front of the cathedral. Several black boys were tap-dancing nearby to an accordion; a painter was sketching the church façade. The bell in the tower sounded the five o'clock hour.

Tom dropped a dime in the boys' nearby hat. More confident now, he said, "We're so close. To where we first met. How about something to drink?"

Over coffee and beignets, they both relaxed. She stopped running off at the mouth; he let himself be drawn out.

"In truth, my real name is Tomas. Tomas Steinberg. From that, you can deduce much more, if need be."

"There is no need," she replied, her tone more suggestive than she had bargained for. He appeared moved and looked away. "I am, however, curious how you ended up here, New Orleans of all places."

Tom let some time pass as they sipped their coffee. In silence, they watched the passers-by, he trying to figure what needed to be revealed, and what did not, to this young woman so lovely to behold and yet so different from anyone he had ever been close to. If he understood correctly, she had a college degree, and spoke some German. Surely, she would be aware of the broad contours of recent history.

"My parents saw the writing on the wall in Germany earlier than most. Most Jews, in any case. They sent me to America shortly after I finished my university studies. I ended up in Texas. You may be surprised but many Germans live there. To a few of them, I was distantly related."

Claire knew nothing of all this, but she beckoned him to continue.

"Eventually, for reasons not clear even to me," he said, "I hopped on a train going east and hopped off with a bunch of—what do you call them?—ah yes, hobos. Right onto Magazine Street."

"From a moving train?"

"Those fellows know how to do it. I imitated them," he explained. "For a week or two I shadowed them, eating off the back porches of people who put out bread, or whatever else they had on hand."

Claire nodded, thinking of her mother. She wanted to take the sensitive young man's hand but limited herself to a bite of beignet instead. He did likewise. The crowd at the café thickened. The traffic did too.

Although she had more questions, Claire refrained from asking them. She did not wish to dig too deeply, hoping that sooner or later she would learn all she needed to know. She looked past him, taking in the other customers, feigning more interest in them than she had. Before long, she turned her gaze back toward him. His eyes shone bright in the dying light.

"All that has happened in your life, Tom—the separations, the strange land you find yourself in. You've had quite an adventure. I don't know what to say about it."

Tom smiled, a little sad at how she put it.

Seeing his face, his liquid eyes, she hastened to distract him. "Unlike yours, my own life has unfolded along a decidedly pedestrian track," she averred.

Tom tilted his head, bemused. "Like a streetcar. You know where it's headed but perhaps not how fast." He eyed her quizzically, his lips not quite breaking into a smile.

Chapter Thirteen

PRICEY BUT NOT PERSONAL

B y the time Claire got off the streetcar and hurried home, her feet were aching. But more tellingly, her heart was pounding.

Once inside, she plopped down on the couch, wiggled out of her shoes, and propped her feet on the coffee table. The radio in the next room was playing, a plaintive voice singing "I've Got You Under My Skin." Coco curled up beside her. Soon her mother walked by, a wicker basket in her arms. She snagged on her daughter's swollen feet.

"You should treat yourself to a comfortable pair of shoes, dear, with lower heels," she ventured. Claire nodded without looking up. "You do know what they're saying now?" At that comment, she raised her eyes, expectant. "There'll soon be shortages—of leather, among other things. Even if there is no war."

"What does Addison think?" Claire asked.

"Your father spoke to him this morning, but, as you know, he does not say much about work on the phone. In any event," she went on, "he'll be flying this time, getting in not a day too soon, on the twenty-third."

Claire began to stroke the cat behind the ears, nestling her head in the feline's fur.

"You do remember that we're having people over that evening," her mother added, more as a statement than a question. Claire looked unenthusiastic. Mrs. Endicott persevered. "You are welcome to invite someone, one of your new classmates, to round things out. I prefer when the guests are evenly divided. Makes the conversation more pleasant."

"I'll give it some thought, Mother, though by now most of the students have scattered," she replied, wishing that Myra were around and would want to be in company during the holiday. Jewish or not, Christmas is Christmas. Or Tom Stone, though she did not know him well enough to propose such a thing and besides, he was male, very male. As well as Jewish.

Things were more complicated than she wished them to be.

"You haven't asked, but I spoke with Helen Carrollton." Claire did not bother to look curious. "Harold and Richard are back from their extended trip. I'm sure they'll have much to recount about things up and down the river. They're looking forward to coming over, though, naturally, you may see Richard before then."

"Not likely before Addison gets home. It's very busy at Rothmann's, and I have an exam to prep for."

Still clutching her wicker basket, Mrs. Endicott shifted her weight as though she had something else to say. The clock on the mantelpiece struck seven.

"I can help you with the laundry, if you like, Mother. I was about to go upstairs anyway."

"No need. Take a bath. Soak your feet. Your father won't be home until after his meeting. We'll have gumbo around eight, if that suits."

Once upstairs, Claire tossed her shoes aside and threw herself across the bed, burying her head under a pillow. How was it, she asked herself, that life had reached such an impasse?

THIS NEARLY WAS OURS

As Myra put it last time they griped about living at home after college: "We both may need to break away before we end up breaking the dinner plates."

And then there was the rest of the world, which also seemed to be going to hell in a hand basket. Myra certainly thought so, after her adventure rescuing her aunt. So too did Professor Calhoun, who would be expecting term papers on the repercussions of the Treaty of Versailles. To what extent, the question was, should Germany be blamed for flexing its muscles after being held in check so long?

She would have liked to discuss the issue with Myra, but then it would come out that it was none other than her friend's former lover in charge of the class. Not only that. She had noticed the professor's barely concealed attentions toward another seminar student, her name frequently on the sign-up sheet for in-office sessions.

To Claire's mind, Myra had escaped the worst. Better not to allude to her erstwhile folly.

While relaxing in the tub, she turned to her own romantic entanglement, as if that were the right designation for it. To fantasize about Tom Stone brought her pleasure, and as she soaped her body, her nipples hardened at the memory of his hand on her arm as she mounted the streetcar that evening. To think about Richard, which of late she only did when her parents brought up his name, only made her feel guilty.

On Christmas Eve, Richard dutifully accompanied his parents for supper and a gift exchange at the Endicotts. The house was beautifully decorated, Edward having gone to a stand near Lake Pontchartrain to acquire a spruce, on which he strung mercury lights and on which Esther hung crystal ornaments and silver tinsel. Addison had mailed home the latest album from Bing Crosby, which played softly on the record player.

During the dinner of roast pork and potatoes, the conversation veered toward politics and the prospect of a widening war in Europe, with the two older men holding forth in full oratorical ardor. Ample drink helped. Edward defended Germany's right to secure lands it considered lawfully its own; Harold argued that countries like Poland had a right to protect their borders.

Claire fidgeted in her chair but said nothing, everything her professors had said about the situation abroad was now a jumble in her mind.

"As long as things don't spill over here," the two men agreed to agree over Esther's lemon custard. "Roosevelt has enough on his plate."

Then, turning toward Addison, Harold asked, "Tell us, if allowed, what you think about the government's next move? If I understand, you are now an insider, being stationed there in DC."

Addison took another sip of his wine and obliged. "It's no secret that the president and his cabinet believe it's better to be prepared than not. Visibly so."

"What do you mean, son?" his father pressed.

"Troop maneuvers are underway." The table looked blank. "Even down here. Basic training camps are being built and recruits are being stationed." Everyone looked nonplussed. "Near where your friend lives, Claire. Up around Alexandria," he added.

"But, in the end, it may all be for naught. No war anywhere," Esther piped up.

No one seconded that view.

Raising her eyebrows, Claire eyed Richard, the only remaining male at the table. About to be a businessman with a title and a dozen regional managers reporting to him. Surely, he should have an opinion, and be able to express it, she reckoned.

After a gulp from his water glass, he mustered a response, something about the treaty that ended the last war, which severely punished the belligerents, and likely led to current hostilities. Beyond that, he faltered, retreating red-faced to his custard.

Heat rose in Claire's chest. Not only was she embarrassed for

Richard, but she was indignant that no one would touch the subject that had become a political hot potato. In years past, she would have remained silent, but she now spoke out, unrehearsed. "It's not only about Hitler trying to take back land. Jews are afraid of what will happen to them if they remain there. And the refugees who do make it here are facing all kinds of roadblocks."

She was met by blank stares. She plowed on, mentioning the rescue operation that Myra and her father had undertaken.

Her father made a face as if to signal that his daughter tended to over-dramatize. Helen and Harold Carrollton exchanged a look of disbelief.

"Leaving your college friend aside, who sounds quite formidable, we can't countenance flotsam and jetsam, from wherever, now can we?" Richard's father rushed to say, attempting to put the subject in its proper perspective. (Whatever that was.)

In the silence that followed, Esther pushed back her chair, stood, and began to fiddle at the sideboard. One of its legs wobbled. The entire piece squeaked.

"Sounds like you need to get someone over here. No way to get it to Rothmann's without risking further damage," Helen jumped in to say.

The change of subject allowed everyone to take a deep breath. "I suspect you're right," Esther replied. She proceeded to pour apricot brandy for the four men and sherry for the women, placing the glasses on a lacquered tray. Addison quickly rose to carry it into the parlor.

Once the dessert plates were removed from the table, the older men repaired to armchairs and Cuban cigars, their wives to the sofa and their thimbles-full of sherry. Claire brought in a plate of pralines and placed it on the table in front of them. No one partook. Addison turned up the volume on the record player a notch. Bing Crosby was singing "I'll Be Home for Christmas."

Quietly, Helen recommended a workman who redid one of her armoires. "Hard to find anyone with artistic bent but this young man was a gem. Varnished the piece to perfection. I'll phone up and have his boss ring you."

Over at the tree, Claire presented Richard with the fancy leather wallet from Maison Blanche, having heeded what her mother had further admonished—"nothing intimate. But pricey it should be." In turn, he retrieved his gift for her from an Adler's shopping bag, a Lalique vase in pale lavender. Definitely pricey, but definitely not intimate.

From across the room, Esther's lips were a thin slit. Conversation died out altogether shortly thereafter, with Richard and Addison making plans to get together before New Year's Eve to hear some jazz in the Quarter and go fishing out on the lake. Richard turned to thank Claire for the wallet before being swept into his parents' Cadillac. "I'll call you during the week," he stammered as they pulled away.

"Well, that was that," Esther said to Edward as they mounted the steps back inside, her tone leaving little doubt she considered the evening unsatisfactory. Addison pulled out his cigarette case and gestured that he would take a walk around the block.

Claire offered to rinse the dishes.

"I believe you've done enough for one evening," her mother retorted, her meaning not hard to decipher.

Sheepishly, Claire went up to bed, scooping up the cat on her way. Once under the covers, with Coco curled up above her head, she went over the evening. She did not regret her outburst, even if it came across as ill-mannered. And even if it sorely disappointed (if not scandalized) her parents.

Further, relations with her purported betrothed had, if anything, cooled rather than warmed, their holiday gifts to each other outward and visible signs of their longstanding but decidedly unromantic attachment.

Worse, Claire now understood that Richard was more constrained by his parents than she was enthralled to hers.

It was not a good omen.

Her last waking thoughts were for the other man now in her life.

Whereas Tomas Steinberg had been forced to fend for himself in a foreign country, with all the obstacles that entailed, he carried himself with more assurance than Richard, with all his privileges and opportunities. If anything, she wished to model herself more on the former than the latter, as outrageous as that sounded.

Chapter Fourteen

SO CLOSE, YET SO FAR

On Christmas Eve, Philip Caxton ordered po-boys and gumbo from a place in the Quarter for his half-dozen workers and dismissed them all immediately after lunch, each with a bonus of $50 left under their plates, under Tom's too, even though he had been there less than a year.

On Tom's way out, the old man handed him a work slip. "Forgot about this. A customer called, said you were recommended that you had immaculate manners," Mr. Caxton explained, pronouncing the word *immaculate* with some amusement.

Tom blushed. He was relieved the other men had already left.

"Anyhow," the old man went on, "the lady said she'd be grateful if you could fix a sideboard next week. In time for New Year's Eve. It's set for 3 p.m. on the thirtieth. No need to come in here that day. The whole town will already be celebrating."

Thoroughly embarrassed but happy for the extra work, Tom put the slip in his pocket and thanked his boss. At loose ends, he took a stroll through the Quarter, stopping sporadically to hear sidewalk music, dropping dimes in a few hats, and eventually entering a joint to buy a beer. Or two. No one spoke to him other than the bartender, who was too busy to chat at length. An hour ticked by. Watching the passers-by on Bourbon Street, especially young couples holding hands, overwhelmed him with sadness. He was sorry he hadn't tagged along with the other workmen, a couple of whom were pleasant enough, and not much older than he was.

For the first time, Tom realized he was not only alone in the world; he was lonely.

Around sunset, he wended his way back to his lodgings, determined to find something to do during the holidays that did not involve his diagrams. He did not want it to end up being a stop in Storyville. As he turned onto Esplanade, he saw a group gathered in front of the boarding house. A couple of guys in nondescript uniforms. In conversation with, of all people, Mrs. Jennings. He quickened his pace.

Before they noticed him, he spotted what they were going on about. A battered wooden trunk stood on the sidewalk. The delivery men were haggling over payment if they were to carry it up five floors. Mrs. Jennings was trying to talk their price down. Loudly.

"In time for once," she groused at her tenant. "This contraption is yours, Mr. Steinberg. Sent by train from Texas. Assume you know what's in it."

Tom began to finger bills in his pants pocket. "What do I owe you gentlemen? It is five floors up, though I can help lift," he said.

"It's heavy alright. Ten dollars would be the going price. Divided between us."

"That's ridiculous," Mrs. Jennings shot back.

"It's worth it," Tom replied, pulling out two fives and handing them over.

"Got to tell you, mister, the lock is busted. Things happen on trains. Not our responsibility," one of the men said.

Tom nodded and gestured toward the entrance.

Mrs. Jennings mumbled under her breath but none of them paid her any attention. She followed them up and halted at the fourth-floor landing where the bottom of the trunk fell off. A half-dozen books tumbled out, followed by phonograph records, a packet of photos—and a gun.

Tom snatched up the weapon and put it in his pocket. The delivery men corralled the books and records. Without a word, they took them upstairs, stacking them in front of the door. A few items of clothing remained half-stuck inside the trunk. Mrs. Jennings jerked them out, wadded them up, and carried the bundle upstairs, grumbling along the way.

Tom meanwhile sifted through the remaining contents, including a cowboy hat, a pair of leather boots, and a gold locket. Its chain had broken. He slipped the necklace into his other pocket. The delivery men returned to haul the broken trunk up the final flight. Mrs. Jennings had already fished out her own key and opened Tom's door.

The woman was incorrigible, he thought.

"Put the trunk against the wall," she ordered the workmen. "The young man fancies hisself a carpenter. Maybe he can salvage the thing. Books can go on the table."

Crossing the room, she dumped the clothes on Tom's bed, several chess pieces tumbling out of a pocket onto the floor. Ignoring them, she jerked the nearby shade to let in the late afternoon sun.

Tom soon clambered up, deposited the boots and hat on a chair and thanked the men for their trouble. In the hallway, he scribbled his name on the receipt and watched the two descend the staircase.

To his consternation, Mrs. Jennings was sniffing out his books and records when he re-entered. Ignoring him, she picked up a volume.

"This one's in German," she announced, accusatory.

"Thomas Mann is one of our most famous writers," he said evenly, hoping that would be explanation enough. She blinked several times, unimpressed.

"This one too," she went on, flipping open another tome. "Since you can read these, what does *'Mein Kampf'* mean?" She pronounced the title well enough for him to understand her.

111

"It means '*My Struggle*,'" he replied evenly.

"Books weigh a lot. No wonder your trunk came apart."

"Indeed," he agreed curtly, hoping that would end the exchange.

"That gun too. Not used to things like that in my boarding house." She wagged her kerchiefed head in disapproval. "Strange, altogether strange."

"Texas is a very different place, Mrs. Jennings. Guns are for protection there." She tilted her head, as though weighing his defense. "My friends there obviously threw in everything I had accumulated before sending it on to me."

He made a tsking sound with his voice and looked at his watch, as though to signal it was late and he had things to do. In his own rented room.

"Left Texas in a hurry, did you?" she tossed out, an insinuation, not a question. His stomach turned over.

She picked up a third book with a bright yellow cover. "Ah, this one's in English. By Ernest Hemingway. You can read it too, I suppose. One of *our* great writers, so they say."

"It's true. *The Sun also Rises* helped me with my English. There in Texas."

At this juncture, Mrs. Jennings seemed to run out of curiosity. Besides, it was getting late, and she could use a jigger or two of bourbon to compensate for her exertions. Keeping her boarding house on the up-and-up was a full-time proposition, especially with all the lowlifes washing up from the riverbanks or jumping off of trains.

Tenants too were a trial. She had always said so, to her husband, to the neighbors, to the cops when they came round. This one here was polite, and paid in advance, but even so, something was off with him. She would stew over it.

Placing the Hemingway on the top of the pile, the landlady wiped her hand on her smock and turned to face her renter. "Don't know about your records, but if you hanker after hearing them: no loud music on the premises. I run a respectable house and aim to keep it that way."

Tomas bowed his head, struggling to keep his irritation in check. But unable to bear another minute, he sidled to the door and twisted the doorknob. "Thank you for all your help, Mrs. Jennings. I am most appreciative."

Once alone, he surveyed the mess on the floor, his eyes searching for the most important thing: his immigration papers stamped on Ellis Island four years ago.

Nowhere to be seen—not stuck in books, not in the pockets of his clothes, not at the bottom of his boots.(Why his friends had bothered with these last, the leather irreparably worn, when he had stressed that New Orleans would not require anything like that, was beyond him. He let out an expletive and paced back and forth in thought.

In a hurry or not, how could he have been so careless or cavalier as to hop that train, leaving those documents behind? If he had never needed to show them, getting by on—what was it: his looks, his charm, official negligence or indifference?—the world was now a more worrisome place. It was disjointed, it was disruptive. And Germans were largely to blame for it.

As for the gun, that was a different problem. He had learned to shoot at varmints out in the badlands, but never saw any need for a weapon in public places, especially around those ubiquitous beer halls they called saloons.

He was no cowboy, as that Texas gal with the twang had quickly observed. From the get-go, Tom knew himself to be different, and different could easily be frowned upon in America as anywhere else.

After checking to make sure it was not loaded, he stuck the thing, a bone-handled six-shooter, in the only chest of drawers in the room, under his socks.

Surely, Mrs. Jennings would not have the gall—

He retrieved a beer from the icebox and began to arrange the titles on a shelf of his makeshift bookcase. In addition to Hemingway, he had acquired a novel by William Faulkner, which had proven too difficult at the time, and another by Sinclair Lewis, which he had managed to read, and admired.

The half-dozen record albums he now examined—three operas in German his parents had shipped him early on, and three others he had acquired in Texas.

These latter were referred to as Big Bands, the same cowgirl with the twang had told him, laughing at his ignorance, pulling him onto that sawdust dance floor, nonetheless. Artie Shaw, Glenn Miller, Tommy Dorsey: their music had rhythm, and thus inspired by their tunes, he had picked up the dance steps.

"Not half bad," the girl had commented, delighting in being twirled around for hours on end. Afterwards, they had screwed long into the night, under the vast Texas sky. She kept her boots on, throughout.

He could no longer remember her name, but the exuberance of their encounter came back to him.

Despite Mrs. Jennings' warning, he determined to browse around Werlein's on Canal Street for a proper phonograph player.

As for the tiny chess pieces, he retrieved a cardboard box, dumped them inside and placed it on the bottom shelf of the bookcase. All those games he had played, first against his father and then against Hans, were now unimaginable. Would there ever be another time for such fun, against anyone?

Determined to throw off his funk, Tom set about, with hammer and nail, to re-attach the bottom to his trunk. "Improve upon what's before you, but always think ahead," Tom recalled his father saying. It applied to more than chess.

When the doorbell rang, Claire raced downstairs to let the workman in. Her mother had an appointment at the beauty parlor downtown and then a ladies' luncheon to raise funds for Charity Hospital.

"I'll forego shopping and get back mid-afternoon if you're too busy to oversee things," Mrs. Endicott had offered.

Claire insisted she could handle the interruption to her studies.

"When you show the fellow the wobbly leg, apprise him of the fragility of the thing," she had gone on. "I have moved all the valuables out of there, so you needn't keep constant guard." Claire had rolled her eyes.

When she opened the front door, it was hard to tell who was more agog.

"What on earth are you doing here?"

"This is Webster Street, right? I've been sent to repair a sideboard." Tom switched his toolbox to his left hand and held out his right. "I had no idea this was your home, but I'm glad it is. Now I can wish you *Frohes Neues Jahr*."

"And same to you, Tom. Happy New Year 1940." Claire shook his proffered hand. Warmly. To dispel any awkwardness, she ushered him inside and straight to the dining room.

"This is the offending sideboard. Personally, I don't mind the wobble or the squeak, but my mother is particular about such things," she explained.

Tom nodded and set about examining the leg joints.

Instead of returning to her room to study, she watched him work, his expression intent. Eventually, from his toolbox, he retrieved and applied a gluey substance smelling of cedar to the planed leg. Reassessing the others, he tightened one, repositioned another.

"Nothing much wrong with this piece, though I reckon it's at least a hundred years old. Helps to keep them maintained, and polished." While he returned his implements to his toolbox and wrote up an invoice, Claire retreated to the kitchen. He soon followed, rinsing his hands in the sink.

"It's not Café du Monde but our coffee does have chicory," she said.

They sipped in silence, his eyes taking in the room and the view out the window. A weeping willow stood near a weather-beaten back fence.

"You have an inviting home in a quiet neighborhood. Very different from French Town."

She hesitated, the compliment, as was often the case, throwing her off-balance. "I like that there are different sections of the city, diverse people in them." Pausing, she added, "The charms of the Quarter, for instance, are considerable."

He smiled, recognizing—could it be for the first time?—that her voice had a seductive lilt. A far cry from a twang.

Since he did not respond to her observation, Claire eyed her watch, calculating her mother would not return for another couple of hours. She took a chance. "I'll show you the rest of the house. Perhaps you'll find something else that needs fixing," she said, more mischievously than she intended.

He gestured for her to lead the way.

"You're right about the furniture. Weighty and old," she chattered on, as they walked through the living room, an alcove with a piano, a sunroom with potted plants, and into her father's study.

"Like my parents, I guess, the furniture," she added.

Tomas smiled at her witticism (if that's what it was) and brushed his hand along a row of books in leather bindings. He paused to scrutinize the authors: Dickens, Thackeray, Austen and on a lower shelf, in gold-Moroccan leather, a set of Sir Walter Scott's works.

"All the Victorians are here," she pointed out, "though my personal favorite is out of reach." Her eyes shifted upward to the top shelf. "George Eliot. A woman writer who was smart enough to know her books wouldn't sell if people knew she was female."

Tomas nodded as though in assent of her sentiment.

For an instant, Claire appeared lost in thought, gazing at the young man's spine as he stretched to pull out one of the novels high up. He held it in his hand, his expression quizzical. The title apparently mystified him.

"*Middlemarch* is complicated. At heart it's about mismatched lovers."

Raising his eyebrows, he replied, "Perhaps someday I'll be able to..."

"For now, I'll show you the upstairs," Claire interrupted briskly. "My room overlooks the street. There's a balcony."

He motioned again for her to proceed, Coco already awaiting them at the top of the staircase. The feline looked disapproving and descended in evident disgust.

In Claire's room, several textbooks and a tablet were strewn across a roll-top desk. Another tome was splayed open, spine-up, on the canopied bed.

"I was studying when you arrived," she said lamely, acutely aware of the flowery wallpaper, the lace curtains, the silk damasked chairs. Too frilly, too girlish, she thought.

Tom took it all in without comment, before noticing the framed photo on the night table. He picked it up.

"It's of my friend Myra and me. In the library at Sophie Newcomb College. We often studied together."

He nodded, then said, "Yes, I remember that day at the café. She looked stricken." He was about to add, "as was I," but checked himself. Instead, he switched gears. "Why don't we?" gesturing for her to raise the French window and step out onto the balcony. Which they did.

"My parents prefer I don't stand out here, making a spectacle of myself, but here we are!"

Of necessity, they stood close to each other, their arms touching, and looked out over the balustrade. Several neighbors were walking their dogs, a slice of the river could be seen in the distance. Potted ferns took up the extra space.

After a beat, Tom asked, "Should I assume you always do what your parents expect of you?" His voice was mildly mocking.

"As you can now attest, not always." she rejoined. They continued to take in the scenery, their eyes turning to the rooftops, other balconies across the street, several church spires. "Home," Tomas murmured, thinking of Lübeck.

Then, as happened often in New Orleans, clouds rolled in, obscuring the sunshine. The wind picked up.

Claire shivered.

He lent his arm to help her back through the opening, closed the window and turned to face her. Her eyes were wide, questioning. He took her hands—clammy to the touch—and pulled her to him. A clap of thunder made her squeeze them tight.

She parted her lips, tilted her head back. Tomas kissed her, at first tentatively, then more probing, her tongue eagerly entwining with his.

Breaking away, he whispered, "You must tell me if you do not want to—"

"No, no. I mean, yes. Here, now, it's what I would like," she burgled, sweeping the opened book off the bed.

Against his better judgment, Tom followed her lead. He was a virile young man, and she a beautiful woman. And there was a waiting bed. Her fingers fumbled to unbutton her blouse. He helped her. Kicking off her pumps, she lay down on the bed, her head propped up on pillows, pulling him alongside her. She seemed avid; he struggled to control himself.

But then they heard a crash. Downstairs. Claire froze. Tom righted himself. Together, they rushed to the staircase and down to the landing. Coco scampered past them on her way up, looking abashed.

Peering over the banister, they could see partially into the dining room, shards of lavender-colored glass strewn about the floor.

Suddenly a voice.

"What on earth? Crazy cat." It was Claire's father, sounding none too pleased.

Tongue-tied, Claire shrank behind Tom, buttoned her blouse, and ran her hand through her hair.

They could hear her father muttering and then the sound of glass being kicked aside.

Within seconds, Mr. Endicott appeared in the hall below them. He looked up, a stunned expression on his face.

"And you would be? Upstairs, with my daughter."

"We heard a noise, sir, and did not know—"

"It's Tom Stone, Father," Claire interjected. "Here to fix the sideboard—and then, the window to the balcony I can never open. That too..." she stammered, her voice quavering.

"I don't have time to go over this, young man. You need to leave. We have a family emergency."

"Of course, sir," Tom replied. Without another word, he squeezed Claire's arm and descended the stairs. Grabbing up his toolbox, he inclined his head toward Mr. Endicott, but the older man had turned away. Mortified, Tom made his way out the front door, pulling it shut firmly.

"What has happened, Father? Is it Addison?" Claire called out as soon as the front door closed. She could hear her father rooting around in a drawer. In his distress, he was still muttering, but she could not make out the words.

Her feet were bare. She dared not come down, nor retreat, until she knew more.

Soon, Mr. Endicott came back into view.

"Your mother slipped while getting off the streetcar on Canal Street. In the rain. She was taken to the hospital. It's her leg, I believe. They may have to operate. She insisted on a bag of things from home."

Claire raced back upstairs, put on her shoes, and gathered up personal items from her mother's room.

"Be right down, Father, with night clothes and things. Does Addison know yet?"

"I'm calling him at the number he left us. Went up to Alexandria on military business."

To see Myra, Claire thought.

119

Part Two

1941-1942

Families signal their patriotism 1942

Chapter Fifteen

WAR CLOUDS THICKEN

Addison and Claire drove together to deliver the sacks of peach hulls Mrs. Endicott had put aside over the past month. When they pulled up, the pier in the warehouse district was bustling.

A pair of workmen, their faces streaked with sweat from the June sun, thanked the two and with little to-do, tossed the sacks onto the back of a lorry, already chock-a-block with crates. From there, the materiel would be transferred onto barges headed up the Mississippi River to munitions plants. The hulls, it was said, would be repurposed as shell casings.

"Anything else you got, especially in the way of rubber—boots, tires, mats—bring them along next time. Barges push off almost daily," one of them said, inclining his head to Addison.

Even though war had not yet been declared, preparations for combat were underway across the country, more and more household goods re-versioned for use by the Armed Forces. And when the Nazis took over Paris in the spring of 1940, the pace picked up.

When that news bulletin came on the radio, Claire was at the antique store helping Lady Monceau, who was accompanied by her married daughter. They were looking for a settee and matching chairs for the latter's Uptown home near Sophie Newcomb. All three women stopped to listen.

"*Mon dieu.* What a tragedy," the elder woman had exclaimed.

For a fleeting moment, Claire thought to herself that she should have traveled abroad when she could have, knowing that for the foreseeable future the City of Light, as well as everywhere else in Europe, would be off-limits. Without commenting on the war, she helped the two ladies settle on an ensemble, elegant enough but also serviceable.

"How Daniel manages to rough up the furniture in that room is beyond me," the Monceau daughter said, as she ran her hand along the upholstery of the couch. The cloth was thick, and likely durable, though Claire was unfamiliar with the material.

"Children do tend to be hard on furniture, but this texture seems practical," she said.

The daughter corrected her. "Daniel and I have no children. My oblivious husband is forever entertaining students in that room. Heaven knows..."

Although agitated by the news from abroad, Lady Monceau scribbled a check for the three pieces of furniture, and thanked Claire profusely. "Otto Rothmann does not deserve you. And did you not say? You would have liked to travel to Paris. A shame, really a shame."

As the months passed, Claire noticed that many people, including professors at the university, grew anxious about events abroad, some of them even reconciled to the idea that America would sooner or later have to step in to shore up allies, especially Britain. Myra, among them.

It was she who told Mrs. Endicott about peach hulls being of use. She had called up to speak to Claire—and to Addison—some weeks before. Claire could not recall exactly what the two discussed —something about Myra's aunt planning to relocate to New Orleans —but when her brother took the phone, she heard his voice modulate an octave lower.

Since childhood, she knew it was useless to press Addison. He was the soul of discretion, which, she reckoned, stood him in excellent stead with the buttoned-up military.

"What do you make of these latest rumors?" Claire asked as they watched a heavily laden barge being tugged out into the river. "You know, the ones about submarines slinking around in the Gulf."

Addison shrugged, as usual noncommittal. "They very well may be true. We've got boats patrolling the coast, volunteers on foot at crucial sites. We'll see what develops."

Claire nodded, wondering what other changes might be in store if the country were drawn into the conflict—or invaded by enemy troops.

For an instant, she thought of the only German she actually knew, and what he might be thinking now that his country had overrun much of Europe. Could he be looked upon askance, as though he were a spy or something? She had no inkling. Tom Stone had not called or dared come by the house since the accident with her mother.

She did not blame him; neither could she shake the thought of him.

"Something's on your mind, Sis. I can tell," her brother said as they pulled away from the pier.

Her turn to evade. "Oh, you know. Mother. Why she's not getting any better."

A flicker of irritation crossed Addison's face as he edged out into the morning traffic.

"That limp may have sapped her energy," she went on. "And Father hasn't made it any easier. I wish they—"

Addison honked the horn at two young boys kicking a ball in the street.

Claire dropped the subject, not wanting to ruin the morning for either of them. "If you don't mind, you could drop me at Canal and Chartres. I've got shopping to do, shoes and things."

"Not a problem. I'm stopping into the office on Carondelet for a couple of hours. But don't forget. The Carrolltons are coming over this evening. Along with others. Mother's made an all-in gumbo."

Claire did not disguise her lack of enthusiasm.

While they waited for the traffic light to change, Addison lit a cigarette. Claire watched a gaggle of girls cross the street, laughing as if there were nothing in the world to trouble them.

"I was thinking," Addison soon said, "that you might have more fun if you invited a couple of your college friends over. That way you won't feel obligated to make inane small talk with Harold and Helen. Maybe you and Richard could—"

"Could what, pray tell?" she interrupted him to ask, her tone challenging.

"Don't jump down my throat. He is our oldest friend—and everyone thinks you'd make an ideal couple. Besides."

"Besides what? Mother and Father want to see me situated, now that I'm all of twenty-three? As though the only way that can be achieved is by marrying someone they think suitable, meaning, financially well-off and morally irreproachable." Her tone was scathing. "You know, like Father: a pillar of rectitude."

Taken aback by her vehemence, Addison backed off. He took a few puffs and tried another tack.

"You might want to clear things up with Richard, one way or another," he suggested, "though hard to imagine a better person than our Richard. You could do worse."

She made a face as if to suggest she did not disagree with his assessment, but that their friend's sterling qualities did not matter to her.

"Not to mention..." Addison hit the brakes behind a suddenly stalled streetcar.

"What exactly?" she asked.

"If we go to war, everything will change, Sis. Myra will have filled you in about what's afoot up her way." Claire nodded noncommittal, calculating that she had not spoken to her friend about any such thing. "Anyway," Addison continued, "it won't have escaped you that all able-bodied men will be called up—and that likely means sent off."

"Sent off? Where do you mean?"

"It depends, but you read the papers. The Japanese have wreaked havoc in China; the Germans have conquered half of Europe and are bombing Britain. We may not be able to sit this out. Even if it means..."

Before he could finish his thought, or she could formulate another question, they had turned onto Canal Street. Claire straightened up in the passenger seat and gathered her pocketbook and hat.

"Drop me at the clock right in front of Adler's. I should get home by 5, if Mother asks."

Unsettled by this conversation, Claire wandered into Adler's to catch her breath and eye a few of the latest gift items the store was promoting. She would need a housewarming present to take to Lena Walenska's new lodgings.

It took longer than the Kaminskys had bargained on for Lena to wrap up her stay in Alexandria and move to New Orleans.

During the winter months, she developed a persistent cough, eventually receiving a diagnosis of croup, which doctors said might have been lurking inside her during her "deprivations" abroad. The illness left her debilitated throughout the first half of 1941, but no less demanding.

"Bring me that Vicks, make me a broth, search out those Beethoven sonatas and put them on the record player." And on and on.

Ilona ministered to her sister's needs in the early morning but, surprising both her husband and her daughter, returned to her job at the local library in the new year. As the weeks went by, she also made it a point to get her hair styled, regularly, at Bertha's salon, and brought home a few dresses on approval from Bauer's— "something with flair," she had instructed Frederick's mother to bring her.

127

If bemused to see her mother critiquing her reflection in the mirror, standing up straighter as a result, Myra did not let on. *Why shouldn't she indulge herself?* she thought. "The dresses become you, Mother."

Ilona promptly bought all three frocks, without consulting her husband or modeling them for Lena.

That her mother went to such lengths to polish her act and re-establish her command of the household, was endearing, but perhaps not essential. Things in the Kaminsky house had already begun to shift.

Since it was left to Konrad to devote his lunch break to minister to his ailing sister-in-law and otherwise keep her entertained until Ilona got home, the effort eventually grew tiresome. Although he was not one to articulate such a thought, his sister-in-law was more of a diva than he had remembered, and his own wife less of a doormat than he had counted on.

It was a rude but salutary awakening.

Still, Myra had come to appreciate her aunt's softer, more sympathetic side as well as her mother's newfound vigor. Not only was the older woman more perceptive than her regal airs portended, but she had zeroed in on her niece's own streak of independence and lent her quiet support.

When she managed to have time off from her job at nearby Camp Claiborne, Myra arranged a couple of quick trips to New Orleans. Her immediate goal was to deliver her aunt's résumé and a sampling of her concert programs from years past to the music department at Sophie Newcomb. On her first visit, she spent most of her day on campus, talking up her aunt's talent, her Continent-wide career, the hurdles she had overcome, the younger musicians she had mentored. The professors seemed interested but reserved judgment, indicating they'd make a decision only once they had the opportunity to interview the applicant in person.

On her second excursion there, a rainy Saturday in April, Myra scouted the residential area, including her old haunts, for a suitable apartment to lease (or buy, if funds permitted)—one large enough to entertain guests, her aunt had instructed more than once. After a few hours, she came away with a few leads, three places for rent on St. Charles Avenue itself—a street whose grandiosity would likely appeal to Lena, she imagined—and a smaller, but charming dwelling for sale within walking distance of the college.

With a couple of hours to kill before her bus back home, Myra decided to pay a visit to the Endicott home, on the off chance of seeing Claire, or even Addison, though she tried to tell herself the latter was an afterthought.

Mr. Endicott answered the doorbell, betraying a flicker of irritation. She could hardly retreat.

"I was hoping, though I would have phoned if possible. However, I wondered if Claire were at home. If not, I apologize for the intrusion," she burbled.

He stared at her damp curls. "Claire and her mother are out. Not expected back until late." All the while, he remained with one hand on the shiny brass knob, as though eager to close the door in her face.

Myra fumbled for something else to say, not daring to close her dripping umbrella. Then she heard a voice from within the house.

"Father, is it that package I'm expecting from DC? Do they need me to sign for it?"

Before Mr. Endicott could answer, Addison materialized in the foyer. Tilting his head to one side, he said, "Is that you, Myra? It's wet out there. Do come in."

She did, dropping the open umbrella on the porch and shaking out her curls before entering.

The two sat in the kitchen, sipping tea and chatting, Mr. Endicott having made himself scarce. Only when they heard the radio in the parlor come on—the news at 6 p.m., a report from occupied Paris —did the two consult their watches. In response, Myra stood and held out her hand.

"I must be going. I missed the bus I meant to take but can catch the last one, if I leave now. Please tell Claire I was sorry to miss her."

Addison looked hard at her, his smile slightly askew. "I mean, well, I also came to see..."

"Of course. Coco. She never gets enough attention."

She blushed. "Indeed. Your cat."

They stood for a moment across the table from each other, neither making a move.

Finally, Addison said, "I'll get the keys. And drive you to the depot."

She did not object.

The sun had made an effort to come out as the rain fizzled. A rainbow arched over St. Charles Avenue en route. Once he pulled up to the busy depot, travelers scurrying about, some with briefcases, a few in uniform, Addison killed the engine. He turned to face her.

"Whatever happens, Myra, wherever we end up—or I am sent—you do know what an impression you have made on me."

She blinked, not knowing how to decipher such an admission. "Hopefully, everything will work out as we'd like," she managed, before putting her hand on the door handle.

Leaning over, Addison placed a kiss on her forehead. In response, she brushed his cheek with one hand, then opened the car door and made her way inside to the ticket window.

Back at the Endicotts, Myra's umbrella remained open on the front porch until Claire and her mother spotted it upon their return.

"Were we expecting anyone this evening, dear?"

"Not that I'm aware," Claire responded.

When they encountered Mr. Endicott in the parlor, he shushed them. The announcer on the radio was going on about ship movements in the North Atlantic—something about a confrontation between German and British vessels. Shortly, he held out a note to Claire. "From your former friend, that Kaminsky girl. Said she could not wait any longer."

Claire took the folded note, unsure what to make of the word *former*. She helped her mother, exhausted after their outing, get settled in her chair.

As she headed to the kitchen to heat up soup for the three of them, her father called out. "Still, she lingered long enough. Waylaid your brother. They might have eaten everything in the icebox. Got rid of her by driving her somewhere."

Opening the icebox, Claire noticed nothing amiss. She took out her mother's soup tureen and poured the contents into a pan on the stove. While she doctored cold cuts, she could hear her father going on about the day's visitor. "Ought to know better, wouldn't you agree, Esther? *Summa cum laude*, my ass."

Her mother must have reprimanded him for his coarse language, though not loud enough to hear.

"All right, all right. At least Addison knows how to behave. With all he has on his mind, he humored the girl through the afternoon. Goes to show."

"Yes, dear. Our son is above reproach. But Myra is a loyal friend of Claire's and helps her parents, a refugee aunt too. Saving the woman from—"

"I'm bringing you both a tray," Claire called out from the kitchen. "Water or sweet tea?"

"Tea for us both," her mother responded.

Fortunately, the subject of Myra Kaminsky was dropped over the soup, sparing Claire from the umpteenth defense of her friend, and Addison's too for that matter. Still, she reckoned, her brother should be able enough to defend his own fondness for her. If that were the right word. Only after doing the dishes and helping her mother mount the stairs did Claire remember to read the note.

It was scribbled in a hurry, but its tone was curated, as Myra may have assumed Mr. Endicott would be curious enough to read it.

Sorry to miss you, Claire, but my trip to town was last-minute.
As you will remember, Aunt Lena decided to move to New Orleans and has applied to our alma mater's music department—Dr. Henson, remember him? Hopefully, the powers that be will see fit to hire her.

Under that assumption, I've been looking around, at her behest, for lodgings.

Anyway, have to get back home. Camp Claiborne is busier than ever, and the military expects everyone, moi included, to show up on time. They did not teach us that at Newcomb, did they? I'm working for some ranking officers: sticklers but decent. Let's catch up soon. Oh, and Addison happened to be around.

He is driving me to the depot. Much appreciated on my part.
Myra

Lena Walenska's letter of acceptance as an adjunct professor of music theory and an instructor of piano arrived at the Kaminsky home in Alexandria in late August, three weeks before the fall term began. She ceremoniously removed it from her bosom and read it aloud to the table, in her much improved, if still noticeably accented, English.

A full table at that.

Mrs. Murkowski had come over with a cured ham and a peach cobbler that morning and was easily prevailed upon to partake of both that evening. She brought along her grandson, Lech, who had taken a few lessons from Lena and, as a result, no longer drove his grandmother to distraction banging futilely on the keyboard. It also seemed opportune to include the Wallensteins, as their bridge four-somes had languished during the past year, and they now rarely socialized as couples.

Finally, now that Myra had returned from New Orleans, Ilona quietly redoubled efforts to cement the relationship with Frederick. Plus, she wished to thank his mother, Flora, and his aunt, Fannie, for their help in updating her wardrobe. She had already raised eyebrows at the library with her attire, (which gave her unexpected satisfaction). For this late summer evening at home, she chose another of her new ensembles, determined not to don an apron. Most of the kitchen chores were now left to their occasional maid, or to Myra, who was pleased enough to see her mother in high spirits.

Over the cobbler and coffee, Lena, having pulled the letter out from her silk blouse, made a show of teasing the two pages from their envelope. A dinner knife was involved. Not to be humiliated in public, she had read it earlier, asking Ilona to explain a couple of the contractual stipulations.

The dinner guests applauded the good news. Mr. Kaminsky rose to open a second bottle of wine and propose a toast to his sister-in-law.

"May this new chapter in your storied life, Lena, be as fulfilling as those that have come before," he intoned.

Myra too had a surprise to divulge. "Provided that it meets your expectations, Aunt Lena, a charming house near the university is for sale, and the owner, who is moving away, is willing to come down on the price. You could walk to the arts building. Not to mention to the streetcar on St. Charles!"

More applause from the assembled.

"You are an angel, Myra. I will want to live there only if it's spacious enough to accommodate you—and indeed the entire Kaminsky family," Lena exuded, tearing up. "To think, only a year or two ago, I was cowering in a barn." She shook her head, simulating distress.

"Now, now. That's over. *Kaputt*," Konrad said, with some vehemence, he, arguably more than she, riled by the memory of all the fear he and Myra had witnessed abroad.

There was murmuring about the state of the world at the table, but no one wished to ruin the otherwise pleasant atmosphere. Everyone downed their wine. Even Lech, no older than fifteen, was poured a modicum.

Finally, Flora and Fannie, slightly inebriated, took the stage, as it were. "We too have news to share," the one piped up.

"No, no. Not us," the other corrected. "Our nephew does. Enlighten them, Fred. We're all friends here."

The young man looked taken off-guard. From across the table, Myra held her palms up to encourage him.

"It's not up to the man in these cases," he acquiesced tentatively, color rising to his cheeks. He stared down table over the head of Mr. Kaminsky. "But, as it turns out, I am now engaged." Ilona's mouth fell open. "Or rather, *we* are engaged. Ruby Tate, that is."

"Why that's splendid, young man. Congratulations," Mr. Wallenstein chortled, tapping Frederick on the shoulder in masculine solidarity. "I knew the world would come right once this damn Depression ended."

Blood having drained from her face, Ilona picked up her water glass and consumed the entirety. The two Bauer matrons chattered on about Ruby's plans for a fall wedding, her promotion at the bank, and her family's general prosperity. Mr. Tate sold Chevrolets; his wife kept the accounts. The only black spot was their ne'er-do-well son who spent his days wasting nickels at the penny arcade.

Not one to hold back an opinion, Mrs. Murkowski had her own (opposing) view. "But Ruby Tate isn't even Jewish. A *shiksa* through and through!"

Something like a smile crossed Myra's face.

Chapter Sixteen

UPS AND DOWNS

Sometimes, on the streetcar ride home, Claire wondered what Myra would make of their fortunes in life. About her own so far, she was disconsolate; about Myra's, she was perplexed.

One thing was clear. They had been misled.

All those professors who had declared their students would be the first generation of women to make the world their oyster. *How gullible we were to have swallowed that*, she mused.

In Claire's view, neither of the two friends had done anything of note, despite their degrees.

Neither had ventured out to Africa to fight malaria or to the Pacific to research the natives. Myra at least had helped to extricate her aunt from the Nazis' grasp and then maneuvered to secure her a teaching position at Sophie Newcomb. Further, she had landed a job to help set up the country's war machine. (If there were to be such a need.)

To be blunt, Myra had focus and conviction, whereas she herself dawdled at a dead-end job, polishing old wood, kowtowing to enti-tled customers, and avoiding her boss's advances. Admittedly, Rothmann's afforded her some economic independence—by living at home she had saved almost the entirety of her salary.

On the plus side, she decided to put it, neither she nor Myra had acquiesced and married the first man who came along with a ring.

But, as they had been promised, the Depression had petered out, so where was all the fun they were supposed to have in their twenties?

Claire would not speak for Myra, but her own social life was non-existent. Even on that front, her friend had arguably scored more highly: she had had a love affair, as ill-advised and ill-fated as it was; she had a faithful suitor in the person of Frederick Bauer; and, most surprising, Addison seemed intrigued by her. The only man she herself spent any time thinking about—however unsuitable to her parents—had not come around since that mortifying encounter with her father. That awful day her mother slipped and fell, her leg twisted underneath her.

She brushed her blond curls off her forehead and shook her head to throw off that memory. To no avail.

Mrs. Endicott's injured leg had not properly healed after the accident. Although she rarely spoke of it, and never in front of her husband, her pain was nagging. Often when she thought herself unobserved, Claire's mother reached for her knee and massaged it; other times, if she moved awkwardly or stood too long, she winced, and sought out a chair.

If Esther Endicott had longed to once again dance—"a simple waltz at a Mardi Gras ball," she had once, (likely under the influence of a little sherry), sighed aloud to her daughter—she had eventually abandoned such a notion.

To Claire's anxious eye, her mother began to look, as well as feel, old. Her complexion sallowed, gray strands streaked her hair. Claire occasionally spotted her dabbing her eyes or scrutinizing herself in the bathroom mirror, the only one Edward Endicott had allowed to be hung in the house.

Claire made attempts to take her mother out on weekends, to eat lunch in the Quarter, take in a matinee, or attend a public lecture. If

Addison were around, she would encourage him to come along. Sometimes, Mrs. Endicott would rally from the distraction; other times, she barely made it through the occasion.

The efforts became tiring for Claire. Her course work began to flag. She made no new friends. Mostly, she spent her evenings in the parlor with her mother, marking up one of her textbooks, while her mother embroidered or listened to the news on the radio.

"Truth be told, I prefer to hear Mr. Roosevelt speak more than any man I've ever known," her mother broke the silence to say aloud one evening. Hearing this pronouncement, her father folded the pages of the paper, rose to his feet and left the room. After a few minutes, Claire fiddled with the dial, tuning to something lighter. At least "Fibber McGee and Molly" made her mother smile.

Although she had not articulated her feelings, Claire was dismayed by the direction they were taking her. As uncharitable as the thought was, she did not want to end up like her mother. Nor did she want to end up marrying someone like her father.

Surely, there must be a way to throw off these despicable thoughts, she mused as the streetcar rattled up St. Charles.

If anyone could lift her spirits, it would be Myra. And Lena Walenska would be entertaining. To the latter's housewarming party she would go, her gift from Adler's in tow.

When Claire arrived at the address right off Broadway around 6 p.m., she could hear laughter from within as well as the strains of a string quartet. Madame Walenska's new abode looked to be a well-appointed shot-gun house with azaleas interspersed with ferns dotting the front garden. Ivy grew on the half-dozen steps leading up to the entrance, clipped to perfection. The place must employ a gardener. She smoothed her dress and pressed the doorbell.

At first glance, it appeared that half the faculty of Sophie Newcomb had shown up to welcome the newcomer to their ranks. Several potted plants, assorted liquor bottles, and a couple of phonograph records had been deposited on a side table. She put her Adler's shopping bag next to a couple of other fancily wrapped presents.

"What a delight to see you, Claire. We were speaking of you only minutes ago. Do come in," Lena gushed. She was wearing a silk gown but more sedate than the ones she had brought from abroad. Before she could respond, Claire was re-introduced to Dr. Henson, who ran the music department, and a couple of other professors she vaguely recognized from her years on campus.

Saving her from any awkwardness, Myra made her way over. "I knew you would manage. How is your mother? And you? Everyone in fact?" Her friend seemed ebullient, her hair shorter than before, straighter and shinier, her make-up more subtle.

Claire, who only ever dabbed her mother's face powder on her nose, suddenly felt that she had let herself go, whereas Myra had fixed herself up. Perhaps the aunt, so used to the limelight, had something to do with it.

"You'll know some of the faculty, but first, let me show you the house. Needless to say, Aunt Lena has great taste in furniture, but we still have a couple of rooms to fill. "Next time I'm down here, you must come along to help us. Perhaps take us through Rothmann's."

Myra took Claire by the arm and led her down the hallway past a brightly lit kitchen. A servant in livery was busily filling trays of *hors d'oeuvres* and setting out liquor bottles. They continued toward the two back bedrooms separated by a bath.

A canopied bed and matching dresser adorned one room, presumably where Lena had ensconced herself. A day coat with swirls of flowers was tossed over the back of a rocker. The other bedroom featured a large chest and a couple of chairs but otherwise was bare. At the very back of the house was an airy room with, so far, only a roll-top desk and a couch. A French window gave onto a small yard. An oak tree stood at the rear, where it shaded a wrought-iron bench.

"The house is charming, and surprisingly spacious. How ever did you come across it?"

"Wore out a pair of shoes or two. You remember Lucille Truard. She knows several old families in the area, faculty types. The owner happened to be a widower, eager to sell and move away."

Claire nodded, impressed, and a little envious.

"Oh, and she is here, our Professor Truard. Brought along one of her Garden District friends. As for the faculty, many have come out of the woodwork. Apparently, cocktail parties are back in vogue."

Claire smiled at her friend's assessment and continued to take in the room.

"You'll be as amazed as I am. My aunt has made quite an impression in two months, planning a concert in support of Jewish refugees next month. Working to get instructors in other departments involved. 'Jews, Catholics, Protestants: we're all in this together,' is how she put it."

Claire arched her eyebrows.

"Despite some of the mean things I said before about her, she is a force to be reckoned with, far from what we imagined back when..." she trailed off.

"What about your parents? Are they here?"

Myra shook her head. "They'll come down soon. Wanted to let the party be Lena's affair. But yes, they're well. Better actually. Especially Mother. More—what would be the word?—*galvanized*."

If only her own mother, Claire thought, could be as energized as Ilona Kaminsky. She shook off the comparison and walked over to the window. Two squirrels were chasing each other up and down the oak tree; a gibbous moon hung over the top branches. Myra had done a good job, and the wad of German marks Madame Walenska had smuggled in must have been larger than anyone imagined.

After a minute or two, the two friends heard a flurry of doorbell rings and louder voices.

"We should get back," Myra said. "I'm an unofficial hostess. Oh, and don't forget. Dr. Penley is here. I specifically promised you'd be in attendance. I know you can talk to him more intelligently than I!"

Once back in the parlor, Claire did spot her math professor, but he was deep in conversation with Lucille Truard and a couple of other ladies. A waiter handed the two young women goblets of white wine and gestured toward the buffet. As they made their way over to the food, Claire heard her name called.

"My dear Miss Endicott. What a pleasant surprise to see you."

The voice was Lady Monceau's. Claire turned and greeted the older woman.

"I told you I had connections here at your college, but I did not know you were acquainted with Lena Walenska."

"She is my friend's aunt. Have you met Myra Kaminsky? We graduated together in '39, only she was *summa cum laude*." Myra inclined her head and smiled at the old lady.

"I believe my friend Lucille has spoken of both of you. Unless I err, she found the Class of '39 to be exceptional."

Both Claire and Myra accepted the compliment, though Claire doubted that their French teacher thought any of her students were that proficient in French, other than Myra.

"I will leave you two to the buffet. But, by the way, I plan to drop by Rothmann's in coming days. Perhaps you will do me the courtesy of helping me choose some pieces for the guest house I'm refurbishing."

"With pleasure, Lady Monceau."

"Otto would have me purchase only Chippendale or Louis Philippe when all I need is something comfortable. Or even modern! I will trust you to point out things that would appeal to a younger person."

"By all means. I shall look forward to seeing you."

With that, the older woman turned and made her way back through the crowd to rejoin Lucille Truard's coterie.

"She seems quite taken with you," Myra whispered, as they picked up plates and forks. "You must be doing something right on Royal Street. We shall see when I bring my aunt. I hope you're working on commission."

"I never thought to ask about that," Claire replied. "Otto Roth-mann's compliments are icky enough. To ask for anything special might make things worse. As soon as I make enough money to..." she trailed off. No need, she thought, to go on about the subject. She scooped a few olives onto her plate and helped herself to tomato aspic.

Letting the subject drop, Myra began to fill her own plate with shrimp and raw vegetables on tiny skewers. Inadvertently she stiff-ened. A voice had pierced the chatter behind them. Claire darted a glance toward her friend, then swiveled to take in the room. Not ten feet from the buffet table stood Daniel Calhoun. She caught the reflection of his gold watch fob.

For her part, Myra put down her plate, took a swallow of wine, and turned around to face him.

Within seconds, his eyes met hers, but the professor immediately lowered his gaze. He looked flummoxed. That was cue enough for Lena to hook her arm around the professor's and usher him toward the buffet.

"I have my niece to thank for arranging all this, finding the house, and organizing the catering. She graduated two years ago—*summa cum laude*—so you very well may recall her."

Before he could find an excuse to escape, he was *face-à-face* with Myra.

"Ah, yes. Miss, Miss Kaminsky," he stammered, "if memory serves."

His cheeks turned beet-red; hers drained of blood. He held out his hand. She ignored the gesture, but she did not walk off. Others milling about fell silent. A waiter handed Dr. Calhoun a glass of wine.

Claire intervened. "I'd love you to show me the kitchen, Lena. I hear you have the latest appliances."

Once the two were alone in the hallway, the older woman halted. "What on earth was that about? With the professor," she asked. "Don't tell me it has to do with Myra's course work."

"You'll have to ask your niece. Keep in mind that her parents know nothing."

"Just as well," Lena muttered. "Should I conclude it's all over and done with?"

"As far as I know," Claire responded, reluctant to go into detail.

They retreated further, into the kitchen itself. In the hope she would be hosting the kind of parties that lit up her life in Berlin and Warsaw, Lena had acquired the latest Magic Chef stove on the market along with the largest refrigerator Claire had ever seen.

By the time they returned to the parlor, Myra found herself swept up in a group including Dr. Werner and Lucille Truard. The latter two were doing all the talking, partly in German, partly in French. Daniel Calhoun was nowhere to be seen. Lena scanned the room for him.

"You needn't bother searching," Lucille said. "Daniel left abruptly, but at least he gave his mother-in-law a lift home. Never can tell with him."

Myra and Claire exchanged a look but did not make further inquiries.

Once the event wound down, Claire retrieved her wrap from the vestibule and said her goodbyes.

"I'll walk you a ways," Myra said. "Be right back," she called out to her aunt.

Out on the street, the two friends exhaled.

"First, despite what just transpired, you look amazing," Claire said. "Is that how you have to dress at Camp Claiborne?"

"It *is* the military, so nothing sloppy or suggestive," she replied, running her hand along her skirt to smooth the pleats. "But this outfit came from D.H. Holmes, a gift from Aunt Lena. To thank me for my leg work."

"It's lovely, the dress, and the house too." In the dark, they slowed to maneuver the uneven sidewalk.

"You look well too but thinner. And yet, you always had an appetite."

"I walk. Practically everywhere."

"But your shoes: gorgeous, higher than what I'm wearing these days. Stock up now. Leather is growing scarce."

"You think we're going to jump into the war?"

Myra shrugged. "Ask your brother. He knows more than us mere mortals."

Mulling this as they crossed the empty street, Claire further slowed her pace. "Should I take it you consider Addison as more than ordinary?"

"Not an unfair assumption," she replied, but without elaborating.

"And that Daniel is no longer in the picture?"

"Absolutely not."

Claire nodded, reassured. "By the way, who on earth is his mother-in-law?"

"No idea. Likely, old Truard had it wrong."

The two hugged at the intersection with St. Charles, promising to catch up properly before the holidays.

True to her word, Lady Monceau did put in an appearance at the antique store one afternoon in early November. Claire showed her practically the entirety of the inventory and before it was over, the old lady settled on a couch, two matching armchairs, and a coffee table. Expensive but not exorbitant, at least by the old lady's standards.

"Oh, I almost forgot," she said as they headed upfront to the cash register. "I will leave it to you to alert me to a desk, if one becomes available. The kind that a young woman, of industry and interests, would utilize to keep up her studies or her correspondence." A quizzical look passed over Claire's face. "Yes. Someone like you, my dear, if and when the time comes."

The time to seize the occasion came quickly for Claire, albeit in a round-about fashion.

Addison phoned one evening from DC, and after speaking with his mother, asked for his sister.

"In case you might be interested, Sis, here's the scuttlebutt. Navy Intelligence is looking to hire locals up and down the coast. It's all about finding those who could assist in deciphering, if not decoding, intercepts."

"I don't even know what 'intercepts' are, Addison," Claire snapped back.

"Enemy messages," he said, a note of impatience in his voice. He had gone out on a limb. The plan was still under wraps.

In the silence that followed, Claire wondered how he could imagine she'd be capable of doing anything like what he was describing.

"If you're not interested, so be it. There'll be other candidates. But you, little sister, did all that studying—German, French, advanced calculus. Not to mention your love of chess—and cross-word puzzles! Why not put all of that to good use?"

"If you think it's worthwhile, but whom would I even call? Especially since I know little about all these other things—decoding and all of that."

"Don't sell yourself short. And remember: everyone is likely to be called upon to take on things they never thought they could do. Especially women."

"I see," she relented, still uncertain.

Addison dangled another incentive. "Unless I'm mistaken, Myra is making a notable contribution to the Army's preparations. Racking up promotions in the process. I thought that—"

"We're really going to war. Is that what you're saying?"

"To paraphrase the song, 'Don't know where, don't know when,' but yes. It's more than likely and probably imminent."

For a few days, Claire mulled the idea that Addison had tossed out, and which he soon followed up, sending her a telegram with the name, rank, and phone number of a commanding officer, one

Vincent Nelson, based in the office a stone's throw from Canal Street.

Dressed in her best wool suit and medium high heels for the job interview, she was hired on the spot as a civilian operative in the Naval Intelligence unit within the Gulf Coast district. Initially, she would report to a junior lieutenant named Robert Forster, her start date the first Monday of November.

On her way to pick up her last paycheck at the antiques store, Claire arrived at 8:30, hoping to complete the task before customers intruded. She headed back to the storage area, past the oak sideboards too bulky to display upfront and glass cases filled with seasonal fare —Mardi Gras beads and boa-feathered hats—to the owners' quarters.

Through the half-open door, she saw her boss. She knocked anyway. Otto Rothmann was sipping coffee, invoices or some such in hand.

"Yes, my dear. Is there a problem?"

"I thought it better to pick up my final paycheck before the store opens so I could thank you personally," she said, smiling politely at him.

He motioned her in and pointed to an envelope on his desk. She hazarded a few steps, leaving the door ajar.

Before she knew it, he lunged at her, grabbing at her arm. She broke free, and without thinking, picked up the nearest object to hand, an antique chamber pot. She tossed it his way. It shattered on the floor. Hearing footsteps from down the hallway, Claire snatched up the envelope and found her way out the back entrance.

Chapter Seventeen

OFF TO WORK

Humiliated by the unfortunate encounter with Claire's father at the Endicott home, Tom had buckled down at his job, determined to make something of himself and to throw off thoughts of the young woman who had caught his fancy.

Fortunately, Mr. Endicott did not bother to pick up the phone and complain to Mr. Caxton that his employee had overstepped his prerogative and—what?—attempted to take advantage of his daughter while on a job assignment. Months passed. No calls, no complaints.

Tom breathed a sigh of relief. This was America, he kept telling himself, and anyone with gumption—a word that did not literally translate into German but which he believed captured the spirit of his adopted homeland—could make it if they stuck to the task.

Outside, in the sunshine, with the sounds of laughter in the French Quarter or the clang of streetcars, life had brightened. Bread lines and soup kitchens had disappeared from cityscapes, including from the Crescent City. People he encountered were smiling again, going to work, skipping their way to school, shopping for Mardi Gras beads or simply having fun.

They did not know what he knew; they had not been where he had been; they did not miss people who had inexplicably disappeared. He wanted with all his might to be like them.

It could be argued Tom had a finer ear or broader experience than most.

War, he knew, had a habit of spilling over borders, flaring up at even minor provocation, and inciting all kinds of rumors. Even the fellas at Caxton's workshop had heard about spies coming down on river boats and enemy submarines prowling the ocean floor.

Tom largely evaded these exchanges, including the jokes about chinks and krauts, and got on with his chisel and saw. Often, after work, he'd duck into a movie theater, and fixate on the newsreels as much as on the main feature. The Nazis had already, he realized, subjugated several European countries he and his family had visited during his childhood. Many of his own people were being rounded up and herded into work camps. The footage became more harrowing as time went by. He teared up sometimes, relieved to be in the dark and alone.

During the spring of 1941, Tom received another letter from Hans. It was waved in front of him by Mrs. Jennings on a hot night in July. She was flapping a flimsy fan with an advertisement for root beer on it. "Friends in high places, looks to be. In the German *Wehrmacht,*" she cackled, pronouncing the military term as *Where Might*. He did not bother to correct her.

When he did tear the envelope open, he was stunned to learn that Hans had been promoted—and would be second-in-command on a U-Boat, likely dispatched to the Gulf of Mexico.

Because of that, Tomas, this is likely the last letter I'll be able to write to you. Know that I did not want things to come to this. As I imagine you did not.

As the months flew by, Mr. Caxton increasingly sent Tom around to private homes Uptown and in the Garden District where his varied skills were put to use, and his behavior was noted as impeccable. If his good looks had anything to do with it all, he was oblivious, unless the lady of the house started twirling a strand of hair or wetting her lips. Conspicuously.

Eventually, even Lady Monceau, a stickler for perfection when it came to the upkeep of her antiques, dropped by the cabinetry shop to extol the young man's talents.

"Come over here, Tom," Mr. Caxton had called out, his employee bent over a Tiffany lamp whose wiring had frayed and base had been chipped. Carefully, he put the top on a pot of glue, righted himself, and wiped his hands on his overalls. He walked over, bashful, vaguely reluctant.

"Lady Monceau did us the honor, Tom. She wanted to thank you for the work on her Chippendale chairs," his boss said, pleased enough but also amused by the interest the young man aroused among the women of his clientele.

The old lady's eyes raked Tom from head to toe, which made him fidget. "Like me, he's from the old country. We had a respect for Art," she declared, pausing for emphasis, "that's lacking over here. I suspect you agree."

Not knowing what to say to this, Tom nodded at her affirmation.

She turned back to Mr. Caxton. "I did come for another purpose," she went on. "We must keep up with the times. I am wanting to update the lodgings above the garage—they were once servants' quarters but simply won't do now. If, as I intend, the space is leased to a young person. In brief, I'd like to inquire as to a quote and to Mr. Stone's availability to take on the project."

After she was escorted out to her waiting car, Mr. Caxton scratched his grizzled chin. "Up to you, Tom. I could send Willie or Herman if you're not interested. What with the other thing you got going on weekends."

"I'll see what she has in mind, and whether I need someone else to assist. It should not be that time-consuming."

"Wish everyone had your energy. By all means, have at it," Caxton told him.

And so, Tom did, showing up in the Garden District early one morning, whereupon Lady Monceau introduced him to her long-time gardener and handyman, Bennie, who was either black or creole or Cherokee, depending on the person he was dealing with.

He and Tom hit it off instantly, and together undertook a makeover of the guest lodge, working off and on through the late spring, whenever materials arrived. With Bennie's radio tuned to some honky tonk station, "from the bayou," is how he put it, the two put in a solid oak floor, rewired the electricity, installed up-to-date plumbing, repaired the rickety stairs outside, acquired new fixtures at cut rates, and repainted the entirety.

Upon completion, Lady Monceau invited Tom in for tea and sandwiches, where they sat in her Chippendale chairs. He did not dare shift his weight.

"There are not many people left with whom I can converse, Mr. Stone, let alone commiserate, but it must be clear to you how dire things are back home, wouldn't you agree? My beloved Paris is being Nazified. Your country, with Herr Hitler in charge, is bent on world domination. Whatever that might entail." She paused to take another sip of the hot tea.

Unsettled by the turn in the conversation, Tom struggled to say something that would not be fatuous or out-of-place. But rather than hit a wrong note, he simply nodded.

His discomfort did not deter her.

"Like so many, my husband died in the Great War, and I and my young daughter made our way here. Margaret is married now, unhappily, but *c'est la vie.*" She gesticulated with her long paper-thin arm, allowing for a response, but she did not wait for one. "I fear those who have not escaped by now will suffer, so I do trust those dear to you will have managed to..." She did not bother to come up with the word.

"I have largely lost contact with family and close friends, but I too still have hope. If only I could—" Discombobulated, Tom swallowed hard, not wanting to tear up in front of the old lady.

"Now, now. One must live as best one can, however one can." Lady Monceau put her porcelain cup down and reached over to the adjacent marble-top table, retrieving an envelope. She held it out to him, wished him well, and instructed him to let himself out the front door.

Which Tom did, overwrought though he was. Bennie was nowhere in sight, so he let himself out of the main gate and walked back toward Canal Street. It was a glorious June evening, and he did not wish to be alone. He headed toward the solace of Storyville.

Later, around midnight, he traipsed back through the Quarter, hurrying past shadowy alleyways and slowing down once when he heard footsteps apparently dogging him. Exhaustion had likely misled him. At the boarding house, he stole up the stairs to his apartment, determined not to awaken Mrs. Jennings.

Only then did he retrieve the envelope from his back pocket. It was a check, a hefty one, drawn on the Hibernia. However tricky it might be to cash, he vowed to take care of Bennie for his efforts. After all, he had not heard that jaunty word *honky-tonk*, let alone the music itself, since those dusty days in west Texas. The thought made him smile.

Several days later, Tom changed into his best (and only) suit to walk over to the bank during his lunch hour. Trying to appear nonchalant, he stepped up to the window and signed the back of the check under the eyes of the teller. It was for $750 from Marie Elise Monceau, under which she had scrawled "for services rendered."

The imperturbable teller pursed his lips. "Do you bank with us, Mr. Stone, or do you have any identification?" Tom shook his head. "Please take a seat while we try to verify the intentions of Lady Monceau."

The process took an hour, Tom berating himself throughout for never having managed to rectify (or even establish) a legal status. What was it? Youthful negligence, insouciance, indolence or some sort of hubris that he would forever be able to get by on his wits and his charm. He could have kicked himself.

In the end, he silently thanked Lady Monceau. Whatever she said in his favor did the trick. The teller, still imperturbable, peeled off seven hundred-dollar bills from a stack, counted them out twice for his customer's benefit and slipped them into a bank-designated wrapper, along with a fifty.

"For services rendered," the clerk muttered, his tone smirking, as Tom reached to take the packet.

Although hot under the collar, Tom took a deep breath. I cannot even defend myself verbally, he told himself, not while being in legal limbo. He stopped briefly at the Acme Bar for a restorative beer before heading back to work.

On his way to the Garden District that weekend with $250 for Bennie in his pocket, the remaining $500 stuck at the apartment in his copy of *Mein Kampf*, Tom had an epiphany. Beyond the work he did for Philip Caxton, he had heard about a government program called Calliope, set up to build low-cost housing in poor pockets of the country. One of the funded projects was centered in a black neighborhood not far from Lake Pontchartrain, the *Picayune* had reported. He had hesitated to show up and apply, but perhaps he could cajole Bennie to join him—and vouch for his character as well as his construction chops.

With a sprawling family all over the city to support, Bennie readily agreed. "I got chilluns and aunts up that way in the ninth ward. Maybe this will help them out. Puttin' a better roof over their heads."

Tom was elated. "If it works out, and we're both hired, bring your radio. For the music."

"No need of that. There's jivin' all the time up that way. You'll like it, however white you be."

Despite his trepidation of government scrutiny, paperwork to join a work crew was minimal. For Bennie, because he already knew half the folks lined up to work, and for Tom, because he was white and employed at Caxton's—and for both of them, because the pay was below the going rate.

Before long, Tom found himself in charge of a dozen-strong crew, including Bennie, on the weekends. He modified the designs he had come up with in Texas, raising the foundations and reinforcing doors and windows. Within weeks, they were pouring concrete and hammering away along several blocks.

Some white folks living in adjacent areas of the project were enthusiastic, showing up with coffee in the mornings or watermelon at lunchtime. Others were suspicious of government intrusion or wary of too many blacks gathered in one place, whether they were working or partying.

Bennie, who was not easily ruffled, often had to diffuse situations that might have gotten out of hand. Music helped too. All kinds of folks, young and old, seemed to possess one or another instrument and if they didn't, they lent their voices to the choir.

Tom had rarely been happier, occasionally spending his Saturday night in one house or another belonging to a black family. On one occasion, a raucous evening with plenty of liquor flowing, things spiraled into a squabble and a stabbing. The police showed up. Although only on the periphery of the altercation, Tom was hauled in along with several other young men. The one with the knife and blood on his arms was booked, all the others let go, but only after fingerprints and mug shots.

"What you needs, Tom, is sense knocked into your head—and that means a woman. You best get youself one or trouble gonna dog you all the way to the hoosegow," Bennie dropped by the station to say as the men were released one-by-one.

After that scrape with the law, Tom made a point of packing it in before things in the ninth ward could take a wrong turn. Still, there were things that made him jumpy. People appeared to eye him from afar, or tail him now and again, though always at a distance.

Tom wanted to ask Mrs. Jennings if any strangers had come round looking for him, but she seemed to have further soured on him. Since she was a tit-for-tat kind of person, he decided to do her a favor. Without being asked, he spent a morning reinforcing the loose banister on the staircase.

When she happened by with mop and pail, all she did was shake her head and mutter, "What's he up to, what's he up to?"

Further exasperated, he asked himself to whom he could turn. He thought fleetingly of Claire, but despaired at what might she think of him now—after all this time. Bennie was black, or whatever he was, and had enough problems of his own. His being on a list—: hell, all blacks were on a list in this country. He'd not trouble the poor gardener with his own worries.

Still, in his most anxious moments, Tom could not shake off the direst of scenarios. If I do end up on some list, suspected of the wrong sympathies, or simply too obviously foreign—German, to boot—what then?

Ironically, and sadly, Tom continued to pocket a goodly amount of money but without anything much to spend it on. Running out of books to stash the bills in, he tried to open a bank account at a different branch of the Hibernia but was rejected.

It was another bad omen.

Chapter Eighteen

IN THE ARMY NOW

Myra returned to Alexandria several days after the party for her aunt, relieved that the celebration had gone well but chafing at the memory of Daniel Calhoun pretending to barely remember her. Innumerable times she had rehearsed what she would say or do if ever they came upon each other again, but when it came down to it, she had been as rattled as he was.

As badly as things ended, he still figured in her dreams. It was all so heady at the time, if in retrospect squalid and demeaning. Especially the abortion, which seemed to her to symbolize everything she had done wrong, and all that she had jeopardized.

Frederick, she no longer needed to worry about in terms of a confession; Addison, she shuddered to think what he might make of her transgressions.

Arguably, the affair had been for Daniel a mere ¢triviality . He had, in her view, trifled with her, and then disavowed her. The *chosen one* indeed.

At least she did not upend the contents of her wine glass on the professor, ruining his three-piece suit at the party, one newer, she observed, than the ones she had been accustomed to helping him remove. In the circumstances, she did nothing except stare at the flustered professor.

He stammered the minimal. "I trust you are well—that everything has worked out for you," he said, more as a statement than a question.

"As well as could be expected," she retorted. Icily.

She would have liked to confide more of her preoccupations to Claire on their walk after the incident, but she had not yet sorted through them. There was, however, some good news back in Alexandria. If she allowed herself to go over the unfortunate encounter with Daniel too often at night, she, fortunately, had no time to dwell during the day.

Overnight, Camp Claiborne had become a beehive of activity, racing to accommodate upwards of 100,000 recruits at a time, which would dwarf the nearby city they were dependent upon. Trains disgorged thousands of recruits every week. Lodgings and facilities were hammered together round the clock, training schedules set in motion, and protocols for interacting with the locals spelled out.

About this last, word had come down from Washington that the customs of the region needed to be respected, or there would be hell to pay.

Of all the local hires, Myra soon stood out as one of the more industrious and innovative. Few had a college degree, even among the males, and none apparently had a diploma with a Latin citation.

Not to mention, this Miss Kaminsky was regarded by a number of the personnel as quite fetching. That counted for a lot in a makeshift town of young males about to be whipped-into-shape.

After a few months of running errands, placing phone calls on behalf of various officers, and ordering goods and equipment from outside vendors, Myra was put forward for a job in the office of one of the higher-ranking officers. Several days after putting in an application, she was ushered into a bare-bones room by a ramrod-straight soldier, barely older than she was. She straightened her own back and bit her lip.

The officer in question, Major Robert Benson, she had been pre-advised, was a demanding sort, whom most everyone saluted no matter how casual the circumstance, but about whom it was said he was no dimwit. He rose when she entered, gesturing toward the waiting chair in front of his desk.

Since the major was a New Englander, with an accent to prove it, Myra quickly intuited he might need advice as to how to conduct himself with the locals. "My hometown is reckoned a sleepy southern hamlet, which is usually interpreted as meaning charming but hidebound," she limited herself to say. He did not ask her to elaborate.

Glancing at her file, he instead asked her to describe her background and what she enjoyed doing, so that her duties could be tailored to her "predilections." The term left her uneasy. She hurried to say she'd be fine with whatever tasks, as long as he and his staff would recognize she had a learning curve to climb.

"Not a steep one, I take it, Miss Kaminsky. I see you recently graduated *summa cum laude*." He pronounced the honorific smoothly, which made her assume he came from college educated stock himself. "Which leads me to ask," he continued, a trace of a smile on his lips, "what is this confounded thing they put in the coffee down here?"

"Oh, you mean chicory. It's a New Orleans specialty, though an acquired taste. Have you never been to the Crescent City, sir?" For an instant, he hesitated, which made Myra think she was not supposed to pose questions herself, especially not during her own job inter-view, and especially not to a major.

"Never been south of the Mason Dixon Line, so you will, if you come onboard, have to save me from any *faux pas*."

At the other end of the room sat an older woman, picking through files on her desk. The woman paused ever so briefly to give her boss a stern glance.

"Whatever I can do to be of help," Myra hastened to say, her tone neutral.

For a moment, the major appeared lost in thought but soon picked up a notepad and rattled off, in a business-like tone, a list of tasks that would be the civilian liaison's responsibilities. They were varied; a few were immediate priorities. Among the latter were contact with the mayor of Alexandria and a scouting expedition for a USO.

After the recitation, he put the notebook down. "How do those sound, Miss Kaminsky? Doable, or not in your bailiwick?" If he used this last word to throw her, or to intimate that women might not be up to such challenges, she relished the idea of disabusing him.

"Doable, certainly, but if I run into initial difficulties, I would look to your capable staff for help." Out of the corner of her eye, she noticed the older woman give her a sideways glance. The young corporal had long since left the room.

Major Benson scrutinized her face for any hint of sarcasm or brown-nosing, but Myra did not flinch. She wanted the job, especially since she had learned that Ruby Tate was vying for it as well. Still, she was hardly desperate. Unless he challenged her further, she would not tout her qualifications. Or thrust her bosom in his face, as Ruby had apparently done at her boss at the Hibernia, and gotten herself fired.

Instead, Myra determined to make the one (and possibly the other) staffer her comrades-in-arm, as it were. Hierarchy, she had read, was crucial in the Army and thus, having those on a similar level on your side was key to getting ahead.

"I did wonder, sir, about the others on your staff, as it would be important to understand their roles, and try to fit in."

Major Benson looked taken aback. He tilted his head to reflect. "Actually, that makes sense. Mackie—over there—has been with the outfit for a decade," he replied, jerking his head in the woman's direction. "Right, Doris?"

"Fourteen years, sir," she called back, immediately resuming her paper-pushing.

"Corporal Hill came down with me from DC. A West Point graduate. We'll see what we can make of him."

Myra nodded but added nothing. The major rose and held out his hand.

"Thank you for considering me," she said.

Then, almost as an afterthought, he blurted out, "You do understand, Miss Kaminsky, this all could end soon. Our involvement may not be required. Our soldiers might not need to deploy." He waved his arm in the air. She was disconcerted. "In short, the camp, all of us, might fold our tents, and *'like the Arabs, silently steal away.'*"

She knew the poem. Longfellow. She paused to dredge up the earlier lines. "In the meantime," she replied, "*'may the cares that infest the day'* not be too onerous." With that, she reached for her satchel on the floor.

Recovering, Major Benson called out, "Officer Mackie, please see Miss Kaminsky out and bring in the next applicant."

Myra could not help but notice the clunky shoes that the older woman was wearing. She decided to adopt lower heels if she landed the job.

Out in the vestibule, three other applicants, two young women and a somewhat older man, were seated on stiff metal chairs, waiting their turns. She did not think her odds very good.

But within a week, a phone call came from Doris Mackie. Myra had gotten the promotion. "Be here, 8:30 on the dot on Monday morning," the woman barked in her official WAAC voice and promptly hung up the phone.

Given that unpromising tone from her soon-to-be colleague, Myra limited herself to formal pleasantries with the older woman and refrained from interrupting her duties unless absolutely necessary. What the woman did all day was, to Myra, a mystery. The same files remained on her desk from week to week. Her WAAC insignia, however, never failed to be pinned in perfect position on her chest

On lunch break, Myra sometimes ate in the enlisted men's cafeteria along with other locals, some of whom she knew from years past in Alexandria. Other times, in nicer weather, she brought a sandwich and fruit from home and ate outside on makeshift picnic tables, alongside Corporal Hill. The young man gradually relaxed, chatting about life up North, his excursions on the Upper Mississippi, his love of ham radios. He was easy-going except when brass approached. They began to use first names.

"If we deploy, I'm hoping to be in communications, sticking close to Major Benson or someone like him." Myra nodded politely. "You see, I'm not that interested in the fighting aspect of war."

Flabbergasted to hear this from an actual soldier, she thought better than point out the obvious: the corporal might not have a choice, whoever his commanding officer. She offered him a roast-beef sandwich, having begun to pack two.

Her gesture worked.

Bright and eager to please, Stephen Hill soon began to demystify equipment she was unfamiliar with. Most notably, he showed her how to operate the office telex machine, a skill she soon mastered. Inevitably perhaps, Myra's alacrity with messages incoming and outgoing far exceeded those of the long-serving WAAC. Without any fanfare, the responsibilities of sending and receiving messages on behalf of Major Benson were shifted over to Myra.

Within a few more months, she was allowed the use of an Army vehicle, having told the major that indeed she could drive, but did not have a car of her own.

"Corporal Hill will accompany you for a day or two, to make sure you don't wreck the thing or come to a bad end," he deadpanned.

She could never tell if her boss was teasing her. "I will make an effort to avoid both of those outcomes," she replied, emulating his tone.

The bantering back and forth did not sit well will Mackie. Major Benson ignored her. Instead, to Myra he said, "Extra challenges; you asked for them. Besides, we in uniform simply don't have the time or expertise to deal with local anomalies. Tedious things or devilishly tricky things."

"Whatever you think I can handle, sir."

He nodded, his mustache twitching, as though uncertain what to make of this young woman, who sounded deferential in one moment and defiant in another.

One day, still early on, Myra zeroed in on the photo of the major, a youngish woman and a small child displayed on his desk.

"My wife prefers the air around Boston and is hell-bent that our son Benjamin gets into Harvard," he said by way of explanation.

"A worthy cause, I'm sure," she said, the "*I'm sure*" sounding faintly like implied criticism. But whether of him or his wife was unclear.

As the months rolled by, Myra felt freer to express her opinions on the state of the camp. She had heard snippets about squabbles between black and white soldiers, even though they were mostly segregated, the barracks for the blacks less comfortable than those for their white comrades. There was griping, name-calling, a few knock-about fights.

How all that might translate if they got into it in town began to worry her. She took her concerns to the major.

"You're an exceptional young woman, Miss Kaminsky. Aware of potential problems, and what might be the repercussions," Major Benson commented. He shuffled the papers on his desk before adding, "not like most women."

"It's because I'm Jewish," she lobbed back. "Discrimination is something we are attuned to wherever we are."

Nodding uncertainly, he dropped the subject.

Mackie kept her head down throughout this exchange, but eyed Myra more attentively as she walked out.

Before long, Myra became the key link to the powers-that-be around town, including the mayor's office and the chamber of commerce, both of which wanted to take advantage of the growing

U.S. military presence on Alexandria's doorstep. And after only a year, she was granted a top-level clearance, something few locals had obtained. As such, she became privy to discussions about the need to house German-born enemy aliens at Camp Claiborne before their likely transfer to detention centers, as well as bonafide prisoners of war.

If it ever comes to that, Myra mused. She could not fathom that it would.

Konrad Kaminsky, still running the music shop and now handling a steady stream of customers, got wind of the impact his daughter was making on the business district. He was uncertain what to make of it.

Thanks in part to Myra's lobbying efforts, a limited number of recruits were bussed into town on Wednesday afternoons and Saturday evenings, local movie theaters selling them tickets at half-price. A couple of bars and the diner across from Bauer's Dry Goods touted *Soldier's Specials* on the days. After huddling with the head of the Chamber of Commerce, a concert in the town's main park was arranged to welcome officers and family members on a Sunday afternoon, and taking Corporal Hill along, she scouted the area for a suitable venue to set up a USO.

At the dinner table one night, her father brought up the topic foremost in his mind. "Seems you've made your mark down at the camp, Myra. In the midst of all those men." His tone made both his wife and daughter look up from their soup.

"We've been curious how they're treating you," he went on.

"And hoping they're paying you fairly," Ilona Kaminsky interjected.

At least, Myra thought, they've abandoned the subject of Frederick. She ventured to reply more fully.

"Major Benson treats me well and I've made a friend in one of his junior officers. A lot of others—Ruby Tate included—would say I have been lucky." She might have done better not to throw in Ruby's name, but it was too late.

"Seems the wedding has been postponed. Again," her mother volunteered. "Apparently, Ruby is too busy now to think about marriage."

Konrad shook his head sideways, a signal of disapproval. "A spoilt *shiksa*," he murmured, barely loud enough to be heard.

Myra sipped her soup, keeping her face as unreadable as possible. Then, to cap the conversation, she said, "As for the pay, Mother, it's almost double what I started with. Not to mention I have the use of an Army vehicle for duties in town."

Her parents looked either sheepish or impressed, hard to tell which. Neither commented further.

However, not long after their own visit to Lena's new home in New Orleans, the Kaminskys returned to the subject that most preoccupied them: their daughter's prospects in a time of war.

"Your aunt was saying when we visited that you—" Konrad began but was cut off by his wife.

"First of all, how magnificently you organized the party for her— and how charming you were to the guests. She kept asking why you did not bring along a *beau*. That was her word, not ours."

Myra braced herself for another discourse on the joys of marriage. She did wish that Addison was a more assiduous suitor, one that she could describe as such, but quickly pushed the thought to the back of her mind. *Where even was he?* she asked herself.

"To cut to the chase, dear, we were thinking about all the soldiers, who, if things worsen, will be shipped out soon, to Europe or elsewhere," her father took up the chorus. "Or will be returning to their own homes, in other states, if not," her mother added, completing the argument.

Myra did not want to lengthen the discussion more than necessary. It was almost 9:00 and she was in the midst of a new novel, *For Whom the Bell Tolls*, and wanted to make progress before going to bed.

163

"What exactly is your point?" she asked, looking one to the other.

"Only that *tempus fugit* and you are now twenty-four."

"Your mother beats about the bush, Myra," her father clapped back. "Eligible men do not grow on trees. Even here in Alexandria. Especially those of our persuasion," he announced, impatient to get to the heart of the matter. "That Tate girl, for example. Word is she's flouncing around all over the place. Leaving Frederick ripe for the picking."

Although amused by the metaphor of a young man growing on a tree like a peach, Myra contained herself. For an instant, she considered a statement to the effect that she was—what? seeing, dating, going with—but none would do for describing her attachment to Addison Endicott. How could she speak of him, whom she had barely ever kissed, when with Daniel Calhoun, she had...

"We can see this is upsetting, which is not our intention," Mrs. Kaminsky wrapped up. "We want you to be happy. Whatever you want to do in life will be fine with us."

"Really, Mother?" Myra shot back, not hiding her exasperation. "It does not come across that way." Ilona lowered her head, wounded by her daughter's reprimand. "Further, let it be said once and for all. I never will be in love with Frederick Bauer."

With that pronouncement, Myra wiped her lips with her napkin, folded it and slipped the silver ring engraved with her name around it.

As she rose to leave the table, her father lost it. "Well then, Missy. What about the *summa cum laude*? What's happening on that front?"

"Fuck the damn thing," Myra muttered on her way out, but not loud enough to be heard.

Her dander still up over the dinner table argument, Myra took the bus to New Orleans early on a Saturday shortly before Thanksgiving.

"I have something exciting to tell you," Claire had said on the phone when they agreed to meet up late that afternoon.

Having banked a tidy sum from the year at Camp Claiborne, Myra headed to Maison Blanche, where, without belaboring the prices, bought a couple of party dresses and a pair of shoes, not too high and not too low. After that, she window-shopped around the Quarter, finding it eerily quiet. There had been practice blackouts over the last few months and ominous signs were posted in store windows. *Loose Lips Sink Ships* in one, *Rags Wanted for Salvage* in another.

It wasn't only at Camp Claiborne that folks were buckling up, she reckoned.

Even the swank Roosevelt Hotel was less than lively, the only other unaccompanied women in the bar two out-of-towners, from their chattering, on a shopping spree for antiques. Claire suggested they start on Royal Street. "Rothmann's boasts the largest selection, but other shops have more reasonable prices." One of the tourists jotted down the street and went back to her whisky sour.

"I take it the job no longer suits you, since you're drumming up business for others," Myra commented wryly.

"Mr. Rothmann proved beyond boorish. I had to toss a chamber pot at him," Claire said, enjoying her account now that the incident was in the rear-view mirror.

"Not the first such boss. They might have pointed out such dangers in that college course on business economics, don't you think?"

"They probably assumed we'd all be married and never have to consider the perils of a workplace," Claire deadpanned.

"Indeed," Myra responded.

They sipped their drinks in silence for a spell, watching the other guests, mostly men in suits, mostly clutching briefcases, who came and went purposefully or took a seat at the bar to while away the hour.

Over in the far corner, a band had set up and of a sudden began a set, beginning with a rendition of "Time After Time." A heavily made-up woman in a sequined gown soon took up a mic and belted out the refrain.

After a couple of more numbers, Myra turned back to her friend. "You haven't given me a clue about your big news. I'm breathless, and in need of something inspirational."

"It came out of the blue—ironically from one of Rothmann's regular customers. She was even a guest at Lena's party."

Flummoxed, Myra gestured for her to go on.

"Lady Marie Monceau, whom I had waited on a few times, offered to rent me her guest house—without my ever having asked. It's in the Garden District, newly renovated, and the price is a steal."

Squelching a twinge of jealousy, Myra jumped back in. "That's fortuitous, which is not a word we get to use often. What about your parents?"

"Not thrilled. But Addison came to the rescue, insisting that many a young woman does such things nowadays. Plus, as I said, I am spending my own money on this."

"When are you moving in?"

"Right after Thanksgiving. A workman is putting finishing touches on the exterior, and her longtime gardener, Bennie, is fitting out flower boxes. There's an imposing iron gate bordering the back of the property, with a key, and a doorbell at the top of the stairs." Claire sounded giddy at the recitation.

"Sounds ideal."

Sensing a note of despondency, Claire shifted gears. "She may not have spelled it out, but I'm certain your aunt would relish having you in her home. It's roomy enough, and you did make the whole thing happen." Myra tilted her head as though considering the idea. "I mean, once these war rumors die down. When you can leave the Army camp and move back here."

"I'm not so sure about that."

"About what?"

"The war thing. It may be only a matter of time."

As that thought sank in, the band launched into a medley of Tommy Dorsey hits. A middle-aged couple got up and did a foxtrot around the dance floor. After a smattering of applause, the musicians took a break.

"It's not just my overly protective parents, is it? What about this Frederick yours are so fond of?"

"Out of the picture. He's engaged to someone else," Myra declared, not wishing to elaborate. What she did want to do was inquire after Addison, but waited, hoping Claire would volunteer his news.

In the interim, she turned the tables. "What about that friend of yours and Addison's—Richard someone or other? Weren't his parents pressing for the two of you to get engaged?"

"Admittedly, *they* were, but *he* isn't. In my estimation, Richard Carrollton is more attached to Addison than to me. Which is just as well."

Puzzled, Myra did not probe further on that front.

After the waiter had poured each of them another flute of pink champagne, Claire made another reveal.

"Since we're talking about men, you do remember the German from Café du Monde, right? We became friendly, by sheer coincidence, but it never went anywhere." Myra raised an eyebrow. "Well, that's not true. It did, become a thing."

At this admission, Claire's cheeks turned pink. Myra intuited it was not from the champagne. She took a sip of her own and held up her glass to invite Claire to elaborate.

"It fizzled because my father came home while Tom was visiting me." Flustered, she covered her eyes with her hand at the memory.

"Surely, though?"

"I believe Tom—Tomas, whatever—was more mortified than I. In any case, not interested enough to persist, which is a shame because in his place I would have...I repeat, *I* would have. Oh, never mind."

Bemused, Myra turned palms up to elicit more details, but her friend ignored the gesture.

After a beat, Claire changed subjects. "They should bring us some peanuts, don't you agree?"

Myra smiled in agreement, but there was no waiter in sight. Instead, she said, "Let's finish this off with a proper toast. How about to peace, prosperity, and peanuts next time we meet up."

Raising her own flute, Claire added, "And to us, finding our way on our own, despite all these obstacles."

"Hear, hear," they both declared, and laughed in concert.

Chapter Nineteen

WHERE THEY WERE WHEN

Shortly before Thanksgiving in 1941, Lena Walenska and Lucille Truard went together to the opera at the Saenger. It had not taken the two professors, proud polyglots and equally unapologetic free spirits, to bond over their European heritage and their own high culture.

Verdi's *Tosca* was on the bill, and they had splurged on choice seats in the orchestra section.

To stretch their legs during intermission, the two ladies stood and scoured the boxes with their opera glasses. Soon they spotted Dr. Werner, who was seated along the left side not far from the stage. He came down to chat, the three of them critiquing the performances, in French and in German, a smattering of English thrown in. Before the lights went down again, a young man seated in the row behind them broke in.

"Pardon me, sir, ladies, but would I be wrong to presume you are European?" he hazarded, in German. They nodded, polite enough. He switched to French. "I don't wish to intrude, but might you have any recent news from abroad?"

The two women looked at each other, but then back at the

young man. He was deferential, and very handsome. Neither Lena nor Lucille liked to think of herself as too old to notice or to care.

Assuming a protective role, Dr. Werner spoke first. "Might you have been a student at Tulane? I run the German department, such as it is," the professor volunteered. He brought out his pince-nez to scrutinize the stranger. "My guess, you must be a native, or barring that, you possess an exceptionally good ear."

The young man inclined his head at the compliment.

"*Malheureusement*, I have not been to the Continent since '35, but my companion is a recent arrival," Lucille offered. "Have you anything to tell this young man?"

"More perhaps than he would want to know," Lena replied, images of her own ordeal flitting through her mind. They were not pictures she wished to dwell on.

"As you know, it's hard to come by up-to-date information, other than newsreels and the like. Oh, and yes, I am German but in this country for several years. My name is Tomas, Tomas Steinberg."

"Are you a Berliner, Mr. Steinberg, an opera buff, or both?" Dr. Werner asked.

Tomas smiled. "I enjoy opera, though I don't manage to attend regularly. Went to university in Berlin but grew up near the Baltic Sea, in Lübeck. You may not be familiar with it."

Turning pale, Lena mouthed something incomprehensible, then gripped the back of her chair to steady herself. After an exchange of glances among the others, she regained her composure. "I am Polish but got out of Germany two years ago, *Gott sei dank*."

"Thank God, indeed," Lucille murmured, echoing her friend.

"But I am acquainted with Lübeck," Lena whispered.

At that point the lights blinked.

Quickly, Tomas leaned forward to invite them all for champagne in the foyer during the second intermission.

During that interval, he learned more than he could have imagined. That Lena had ended up in Lübeck after her colleagues at the university were fired, detained, or otherwise dispatched with—her voice quivered at the telling—and that her brother-in-law and his daughter came all the way from Alexandria to extricate her from "dire straits."

"A very resourceful young woman, this Myra Kaminsky," Lucille rounded out the account. "One of our best students at Sophie Newcomb as well as my friend's niece."

Tomas's face lit up. "How amazing. I know that name. Might she be a friend of another graduate, a recent one named Claire Endicott?"

Lucille looked startled. "The two were study partners, as I recall. How is it you are acquainted with our free-spirited Claire? She too was one of our favorite students. Very conservative parents, however."

Delighted though he was by the connections, Tomas held himself in check.

"I had occasion to meet Claire's parents, but I have lost contact. I believe her mother suffered an accident. Of some sort." Tom tried to sound vague, and not too eager.

"From what Myra told me, Mrs. Endicott is managing well enough," Lena said. "Her daughter has found rooms of her own in the Garden District. Admittedly, over a garage of some sort, but nonetheless."

"Didn't Marie tell you, Lena? It was she who offered up her own guest house. They had met at Rothmann's, where Claire works. And to think, she so wanted to visit Paris, but given the givens, has had to settle for, well, this commercial job."

Tomas sipped his champagne as the two women continued their back and forth.

"The world now weighs on all young women," Lena rejoined, "but they may soon be called upon to do more than the mundane if things degenerate further." She waved her free arm theatrically to emphasize her point.

"Claire will at least have the pleasure of Lady Monceau's occasional company," Lucille hastened to remind, and then added admiringly, "which cannot but be beneficial."

Gobsmacked though he was by all this intelligence, Tomas remained mute. Had he heard right? Claire Endicott is now the tenant in the guest house he and Bennie refurbished with such care.

If the lights had not dimmed, he would in his ebullience have hugged them—and bought them all another round of champagne.

On a bright Saturday afternoon in early December, Tom headed out, a bouquet of flowers in one hand, and hopped a streetcar crowded with passengers going up St. Charles Avenue. Passers-by hurried along the sidewalks, shopping bags in hand.

His heart was pounding. How serendipitous was it that he had discovered where Claire now resided—and that he himself had worked to fix up. Did he dare let her know that? Or that he had made the acquaintance of two delightful (and loquacious) older ladies who, in the course of an ever so interesting conversation, mentioned both Myra and Claire.

She might, admittedly, listen to this babble and then slam the door of her apartment in his face. And lock it. He knew it locked. Securely too. He had installed the thing himself.

He jumped off the streetcar after the fourth stop and considered turning around and heading home or out to the construction site. Tom looked around for a public receptacle in which to dump the bouquet of red roses, made even more abundant and fragrant with snips of juniper. It was the most expensive arrangement in the shop on Canal Street.

Instead, taking a deep breath, he approached the iron-gated property where the young woman he could not get out of his mind purportedly lived. Surely, the two ladies, professors both, would not have erred in their description of a guest house above the owner's garage.

He decided to do the proper thing and try the front gate, with the idea of presenting himself to Lady Monceau. The flowers would be for her, but then he would, if all went well, mention that he was an acquaintance of the young lady who had moved into the guest house. Might she be amenable to his knocking on her door in case she were at home?

Pulling up in front of the main gate, he tried the bell. Normally, it would alert Bennie in the nearby box to an arrival, but a quick glance indicated it was empty. Tom was about to desist when he spotted his friend pushing a wheelbarrow.

Bennie left his load and hurried over, swinging the gate open.

"Why, Mr. Tom? Whatcha' doin' here?"

"You won't believe me when I tell you."

"If you be lookin' to see the mistress, she ain't here. I took her over to visit her daughter, over near the college."

"She might not believe me either. I know the young woman who is renting the guest quarters." He tilted his head in the direction of the garage.

"In that case, this Miss Claire may be at home, or she may not be at home. She 'spectin' your visit?" the gardener inquired.

"No, I mean, yes. I believe that she is," Tom replied, determinedly. He had gotten this far and did not wish to be dissuaded.

"Ain't nothin' I would be 'spectin, but you look to be wantin' to try your luck. Mighty pretty, this Miss Claire." Bennie opened his eyes wide for emphasis. He accompanied his friend a few yards, picked up his wheelbarrow and headed toward an assortment of flowerpots.

Tom walked briskly across the lawn, banana trees to one side, azaleas to the other. As he rounded the back of the main house, he could hear the crackling of a radio, classical music, coming from the garage structure. He mounted the wooden steps and knocked at the door.

At first sight of Claire, he was taken aback. She seemed not as surprised as he was. Rather, she appeared more poised, something about her posture signaling a self-assurance he did not remember.

"Whatever are you doing here?" she began, dispensing with preliminaries.

Before he could respond, she motioned him in, relieved him of the flowers and stuck them in a vase.

Oddly, for a Saturday afternoon, she was dressed in a dark wool suit, matching heels and a loosely looped gray silk scarf, all of which offset her pale skin. Her hair was chopped short in the kind of bob he had come to observe on stylish young women, like those at the Saenger or the fancy restaurants in the Quarter.

Unsettled by her appearance, he looked around the room, which he and Bennie had so labored over. Several other vases were already filled, one with hibiscus blossoms, another with some purple flower he did not recognize. His first thought: several other young men must be paying her court.

"I must ask how your mother is doing—and the rest of your family. I would have—"

"It's not your fault. Things were difficult after the accident. Not to mention my father who..." She twirled her wrist to suggest things she had no control over. "Mother has largely recovered, physically, that is. A slight limp but nothing worse than that."

Tom nodded, remembering the evening he had gone over to apologize for that confrontation on the staircase and to inquire after Mrs. Endicott's injuries. Replying tersely, Mr. Endicott had shut the door in his face. Or the time, more recently, he had lingered outside Rothmann's around closing time, only to be told by the owner that Miss Endicott had resigned, suddenly. "Taken a government job," the old lady had added.

Claire would know nothing of these attempts to re-establish contact. It did not seem worthwhile to bring them up.

"Mainly, I have wanted to know how *you* are, Claire—especially with talk of war."

"Ah, yes. Submarines in the Gulf. In fact, it's what I do now; work for the Navy. We track the movements of supply ships. And other things. Anyway, none of it can be discussed."

"Understood," Tom replied. "I've seen that poster. *Loose lips sink ships.*"

She shook her head but did not elaborate. His eyes fell to her hands. She was wearing an emerald on her left hand, a ring he had not noticed years before. Perhaps she was engaged, and the young man was assiduous about flowers.

"As you can deduce, my landlady's gardener is instructed to keep the main house supplied with cuttings. I benefit too. I take it Bennie let you in?"

"He could not stop me actually."

Smiling for the first time, Claire invited him to take a seat.

"By the way, you would not have found me earlier. I just returned from the office. A lot of messages to be transcribed and what-not."

"Am I intruding, or putting you in an awkward position?"

She gave him a quizzical look, the edges of her mouth curled upwards. "Not as much as the last time," she replied, turning away to fiddle with the coffee pot.

"I meant, since you have a job with the American military, and I am, when it comes down to it, German by nationality."

She laughed. "I have the most basic of government clearances, so to compromise me would not get you very far," she said, self-deprecatingly. "But you will be amused to know, all those late nights studying German case endings have paid off," she added.

"*Daß ist wunderbar,*" he replied. After a pause, he added, "I have wondered myself why the language clings to the neuter case when masculine and feminine would appear to do the job just fine."

Something in his tone made Claire blush. She arranged the cups and saucers and was glad to have her back toward her guest. After an interval, she said, "I did not even ask, assuming you'd enjoy coffee at this hour. It is how we met. At Café du Monde. All that time ago."

"I remember it well," Tom responded, the memories of that fraught spring flooding back in—Havana, the hapless ship, one setback followed by another. And two beautiful girls seated nearby, sipping coffee, beset by their own problems.

When she brought the tray out to the sofa, Tom cleared a space on the small table in front of them.

"I must say you have decorated the place charmingly," he blurted out.

"Like most of the furniture, the cookies are courtesy of my land-lady. Lady Monceau orders from the best shops, so please, indulge. I do not dare eat them all."

"You could with no problem. I mean, you look lovely as you are," at which point Tom faltered, wanting nothing more than to take Claire in his arms. Instead, he forced himself to drink the hot coffee and munch sweets. Anything to choke off his desire.

"So, you have not said. However, did you find out where I live and why ever did you decide to come over?"

They went on like this for a good half hour, he describing the encounter at the opera house and then filling her in on the so-called Calliope project, building affordable housing in the outer wards, she going on about her mother's recovery and determination to walk unaided.

"And your father?"

"You saw how he is. Set in his ways. Not pleased with my choices."

"And what would those be exactly, *your* choices?" he asked, reckoning that living on her own, unmarried, did not sit well with him.

"Oh, you know. Living here, for one thing, taking further courses at the university, not being married, changing jobs so abruptly." She turned her gaze away, focusing out the window on the crepe myrtle tree. Mockingbirds were bustling about in the top branches.

Tom kept his eyes on her changing expression. Her lips were unusually mobile, as though she had more to say but couldn't.

"May I ask, is his concern hypothetical or does your father have a suitor for you in mind?" He posed the question in as dispassionate a tone as he could muster.

Claire tilted her head side to side. "You might say so. As is often the case, a childhood friend. His parents and mine are—she rubbed her two index fingers together—suffocatingly close."

Tom nodded, comforted by the use of the word *suffocatingly.*

"And is the young man similarly so?"

She crooked one side of her mouth, thinking through a response. "Actually, Richard," she spoke his name with deliberation, "is closer to my brother Addison than to anyone else in the family. Not suffocatingly but assiduously so."

Tom raised an eyebrow but did not press the inquiry.

For a moment, some further thought flickered through Claire's mind, but it dissipated before she could voice it.

Instead, she retreated to safety. "Whatever the case, time and circumstance may change things," she said, trying to sound worldly, or at least beyond the need to dwell on the intentions of potential suitors.

But, in Tom's view, plenty of time *had* passed, and circumstances *had* changed since their last frustrating encounter. To drop the subject now might make it irretrievable. He took a deep breath.

"As you know, nuance in another language can be tricky, if not treacherous. Bear with me." She nodded, wary. "Are you saying you do not love this Richard—or are you saying that there might be someone else—(he hesitated, a catch in his voice)—who interests you more?"

She drank the last of her coffee and placed the cup on its saucer. "I would say I am not in love with Richard, but I do not know the answer to your second query."

As the sun began to set, Tom reluctantly took his leave, venturing only to invite her for dinner in the Quarter— "in coming weeks."

She looked as though she liked the sound of that. He would mail an invitation to her apartment. And then he left, descending the stairs swiftly so as not to linger and try to kiss her.

For all I know, she is essentially betrothed. Still, she has to eat. It may as well be with me, Tom told himself before grabbing the first streetcar headed toward the Quarter.

On Sunday morning, Claire accompanied her parents and her brother to the church service on Napoleon Avenue, where, as usual, they ran into the Carrolltons in the nave.

Lunch at the Endicotts afterwards was agreed as the two families entered their adjacent pews.

"It'll still give us time to take the boat out on the lake, if we don't sit around listening to them lament the state of the world. What do you say?" Addison whispered to Richard. "You too, Sis, can tag along." Claire rolled her eyes.

Over a shrimp salad, tomato aspic and an assortment of cheeses, the lunch conversation inevitably turned to military maneuvers along the coastal waters—no one in agreement as to how likely "the enemy" could attack American soil via the Gulf of Mexico. Nor how close Roosevelt was to putting the country on official war footing, or against whom.

The men left Claire out of the discussion, despite her knowing almost as much as anyone what the Navy's plans were for protecting the Louisiana coast. There would be a contingent of local volunteers to patrol by land and Navy boats to ply the inland waterways. She wondered what Tom would have made of it all, especially the aspersions cast upon Germans, and how uncomfortable he would be made to feel.

Once coffee was served in the parlor, Claire came round with a tray of pralines. Only the men partook. Then the two older men brought out their pipes, while Addison excused himself to go upstairs to change for the proposed jaunt on Pontchartrain.

Despite a disapproving glance from his mother, Richard, looking sheepish, soon followed him.

Not a minute later, Helen Carrollton turned her guns on Claire. "So, my dear, how do you suffer living above a garage and how long do you intend to keep up that arrangement?"

"It's working out fine. Thank you for asking," she deadpanned, silencing the woman. Without lingering to endure another such salvo, she got up to refill the men's coffee cups and pour the remainder into a thermos for the two younger men to take on their boating excursion.

His pipe filled, Edward flicked on the radio. Oddly, he had trouble alighting on a station. Finally, a breathless voice could be heard. He stopped fiddling with the knob.

"What is the man saying?" Harold demanded.

"Something to the effect that this is no drill."

"Turn it up, turn it up."

The ladies across the room ceased their chatter. The secret to Esther Endicott's spiced aspic would have to wait.

Slowly, the group pieced the radio reports together. Japanese planes attacked a military base at Pearl Harbor. In Hawaii. That very morning. A surprise assault. American soldiers were killed, ships were sunk, planes destroyed.

Without a word, Edward got up to look out the front windows, up to the clear blue sky and down to the empty street. He jerked the curtains closed.

Claire went to the staircase. "Get yourselves down here, you two. Looks like we're at war."

Not long afterward, the phone rang. It was Myra. She was at her desk at Camp Claiborne, twenty miles outside Alexandria, having been called to work as soon as her boss, the high-ranking officer she had talked about, had gotten word from his superiors in Washington.

"Major Benson actually said, 'It's now all hands-on deck.' There'll be a huge influx of recruits here in Louisiana within weeks." After this breathless rundown, Myra shifted tone. "I didn't mean to go on." She paused. "And how are you, Claire—and Addison?"

"I think we're all in shock."

"The whole country will be as soon as this thing registers."

Claire could hear noises in the background, like a teletype machine. And male voices in the room with Myra. Perhaps it made sense to contact her own boss, even if it were a Sunday.

Chapter Twenty

A QUICKENED PULSE

Throughout that same December Sunday afternoon at the construction site, Tom took a few minutes off to drink a beer along with Eddie, an affable sort, and adept with a hammer and saw. Several of the local blacks under Bennie's guidance kept up the heavy lifting, punctuating their labor with song.

One tune in particular caught Tom's fancy. *"Go Down, Moses,"* which they managed to harmonize despite the hammering. Although he did not know the word *spiritual* applied to such music, he found the performance soul-enriching. It was not an emotion he often felt, or would know how to share, but certain music brought it on.

He decided it was past time to acquire a record player as well as a radio, however much his landlady would look askance. It might enliven his solitary evenings in his still spartan lodgings.

Once Tom took leave of the other workmen that afternoon, he headed straight home where he sponged off in the make-do shower, humming the refrain of that spiritual. Still bone-weary, he collapsed into bed.

The next morning, he sensed something was off as soon as he came down the stairs.

In the hallway, Mrs. Jennings was mopping the floor with more vigor than usual. She mumbled as he passed by with his usual greeting.

"You best be thinking 'bout moving on—you being German and all," she ventured, looking more put-upon than usual.

"What is the problem, Mrs. Jennings?" he paused to inquire, glancing at his wristwatch. It was already 8:15. "We can talk about whatever concerns you have this evening, if you like."

Her eyes narrowed. She plunked the mop in a bucket of smelly water. "You ain't heard, huh?" He looked blank. "We'll soon be at war. Japs bombed Pearl Harbor. Philip Caxton will know all about it."

It was the first time he'd heard anyone address his employer by his first name.

He raced to work, where the radio was tuned, loudly, to CBS News. Mr. Caxton was drinking black coffee and pacing the sawdust floor. The morning paper was spread out on a worktable. The few employees in the warehouse were chatting when Tom entered. They did not appear to eye him any differently.

Around eleven, they gathered to listen to an address by Roosevelt describing the deadly assault as "a day that will live in infamy." One of the workmen asked the nearest to him what *infamy* meant.

Tom leaned against a sawhorse to take all this in. Especially what it would change for young men in America. German-born men as well. The commentators on the radio rattled on. At one point, Mr. Caxton passed by and patted Tom on the back.

By Monday evening, the country was officially at war against Japan.

After his initial bewilderment, Tom began to consider his options. How quickly things might change in the country—and how drastically—might very well depend on Hitler's next move. Hopefully, the *führer* would lie low, having already done enough damage and occupied enough territory to both Germany's east and west. What more could the tyrant want?

Getting more worked up, the other men in the shop went on about "kicking some Jap ass." Tom focused on the cantankerous table legs in front of him and kept his own counsel.

After work, he noted clusters of men gathered along the sidewalks or outside the bars, apparently going over matters. Like, from what he could make out from snatches of bravado, what "*we*" would do to these slant-eyed Nips. In no mood to join in, he moved purposefully.

Back at the apartment, he retrieved a possible number to reach Hans at the naval base on the Baltic. Unless he erred, phone company headquarters were right off Canal Street and open round the clock. Nighttime in New Orleans would be the next morning in Europe.

His hunch worked. He was allotted ten minutes for the trunk call, paying $10 upfront.

"This will be the last time we are likely to speak," his childhood friend said over a crackly line. "I believe it is a matter of time—very short time. Understood?"

"*Ja, Ja*, but my parents, Hans? Have you any further idea where they might be?"

"Last I heard, still in the countryside near home. But likely as not, that won't last," he replied, sounding hurried, or evasive.

Whatever else, Tom's own parents helped raise Hans—a penniless orphan, albeit as Aryan as they come—and now, as a German military officer, he could hardly be bothered. Holding the receiver tight to his ear, Tom put aside his own exasperation. If this were to be his last communication with his childhood friend, he had to turn to the other person on his mind.

"And Katrin? Do you now know in what country she ended up?"

"It was random, the lottery process onboard the *St Louis*," Hans replied with flat affect. "I was not privy to their lists."

In the silence that followed, Tom could detect faint voices over the trunk line.

Then Hans came back on, and in a different key, said, "You

should know, Tomas, I did not augur any of this. You do understand, right?"

"Yes, I understand."

A knock rattled the glass on the door of his phone booth. Tom looked up. The clerk mimed that he needed to cut the conversation off.

"I have to hang up now, Hans. Be safe."

"You, too. Oh, I forgot to say. I will have a U-boat. Second-in-command. Orders just came through."

The line went dead.

Discombobulated, Tom ambled aimlessly through the Quarter. Passers-by walked more determinedly, heads up, eyes alert. He would have liked to see Claire, especially since he figured she worked in the imposing building on Carondelet where people in uniform came and went.

Within a couple of days, Tom realized Hans was right about how things would unfold. Hitler declared war on the United States. Hours later, Roosevelt returned the favor. That same day, Congress ratified the presidential decision. The country was at war on two distinct fronts: against Germany in Europe as well as the Japanese in Asia.

Within weeks, millions of young men lined up for and received orders to report for duty.

A phone call from the Admiralty's office in Annapolis came for Addison within hours of Roosevelt's declaration of war. He would be in charge of organizing patrols along the Louisiana coastal waters to detect German U-boats and any other suspicious activity.

Although pleased to see his son in uniform, and with an additional stripe, Edward Endicott was disappointed that his son did not receive a more prestigious commission onboard an aircraft carrier. For once, he kept his chagrin to himself. Esther Endicott was simply relieved to have her son close to home.

Despite efforts by his mother, and his friend Addison, to dissuade him, Richard Carrollton marched into the draft office downtown the day after Christmas and received orders to ship out from the West Coast for the Pacific theater.

"This is indefensible," his father sputtered when told. "Underselling yourself yet again. And for what? To fight for islands no one here has ever even heard of."

Although less vocal, Helen Carrollton was similarly distressed. "With all our money, you'd think we'd be able to avoid this," she complained to her husband, though not directly to her son.

Despite their less than patriotic fervor, the Carrolltons made a last-ditch effort to convince Richard to propose to Claire before his departure. Simultaneously, they tried to guilt the Endicotts into pressuring their daughter to accept.

"A proper understanding between the two would strengthen Richard in his resolve and protect him. It would be like having an extra plate of armor," Helen lobbied Esther over tea shortly after her son's enlistment.

Aghast at her friend's nerve, Mrs. Endicott resisted the request. Nor did she or her husband directly broach the subject with Claire. Rather, they encouraged her to travel out to the West Coast to see Richard off.

"How could I possibly?" Claire objected. "All of a sudden, the job I do matters. We don't know where enemy ships might be in the Gulf. And I'm sure Richard would understand."

Up in Alexandria, things were not that different.

To impress both Ruby and Myra, Frederick immediately turned over the running of Bauer's Dry Goods to his mother and aunt and volunteered for the Army's procurement unit.

"Or whatever else the country might have in store for me," he told the two old ladies, when handing over the keys to the store.

Still officially engaged to be married to Ruby, Frederick none-theless went over to the Kaminskys to say his goodbyes.

"You do realize I wanted things to be different," he confided to Myra's parents, "but she..." He trailed off, shaking his head in resigned disappointment.

Ilona nodded in sympathy and urged another blintz upon him; Konrad puffed on his pipe and kept his own counsel.

Around 8:30 that same weeknight, Myra returned home from Camp Claiborne. She wished Frederick well but did not counter him when he blithely maintained "the whole thing" would be over before they knew it.

Mere days after Christmas, Frederick boarded a caravan of troop trucks to New Orleans for the train trip to Providence, Rhode Island, and then onwards across the Atlantic.

Word had it Ruby had not bothered to see him off.

Chapter Twenty-One

NOTHING IS BLACK AND WHITE

In record time, Camp Claiborne revved up its war machine to full throttle. Recruits poured in. Seasoned and reliable locals like Myra were cajoled upon (and generously recompensed) to give up their weekends throughout those first frantic weeks after Pearl Harbor. No one had a clue how long the mobilization would last.

To the consternation of Major Benson, Myra found herself pulled in different directions. She was borrowed, as it were, by officers in other departments, not only to schedule leisure time and leave but also to intercede when tensions flared among the troops. Most notably, among white and black soldiers, the latter outnumbered by a substantial margin.

At the same time, relations between the town and the camp began to fray. Scuffles broke out, a few knives were unsheathed, a shop window or two was shattered.

"We ought to limit the number of recruits who get leave to go into town," Myra told two superiors after she had heard complaints from the mayor's office. "Crucially, we need to prevent blacks and whites from mixing it up on the same evening or in the same vicinity of town."

She received a quizzical look from one of the officers, a condescending shrug from the other. Nonetheless, she persisted. "Whether from your vantage point you think it's right or not, the races down here are segregated. That practice isn't going to disappear overnight."

The two officers looked distracted, or bored. She changed tack. "If you'll permit, I'll work up a plan. Staggering the buses into town as well as tightening the prerequisites for a pass."

"Who is it you are assigned to, Miss, Miss...?"

"Kaminsky," she reiterated, irritated. "I've been with Major Benson for more than a year."

They both nodded, knowingly. "We'll be in touch with him. You need not fret," the condescending one said.

Staring at his watch, the bemused one added, "You are dismissed. We've kept you beyond the official end of your civilian workday."

Frustrated with the two officers and with Army procedures in general, Myra wanted to point out that most all her workdays dragged on into the evening, but she told herself to desist.

After this unsatisfactory exchange, she returned to Major Benson's office to gather her things, including the key for the Army car at her disposal. Doris Mackie was still at her desk, hunched over pages from a different stack of folders than usual. The Army-issued clock on the wall read 19:10. The older woman looked up.

"You look beset upon, Miss Kaminsky." It was rare Mackie made a comment. This one was not wide of the mark.

"I was pondering whether higher-ups in the Army are all as immoveable as the ones I've been dealing with," Myra said, not as a question but as a statement of fact.

"Dunderheads does come to mind," Mackie responded.

It was the most prolonged, and satisfying, conversation the two had yet indulged in.

Not three nights later on a chilly Saturday, all hell broke loose in downtown Alexandria. Specifically, Lee Street, which ran through the Negro commercial district, was turned into a war zone.

A few white thugs got into an altercation with a cluster of black recruits coming out of the movie theater. Racist slurs were hurled. There was push-back. The whites drew guns.

Myra got a phone call at dinner with her parents and Myrtle Murkowski, who had brought along her famous sweets, was winding down. A breathless voice.

"I'm sorry. Say that again."

The frantic assistant to the mayor unleashed a torrent. "They're throwing gas bombs and guns are being fired. Your people from the camp, Myra—the black ones—are caught up in it. The mayor wants you down there. To intervene. He says people have been shot. On the ground."

"Slow down, ma'am. Where's this happening?"

"In front of the Ritz. You know, the Negro movie house. An argument with the police. It's chaos. The mayor said to be careful. Stay on the sidelines. To identify people."

"I'll be there as soon as I can."

Myra hung up the phone and collected her wits. Peering back into the dining room, she forced a smile. "I've got to go into town. The mayor needs my advice on things going on," she said. "Lovely to see you, Mrs. Murkowski. As always, your desserts," she added in a tone to suggest the little pies deserved their city-wide reputation.

She ran up the stairs to grab a jacket, change out of her heels, and grab the key to the Army car.

As she fumbled with the front door, she caught the tail end of the widow's remarks.

"Quite a figure now she cuts, your daughter. Imagine being called out by the mayor, at night, she still a single woman. Times are mighty strange now."

Once she approached the edge of the Lee Street area, Myra parked and got out. She could smell smoke and hear sirens. A couple of ambulances whizzed by along with police cars. She turned to a man in a crowd that had gathered up ahead.

"What's going on?"

The man looked at her askance, then turned away. Another spoke up. "Coloreds from the camps came out of the movie house. Caterwauling or something. An MP beat up on one of 'em, and then they all went at it."

"As if we didn't have enough problems with our own," a third volunteered. "They're invaders. Think they own the place."

"Any idea where the mayor might be?" Myra asked, not wanting to get into an argument. "Looks like things are winding down. Ambulances have come and gone, right?" No response from anyone.

Myra lit off down Lee Street, past the YMCA, a grocery store, and a barbershop. Shards of glass littered the sidewalk. The residue of smoke bombs burned her eyes. Soon, a couple of MPs blocked her way. She flashed her Army pass.

"I've been asked by the mayor's office to come down here. To identify anyone I can."

"The bodies are mostly blacks. Be our guest."

As she got closer to the scene of the scuffle, Myra noticed white sheets covering bodies on the ground. A medic was tending to a man who appeared to be bleeding but conscious; a couple of others, who looked to be ambulance personnel, were hoisting a man, not in uniform and apparently gasping for air, onto a gurney.

Out of the crowd came a voice calling her name. "Miss Kaminsky. Thank God."

"Mr. Mayor. What has happened here?"

"Not good for the town at all. You'll need to make that clear tomorrow to the camp commanders. Things got out of control, out of control."

"Have you called the Claiborne commander yourself, Mr. Mayor? Are officers on their way from Claiborne?"

"No idea. The MPs are responsible for reporting it upwards." The mayor, glistening with sweat, wiped his brow and barked out an order to an underling nearby. "Handle the press, Wayne, and make short shrift of it: a melee, a little property damage, negro soldiers gone berserk."

"But sir, what about the gunshots? Those bodies back near the theater?" Myra interjected.

"There'll be an accounting. But first thing in the morning—to hell with Sunday—you get down to Claiborne and let the brass know that we ain't tolerating any more of a ruckus like this."

Having relieved himself of indignation, the mayor turned back to his inner circle, leaving Myra to fend for herself. Slowly, she made her way back up Lee Street. On her way, she made a mental note of six bodies in front of the movie house, a pool of blood having collected around the outlines of two of them. She would have accosted one of the medics but their ambulance, the last one on scene, had pulled away. She spotted two more bodies in front of the barbershop.

Near where she parked the car, she was stopped by two city cops, ordering her, despite her Army pass, to vacate the area. When she turned back around, one was barking commands into a walkie-talkie, the other was cordoning off the main drag and side streets.

Her eyes were watering, her stomach was churning. Once beyond Lee Street and the acrid smells, she veered into a darkened alley and vomited. She had been an unwitting witness to a massacre.

So, this is what war is like, she thought.

When Myra entered the house as quietly as she could, her father was pacing in the parlor, her mother knitting. Mrs. Murkowski was nowhere to be seen or heard.

"Abe Wallenstein rang up after you left, Myra. Said there was a riot on Lee Street. They could hear gunshots." Her father spoke as though she were somehow at fault.

"Please don't tell us that's why the mayor telephoned you," her mother interjected, shaking her head as though she knew the answer would not be to her liking.

"Yes and no. It was all over when I arrived. But there were—"

"You can tell it all to that major you work for. He too called. Left a number. Said to ring him at whatever hour." Mr. Kaminsky pulled out a notecard from his vest pocket and handed it to his daughter.

Out in the hall, Myra picked up the receiver and waited for the operator, wishing that the family had thought to have another phone installed upstairs.

After two rings, Major Benson picked up. "About time, Myra. Do you know anything about what happened in your town this evening? With our men."

As dispassionately as she could, she recounted what she saw, including lifeless bodies on the ground. He interrupted several times, with a few unexpected questions.

"You're privy to our Weekend Liberty passes. For the black soldiers as well. How many would you estimate we gave out for this evening?"

"The files will have an exact tally, but I would estimate 200 to 300 for the blacks. As I've argued before, large numbers could be troublesome."

Major Benson ignored this last comment. "What are the locals saying caused this, this incident?"

"Something trivial—like swaggering or cavorting in front of the movie theater. Drink could have been involved."

"So, black soldiers started it?"

"Not necessarily. More like an MP got into it with a soldier and began to beat him up. Other soldiers intervened. Things got out of hand."

"Ergo, it was *our* blacks, not those from Livingston or the other camps?"

"I don't know, sir. I noticed buses marked both Claiborne and Livingston parked along side streets." She could hear the major sigh in frustration, perhaps with her or with the situation itself.

"What I'm trying to get at, Myra, is how many, if any, of our men were involved in the ruckus. Commander Holiday is convening at 9 in the morning and will want to know the facts."

"I understand," Myra said, accustomed as she now was not to volunteer anything unnecessary.

"Without making the thing any worse than it needs to be," he added.

At that off-handed aside, Myra bristled. "In terms of facts, Major Benson, I can say that I counted six dead bodies, all in the proximity of the Ritz theater, and two others, at a minor distance, in front of a barbershop. That eighth was uncovered as yet, and in uniform, as presumably were the others. He looked to have been hit by a bullet in the chest as blood was pooled around him there."

After a little more back and forth, in testier tones, Major Benson said he needed to ring off, but would see her in the morning. He did remember to thank her for her "commitment to duty."

Disheartened, Myra hung up and returned to the parlor to bid her parents goodnight.

"They had no right to get you mixed up in this, Myra. None whatsoever," her father fumed. He rapped his pipe on his smoking table for emphasis.

The next morning, Myra drove to the camp before the sun had risen, convinced that she had happened upon a fatal rampage in her own hometown. Being black is dangerous in and of itself, she knew, but being black in military uniform might actually make things worse.

After strong coffee at the enlisted men's canteen, she made her way over to the Records office to check the files for the names of all those with Liberty Weekend passes. Against those, it could in theory be ascertained what soldiers never returned to base when their passes expired.

To her frustration, the file for January 10, 1942, had not yet been placed in the cabinet, or had been removed.

After that, Myra walked back to the major's office, and was the first to arrive. Mackie showed up at 8, Corporal Hill at 9, come to say his goodbyes.

"Obviously, I missed a big deal last night in your neck of the woods, Myra. I'd have relished being there to record it all."

Myra managed a faint smile. "Hopefully, you won't have to see anything like that once you're overseas. Whereto, can you say?"

"Only that it's to Hawaii, and then on to some God-forsaken island the Japanese are enamored of."

"Keep your sense of humor, corporal. It'll come in handy."

She held out her hand to shake his, but instead he hugged her.

Struggling to keep her focus, Myra went to her desk, took out pen and paper, and began putting down her recollections of the incident the night before.

Before long, Mackie piped up. "This is the Army, Myra. A lot of things get buried, not just bodies."

It wasn't until the end of the day that Major Benson burst into the office with papers in his hand. Without a word, he made a beeline for his own office and slammed the door.

Minutes passed.

"If you want to tell him what you yourself witnessed, you should do so now," Mackie said. "Otherwise, a different version may prevail."

Taking a deep breath, Myra got up, tapped at the door, but did not wait to be invited in.

Major Benson looked up but did not ask her to sit. "Mainly, I would like to know why on earth you found yourself in that mess last night."

"The mayor's office rang me. I got there as it was winding down. But it was more than a mess, sir. More like a massacre."

"You were unscathed. That's the important part." He forced a smile. When she did not budge, he cleared his throat. "In any case, we've looked into the matter. The issues will be addressed."

Myra remained at attention.

Apparently disconcerted under her gaze, the major fussed with the photos on his desk and then rattled the documents in front of him.

She thought his hand trembled. She planted her feet more firmly.

"But yes. We owe you thanks for your representations in the matter, Miss Kaminsky."

"As I mentioned last night—and I apologize for being scattered then—I counted eight bodies on the sidewalk. Plausibly, they were our soldiers." Major Benson tightened the muscles of his jaw. "I made an effort this morning to match the files, so we can know for sure."

"Whatever are you talking about, Miss Kaminsky?" he demanded, his tone sharper.

"The names of the black soldiers who had a liberty pass, against all those who can be accounted for today as having returned to base."

Major Benson stared down at the report in front of him. "As I said, we've already dealt with the incident. Commander Holiday has signed off on the investigation. He and his staff members have spoken to the local authorities in Alexandria as well as to the press."

Myra felt as though she had been sucker-punched. She opened her mouth to speak again but could not find the words.

Major Benson looked up at her, his eyebrows arched, more challenging than expectant. "So now, if you'll excuse me, we have a war to win."

Myra waited until dusk before leaving the office. Mackie's parting words were "Watch your step, Myra."

Her murmured response, "Thank you, Doris." It was the first time she had used her colleague's first name.

Rather than heading out the main gate, however, Myra detoured down a side road to the area where Camp Claiborne's black soldiers were bivouacked. She had been over that way before, but only now did it strike her how ramshackle the buildings were, how few the amenities.

A handful of black soldiers walked by her vehicle on their way ostensibly to the commissary, it too haphazardly erected, poorly lit. If they saw her, they gave no indication.

Deflated by all that had happened in the last twenty-four hours, Myra could not fathom how to accost these men or inquire as to what they might know about what transpired on Lee Street. Within a couple of minutes, she pulled away, not wanting to risk an MP shining a flashlight in her face.

Once home, Myra put on as chipper a face as she could, declining dinner but joining her parents in the parlor. They were listening to news from the front, specifically reports of Japanese attacks on islands in the vicinity of the Philippines. They handed over the Sunday paper to her.

The headline of the *Daily Town Talk* read: "No Deaths, 28 Injured in Lee Street Uprising." Further into the account, the Camp Claiborne Commander Ralph Holiday was quoted in an official statement: "None of our boys participated in this unfortunate outbreak."

"That was a dangerous thing you did last night, dear. We're relieved you weren't hurt," her mother said. "And," her father added, "that you managed to help the powers-that-be down at the camp. They must be proud of you."

Pleading exhaustion, Myra went upstairs, drew a long bath and went to bed. She would have liked to talk over all that had happened with Claire, who, now that she too was exposed to military protocol, might sympathize. Addison, too, she thought about, wondering what he would have said or done, in her shoes, or, more pertinently, in those of Major Benson.

Chapter Twenty-Two

SUSPICIOUS EYES

As winter set in, shortages took hold across the country. New Orleans was not spared. Before people knew it, sugar, coffee, canned fruits and vegetables, butter and, the final straw in Edward Endicott's estimation, meat were rationed. Cotton and wool, leather and anything made of rubber, including car tires, sold at a premium, though for the moment alcohol remained available, and in greater demand.

Having doled out bread and milk to all comers during the Depression, Esther Endicott converted the backyard into a victory garden.

President Roosevelt urged folks to embrace the war effort, in whatever way, shape or form. Most did. Businesses were transformed overnight; factories were retooled to make munitions; women en masse took up jobs they had never imagined doing in their lives.

Esther rose at dawn to assist the Red Cross, driving a van around the parish to deliver supplies to hospitals, clinics, and warehouses along the river. The pain in her leg subsided.

Helen Carrollton was shamed into taking part, spearheading the distribution of blackout booklets throughout the city.

Every evening, Edward combed through the *Picayune* to find that something else now required a ration card, or was no longer in stock, or had been repurposed for the troops. Remembering (vaguely) his own role in the Spanish-American conflict, his gripes soon subsided. "This is war, Esther. No different from what we went through in '98 and again in '17."

And as she had always done, Esther accepted her husband's viewpoint, though she pointed out that this time the war was closer to home.

Blackouts became common. Bourbon Street was no longer raucous. Fewer young men were out carousing, and those who were around were often in uniform, and hence held to a somewhat higher standard of conduct.

Tourists too made themselves scarce. Café du Monde lost its mojo, serving a few sailors on leave, lonely old ladies, and an occasional clutch of schoolgirls.

All around town, people kept their eyes peeled and their ears open. Everyone, it seemed, had the jitters.

Like most people, Claire kept her head down at work, bent on doing the best job she could decoding intercepts, translating and re-summarizing them for her superiors. Some of the messages were worrisome. U-boats were detected in the Gulf on a daily basis. There was talk of enemy agents penetrating the coastline and making their way into the city.

During a fraught day in late January, her supervising boss, Lieutenant Nelson, rushed over, waving a German intercept in his hand. "Can you make heads or tails of this?" he asked, breathless. "An entire flotilla may be headed our way."

She glanced at the writing. "The Germans are calling this Operation *Paukenschlag*, which roughly translates as Operation Drumbeat," she said. Quickly, she scanned the rest. "Looks like they're deploying six or seven U-boats to what they call the Louisiana sector."

"Damn," Nelson let out, and hurried back to the operations

room, where he and other officers huddled around a map on the wall, putting pins where they suspected a threat. Next to the map, they kept an outsized calendar updating U.S. ship movements into and out of the Gulf.

The very next day Junior Lieutenant Forster invited Claire for lunch nearby.

"I'd like to try this po-boy thing"—he was from Idaho—"if that appeals to you. If not, name your poison." He spoke in staccato bursts, as though his thoughts moved too swiftly for his words to catch up.

Over muffulettas, he explained more about the scheduling of convoys, some carrying cargo, others transporting troops, which made their way through the mouth of the Mississippi River and into the Gulf of Mexico. "What we're trying to do, I think you already have deduced." He looked her way, flipping his sandy blond hair from his forehead. She smiled politely but did not respond. "Stay one step ahead of the Krauts. Alert the convoy whenever a German sub is detected in the area."

Between bites, Claire asked, "I keep hearing about blimps. What do they do?"

Forster looked taken aback. "You gals aren't supposed to know everything," he said, rubbing his thin blond mustache. She looked at him, bemused. Secrets were hard to keep in such an office. "But yeah, you're right. We're all in this together. Besides, you've filled out all the paperwork. We know all about you."

Claire stiffened, picking up the menu to divert attention. "We could split a slice of carrot cake, Lieutenant. They may have more sugar on hand than we do at home."

"By all means," he rejoined. "And please call me Robert."

"Lieutenant suits you fine. I am still curious about the blimps."

He glanced around to make sure no one was listening. "We field a handful of them at night," he whispered, conspiratorial. "That's when the subs surface, stalking their prey, as it were. Often, the enemy can spot our convoys from the shadows they throw on a coastal town and fire their deck guns. One more rationale for blackouts."

She nodded, not fully grasping the picture but figuring it better to drop the subject.

Over coffee and carrot cake, the officer asked her where she lived and what she did in her spare time. Claire was vague, and vaguely uncomfortable. She liked the junior lieutenant well enough, but she liked the job more.

When the bill came, she insisted they go Dutch. He objected; she insisted. And then asked, "You still haven't explained."

"What?' he asked, eager enough.

"What happens if we can't determine where they are, the U-boats?"

"Then the convoy risks being struck by torpedoes. Even sunk. You'll know when that happens."

It did not take long for such a misfortune to rattle the office.

Communications with a convoy headed out into the Gulf had been lost during the night, fifty miles southeast of New Orleans. Coast Guard reports came in the next morning that two destroyers had limped on to Mobile, but the troop ship they had accompanied had been damaged by U-boat torpedoes and sunk. Only a few bodies had been recovered. The ship had carried upwards of four hundred soldiers bound for, if Claire heard right, some town she had never heard of in Libya. In a quiet moment, she flipped open her atlas to locate the destination, a place called Aran.

There was less horseplay and more smoking that day. Somber-faced officers from the other floors gathered to discuss repercussions. Secretaries were summoned to take notes or field messages. Claire was asked to man the telex machine, monitor the telegraph, and await the drafting of a report to Naval Command in Annapolis.

At the end of the day, she retreated to what was called the Ladies Room, which included a couple of armchairs and a poorly maintained rubber plant. It served for the female employees on the two top floors of the six-story building.

She splashed water on her face and dabbed at it with a linen cloth embroidered with the Navy seal. As she pulled out her compact, another woman exited one of the stalls, joining her in front of the mirror. She was unusually tall and held herself at the ready.

"Leaves me queasy when there's an incident this bad. Damn Germans," the woman said.

Claire recognized the voice. She turned her eyes the speaker's way. "I beg your pardon. Don't we know each other? From Sophie Newcomb. You're Myra's friend, from downstairs. You helped us—" She stopped herself in mid-sentence.

Unconvinced, the woman scrunched her forehead. "Oh, yes. Myra Kaminsky. And I remember you, coming over to visit her."

"Exactly. I'm Claire Endicott. I started here a few months ago."

"Me, a year or so already. Bernice Fleischer. I'm special assistant to the commander. Top floor. Not what I expected to be doing after college, but that would be true for all of us, right?"

"Indeed. So, how long do you think this will last?"

"What, our jobs, or the war?" Claire felt naïve to have asked, but Bernice did not seem to be judgmental. "My boss says, quoting someone or other, 'The best laid plans of mice and men.'" Claire nodded her head in tacit agreement. "Judging from how badly things are going in the Pacific, and right on our own doorstep, I predict it's going to be a while."

At that point, Bernice began to wash her hands, scrubbing hard to get ink off her fingers. "Had to draft a number of letters today. Condolences," she volunteered. After a beat, she shifted gears. "By the way, how is Myra?"

"Working at Camp Claiborne. She's liaison with the powers-that-be in Alexandria."

"Few were as smart as she," she said, "except for that personal episode. Well, you know what I mean." Bernice dried her hands, ran a comb through her coal-black hair, and retrieved a bulky briefcase from the nearby table. "Got to fly. Meeting someone. See you around."

Claire lingered a few minutes, seating herself in one of the armchairs to change out of her heels—leather shoes were becoming scarcer by the day—and into an old pair of flats. As she got up to leave, something on the sink caught her eye. It was a ring, a central diamond surrounded by a dozen tiny ones. Bernice must have taken it off, she surmised, and distracted, forgot to put it back on. It was past six now. She dropped it in her own bag and snapped it shut.

The next morning, Claire took the elevator to the sixth floor and deposited a tiny, wrapped box on the desk in front of Bernice. Several of the men in the room turned to watch but soon went back to whatever they were doing.

"Don't tell me," Bernice exclaimed. "I thought it was lost forever. You are more than kind—: you're honest."

"It's a beautiful ring. The man in question has excellent taste."

"No, no," Bernice said quietly. "It's not what you think. It's my Czech grandmother's. She sent it over a couple of years ago, with some other jewelry, knowing that she..."

"Oh, I see," Claire replied, disconcerted.

"I wear it," Bernice whispered, "both to honor her, and to deter unwanted interest." Her eyes swiveled to suggest the men who sat across the way.

Claire nodded, it not lost on her that Bernice was an arresting figure, and one of the few females on the floor.

That weekend after the loss of the convoy, Claire took a streetcar to Canal Street, determined to shop for shoes, both high heels and flats. Something to cheer herself up. On her way out of Maison Blanche, she literally bumped into Tom, who appeared to be rushing into the store. They both blushed. He recovered first.

"I did not forget. The dinner I invited you out to. But I figured things might have changed for you."

THIS NEARLY WAS OURS

She eyed his face, wondering what 'things' he might be referring to and whether things might have changed for him. Several customers eyed the two curiously. They were blocking the main entrance to the store.

"We should move aside," he said, taking her arm and moving a few paces down the sidewalk.

His touch stirred something in her. "I'm on my way home. If you like, come over later. Around 8 or 8:30. We can have whatever I can throw together. If that suffices?"

He looked at her, his gray-green eyes softer than she remembered. "I will be there, with a bottle of wine. There's no way I can compete with Bennie's flowers."

She laughed, a clear bell-like sound. Her mood had lifted. She rustled around in her pocketbook and pulled out a long key. "Bennie has taken to locking the back gate after dark, afraid, he says, of German spies getting in." When she saw Tom's face fall, she instantly regretted the remark. "Anyway, let yourself in and knock on the door when you arrive."

He took the key and watched her cross the street toward the streetcar stop. He forgot his shopping errand altogether, hurrying home back along Royal Street, where a streetcar was inching its way along in front of him, its destination *Desire*. He had been to that street somewhere in the ninth ward to meet Bennie's family. But seeing the word written on the streetcar stirred something else in him.

Claire took a bath and put on a wool skirt and silk blouse, neither too casual nor too formal. She did not let her mind wander to other details of her attire, or her body, forcing herself instead to throw together a vegetable salad and boil some shrimp.

At 8:30 sharp, Tom knocked on the door, a bag with two bottles of wine in his arms as well as a small book. He placed the two bottles on the kitchen counter, remembering how difficult it was to install but how well it looked once completed.

"How do you like your kitchen space? It was the only hard part in putting the whole thing together."

"I'm very happy with it, though don't get your hopes up that the cooking here is anything to write home about," she replied, again thinking that almost everything she uttered could cause discomfort for this young man. Did he even have a proper home to write to?

"Why don't you open whichever wine you prefer. I'll unwrap a couple of cheeses," she said, turning to open the refrigerator.

Soon, they toasted the war effort with a French burgundy, but neither felt like belaboring the subject. Instead, Tom pulled the book in gold trim out of his pocket and handed it to her.

"It's one of the few things I brought from home, those years ago. Rilke is one of my favorite poets. Your German is so good you will appreciate it. And to be honest, I wanted you to be reassured that not all things Germanic are evil."

Moved by his gesture, she replied, "I do know that. You can hear the music, right? What would the world do without Bach," she asked rhetorically.

To collect himself, Tom walked over to one of the two windows. It faced east. The crepe myrtle was beginning to leaf out and would soon sport its watermelon-colored blossoms.

After a few more minutes, Claire brought out her salad and chilled shrimp, which they took their time eating. She asked if he'd ever eaten gumbo. He hadn't. He asked if she'd ever traveled to Europe. It almost happened but didn't.

Eventually, Bach gave way to Beethoven and then on to Schubert and Mendelssohn. She asked him if he played an instrument. He said he had studied the piano, haphazardly, but enjoyed it more with his childhood friends, Katrin and Hans. "It's how we first learned English. Playing the songs of Thomas Moore."

She looked surprised. "You mean, like 'Believe Me if All Those Endearing Young Charms...?'" she asked. He nodded. "A shame, I guess, that no one speaks like that anymore. But we do still, occasionally anyway, sing those songs."

Later still, they sat on the sofa and Claire asked Tom to read one of Rilke's poems. "Slowly," she said, "with feeling."

He looked at her, questioningly. "Yes," he eventually said. "It is what we shall do."

He thumbed to a lyric simply called "Love Song." He read it first in German, and then in English. Then he coaxed her to read it along with him, with the requisite rises and falls of the language. Together they recited the lines, "How shall I hold my soul, so it does not touch on yours. How shall I lift it over you to other things?"

"You may keep the book for as long as it brings you pleasure. I know most of the poems by heart anyway," Tom said.

After they finished the wine, Claire lit a couple of candles, lowered the shades on the two windows, and turned off the lamp.

"If there is a blackout," she said, half-jokingly, but also as a signal of what was to come, "all we have to do—this one is yours, the other, mine—is blow them out."

She placed one on the right side of the bed, and the other on the matching stand on the other side. And in that flickering light, she invited him over. As she had more than two years ago, when, like now, she had kicked off her shoes and positioned herself on the edge of the bed.

Tom inhaled deeply to calm his racing heart. He took her in his arms, and delicately undressed her. She was less shy about her body than he expected, her breasts so eager he had to look away. With her help, he slid back the coverlet on the bed, and lay her body on the cool sheets. She did not cover herself nor avert her eyes from him.

"You must tell me if this is what you want—and stop me if you do not," Tom told her. He had fantasized about making love to her more than he cared to admit, but now that the time had come, he was more nervous than he had anticipated. He fumbled with his own clothes, dropping them on the floor, and then lay down as gently as he could next to her. His excitement was visible. She showed no sign of embarrassment.

"I have imagined this off and on, so, yes, this is what I'd like." She leaned into his body, her breasts touching his chest, her lips finding his.

A practiced enough lover, Tom made an effort to control himself and to think of her, younger and less experienced. For a few minutes, they kissed, their tongues intertwining, their breaths shallow.

Be gentle, be gentle, he told himself. With care, he explored her curves and hollows with his fingers, then with his tongue, and then with his penis, only coming inside her after pleasuring her as fully as he could. She moaned, he gasped, she came, he followed her. Then again, after some water, candles still lit, Claire did the same to Tom, learning his body with her hands, then with her lips and finally with her mouth. They tasted what was of each other they could until they could do no more.

Neither Claire nor Tom professed undying love during this first night of lovemaking, but a goodly portion of their days going forward was devoted to anticipation of the next time they would be in each other's arms. War or no war.

Often, Tom would await her outside her office, and they would take in a movie or go eat somewhere, usually nondescript places along Magazine Street. Other times, they would head back to her place. The disapproving eye of Mrs. Jennings as they mounted the stairs together at his place queered them both.

Claire walked with a lilt, and with an appreciation of her body she had never had before. Her parents noticed but had no idea to what to attribute this unexpected ebullience. Neither apparently did her colleagues at work, though she had noticed that the men eyed her more curiously than they had before. Lena Walenska and Lucille Truard commented to each other on their young friend's surprising *présence*, in the French sense, and attributed it to her newfound independence.

Myra, who took a long weekend in April to return to New Orleans, immediately sensed that Claire was wound up like a top.

"Whatever is going on with you?" From Claire's crimson cheeks, she guessed correctly. "Who is it and what and when?" she asked as soon as the two were ensconced in the guest bedroom in her aunt's house. "I didn't think there were any eligible young men left in the city—unless in uniform!"

It was only later, after telling Myra about meeting up with Tom Stone yet again that she realized something bothered her. It was a niggling sensation that Tom might be vulnerable: not only disliked by her parents but eyed suspiciously by the authorities. America was at war; Tom's home country was the enemy. Being Jewish did not change that basic fact.

Still, it was marvelous to be in love, so Claire let her reservations go for the time being.

As for Myra's mood, she was still rattled by the reaction of the camp and the town to the Lee Street incident, which no one wanted to talk about, let alone tell the truth about.

When her aunt Lena asked about the melee that had taken place, she gave a perfunctory explanation and moved on. Nor did she say much about Major Benson, who had tried in his way to make amends for dismissing her account of the violence. On the one hand, he invited her out to dinner several times (overtures she rebuffed), and on the other, he let her off early on Fridays (which she readily acquiesced to).

Myra's parents found her more subdued as the months went back. However, she did what she could around the house and took them out to dinner or the movies at least once a week.

A war was on; things weren't going well on any front. Battles were being lost right and left in those early months. Her own problems would have to take a back seat.

One morning, Myra walked into the office to find Doris Mackie with a long face. "He'll want to tell you himself," she mumbled, jerking her head toward Major Benson's open door.

"Whatever is the matter?" Myra asked.

"Go on in."

She did and stood at attention in front of the major's desk. He was looking at a telegram. The cross-hatches on his forehead appeared more prominent than usual. Thinking it would not be good news, she spread her weight evenly between her feet.

"Turns out, Myra, that we've lost one of our own. Corporal Hill was fatally wounded in the line of duty."

The blood drained from her face. "Where? When? He's only been gone since—"

"He was manning a radio transmitter during a skirmish on some island in the South Pacific. His remains will be shipped to his family in Minnesota. I will be sending condolences on our behalf."

She stiffened, unable to move.

Shortly, Major Benson looked up. "You are dismissed, Myra. Should be a busy day."

Chapter Twenty-Three
EVERY WHICH WAY

By May of 1942, Philip Caxton had decided to convert his forty-year-old workshop over to the war effort, which, to begin with, meant a Navy contract to produce crates for the shipment of maritime supplies overseas.

"Antiques, my dear lady, will have to bear up for the duration," he told one customer who wished to have a dozen Louis Philippe chairs refurbished, war or no war.

"And how long will that duration be, Mr. Caxton?"

"No idea, Mrs. Lind. You will have to ask Herr Hitler."

Insulted, she hung up the receiver. Caxton chuckled. He had turned sixty-five and, in his own estimation, allowed to say what he thought.

The business decision was practical as well as patriotic. His younger employees had been called up in the weeks after Pearl Harbor. Except for one deemed unfit, they had, to a man, already shipped out for Europe or for the Pacific.

It did not escape notice, however, that his favorite employee was conspicuously not among them.

"As much as I'd like to keep you around, Tom, you could do

more. For the war effort, and for yourself." Tom looked stricken. "Frankly, you need to do more so as not to arouse suspicion," his boss further opined.

"I am aware of that, sir. But I have no papers. No past I can easily account for. That had not been such a problem, but now, with the war, it is worrisome."

Caxton wrinkled his brow. "Don't matter how you put it. These are parlous times," he declared, rattling off the battles in the Pacific which had not gone well. Tom nodded, having followed the same newsreels and newspaper reports. "Everyone has to play a part," the old man went on, puffing away on his pipe. It was past five o'clock. He had sent the office accountant, an older man, home, and hung out the *Closed* sign.

Tom glanced at his own watch, but was too polite, or beholden, to leave until dismissed.

Caxton changed the subject. "I figure you've been preoccupied. Anything you want to tell me?"

Although his first instinct was to say no, Tom liked his boss, and had no other male to confide in. "It's a girl. I'm in love with her, but nothing can come of it. She's—here his face lit up as though to affirm his enchantment and then fell as though to suggest the obstacles in his way—she's wonderful, but I'm in no position..." He shook his head in dismay.

Caxton refilled his pipe and propped himself against the nearest sawhorse. Eyeing Tom in profile, he was reminded of his own son, same angular facial planes, same gentle demeanor, but also, the same tendency to evade. He tried to retrieve what had so exasperated him about his son but failed. Philip Jr. had died ten years before, a freak accident on the lake. Caxton's wife faded away within the year. He threw off the memories and got to the point. The girl in question could wait.

"You can do more than repair hinges, Tom. And leaving aside your love life, a challenge would be good for you. You might help the war effort and keep yourself out of harm's way. You don't want the Feds waving the Alien Enemies Act in your face."

"What do you have in mind, sir?"

Caxton went on to describe the conversion of factories into munitions plants around Lake Pontchartrain. Including a facility to make amphibious landing vessels. "I know people up there, including the engineer overseeing the design of these boats. If you're interested, I'll write you a letter of introduction to this Higgins fellow."

Given the growing need for skilled labor, few questions were asked up at the industrial site along the lakefront. Tom Stone presented well, and Caxton was a known quantity, one who could write a convincing letter.

For a while, all worked out. Tom rolled up his sleeves and quickly got the hang of the project. In his deliberate way, he helped make the vessels lightweight but sturdy, the front flap flawlessly functional. Higgins and his subordinates liked his design suggestions and his unstinting work ethic. He showed up early in the mornings and never left work until after his superiors did.

But Tom also began to fret.

People at work gossiped about the lists that the State Department was compiling around the country, especially in vulnerable coastal cities like their own.

"You can end up on the *A*, *B*, or *C* list," he overheard one guy say. "They nabbed one of my neighbors. An Italian fella who pushes a food cart. Guy wouldn't hurt a flea."

Tom did not join in these conversations, but he did read the papers more thoroughly. He kept his now illegal short-wave radio hidden under his bed, but instead of listening to Beethoven, he kept it tuned to news about the war, what was happening on the home front as well as abroad.

Almost every week, Japanese families were herded into camps out in California. Germans too, judging from gossip he picked up here and there. The kiosk on Canal Street stopped carrying German newspapers printed in American cities.

Sometimes during the nights that he spent with Claire, she would awaken to find him with his eyes open, smoking a cigarette and staring at the ceiling.

"Is something wrong, darling? Something I said, or did?"

At these questions, he would stub out his cigarette and take her in his arms. Making love was the best way to snuff out the cares of the day.

Although she did not know the specifics of Tom's past, Claire knew not to broadcast anything about her relationship around the office, limiting herself to vague references, even with Bernice from upstairs. They had fallen into the habit of grabbing lunch together when things were not busy in the office, which also helped her avoid overtures from Junior Lieutenant Forster. For a time.

Unfortunately, and to Claire's unbeknownst, the lieutenant had become obsessed with her. He popped over to her desk with the minimal of excuses, offered unwanted advice, and bestowed unwarranted praise on anything noteworthy she decoded or translated for her superiors. Other men in the office rolled their eyes, but kept their mouths shut.

The young officer's attentions eventually followed her out the door. He trailed her to the Garden District, hopping the same streetcar at the last minute and jumping off after her stop to double back. He watched her unlock a high iron gate and engage in conversation with a Negro holding a rake.

The lieutenant might have let it go at that, but one late Friday evening in May, after a trying week of multiple ship losses and casualty reports to file, he watched as a young man met up with Claire on Carondelet and accompanied her home. Oddly, it was the *man* who pulled out a key to open the gate and follow her up the stairs to the guest house. Forster lingered on the sidewalk for an hour, but no one came out. Early the next morning, he returned in time to see the young man leave and grab a streetcar back downtown. From there, he trailed him to an inauspicious boarding house on Esplanade. He jotted down the address.

A few days later, Forster took a long lunch break to strike up a conversation with the voluble landlady.

"A strange young man, Mr. Steinberg, or whatever his name is. Pays on time, mind you, but keeps secrets up on that top floor."

"Like what?" Forster persisted.

Mrs. Jennings crooked her head. The woman expected to be paid for anything more incriminating. He slipped her a five-dollar bill. On cue, she rattled off a laundry list of questionable items she had come across in her "otherwise respectable" house—a gun, letters with Nazi insignia, an illicit radio.

Anonymously, the junior lieutenant passed on what he had gleaned to the Navy's domestic intelligence unit—and left it at that.

Then one weekend when Claire was called upon to work—reports had surfaced of more U-boat incursions in the Gulf—Tom joined several men from his work site to fish in the marshlands south of New Orleans. He had rarely fraternized with other males, nor had he been fishing since childhood, but it seemed sensible to get his mind off his troubles.

On the second day, their boat ran aground. Before they knew it, a brawl with some Cajuns broke out. Fists flew; drink made things worse. A nearby coastal patrol unit stepped in. Along with several others, Tom was questioned and ID-ed.

He did not mention this misadventure to Claire. She had enough on her plate.

As she had described it to Tom, every time the telex machine clicked on and a message crossed the wires, a hush would fall over her office.

"From what the higher-ups say, U-boats have stepped up their attacks around here, sinking or damaging cargo or troop ships at the rate of six or seven a month," she told him. "Casualties are mounting on our side. Everyone on Carondelet is tense."

He nodded sympathetically, thinking of Hans, and where his

childhood friend might be. How ironic that their lives had so diverged. He did not speak of this either to Claire.

Not a week later, on a scorchingly hot afternoon in mid-July, a firestorm raged off the Louisiana coast near Grand Isle. In Claire's office, everyone scrambled.

Smoke was soon visible in the sky over Canal Street. This was one skirmish that could not be withheld from the press or the public.

"It's a tanker. The *Benjamin Brewster*," one of the officers on the phone yelled. "Torpedoed and on fire. There may be survivors."

The ship's manifest bore him out. About half the crew was lost but a number aboard did, despite the flames, manage to detach rowboats or swim to shore.

Addison was among the Naval bigwigs dispatched to oversee the rescue effort.

"The problem is," he said over dinner with Claire and their parents that Sunday, "the more these reports get out, the more the Nazis step up their assaults. Beyond the subs themselves, they're clearly getting help from inside the country."

"You mean, like spies in our midst?" Esther inquired over the vegetable salad. Roast beef had been relegated to holidays or birthdays only.

"Something like that," Addison said. "The government has lists —Japanese out on the West Coast, but also Italians and Germans. Not everyone in our midst supports the war effort."

Claire broke her silence. "Has anyone—an Italian or a German— been arrested around here?"

"You know the protocol, Sis. It's all classified but yes, we receive indications now and again. Sometimes anonymously. The FBI follows up."

More perturbed than ever, Claire declined a slice of her mother's lemon icebox pie and spent the night in her childhood bed. Laying there, she had an eerie feeling of having been followed herself—when alone or when with Tom. She could not pinpoint the occasions or who it was that might be so interested in them.

Making it worse, her brother had not stopped with mention of the supposed lists. Anyone determined to be a threat is sent off to camps—*interred* was the word Addison had used—for the duration. Where such camps were and what went on there he had not said or did not know. As for the duration, no one seemed to have a clue how long this war was going to drag on.

It certainly was not going as well as it might. Of that Claire had no doubt.

At the end of the month, things did get worse. Claire intuited the bad news when the commander from upstairs burst into the office at 8:30. Everyone scrambled to their feet. Bernice followed behind her boss, notebook in hand. A couple of other officers from the sixth floor brought up the rear.

"What I have to say does not leave this room," Commander Owen Lassiter began. No one spoke. "A passenger steamer, the *Robert E Lee*, of all things, has been scuttled in the Gulf. Multiple casualties. We shall know more later today. Meantime, and this is the only good news, one of its escorts—what is its number, Morrison?" he demanded, scanning the room for his underling.

"Number 566, under a Captain Claudius, sir," the junior officer called out, saluting as he did so.

"Duly noted. Apparently, the escort gave chase and dropped a depth charge on the U-boat. There were explosions. We'll know more on that score in due course." He turned to converse briefly with a couple of other officers. All in hushed tones. Claire could not hear what was said.

The commander then surveyed the assembled again, nodding appreciatively. "Though we probably won't have to worry about that sub anymore, folks, we have a lot else to contend with to get through this minefield. No pun intended." For an instant, his jaw relaxed. He had come close to making a joke.

The handful of women in the room, including Bernice, smiled.

215

The men in the room remained stiffly at attention. The commander glanced at his watch. "You may proceed with your day. And the slogan was never truer: *Loose lips sink ships.*"

With that, Commander Lassiter turned toe, followed by his entourage.

Naturally, the loss of an American passenger ship in the Gulf became front-page news, making the city ever more jittery. Addison was authorized to double the number of volunteers scouring the lower Mississippi for anything suspicious as well as to launch more patrol boats to police the Gulf as far as Mobile, Alabama.

Without making a formal commitment, Tom and Claire rarely discussed the particulars of their respective jobs, each wanting their relationship to provide a haven amidst such upheaval. Still, it was hard to shut out everything having to do with the war.

When he saw the news about the confrontation between the *Robert E Lee* and the U-boat, he rifled through his things for Han's last letter. His friend had indeed made an offhanded reference to his vessel being headed across the Atlantic toward the Gulf.

"It occurred to me, do you ever see the manifests of enemy subs or the names of the captains, things like that?" Tom asked Claire casually after they had gone to see a movie about Dunkirk. It was mid-August. The weather had started to break, huge drops began to fall as they made their way back to her place.

Non-plussed, Claire equivocated. "Not really. We've not succeeded in disabling, let alone sinking, many enemy subs." Tom struggled to open the umbrella. "Why do you ask?"

"Just curious." They picked up their pace as the rain pelted them. Claire's umbrella was not designed for two. Tom held it over her as best he could. "Sad, though," he continued, almost as an aside, "to perish at sea and not be identified."

"From the little I understand of Germans, they likely keep meticulous records of their soldiers. Wouldn't you think?"

"I suspect they do," he said, something in his tone rueful or resigned.

Claire was troubled by the exchange but could not say why. She let it pass. The rain kept on.

The two lovers were drenched by the time they mounted the stairs. Tom fetched the key from his pocket and Claire retrieved two letters from the mailbox, one from Myra and the other from Lena Walenska.

After drying off and taking off their wet squeaky shoes, Tom poured them a glass of wine. Claire cut open the envelopes.

"This should be fun," she soon said. From across the room, Tom looked up, expectantly. "Myra's aunt is performing at the college mid-September, Chopin naturally, and the Tulane orchestra is playing Elgar. It's a fund-raiser."

"You must go by all means," Tom said.

"You too. Myra spoke with her aunt—and explained that you and I know each other well. You are specifically invited."

Tom looked dubious but did not object. "Perhaps I did not tell you. When I met them at the opera, I discovered Madame Walenska and I have Lübeck in common. And they were both lovely to me, she and Professor Truard. They both spoke highly of you."

Later, they made love with care, each burdened by the secrecy of their relationship and beset by premonitions.

The concert was an elaborate affair, well-attended by alumni and Crescent City luminaries as well as by college students and faculty. Myra came down from Alexandria with her parents, bringing along her colleague Doris Mackie, whom she described as a mainstay officer of Camp Claiborne.

Claire persuaded her father to attend, her mother having taken to her bed with a headache. Addison had received an invitation directly from Myra and showed up on his own. Tom did the same, sitting discreetly in the row behind Claire and her father.

"You do remember Tom Stone, do you not, Father?"

Tom held out his hand. Mr. Endicott barely nodded. Addison,

by contrast, shook his hand warmly. He had heard the name Stone before, from somewhere, but not, unless he erred, from his sister.

"Are you in the service, Tom?" Addison ventured.

"I'm working out at Lake Pontchartrain, on the landing vessels project."

"Excellent. We've been hearing good things about its progress."

They might have continued to chat, but the lights dimmed. Opening remarks were made by the college provost, followed by the Pledge of Allegiance. Everyone stood.

Once the curtain went up, Lena Walenska was revealed in a lavender gown, less ostentatious than the attire she had brought with her from Europe but flattering, nonetheless. Beaming, she took a bow and situated herself, with studied flair, on the piano bench. Having had a year to practice on the college Steinways and revive her technique, she performed flawlessly. The orchestra acquitted itself with the requisite fervor that Edward Elgar's second symphony required.

After the concert and the collection of donations, family and friends gathered for a late-night supper at Lena's home. At one interval, Tom fell into conversation with her about her time in Lübeck. The town had its charms, she told him, but, as she delicately understated it, "It was not a happy time." He nodded sympathetically. "Mind you," she went on, "I had my piano students, so I made ends meet, but even they—or their parents—were targeted."

"It must have been unnerving," he offered up.

"Yes, poor Johan, he was gifted." She shook her head in dismay. "Only Katrin, a lovely girl, somehow managed to get out. Helped by an old family friend, I was told. She secured passage on one of the last refugee ships out of Hamburg."

Dumbfounded, Tom's mind began to race. "I must ask," he stammered, "but do you remember this Katrin's last name?"

"Let me think. Her mother was Swedish, the father was the one who was Jewish. They both—" She gestured to indicate the unthinkable. "His name was Klein, no Kleindorf. That was it."

His breath shallow, Tom made his way over to a couch.

Claire soon joined him. "Are you alright? You look like you've seen a ghost."

"Rather, heard about one."

"Meaning?"

"Lena Walenska apparently gave piano lessons to the family friend I told you about. The one I went to Cuba to meet. You remember, right? Katrin was on the *St Louis*."

"The ship that was forced to turn back. Does Lena have more information?"

"She herself ended up in hiding. She would not have known anything more." Claire nodded, trying to process the contour of the story. "Hans, my other childhood friend, was uncertain to what country Katrin would have been sent."

"I'm so sorry," Claire said. She had never seen Tom so disoriented. Even if it were because of his attachment to another woman, she was moved, and loved him more for it.

Before long, Lucille Truard and Marie Monceau wandered over to speak.

"I trust you are well, my dear," the professor began, addressing Claire. "And still finding use for your language skills."

"Yes, I do. I owe you a debt of gratitude."

The French teacher patted her on the arm. "*Très bien*," she mumbled.

"I hear from Bennie that you leave early in the morning and often work late there on Carondelet," Lady Monceau added. "Distressing news. Losing ships before they even manage to cross the ocean. Must be stressful what you do."

Claire nodded her head in tacit agreement, not knowing how to respond to such comments, or whether she should. She was recently given another security clearance, though not as high as her friend Bernice's. Even so, she had become more circumspect.

Lady Monceau turned her attention to Tom. "I suspect you are busy too, Mr. Stone. Bennie says the noise of hammers never ceases on the lake, and that you often have to be dragged away from it all."

"He exaggerates, Lady Monceau. I'm simply trying to do my part," he managed, ill-at-ease under her gaze.

She reached out for him to squeeze her hand, then glanced from one to the other. "I'll expect to see the two of you soon for afternoon tea. All work and no play—you do know what that bodes."

Later that night, Claire asked Tom if he was feeling less upset.

He hardly knew where to begin, so tried to limit the things preying on his mind. "Not to alarm you, but I keep imagining eyes upon me, at the strangest times." The muscles in Claire's face twitched but she said nothing. "The worst thing is I worry that somehow you will be implicated in whatever I might be accused of doing."

Claire swallowed hard and considered her next words. "The war is getting to both of us. But I love you, and I am tired of having to hide the fact, when I would rather celebrate it." She leaned over and gave him a kiss.

"Let's be clear, though," Tom replied. "The fact is not hidden from anyone. All they have to do is look into my eyes."

"And into mine."

Chapter Twenty-Four

INTO THE UNKNOWN

Six weeks later, Addison drove to Camp Claiborne on a Friday evening. He had not reckoned on the rain. A trip he had heretofore made in two hours took three. Since he was dressed in full naval regalia, the guard at the main gate went out of his way to help the officer find Major Benson's quarters. He was escorted by a recruit to the reception area. An older woman came out to receive him. It was Doris Mackie.

"I did not breathe a word, Commander Endicott. She's at her desk. I myself will be leaving now. The major had a meeting offsite. Not likely to reappear this evening."

"Thank you, Doris. And you may call me Addison."

She saluted; he touched his cap. She turned the knob for him and left.

When he opened the door, Myra had her head lowered, the receiver to her ear, taking notes. She was oblivious to the intrusion.

"That's correct, sir. Mr. Louis and his entourage will be met at the airport and transported here by Army bus. Yes, they'll be lodged in guest quarters." She proceeded to scribble whatever was being relayed to her over the phone. "I do understand the concern. Open seating at the match or no bout," she repeated, and then, after a pause, added, "as it should be."

After ringing off, she jotted down other particulars. Finally, she stuck her pencil in a soup can along with others.

Addison took a couple of steps and cleared his throat.

"What on earth? I had no idea," Myra blurted out, brushing stray curls off her face. For weeks, she had been meaning to book a haircut at Bertha's but had not found the time.

"I hope I'm not interrupting. But I wanted to speak to you first before anyone else." She looked anxious. "Nothing like that," he rushed to specify, dismissing anything tragic. "Might I drive you home?"

"I need to leave a note for the major. Joe Louis is to do an exhibition bout here but won't oblige unless there's open seating for blacks and whites."

"As it should be," he replied, repeating her phrase.

"Since I'm liaison, smoothing the way falls to me," she said. "And to think, two weeks ago, I did not even know who this person was."

"The Brown Bomber," Addison chuckled. "All the men will be clamoring to get in."

"Even though you are Navy, we might could wrangle a pass. It's in mid-November."

Addison's face fell. He looked around at the room, three desks piled high with paperwork, a couch, and a water-cooler. Through the open door to the major's office, he could see a more imposing desk. It too was covered by folders, a Dictaphone and several framed photos. "I assume you like your superior," he asked rhetorically.

"Well enough," she replied, with no elaboration. Instead, she stood and walked a note into Major Benson's inner sanctum, placing it in his wooden inbox. She doused the lights, grabbed up a leather pouch, and turned to her visitor. "Ready if you are."

They drove for a few minutes in silence, concentrating on ruts in the road which had worsened in the latest round of fall storms. Once the downpour let up, Addison spoke up.

"You know better than most that things are not going swimmingly, right?" Myra nodded, tightening her grip around the passenger door handle. "As it turns out, I've been assigned to an aircraft carrier. My orders came through the other day. Unless the date slips, I'll be headed to the Pacific by Christmas."

Myra could feel her stomach turn over. She closed her eyes tight, willing herself to remain professional. "What exactly is the job, if I may ask?"

Addison slowed to dodge a fallen limb. "You know how these things work. It has to do with intelligence coordination under the Pacific Command fleet. There's a promotion involved, though that hardly changes things."

He sounded self-deprecating, but Myra suspected (and hoped) he was also reluctant to be separated from home (and from her).

Recovering, she asked if he had informed his parents and his sister. He had not yet had the courage, he admitted. "Mother will take it hard. My father will be of a mixed mind. And Sis you know better than anyone. She'll be fine."

"I wouldn't go that far about Claire. She depends a lot on you. But she will understand." Myra could feel her eyes filling up but forced herself not to cry. "We all do," she added softly.

That evening, the Kaminskys pulled out all the stops to make the newly minted naval captain feel welcome.

Ilona brought out her best china and served up the beef stroganoff she was planning to feature the following evening. Myrtle Murkowski popped in midway through the meal, having noticed the strange car at the curb. Too late for the rationed beef, she indulged in two servings of apple crumble.

Once they retired to the parlor, Ilona brought coffee for the group and Konrad tuned the radio to his preferred music station. "Hard to sleep at night if we listen to the news from Europe. We tend to do that in the morning and then the papers in the afternoon. But you have a first-hand grasp of how things are proceeding, Captain Endicott. Can you tell us anything?"

"Please call me, Addison. And, although I'm in Intelligence, I know little more than what you read or hear."

Konrad began to prepare his pipe. "How about around New Orleans?"

"I'd say the situation in the Gulf has improved. We believe the Germans have shifted a number of subs out of the area. As for enemy aliens or Nazi or Fascist sympathizers, they continue to be rounded up around the country."

Silence followed as some baroque concerto came on. "Hard to do without German or Italian music though," Konrad mused.

Eventually, Myrtle piped up. "I almost forgot. Flora received a letter from Frederick." The Kaminskys nodded. "He is a childhood friend of Myra's. Family owns the main dry goods store in town. Fred had begun to manage the store when—you know, Pearl Harbor."

Addison glanced at Myra, but her gaze remained resolutely trained on the magazines on the coffee table. "And where is Mr. Bauer serving, Mrs. Murkowski?"

"Half the letter was blacked out, so poor Flora is not sure of much. But she believes he has been fighting in North Africa, chasing this Rommel the Fox, perhaps not personally but you understand. From there, it's anyone's guess." Flustered, she desisted. The others smiled. Ilona poured her neighbor some more coffee. "He did ask after Myra naturally. That part was not blacked out," Mrs. Murkowski added, pointedly.

This time, Myra rolled her eyes.

"So, Captain, I mean Addison," Ilona asked, "how long are you likely to be out in the Pacific and does your boat have a name?"

"It's not a boat, Ilona, it's a ship, or rather, a carrier. There are only so many in the Navy, but I'm sure the captain would prefer not to say which he'll be sailing on," Konrad interposed.

"That pretty much sums it up," Addison replied, more amused than offended by the questions thrown at him.

While Ilona prepared the extra bedroom for their unexpected guest, Addison and Myra walked Mrs. Murkowski home. The rain had stopped but the wind had picked up. On their walk back, he took her hand. "It's hard to know what to say, because I studied and trained for this for so long."

She looked sidelong at him. "But?"

"There are things and people I shall miss." In the dim light of the streetlamp, he looked stricken.

This was not music to her ears; it was dissonance. She put her lips together tightly.

"I suspect that sentiment describes what every soldier feels upon being uprooted from hearth and home," she replied, her tone matching the chill in the air. In her head, she counted the times the two had kissed. Only a handful, when in her case, she had done things with another man about which she could (or would) no longer put words.

Addison came to a stop and distractedly kicked a can off the still slippery sidewalk. Myra stopped alongside him. She dropped his hand.

"This damned war. Hard to know what will happen, and how unfair it is to assume anything. But you will be in my thoughts: you, my parents, Claire, Richard. I'm not a very demonstrative person."

If stunned by how mealy-mouthed this confession sounded, Myra was also struck by Addison's pained expression. Part of her wanted to slap him, but the other part urged her to be supportive. The man was about to put his life on the line against the Japanese, for heaven's sake.

She managed a wan smile and took his hand again. Together they mounted the steps to the house.

The next morning, Ilona outdid herself again, whipping up vegetable omelets, toast, and coffee. No one said much at the breakfast table, but afterwards, Addison thanked the couple profusely. "I'm expected for a briefing at noon," he explained. "Otherwise—." His face was flushed. He was floundering.

"You will keep me posted, so I can come down to see you off?"

Myra asked as he pulled the keys from his dress pocket to open the car door.

"I shall count on it," he said, glancing up at the front windows where the elder Kaminskys were looking out. He placed a kiss on Myra's forehead, adjusted his cap, and headed off.

"Why ever do you think he came up here, Konrad?" Ilona whispered to her husband, as Myra came back through the front door.

"Not a clue," he murmured.

Later that Saturday, Myra walked into Bertha's beauty parlor for what was advertised as *The Works*.

Major Benson made a point of commending Myra for her role in orchestrating the Brown Bomber's exhibition bout and helping to bring it off without incident. She had lobbied for a random lottery so that interested blacks, of whom there were many, would be as likely to draw an entrance ticket as their white counterparts. The allotment for town folks and officers' guests she managed to keep to a minimum.

"It's Mr. Louis's wishes that this be for ordinary soldiers, is how it was put, and I gave my word—and that of the camp—that they would be respected," she had told Commander Holiday when he accosted her in the officers' commissary.

"Benson's young woman is apparently not to be toyed with," he purportedly snorted to his subordinates. Word got around, (if it hadn't already in the wake of the Lee Street riot), that the Kaminsky girl had a mouth on her.

In the event, the match was a sold-out affair, and blacks and whites banded together in their enthusiasm for the blows exchanged in the ring, rather than among themselves. Extra security, which Myra also urged upon her superiors, helped keep things in check.

"Oddly, though, I did not spot you at the match, Miss Kaminsky. I had understood that a visitor, a Naval man, had been by to meet you shortly before. Surely, we could have found a pass for him," Major Benson said.

It wasn't precisely a question, so Myra let it hang in the air.

"On shore leave, was he? Or one of those desk-bound types, in his starched whites and all." The major took a long drag on his cigarette and blew a smoke ring in her direction.

She picked up the gauntlet. "The captain is Naval Intelligence. He's to embark for a command in the Pacific." She held his gaze until his own faltered.

"I see," he went on. "Intelligent like you—*summa cum laude* and all." Her face telegraphed that the honorific was neither here nor there. "Which reminds me," he added more briskly. "My son did get into Harvard. Winter semester. Which means my wife," he further revealed, picking up one of the photographs on his desk and flicking dust off it. "My wife will be joining me here. For a stint."

"How nice for you," she replied, as neutral as possible.

Major Benson tilted his head ever so slightly and raked her body from head to foot. Myra did not flinch. "I believe you are sporting a new hairdo."

"If that is all, sir, I'll get back to my desk. I understand our first tranche of POWs will arrive by the spring. Construction is already behind schedule."

"Have at it, Miss Kaminsky. Have at it. We wouldn't want the Germans to find us ill-prepared, now, would we?"

Myra thought better than to respond to that dig. For the first time, she wondered if he were embittered by his own, admittedly unexciting, desk job, or by the toll age itself had taken on him.

When she returned to the outer office, Doris shook her head, a prelude to one of her unvarnished (even if unsolicited) opinions. "He is a piece of work, our major," she said loud enough for Myra's ears.

"I have noticed," Myra mouthed back.

"He may be smitten by you; he may be beholden to his wife. But he is married to the Army, no matter the cost."

During the last week of the year, Addison's final orders came through, leaving him no time to do anything except pack and tell his family goodbye. He left his mother teary-eyed, his father stoical, and his sister doing her best to be upbeat.

At the last minute, before his already battle-weary ship pulled out of San Diego en route to unspecified islands, he rang Myra at Camp Claiborne.

The conversation was short. Worse, it was stilted. He could make out the clicks of a telex machine in the background, male voices barking commands. Discombobulated, he asked how the boxing match went—Myra had not in the end sent him an invitation.

"A knockout, in the seventh or eighth round, I forget which, but mercifully no punch-ups among the recruits," she said.

Static came on the line. He needed to hurry to switch gears.

"When they let us write," he began, then faltered. The prospect of the vast ocean in front of him was daunting.

"Yes. When they let you write," she responded in the same key.

He could not find more words.

Hanging up, Addison looked out at the metallic surface of the water, seagulls cavorting overhead, huge ships slipping in and out of the bay. At 22:00 that evening the newly patched-up *Saratoga* set sail.

Part Three

1943-1945

*American soldiers celebrate the liberation
of Rome 1944*

Chapter Twenty-Five
EVERYONE IS SUSPECT

T he second year of all-out war against the Nazis and the Japanese began on a bleak note. Fierce battles raged, casualties mounted among the Allies, and sacrifices on the home front worsened.

"The most terrible thing for us all," Helen Carrollton confided more than once to Esther Endicott, "would be an unexpected knock at the front door. Men in uniform standing there with long faces."

After that utterance, the two sipped their sherry in silence. Helen thought of her son, hunkered down on some god-forsaken island overrun by poisonous snakes as well as by equally venomous Japanese soldiers. Esther pined for Addison, who, she imagined, was breaking his brain over conflicting attack plans proposed by competing admirals, his carrier all the while under threat of kamikaze attacks.

The women's respective husbands had not lent much reassurance. Having egged on Richard to "be a man," Harold Carrollton had grown dubious about his son's fitness for the Marines. He now drank more whiskey than was his wont. With Addison essentially "lost at sea," Edward Endicott had grown morose, withdrawing to his study to re-arrange his old war memorabilia.

Sundays were the only reasonably placid days for either set of parents. Claire rarely failed to appear, accompanying her parents to church and then either out to lunch or, weather permitting, a walk in Audubon Park. She weeded her mother's victory garden and played chess against her father. Occasionally, the three would gather round the piano and sing a few old favorites.

Meanwhile, city, state, and federal agencies—sometimes in concert, sometimes in competition—accelerated their attempts to root out suspicious characters, collaring any questionable male who might be a threat to the security of the country.

Eventually, separate reports filed to Naval Intelligence—the first, an internal dossier, (sent anonymously) and a second from the Coast Guard (signed by a Captain Perry)—wended their way to the local office of the FBI. They both regarded one Tom Stone, also known as Tomas Steinberg. Within a few months, the reports were shifted from the box marked *routine* to that marked *priority*.

Neither Tom nor Claire had any inkling how close he was to being fingered.

Instead, the two lived for their times together, nestled into each other, "like spoons," she had laughingly described it to him. When they weren't making love, they would dine by candlelight, or play a game of chess, or listen to music. Rarely did they go out, except to catch whatever movie was playing at a small theater nearby.

In February of 1943, however, they ventured downtown for a new film starring Humphrey Bogart and Ingrid Bergman. The newsreels that preceded the feature showed snippets from both war fronts.

In operations in Sicily, American troops had, after sizable losses, made inroads against the Germans and their Italian allies, finally taking Palermo, and pushing enemy troops back onto the mainland. All the American G.I.s caught on camera seemed to be smiling. In the Pacific, footage showed plane after plane taking off from a carrier en route to bomb some island whose name Tom and Claire instantly forgot.

"There's a map in our office, but it's hard to remember which sea is which, which islands are the Marianas, which, the Marshalls," Claire whispered.

"Seems like another war entirely. Not like Europe at all," Tom replied.

"Our supervisor said we're 'island hopping,' forgoing attacks on those that are fortified by the enemy and focusing on those where we might gain a foothold. And build an airstrip." Somebody in the row behind shushed them as the movie began.

Engrossing though it was, the three-way love story in *Casablanca* was not the only thing that grabbed Claire's attention: it was the so-called letters of transit. Tom's body had tensed; the plot device of the much-sought-after documents struck close to home for him.

Afterwards, as they were walking out, Claire heard her name called. It was Bernice, arm-in-arm with another woman.

"How nice to see you here, away from the office. What did you think of the movie?" she turned to ask.

"A beautiful story, wonderful actors, and a message for us all," Bernice ventured.

"And what would that message be, do you think?" Tom asked.

"Sorry, I should have introduced you two. Bernice works upstairs from me. This is Tom, Tom Stone."

"Oh, and this is my friend, Teresa Johnson. She works at the ship-yard now. As a riveter," she explained, apparently proud to herald the designation.

For an instant, Tom thought to mention he worked at the same place, but something stopped him. He had become reticent with strangers.

"Well, I'm no critic," Bernice replied, "but it's what the Bogart character says in the final scene. 'The problems of three little people...' when the world is coming apart. To me, that's the message."

"Absolutely," Claire said.

The four stood there awkwardly as other moviegoers made their way in or out of the theater.

Then Teresa piped up. "I liked the movie too, but I didn't under-stand about those letters they were all desperate to get hold of. You know, the ones hidden in the piano at Rick's place."

Bernice, who was familiar enough with Teresa's limitations (though not embarrassed by them), was also sharp-eyed. She looked closely at Tom while she responded. "To a lot of people, so-called letters of transit might not mean much, but to others of us, with family over there, exit papers would be lifesaving."

Hearing that deft explanation, Tom gave Bernice a nod of recog-nition. He held out his hand. "It was lovely to meet you both." The two women soon locked arms and took their leave.

Later, over beer and oysters at the Acme Bar, Claire asked Tom what he thought of the evening.

"If you're asking if I enjoyed the movie, it would have been hard not to." He paused to squeeze lemon juice on an oyster and down it with a couple of crackers. But if you're referring to letters of transit, they did remind me of people back home—and what might have become of them."

Claire nodded her head. "It's possible, isn't it, that some have found safe haven or hidden out with the help of strangers. Like Myra's aunt did for a spell."

Closing his eyes briefly, he let her words assuage some of his anxi-ety: about his parents who were God knows where, a cousin in Hamburg who sold books, a great aunt in Berlin, and poor Katrin. Pointless to burden anyone else since there was no longer anything to be done. At least not from afar.

More briskly, he said, "You do realize your friend is Jewish, right? She picked that up about me with no trouble."

Claire tilted her head. "It would not matter to me one way or the other. As you should be keenly aware."

"It's the name thing, Claire," he pressed on. She looked up puzzled. "I came up with Tom Stone that first night I met you and your parents. It's not that I don't feel Jewish. It's that I did not want *not* to be able to know you. If that makes any sense." Claire picked up her water glass and drank half of it to gain a beat. He kept on. "It was naïve to think such a thing does not matter in this country. It does, and to your parents too."

There was an edge to his words, which stymied Claire. She knew that Tom had assessed the situation accurately enough. That she ignored how her parents—perhaps even her brother—felt about her friendship with Jews, first with Myra and now with him, did not make their disapproval any less deplorable, or any more tolerable.

Arguably, though, she now had some personal agency—something she and Myra had both explicitly vowed to obtain. Among other things, she could indulge in a love affair without her parents' interference. Indeed, without their knowledge.

She looked across the table and smiled.

"Enough of all this," Tom said softly. "Not everything can be resolved in one night. Let's order lemon pie and then we'll go to my place if you like." She nodded in agreement.

Around 4 a.m. on a rainy night in May, Tom was jolted awake from a rare deep sleep. He could make out a sliver of light from the hallway of the boarding house.

"Mr. Stone. FBI. Open up, sir. Federal agents."

Hurriedly, he tossed the newspaper off the bed—he had fallen asleep reading about an uprising in the Warsaw ghetto—and fished around for his robe. "In a minute," he called out, pushing his feet into a pair of worn slippers.

A key turned in the lock.

When the door opened, two burly men in ill-fitted suits pushed past Mrs. Jennings. Practiced at intrusions, they immediately flicked on the overhead light. Tom blinked.

"You are confirmed on a list of possible enemy aliens, sir. We have orders to take you into custody. Your lodgings will be searched for anything deemed illegal in wartime."

"I knew it, I knew it," Mrs. Jennings wailed, presumably referring to her tenant.

The two agents ignored her. "Do you understand, sir?"

"I do, yes." He looked around the room, trying to pinpoint what might be incriminating.

"Don't make a commotion. I run a respectable house here," Mrs. Jennings mumbled, wringing her hands.

Tom turned to the two agents. "Might I see the information you have? I work up at the ship-building project, on the lake. I've done nothing wrong."

"Says different here," one of the agents replied unsympathetic. He had been through this process before. "Do you have a lawyer?"

"Of course not. But may I call someone who can speak for me— oh, what is the word in English—*vouch* for me?"

"Is it correct you are a German national? If so, please produce your papers."

The back-and-forth went on rapid-fire from there, it becoming obvious that Tom was "in hot water," as Mrs. Jennings put it. She appeared to be gloating.

Before the day was out, Tom was questioned at the FBI field office, which subsequently alerted the office of Naval Intelligence, domestic division. He was escorted over to that building, the very one Addison Endicott had worked in and where he had seen the name Tom Stone, also known as Tomas Steinberg, some months ago in an anonymous report. The next day, Tom was allowed to call his old boss, Philip Caxton, who came over within an hour, and his supervisor at the Higgins boat project, who would be available to speak the next day on site at Lake Pontchartrain.

Caxton did vouch for Tom's probity and diligence but could not shed light on his erstwhile employee's past or his present associates. "Kinda a loner," Caxton went on, other than that his former employee had a "lady friend," as he termed it, but did not know her name.

The supervisor up at the boat factory had nothing ill to say, albeit nothing illuminating. "We need good men, who know what they're doing. He's one of them," was the best he could muster.

Unfortunately, Tom's interrogation did not go well. He would not come up with any other character witnesses, and adamantly refused to comment about any alleged lady friend.

Yes, he had been to Cuba in 1939, but it was to meet a childhood friend, not a fellow spy who reportedly had been aboard the same ship as she, and who purportedly came ashore in Havana for the days Tom admitted to being there. As for his processing at Ellis Island in 1936, he had not a shred of evidence, admitting that any papers he had in his possession were misplaced during his years in Texas. All he could argue in his own defense was that he was Jewish and thereby unlikely to be a supporter of Nazi Germany.

His interrogators, phlegmatic and skeptical, took all this in but appeared not to appreciate his logic or his sarcasm. They gave him cigarettes and a root beer and kept him for another night.

Once his lodgings were searched, things went from bad to worse. The police turned the place upside down, finding not only his radio but also his bone-handled six-shooter, his copy of *Mein Kampf,* and his letters from home—written on embossed military letterhead— and sent to him from a maritime officer named Hans Durst. A U-boat captain, no less, if they translated rightly.

"Yes, I know Commander Durst. Hans was a childhood friend. We were in contact because I wanted whatever information he had regarding my own parents."

As bad as things appeared, Tom resisted involving Claire in his troubles, not admitting to their friendship, despite sharp questioning from a Navy officer brought in for the purpose. "So, am I to take it that you are, you know, one of those?" the officer asked, making a fey gesture in hopes of getting a rise.

"Far from it, sir," Tom replied, calculating that being pegged as a homosexual spy would make things even more dire. "What I do know of ladies, I have, if you must know, learned from the ones in

Storyville." As little as he wished to bring this element to the fore, his interviewers snickered and moved on.

After three days of little food and less sleep, Tom was accompanied back to his ransacked lodgings, where he was allowed to change clothes and pack a single suitcase. His minder, a junior lieutenant in the Navy who had volunteered himself, waited outside the door, whistling.

Tom dressed hurriedly and then felt under a loose floorboard. He had stashed all the cash he had saved over six years in a leather pouch. Perhaps it wasn't so bad that the Hibernia had turned him away. With no time to count the bills, he stuffed the pouch in his boot and slipped his foot in. There was little else left in the room that he wanted. They had smashed his cowboy hat, broken his records, scattered his draughtsman's tools. At the last second, he spotted the gold locket with his parents' pictures lodged against the table leg of his desk. He slipped it inside his shirt pocket.

"A chapter is closing," he whispered to himself. "Another will begin."

As soon as Myra got to work on a bright spring morning that same week in May, Corporal Evans called out from across the room. Few things came out of this officer's mouth that weren't either threatening or insinuating. She and Doris both missed his predecessor, but there was nothing to be done about that.

"You're wanted over at the detention center, Bldg. H, wherever that is. They've brought in a suspect who is Italian, or German. I forget which. They said you might could translate."

Doris looked up from her own desk. "Nothing else urgent this morning, Myra. Go on over. And the unfortunate creature in custody is German, not Italian."

Myra glanced inside Major Benson's office. He had taken to arriving later than usual in the morning, if at all, now that his wife had come to town. Several more framed photos now graced his desk.

She left her briefcase on her own desk, picked up a notepad and headed across the camp by foot.

These were not sessions she relished. Most of the detainees processed at the camp did not appear to pose any immediate threat to the country. In many cases she had observed, they were simply dyed-in-the-wool conservatives who missed their homeland and still thought of themselves as staunchly German. In only a few instances, they were overtly sympathetic to the *führer*, and had either distributed leaflets or attended clandestine meetings where money was raised for the Nazi cause.

Incarcerating such folks was an overreach in Myra's view, but as Doris had remarked, no one in uniform cares what civilians think. "In war, governments are as liable to behave badly as they are to behave well," she had commented more than once.

Hard to argue with that, Myra thought. She had seen the news-reels: mostly, those rounded up were Japanese Americans, entire families now living behind barbed wire, mostly in California. She had assumed that was the end of it.

But sometime in late 1942, Camp Claiborne was designated to handle suspect Italians and Germans from the region, most of whom ended up dispersed to one detention center or another: Italians to facilities in the Midwest; Germans to a camp in Texas, though word of late was that it was now over-crowded. Another center had recently been commandeered from the Army in the upper Midwest. Somewhere very cold, if she remembered rightly.

In war, vigilance can spill over into vengeance, Myra had come to think.

She quickened her pace past the officers' club. From the tennis courts behind it, she could hear the thwop, thwop of balls against rackets. An odor of detergent from the nearby laundromat wafted past her.

An MP greeted her at the entrance to the metal roofed Bldg. H.

"I'm wanted for an interrogation. A Sergeant Connors called

239

over to Major Benson's office. I'm fluent in German, if that is what's needed."

"Yes, ma'am." He glanced at her pass. "The suspect speaks English but it's better to get things down as precise as possible." He escorted her inside.

Peering through one-way glass into interrogation room two, Myra was instantly bowled over. Tom Stone, his face drawn, shoulders hunched, was seated across from an officer scribbling in a notebook. A tape recorder sat on the table. An ashtray held a number of butts.

Her heart began to pound. There must be some mistake, her first thought. Her second was to be more circumspect. Straightening her back, she knocked on the door. A sullen-looking officer opened it.

"Yes?"

"I'm Myra Kaminsky, civilian liaison with Major Benson's office. I speak fluent German."

"Never hurts," he replied, unimpressed. "Sergeant Connors." He flicked his hand to beckon her in. Tom looked up, his eyes wide as saucers, but quickly checked his own surprise.

"We've established worrying irregularities with this Mr., Mr. Steinberg," the sergeant summarized, glancing down at his notebook. He switched the tape recorder back on. "Joining us is a Miss K somebody or other, assigned to Major Benson's office. Fluent in German."

"Myra Kaminsky. Civilian liaison," she enunciated distinctly.

"Right. Miss Kaminsky has joined us as we finalize our interview." Connors swiveled the notebook so that she could read the notes he had taken.

"As you can see, these are serious findings, which under the Enemy Alien Act call for indeterminate interment."

"But what has he actually done, this young man?"

"It's a long list. To begin with, suspicious loitering, having been trailed for months. Mysterious blueprints worked on in the dead of night. An unexplained trip to Havana, including proximity to known spies. In addition, a search of Mr. Stone's lodgings turned up an unregistered firearm, an illegal radio, and a copy of Hitler's manifesto."

Myra looked flabbergasted and held her tongue.

"Which brings me to..." The officer turned the page of his notebook. "Yes. Some compromising letters from a German military officer. It's these we'd like you to take a look at."

With that, Sergeant Connors opened a separate folder marked *Evidence* and passed several letters written in German to her.

She looked over at Tom. He had closed his eyes and was shaking his head sideways. Utterly dejected.

"As you can see, he's also uncooperative, refusing to reveal an accomplice. A so-called lady friend."

Myra glanced at the envelopes; the gold embossed insignia of the German Navy was hard to ignore. She scrunched her brow but said nothing.

In reaction, Tom pulled himself together and sat up straighter in the metal chair. "I've told the sergeant that these letters are from a childhood friend, Hans Durst, who is in the German military."

"Why on earth, Tom, would you be so careless?" she lashed out in German before catching herself. Her tone suggested mixed emotions, both criticism of his recklessness and sympathy for his plight.

The sergeant looked confused. "What did you ask him?"

"It's possible there are harmless explanations for most of this," she said.

Another knock came to the door. Connors rose, hit the stop button on the tape recorder, and left the room.

Myra and Tom both spoke at once. "You go ahead," she whispered. "*Schnell!*"

"You're right. I have been negligent. I have no papers to prove anything, not even my real name." He began to wring his hands. "But remember, whatever they want to do with me, Claire must not be drawn into this."

"Does she know anything? Is she involved?"

"Nothing like that. She's aware of my childhood friends, but that's it. If her name surfaced, she'd forfeit her clearance and probably her job. Not to mention what her parents would think or do."

Tom looked more devastated than she had ever seen a man. She had no idea what to say. He continued to plead. "Please help me protect her, Myra. She mustn't find out or try to intervene."

"I need time to think this through."

"Of course. Again, whether I end up in prison or deported, I do not want to ruin Claire's life."

She looked at Tom's distraught face. His eyes were about to brim over. She reached over to squeeze his hand. "If only I were a lawyer."

The voices in the hallway died down. Looking harried, Sergeant Connors stuck his head back in. A younger officer stood at his shoulder. "There's been an incident in another part of the camp, Miss—I keep forgetting."

"Kaminsky," she replied.

"Appreciate your help. If you'd type up translations of those three letters, they will go into the dossier. That way we can wrap up within the day tomorrow."

"No problem."

"Meanwhile, the corporal here will figure out what to do." The unnamed subordinate looked flummoxed at the prospect.

Myra took a deep breath. "Let me understand, Sergeant. Mr. Steinberg has not been charged with a crime. He has been employed, reliably and without incident, at the New Orleans shipyards, specifically on those amphibious landing vessels. I am prepared to take responsibility for him until a decision is reached. Meaning, he might, if agreeable, spend the rest of the day and night at my parents' home in Alexandria."

The sergeant looked dubious. Undeterred, she added, "As is legally the case, he has not been arrested. And, as you will have further observed, he and I are both Jewish. He'd like to be with his own kind until he knows what the government plans to do."

Myra had rarely spoken with such conviction, at least not to those who were imbued with authority over her. She trained her eyes on the officer's face. He glanced at the corporal, who gestured to indicate the issue was beyond his meager pay grade.

"Unorthodox, but if you're willing to shoulder the responsibility, have at it. He needs to be back here by 11 sharp tomorrow for a final determination." He turned toward Tom. "Understood?"

"Yes, sir."

"Miss Kaminsky, don't screw up."

Within minutes, the corporal accompanied Myra and Tom out of the building.

Once out of earshot of the junior officer, she said, "Act normal. We're going to stop briefly in my office and then take a camp car home. You are okay with this, right?"

"What do you think?"

In the car back to Alexandria, Tom rolled down the window to feel the rush of fresh air.

He spoke first. "I can't thank you enough, Myra. You were amazing. I never thought that officer would let me out of his sight. Like I was a common criminal."

"I surprised myself, but the spiel seemed to work. By the way, I told my parents you happened to be up this way. You can fill them in as you see fit. They'll be delighted to see you again. Plus, my mother is a great cook." She glanced over as he wiped away a tear. "You do look famished."

"These last few days are a blur. Beginning with the revelation of some anonymous naval intelligence report about me. Strange, right?"

Indeed, she thought, not knowing what to make of that. She let it go.

"It might do us both good to have a cigarette," she soon suggested. "A pack's in my bag, if you want to root around."

He did, lighting a Camel first for her and then for himself. He had not felt this relaxed for days. In fact, he wasn't sure what day it was. In a few minutes, he returned to the issue closest to his heart.

"Claire and I were planning to go out on Friday evening to a concert in a church off Napoleon Avenue. Where we know no one. It's ridiculous having to keep things secretive, but that's how it is."

Myra nodded, recalling what her clandestine love affair with Dr. Calhoun had been like. It seemed a lifetime ago, but it also seemed that the professor's feelings for her could not hold a candle to what Tom's were for Claire. She was in awe.

"So, Tom, I'd say we need to stall until you're in the clear, or whatever. Hopefully tomorrow."

"Which is what day? I've lost track since they picked me up."

"Tomorrow is Friday. Since Claire is expecting you to meet her, we're going to improvise or obfuscate or some other fancy verb which means *to lie*. Not that I like that." She paused, then shifted tone. "Don't you think she deserves to—"

"To what? Have her life turned upside down because of me? No, whatever we have to do to shield her, we do. And you are not to shoulder any blame for my—whatever it is, negligence, obliviousness, hubris." He waved his cigarette in the air to suggest all three failings. "It's all on me." Here he mumbled some Teutonic expletive Myra did not recognize.

"Don't beat yourself up. There's a war going on. Everyone is rattled. Our government overreacts. But the war will end. At some point it will end."

"Not a day too soon," Tom concurred, and finished his cigarette in silence.

When they entered the Kaminsky home, Myra could smell borscht. Her parents greeted Tom in a rushed mix of German and English. Myra rolled her eyes when she caught his, but he was smiling. There was warmth in her family home, and this luckless young man was enveloped by it.

Over the borscht and an equally hearty red wine, they talked about the old country—Poland, Germany, and those summer jaunts to the Baltic beaches, which Tom too had taken with his family. It did seem a lifetime ago.

Konrad could not help but bring up what had recently transpired in Warsaw. "They had to revolt. How could our people not stand up to this latest atrocity of Hitler? Cost what it may." His face reddened as he spoke.

Ilona plopped a second *pierogi* onto her husband's plate to calm him down. She then turned to address their guest.

"Tell us, Tom, what, if anything, you know of your own family. Have you heard from them?"

It was too late for Myra to ward them off the subject.

Tom took another sip of wine and unburdened himself, mostly in German. "Sad to say, I know little. Letters from my parents ceased shortly before I came to New Orleans. In their wake, I received only sporadic bits and pieces, from an aunt, and a cousin. Rumors, wishful thinking, conjectures, none of them reassuring. In his last letter, my friend Hans mentioned a camp called *Neuengamme*. It used to be a brick-making factory in the area. Perhaps they repurposed it."

A hush fell over the table.

"The problem now is that our own government, and the military, are suspicious of people who are Japanese or Italian or German, which means a lot of folks are getting swept up on the slightest of pretexts," Myra said to break the spell. "That's why Tom ended up at Claiborne, and why we'll go back tomorrow morning to straighten it all out." She did her best to sound encouraging.

"We would have hoped to have you for the entire weekend, Tom, but you must do what is necessary," Ilona said. She soon excused herself to the kitchen. When she returned, she was holding a silver platter aloft. "When Myra phoned, I baked a cake with fresh Louisiana strawberries. Something sweet will do you good."

"I have not eaten so well in a long time, Mrs. Kaminsky. I will not soon forget your hospitality. Whatever happens."

After dinner, he took a long shower while Myra fixed up the guest room.

"Get some sleep, Tom. Tomorrow could be trying," she said, awkwardly patting his arm. As soon as he turned out the light in his room, Myra set about to translate the letters from Hans. She grew more concerned with each one, especially the last. There was no way to downplay the closing sentence: Tom had been corresponding with a U-Boat commander patrolling the waters of the Gulf of Mexico.

Out of earshot of Tom, Myra gave parting instructions to her parents. "If Claire rings, do not mention Tom or that he was here last night. If she asks, say I've been working non-stop at Camp Claiborne but that I'll call her during the weekend."

Her mother looked perturbed but nodded her acquiescence.

The two young people drove in silence most of the way, Tom again rolling down the window to enjoy the spring air. A few miles from the camp, he spoke up.

"I slipped something into the top drawer of the dresser this morning," he said. Myra glanced over at him curiously. He was looking straight ahead, his jaw set. "If all goes well today, you can return the pouch to me. If not, the packet is for you and Claire to share. You are best friends. You two will figure it out."

Predictably, things did not work out well. By the end of the day, the wheels of military machinery cranked into high gear, and Tomas Steinberg, alias Tom Stone, was processed and ordered to be confined at a facility for enemy aliens in North Dakota.

"For the duration," the sentence read.

Despite Myra's vocal protestations.

"Piece of work," one of the MPs spat when she objected to Tom's being handcuffed for his transfer. "Jewish whore," his colleague rejoined.

She did not have the energy to call them out for their actions. She returned home that evening more dejected than she had been since the race riot on Lee Street. Worse, she had no idea how she would convey to Claire the bad news about her lover.

Chapter Twenty-Six
A WORD TO THE WISE

Once she did find out what happened, Claire cried off and on for a week, berated Myra on the phone, refused to eat, and did not go to work. It was Bennie who finally coaxed her into eating some gumbo one of his children had cooked up. "Specially for you, Miss Claire." His soothing voice calming her down enough to listen to reason.

"I know'd he done nothing wrong, but the cops is the cops, and they done come a'lookin, up at the shipyard. I 'spect Mr. Tom did not want you to get in no trouble, Miss Claire. So, I played even dumber than I am," Bennie said.

The following weekend, Myra drove down to New Orleans, rang the guest house doorbell, and stiffened her resolve. When Claire opened it, she thrust a letter at her Tom had scribbled that night at the Kaminsky home.

"I can fill in the blanks after you read it," she said, averting her gaze from Claire's swollen eyes.

Claire took the letter and gave Myra a perfunctory hug, at the same time apologizing for calling her a false friend and thanking her for doing whatever she could to defend Tom.

While Myra unpacked the sandwiches and sweets her mother had put together for them, Claire tore open the envelope. It contained only a *C* to represent her name.

Dearest C,

The worst possible thing would be for you to be caught up in this unfortunate circumstance. If and when I can be in touch without conse-quences for you, I shall do so. Please know that wherever I am, you are in my thoughts. Go about your life and may it unfold in joy and happi-ness as mine has in your company. Do not blame Myra for any of this. She did her best to plead my case, but alas, the war has caught up with me. I took too much for granted and must pay the price. One final thing. I entrusted a pouch to Myra. You and she will figure out ways to use it. The money would be of little use to me in the camp. In fact, it would likely be confiscated. The war cannot end soon enough.

Yours, Tom

Refolding the single sheet of notepaper, Claire slipped it back in the envelope. Although distressed, she no longer had the energy to cry.

Within a few minutes, Myra brought a tray of sandwiches and fresh strawberries over to the coffee table as well as two glasses and a wine bottle.

Claire forced a wan smile.

"Like old times. At your place, except everything has changed," she murmured.

"First things first. You must eat something. Then we can talk all this through."

"As commanded," Claire said. She picked up a ham and cheese sandwich along with a vinegary pickle. The food revived her.

"Mothers are a mainstay in crises," she announced. Myra nodded. "Except when they don't know there's a crisis. If I could have confided in mine, I would have."

"Don't berate yourself, Claire. They're a different generation, with different values. Remember the thing with Daniel? I could never have told my parents about that. About some things, we have to rely on each other."

"I know. I never should have doubted your intentions." After a pause, Claire returned to the questions Tom's letter raised. "He mentions a pouch. Do you know what he's talking about?"

Myra crossed the room to retrieve her bag. She plopped it down on the couch and pulled out the pouch. Claire unsnapped it and reached in, pulling out a stack of bills. She shuffled through them, estimating upwards of five to six thousand dollars, largely in hundreds. Separately, with a silver clip around them were a couple of hundred Deutsch marks.

"A sizable sum. Why did he not put it in the bank?" Claire wondered aloud.

"Because he couldn't," Myra replied. "Seems he had no official identification, and never bothered to impose upon anyone to vouch for him."

"But I would—"

"It would have had to be a man, to open a bank account," she rejoined. "Like for most everything else," she added drily.

Claire shook her head in resigned agreement. "It may have to be your father who opens an account in his name. Mine..."

"The least we can do," Myra said.

For a few minutes, they ate strawberries and sipped wine. Color came back into Claire's cheeks.

"Tell me, Myra, why on earth are they sending him to North Dakota?"

"All I know is that, if it's like the situation for the Japanese in California, it's not exactly a prison and not exactly a summer camp. Something in-between, not awful but not idyllic either. Though Tom should not be there in any case."

"But you're saying that that ship has sailed?"

"For the time being."

Newly distressed, Claire rose and opened the window to let in the fresh air. The scent of jasmine drifted into the room. She put a record on the turntable and returned to sit next to her friend. A plaintive flute started up; strings soon joined in.

"I am thinking that you would make an excellent lawyer, Myra, and that I wish you already were one!" Her friend raised her glass in tacit agreement. "In lieu of that," she continued, "I'm glad Tom's final evening could be spent in your family's company. If only mine were different, we wouldn't have gone about things the way we did."

Myra nodded, thinking it best not to comment about anyone else's family foibles, or failures, especially not her best friend's. The comment did, however, make her wonder whether Addison's attitudes more closely mirrored his parents' or his sister's. She started to ask what they had heard from him, but Claire broke in.

"The other thing I can't fathom is how the FBI got wind that Tom's behavior was questionable. Did this come out at the interrogation?"

"From random remarks I heard, two different sources implicated him. One document related to an incident down in Cajun country." Claire nodded, recalling that Tom had mentioned that escapade. "The other," Myra continued, "came from Naval Intelligence, whatever that implies."

Claire's face clouded over. "But how could that be?" she puzzled, not expecting a response.

Myra gave her none. Rather, she got up to turn the volume up on the record player. "Let's listen to Glück, then take a brisk walk." Claire managed a faint assent. "And tomorrow, you should go to church with your parents, while I go to synagogue and check on my aunt. Remember, I'm counting on you to buck up and get back to work on Monday morning. Okay?"

Claire smiled and did as her friend requested.

To divert attention from her still puffy face, Claire donned an elegant summer suit, a powder-blue affair with a ruffle at the hemline, and her only high heels that were not scuffed. She dabbed on some make-up and donned sunglasses on the streetcar. On the office elevator she ran into Bernice.

"Haven't glimpsed you in a while. Everything copacetic?"

Claire hesitated. The three male employees in the car glanced their way. "I was under the weather, but I'm better now."

Bernice eyed her more critically. "You look thinner. Wouldn't mind shedding a few pounds myself." Claire managed a tight smile. "Anyhow, things are cheerier these days. The team will fill you in."

The doors opened on the fifth floor. She alone stepped off.

The first thing she saw in the office was a vase of red roses on her desk. Unnerved, she walked over, deposited her briefcase on the floor and took a seat. Several documents, with attached notes, stood in a small pile in front of her. Things to take care of. She inhaled deeply and willed herself to relax.

"Welcome back," one of the stenographers called out. Another said, "You'll be thrilled to know we have a new coffee grinder in the kitchenette. Courtesy of Commander Lassiter upstairs." Claire nodded her approval.

She was deep into translating an intercept from a vessel off the coast of South America when a voice jarred her.

"Thought you'd be back today. Flowers always become a pretty lady," Junior Lieutenant Forster chirped, having materialized at her elbow. He had a habit of flitting about whenever people were deep in concentration, and alighting way too often near Claire's perch. A few eyes cut their way.

She stifled her irritation. Barely. "They are lovely, the flowers. They brighten the entire room."

"In any event," he went on, ignoring her tone, "we're glad to have you back. Lunch on me as soon as you catch up." He tapped her desk twice with his hand, apparently for emphasis. She had forgotten how irksome his presumption was. The stenographer who sat in Claire's line of sight rolled her eyes at the scene.

After a restorative cup of newly ground coffee around 11 a.m., Claire was summoned to her supervisor's office. Lieutenant Nelson beckoned her to take a seat. She flipped open her notebook, ready to take notes.

"Nothing urgent, Miss Endicott. First, I trust you're recovered." She nodded affirmatively. "As you will have noticed, things have quieted down in the Gulf, though they've picked up elsewhere. Several Allied oil tankers have been torpedoed off Brazil." She nodded again. "We're instructed to monitor enemy attacks up and down that continent's east coast. New codes to puzzle over," he added.

"Yes, sir," she said. "I'll get with the team on this soonest."

At that moment, one of the stenographers appeared at the door. He waved her away and returned his attention to the young woman in front of him.

"Do I remember rightly you have a brother in Intelligence, out on a flattop?"

"The *Saratoga*," she replied.

Two lights on the lieutenant's phone panel began to blink red, which meant calls had come in. He pressed one of them. "Yes, Bernice." He puckered his lips. "Of course. Be up there in five." He turned back to Claire. "As I've stressed to all our civilian employees, especially our contingent of females, discretion is of upmost importance in our line of work."

Claire's heart dropped like a stone.

"A young man with ties to Nazis was identified only weeks ago, and it appears he had some connection with Intelligence personnel here." Lieutenant Nelson's steel-gray eyes fixed on hers. She dropped her gaze but tried not to flinch. To steady herself, she concentrated on the hum of a motor powering the aquarium against the far wall. Colorful fish were darting among coral reefs.

Lieutenant Nelson glanced at his watch. "Suffice to say, Miss Endicott, you are a very attractive young woman in a very crucial role. A lot of lives are at stake."

"Yes, sir," she replied. "I am aware of the implications."

He looked away, his head bobbing from side to side as though weighing options.

"Anyway, better news coming out of the Pacific. Your parents must be proud of your brother—and of you."

Overwrought, Claire held back tears, blinking several times in rapid succession.

Fortunately, the lieutenant began gathering dossiers and stuffing them in his briefcase. "You are dismissed, Miss Endicott. Don't overdo it your first day back."

Several days later, Bernice enticed Claire to take a break for lunch at a diner in the warehouse district. A few prosperous looking lawyers with leather briefcases and a look of entitlement occupied the two tables at the windows. Tough-looking men in overalls and a few women not that dissimilar in attire or demeanor took up the rest. A briny smell suffused the air despite the efforts of ceiling fans.

The two young women ordered shrimp salads and iced tea.

"My treat," Bernice said. "But that means a dessert as well. You look like you need to bulk up."

"Thank you. It is good to get out of there sometimes."

While they waited for their order, Bernice pulled out a pack of Camels, offered Claire one (she declined) and lit up. "Since we met at Newcomb, you may not have realized, but I was born around here. It was rough and tumble then, and now with the war, noisy again day and night."

Not knowing what to say, Claire nodded. She had never given much thought to Bernice's background, other than the fact she was Jewish. But here she was, another young woman trying to make it in a man's world—a military one at that—and the only other one besides Myra with whom she had developed any rapport. "Do you still have family around here?"

Bernice drew deeply on her cigarette. "My father died at Verdun in '17, my mother during the Spanish flu. I was raised by an aunt not far away, over in Metairie."

"I'm sorry. I did not know."

Bernice went on. "Not much to do out there, but my aunt, with her 'old country' values, was bent on my getting ahead. Hence, I studied. *Et voilà*: full scholarship to Sophie Newcomb. I was the token Jewess in '37, just as Myra was in '39. An informal quota, but all the same."

At that point, a harried waiter plopped two salads down and poured tea into two tall glasses with ice. "No lemons today. First, it was the rinds they needed. Now it's everything. Sorry ladies."

"*Nada problema*," Bernice said drily. They both spooned a teaspoon of sugar into their glasses.

Bernice ate with relish, breaking off a piece of French bread to accompany her salad; Claire picked at hers but kept at it to be polite.

"I was asking myself," Bernice tossed out, "about your young man. The one we met at the movie theater that night." Claire stiffened. She picked up her glass and drank most of the tea. "My friend Teresa thought he must be on shore leave. He seemed jumpy."

In her head, Claire calculated the odds. How likely could it be that a second person at the office was suspicious of her love interest and whether she had been compromised because of it. She skewered another shrimp and dipped it in a ramekin of tartar sauce. "I don't know about any nervousness," she replied, vaguely dismissive of the subject. "He likely had a long day."

Bernice's brow twitched. She lit another cigarette.

The waiter soon returned, picked up the salad plates and the basket of half-eaten bread. "We do, however, have a few desserts today. Strawberry shortcake, peach cobbler, chocolate pie."

Claire shook her head in the negative.

"How about coffee?"

She nodded.

"That will be two cups, right?" the waiter asked.

"Yes, and the bill," Bernice said.

When the coffee arrived, Claire sipped hers black, figuring she might need the extra jolt of caffeine to get through the afternoon. Bernice spooned her teaspoon of sugar in hers and stirred it in slowly. Finally, she said, "I was thinking..." Claire looked up as nonchalantly as she could. "Whether your young man—Tom, right? Stone, unless I err—is still here or not. You cannot be lacking in admirers."

At this unwanted comment, Claire made a face to suggest such an idea was boring to her and irrelevant to the conversation at hand. Bernice ignored both conjectures. "You need look no further than the office, from what I observed. A dozen roses awaiting on your first day back."

"Lovely of the fifth floor to do that," Claire parried with a straight face.

"Another time, while I was waiting for Teresa out front—she's invariably late, all that riveting—there he was smoking, *lurking* is more like it, on the far side of the street." Claire looked flummoxed. "Junior Lieutenant Forster, I mean." Claire flexed her lips to mean *so what*. "Shortly, you came out of the building, wearing your flats, oblivious. You headed toward the uptown streetcar stop. Within a minute, Forster ditched his still burning cigarette, took a look around, and set off in the same direction."

While Bernice rummaged in her pocketbook to pay the bill, Claire scrolled through her mind. Could it be that this officer was so besotted that he had routinely followed her? Or worse, that he had finagled to have her lover removed from contention as a rival? She shook her head in an attempt to shake off such suspicions. Unsuccessfully.

Before they rose to pay the cashier and leave, Claire's and Bernice's eyes met. It was a meeting of the minds.

"If and when, Bernice, there is an opening upstairs, on the Commander's staff, I would very much like to be considered."

Leaving cash and the receipt under the sugar bowl, Bernice gave Claire a knowing smile. And said, "It is true that the view from the sixth floor is quite clarifying. I think you would thrive there."

Chapter Twenty-Seven

LETTERS FROM AFAR

"You are a very opinionated young lady, Miss Kaminsky."

Myra swiveled to see Major Benson several feet behind her, waiting in line for cake and ice cream in the commissary. Officers and guests had gathered to celebrate Commander Holiday's birthday, and his imminent departure for Washington, where a promotion awaited him. Several of the men in line swiveled to hear the exchange with the young woman.

"You are correct, major, at least when I have strong feelings about something."

"Detainees, for example? We mustn't be naïve about enemy aliens. Especially in a time of war."

She thought about letting the comment fizzle out, and inquiring after his wife, but the injustice of Tom's treatment grated on her.

"If you're referring to the German who was processed last week, then yes. I was convinced he was careless in his behavior but hardly a criminal."

"You took a lot upon yourself, taking him home, and no one there to stop you. Most irregular."

"Mr. Stone held up his end—that must count for something—and is now merrily on his way to the frozen tundra of the Dakotas," she retorted, the sarcasm not lost on anyone in the vicinity. Several in line exchanged bemused glances. The major was not one of them.

"That incident aside, we have a contingent of POWs headed our way. You have been requested to assist with their processing. I trust you will handle that undertaking by the book."

Myra nodded in compliance. With her plate in hand, she made her way to a table with the mayor of Alexandria and several other local dignitaries. Doris Mackie sat at a nearby table with other WACs, as they were now being called. Major Benson took his place on the dais along with other high-ranking officers.

Looking around the room, Myra noticed only one black soldier, his stripes indicating he was a sergeant. He stood at attention in the back, sipping iced tea, no plate in hand. There had been grumbling among the Negro soldiers that the newly constructed facilities for the POWs were more elaborate and comfortable than their own. She wondered if Holiday's replacement would run things differently.

Later that afternoon, she asked Doris. "What do you think? Will things improve under the new commander?"

"I would not count on it, Myra. The Army accommodates. If anything changes, it'll come first from Roosevelt and filter down. Essentially, if you rock the boat in the military, you tend to get thrown overboard."

"So I've noticed."

"It's a Friday. It's the summer. Go home and be with your family."

Which Myra did, wishing that she had thought enough to invite Doris to their home for a meal. Others of their small circle, including the Bauer sisters, did show up that very evening, Ilona Kaminsky's *pierogis* hard to turn down.

At the dinner table, no one brought up details of the Warsaw Uprising, which the papers had moved on from, leaving the estimated death toll of Jews at the hands of German stormtroopers at roughly 10,000, the entire barbed wire enclave bulldozed. Myra had picked up at the camp that the remainder of residents trapped inside that ghetto were herded to a camp called Treblinka. Everyone at the dinner table knew that name and what it meant. No one mentioned it.

Instead, Flora Bauer brought out a rolled-up scroll and announced it was V-mail from Frederick.

"Where is he, how is he?" everyone asked at once.

"You know how the Army is. All letters are censored. We believe he is in Italy."

"Read us what you can, Flora. We are all ears," Konrad ordered.

A florid person made more ebullient by the wine and a captive audience, Frederick's mother provided excerpts.

By the time you receive this you will know the name of Bizerte, the last port in North Africa to fall to us. Behind us blood and sand and the bodies of too many of our fellow soldiers. Our captain says 250,000 enemy combatants have been taken prisoner.

"Unfortunately, the rest of that paragraph is blacked out. Does anyone know where Bizerte is?"

Since no one spoke up, Myra did. "On the coast of Tunisia."

"Is there more?" Myrtle Murkowski asked.

Flora obliged.

We crossed a stretch of the Mediterranean by moonlight, landing in Sicily in the early morning hours. We sat crouched in the vessel for hours, the water lapping at the keel. I could sense my comrades' heart beats as they could mine. It seemed so intimate and yet we knew that

3000 other boats just like ours were making the same voyage at the same moment. Can you imagine a thing being eerie and invigorating at the same time? So it felt. Soon, I could feel my stiff legs gather strength as we touched terra firma.

Overhead, planes buzzed, giving us cover. We hunkered down, drank water, and ate from our rations. A far cry from pierogis or gumbo, but so be it. Before us is the entire island, at first glance, lush and fertile, olive trees, rolling hills, even, for the moment, the chirping of magpies. Beyond this vast expanse the entire length and breathe of Mussolini's Italy awaits. 'Avanti' is their word for onwards.

There was silence at the table as everyone took in this graphic account. Myra was disconcerted. Little more than a year ago, her childhood friend was ordering men's button-down shirts and ladies' corsets; now he is exchanging enemy fire with Panzer troops in the rugged terrain of a Mediterranean island.

"Where would you reckon that they are now, Flora? Does he go on?"

"A lot is blacked out, but yes, they have taken Palermo. It has been in the papers but not like he puts it."

Never thought I could walk so far in my wildest dreams. The days were sweltering, then rain fell until our boots squeaked and we were drenched to the bone. But we marched on, a hundred miles in four days, skirmishes along the way bogging us down. Fortunately, tanks both proceeded and followed us. And then, rounding a bend, we were at the outskirts of Palermo. Domes glistened in the sunshine. Even brighter and more welcome were the dark eyes of Sicilian girls waving white handkerchiefs from stone balconies. In the evening accordions and dancers in the streets took over.

We ate, drank the reddest of wine, laughed to be alive. I thought of

Coleridge, that poem we all loved—Myra will remember it. Who would want to awake from that dream?
Though we will. General Patton will see to that!

Flora desisted. "The rest is censored except for the end. He sends regards to all of you."

Everyone relished this account, its vividness greater than what they were accustomed to from the newspapers or from newsreels. To Myra's mind, Frederick did have a flair back in high school, which for reasons she never bothered to plumb, he squelched, or was obliged to squelch. By his now deceased father, he having been the embodiment of dry goods.

Abe Wallenstein proposed a toast. "To our Frederick," he proclaimed. "To victory," Myra's father seconded.

Back in New Orleans, letters arrived from the Pacific theater as well, though given the distances and the logistics, with longer delay. They were heavily redacted. Still, some did get through, including a few from Richard, who found himself, as his mother put it, afloat somewhere in that boundless ocean.

Helen Carrollton wasn't exaggerating. At the fanciest bookstore in the Garden District, she bought the largest and most colorful of maps illustrating that side of the world, from the Aleutian Islands off Alaska to the Solomon Islands north of Australia and all the chains dotting the waterscape up to and including the empire of Japan.

One Sunday after church, she told her husband to rush home and bring Richard's latest letter over to the Endicotts. As he often did, Harold looked less than enthused by his wife's request. Not wishing to make a scene in front of the Presbyterian congregants, he obliged, grumbling to himself as he skirted the minister without speaking. Helen meanwhile rode with their friends alongside Claire in the back seat.

"I have not seen you to ask, Claire, but you may well have received your own correspondence. If you care to share any of what Richard might have said, that would be welcome."

Coming to her daughter's rescue, Esther Endicott jumped in. "V-mail is erratic at best in the Pacific. Not to mention that time to write must be very limited."

"Even from Addison, news is scant. He did finagle a trunk call last month, but we don't know from where. He sounded good, the little we could hear," Edward Endicott added.

"No doubt your own job is intense, my dear," Helen continued. "We noticed that item in the *Picayune* about our code breakers who located that awful Yamamoto. Up in a bomber, he was. Our pilots shot him down." Claire nodded her head. "You've been so scarce all these months that we assumed you were doing all the decoding."

Reminding herself that Helen Carrollton had a gift for needling, Claire smiled politely. "The Navy relies on an army, pardon the pun, to do this kind of work. I play a very small part."

"I see," Helen lobbed back, as though this was a pathetic admission that the younger woman's job was little more than a trivial pursuit.

So cutting her comments, Claire thought, and so irritating to be on the edge of her knife. She longed to pull out a cigarette and blow a smoke ring in the older woman's face.

But the car had pulled up to the front curb, Claire's father bringing it to a jerking halt. Perhaps he was as put off by Helen as she was.

Sunday dinner restored everyone to a better mood.

Esther had baked a sea bass, the largest she could find in the market, and smothered it with cherry tomatoes. Yellow squash and green beans as well as lettuce, peppers and cucumbers from the garden filled out their plates. The first Georgia peaches of the season were served for dessert.

Afterwards, Claire and her mother wiped down the table so that Edward could spread the map. Claire found it less factually accurate and more fanciful—sketches of dolphins frolicking off the coast of the Philippines—but did not say so. It might be best for the assembled not to know where any given U.S. soldier might be. The Japanese fighters gave no quarter and were dug-in literally and figuratively.

After a spell, Helen put down her coffee cup and retrieved the letter from her pocketbook.

"A couple of excerpts will do, Helen. We don't want to bore our friends," Harold stated. It was tantamount to an order.

"Well." She harrumphed. "It is from your only son, so I would think—" She cleared her throat. "Besides, most of it is blacked out."

Dear Papa and Mama,

I shall trust the heavens that you receive this letter, as inadequate as it surely is, and censored to boot. More fervently, I trust you are both well. Addison too. I did receive the news that he had embarked on the Saratoga, *but I have no information as to where any carrier might be headed. Except the one I'm on: the* Helena, *which is not a flattop but rather a battered cruiser, with lots of experience at its back!*

Unlike the Gulf of Mexico, the vast emptiness of the Pacific Ocean unsettles the soul. Thus, of whatever rank or condition, we are all elated to spot seagulls. They herald land. Sadly, that joy soon dissipates. It is followed by sure knowledge that we will be amphibiously disgorged onto whatever island we have been ordered to wrest from the enemy. This, I have gone through several times already.

As this letter attests, I am still here to tell of it. To be more specific...

Here, Helen dropped her recitation to say that the following lines were blacked out. The faces at the table were taut. Edward poured Harold some cognac, filling his own glass as well.

The tone of the letter struck Claire as bitterly frank. Her childhood friend was not pretending to be island-hopping with a bunch of other young men for fun.

Notwithstanding, Helen plowed on.

Of late, we have been through a series of skirmishes, and they have gone less badly for us than for them. Because of its strategic importance, I won't divulge the name of the island we took in late June, but it was a good effort. For all we are told, it may have already been in the news back home, part of the so-called New Georgia Campaign. We came ashore with weapons and supplies in support of Army comrades, and what did we see? A high mountain staring us in the face, which meant we might use it to our advantage. An observation post, ready-made. Meanwhile, we huddled among the huge trunks of trees none of us knew the name of, but were glad for, nonetheless. Also, glad for chocolate bars. Two days went by before we were strafed, and then assaulted by land. A buddy of mine did not make it.

There were others. In fact...

Richard's mother paused again, her face distorted, as though the tone of the letter was only now hitting her.

"Shall I get you some iced tea or water?" Claire asked her quietly.

"No, no," Helen said, her voice faint. "The rest is redacted," she explained, "except for the ending." She turned toward the two men. "Do you see anything on the map that suggests where he might be?"

Claire had already calculated that Richard was involved in one or another battle for the Solomons. She thought better than to say so. Things in that part of the Pacific were touch and go.

"He mentions the name of the campaign but doesn't give us any geographical clue, does he, Edward?"

"It might be the Solomon Islands, which are closer to Australia than to Japan. We believe Addison's carrier, if he hasn't been transferred elsewhere, is further to the north, nearer the Marianas or the

Marshalls." Edward indicated with his finger where those two chains were on the colorful map, not far, Claire noticed, from the frolicking dolphins.

Helen could not be deterred.

We are in such cramped quarters here that it is hard to imagine life anywhere else.

I'm sure the home front can't be a barrel of laughs either but from what we are told everyone—even women and school children—are doing what they can to help the war effort. Do keep me in your prayers as I will all of you.

Your son, Richard

Esther broke the ice. "You did a marvelous job, Helen. We are all thankful that Richard is doing what he can. If and when we hear from Addison, we will let him know about his friend. Perhaps communications are easier within the Navy." She looked across the table. "What do you think, Claire? Is that the feeling within Intelligence?"

"Seemingly so. It would be comforting for the two of them to be in contact."

During the following week, Claire did inquire about intra-service mail, asking not Junior Lieutenant Forster but their supervisor, Lieutenant Nelson.

"Might be feasible for the two, given that your brother is a high-ranking officer. Are you aware what ship his childhood friend is on?"

"In a letter written in late June, he mentioned the cruiser, *Helena*."

The lieutenant looked puzzled. He flipped through a folder on his desk. "It's not yet public knowledge, but the *Helena* was sunk, a week ago, at a place called Kula Bay."

Claire, her face gone pale, opened her mouth but no words came out.

"Nothing about casualties as yet," the officer continued neutrally. She nodded, raising her eyes to the map on the wall behind him. "Sorry," he said. "I didn't mean to—"

"Thank you, sir," she replied and quickly returned to the outer room. The numbers and letters of the coded message she was assigned to work on remained a jumble for the rest of the day.

Chapter Twenty-Eight
LEARNING TO SURVIVE

How desolate a landscape, Tom thought, as the Army truck drew close to its final destination. Along with several other detainees, none of whom had much to say, he was seated in the back of the vehicle, with a view out the rear. They had driven for several hours from the train station at Bismarck, a nondescript town with not much to recommend it. Further depressed he became when he caught sight of a high double fence along the side of the road. The outer layer was topped by coils of barbed wire. Approaching what appeared to be the main gate, they all spotted a guard tower at the far end of the enclosure. A figure was standing at the edge of the tower, a rifle at the ready.

"It's a goddamn prison, that's what it is," one of the men, a grizzled sort with a bulbous nose, muttered. His English was more colloquial than Tom's. Hard to imagine him as an international spy, Tom thought. Hard to imagine himself as one either.

One of the other men, who said he lived in New Jersey since emigrating in '38, offered him a cigarette. He accepted, drawing in the nicotine to calm his nerves.

The check-in operation took a couple of hours, even though the two custodians greeting them were business-like and efficient. Tom counted four floor-to-ceiling shelves stuffed with folders in the tiny reception, presumably information on all the detainees. At least a thousand such souls, he reckoned. He filled out the paperwork as best he could, indicating "soon to begin the process of naturalization," where it asked for legal status.

Neither of the two officials questioned his answers.

Two of the four men he traveled with were assigned to a shared facility on the east side of the camp, until their wives arrived. As single men, Tom, the young detainee from New Jersey, who gave his name as Gunther Gersh, and the grizzled sort, who gave his name as Dieter Benz, were to be lodged on the west side. After signing more documents, each of them was handed a folder.

"Inside your packet, you will find a map of the camp with all the buildings marked for your convenience. You will be required to participate in the upkeep and improvement of the camp as well as purchase basic items from the general store for your own use," the senior of the two officials, a Mr. Dirksen, explained.

The men snorted in acknowledgement.

The other official then indicated the large building straight down the road in front of them. It had a horseshoe driveway in front and a couple of struggling sycamores out front. Several official-looking cars were parked outside, including one with a siren atop marked BPD. "You will be accompanied to what we call Building A, where the bank is located. You may also rent, for a modest sum, a box for any valuables you wish to store there. For the duration."

Dieter guffawed. "The duration, huh."

"We're in a war, gentlemen," Dirksen reminded them. "It behooves you to abide by the rules. It'll make your stay less burdensome, and our jobs less tiresome."

Lying on his assigned cot that November evening of 1943, Tom could not but think of the so-called work camps back in Germany. But what was going on there was, if rumors were true, much worse

THIS NEARLY WAS OURS

than here. He shuddered to imagine. His own situation was bad enough.

It had been hard to fill out the form earlier where he was asked to indicate Parent Names and Address, as well as Spouse and Children Names. So many spaces left blank. He felt alone in the world.

If only he had better kept up contacts—the cousin who lived in Hamburg and ran a bookshop, his great aunt Matilde who lived in Berlin and engraved jewelry for a living. More crucially, the tenuous link with his childhood friend was now severed. What an irony, he realized. As Myra had hinted, that handful of letters from Hans became the single most damning piece of evidence against him.

Before he fell asleep, Tom determined to write to all of them back home, at whatever last address he could dig up. One of the many things he had forgotten to ask earlier was if mail was allowed, and if it was censored. And even if permitted, how on earth would he now communicate with Claire without compromising her position? And what about access to newspapers or to books?

It was all too much.

The wind rustled the windows of Bldg. 4 West, the air crisp and cold. It was only November, a month when evenings were still balmy in New Orleans. Apparently not here. The camp was almost in Canada, for God's sake. Gunther, the detainee who had, solely out of curiosity, attended a pro-Hitler rally in New York City, said that the Dakotas were reckoned as frigid as anything in the Alps.

Tom remembered those winter holidays fondly, first with his parents, and then with Hans and Katrin. But, from the look of things, there'd be no skiing or sledding or ice-skating at Fort Lincoln. He pulled the pea-green Army blanket up around his chin and tried to refocus.

Myra had insisted that these internment camps were—how had she put it that awful final day at Camp Claiborne?—"not that dissimilar from an old-fashioned summer camp." These places would have amenities. Campers were encouraged to participate in the life of the place. "It would help to do so," she had advised him. "Better treatment would be in store. Early release might be possible."

Bone-weary, he eventually went to sleep trying to keep this optimistic version of his predicament at the front of his mind.

aAs the months went by and the cold took hold, Tom came to agree that Fort Lincoln was most assuredly a prison. Every time he looked up, he could see one or another of the four guard towers and the ten-foot-high fences that ringed the place. But he kept telling himself, with the right attitude it could also be endured as a *summer* camp, albeit an endless one.

He set about to make himself useful. For one thing, the camp was in a perpetual state of being expanded or reconfigured. Within a few weeks of arrival, he was volunteered to help design a gymnasium, both for sports activities as well as communal events, like the occasional movie or lecture. He even helped build a mini ski slope for the kids in the camp.

It did not take the organizers long to figure out that Tom was adept at deciphering blueprints, ordering materials, (without exceeding the skimpy government budget), handling tools, and overseeing the construction operation.

"Say, where did you learn all this?" Gunther asked him one day, as they took a smoke break.

"I studied architecture. In Berlin, before I emigrated," Tom said, not wanting to go into detail.

Gunther offered him another cigarette. "I myself did math. Came over to study at Princeton. Einstein is there, a lot of others too. But it didn't work out. I drifted away, toward the wrong crowd."

Wanting to leave things at that, Tom changed the subject. "What do you think about erecting a stage at one end of the gym? Shouldn't cost much and might be useful. Especially since kids here don't have much to do."

"Yeah. Who knows? Maybe they'll end up on Broadway."

"You work up the measurements. I'll run it by the foreman."

Word soon got around that Tom Stone was no slouch in the work department and easy to work with.

The foreman, a local fellow named Olaf Hendricks, came to rely on him to move the gym project along, and bring it in on time and under budget. Including a workable stage with rafters for lighting fixtures overhead and a small orchestra pit below. By the spring of 1944, the gym was functional. The teachers at the school were ecstatic, students performed "Peter and the Wolf" on opening night, and young and not so young male detainees took to the basketball court the very next day.

Tom received a public commendation from the foreman and a positive write-up in his file from camp director Dirksen.

For the first time since his internment, his heart felt less heavy. He had, during his so-called down times, penned letters to the cousin in Hamburg and his great aunt in Berlin but received no replies. It took him much longer to compose a letter to Claire, addressing it to Myra at her family home in Alexandria. He struggled with the tone more than the grammar. In the end, he adjudged it stilted but, after crumpling reams of paper, he sent a version. Censors be damned.

Claire,

There are many things I need not tell you. You know what they are. I will only add that I trust you are relishing your life despite the war and everything it has brought upon us.

Presuming you will want to know about my life here, so far away, it is not so dreary.

There is camaraderie and kindnesses abound. I have reflected on my own failings, which are many. In response to that effort, I am doing my part to make this camp a better place for its detainees. We are in the midst of a building project, which they may not want me to elaborate on, but which will be a boon to the community, especially to the children. (There are a few families interred here as well as single men.) We do get word of how the war progresses, and I am encouraged, as no doubt you and your family are, that hostilities will soon come to an end, and our side be victorious. For reasons you will understand, I will leave it at that.

Tom

Not long after the opening of the gym, camp director Dirksen approached Tom about another idea: adding a row of cottages to accommodate incoming detainees with families. "Other camps are overrun. We don't want to be caught unprepared. As long as you can stay within budget and move things along, you can pick and choose the work force."

Tom had learned to bargain. He'd get to it right away, but there were two requests that he had been "fielding" from other detainees. "If possible, from townsfolk and others of your acquaintance, sir," he began, hoping to compliment him enough to maintain his attention.

"And what would those be, Mr. Stone?" Dirksen asked.

"More books, for the adults. Novels set in America. Also, poetry and history. There's a small room over in Bldg. A, which seems not to be utilized. We could install shelves and a couple of desks. Even create a check-out system. Gunther, you know him as Mr. Gersh, could take that on. He's a math whiz. If you agree."

The older man found it impossible to say no to that, so Tom came out with his other request. "Every stage needs to have a piano. Any old instrument will do. You might be amazed at how many people love music here. It is one of the glories of Germany—as we once knew and loved it. Wouldn't you agree, sir?"

Flabbergasted, the director sputtered a response. Dirksen had not thought favorably of his native country for well-nigh a decade. So odd to be hearing this encomium from a detainee, who, if he remembered rightly from his file, was Jewish by birth. But he would ask his wife whatever happened to the old instrument they had early on in their marriage.

Cottages began to go up over the summer months. Piles of books began to arrive at the main gate from citizenry in the area as well as from camp staff members themselves. And, before a new school year began in September, a Steinway upright, newly polished and tuned, and with only a few scuff marks near the pedals, was delivered to the gym.

Of all people, Dieter, as grizzled and grumpy as ever, became the one to inaugurate the instrument. The sound of a Bach fugue carried through the open windows. Everyone within earshot stopped what they were doing to listen.

About the time the piano arrived, Tom received his third letter from Claire, this one more impersonal than the preceding. She brought him up to date on the war in the Pacific, including inroads the Allies were making in the Philippine Sea, and the letters from her brother and their childhood friend Richard. She referred to work in the vaguest of ways—"going well, always lots to do"—and slipped in names of people he would remember, most notably Myra, Lena Walenska, and Marie Monceau. There was much she did not say.

He read the letter over three or four times for any missed clues. To no avail.

That November of 1944, the entirety of the Fort Lincoln camp was invited to day-long screenings of a new movie in the gym. To the unbeknownst of the camp organizers, the film cans sent along from Bismarck contained a newsreel as well. Thus, before the feature, the detainees were treated to footage from Pisa, with smiling Allied soldiers hanging out the American flag from the Leaning Tower, and then from a tiny island in the Pacific called Peleliu, where the Marines looked unusually bedraggled. The latter section left most of the audience in silence.

Then *Thirty Seconds over Tokyo* came on. Almost everyone was riveted, cheering each of the B-25s as they took off from the carrier on their way to drop their bombs.

Coming back from the movie, and a couple of beers with

Gunther thereafter, Tom tripped over a pickle barrel in front of the general store. Within a minute, his left hand swelled to twice its size.

"Wow, man, you need to get that checked out," Gunther said.

"At this hour?"

"Someone is always on call."

His friend took him straightaway to the infirmary, where the nurse on duty led him into a brightly lit space. Big-boned and buxom, Ingrid, as her badge indicated, set about cleansing the area.

"You smell like vinegar, Mr.—?"

"Tom, Tom Stone. I fell over a pickle barrel." Gently, she felt the fingers and wrist.

"Hope it's not broken. Lots to do around here," he threw out.

"For all of us," she said laconic. He liked her no-nonsense tone. "As usual, bad things happen when the doctor is not around. I'll make a splint, and first thing Monday morning, you get yourself back here. Dr. Katz will do whatever needs to be done."

While she cut up cloth and latched three wooden sticks together, Tom looked around the room. Two framed certificates hung on the far wall, which he presumed were there to reassure patients that a bonafide doctor was available. Cut-outs of colorful birds, likely scissored from a magazine, were affixed to the nearby wall.

Funny, he thought, that he had never been inside the place, though he had heard of children going there with cuts and scrapes.

"Hard job working the night shift, especially if others have done stupid things like me," he said by way of making conversation.

"Since my husband died. Keeps me busy. Is good to be helpful to other people, *Ya?*"

"Indeed," he replied. It occurred to him that he had not been in close proximity to a woman for upwards of a year, nor exchanged more than a sentence or two with any, other than official information. Prison is more than a place. It's a state of mind that can take you over, he thought.

"You may feel this," she said.

He winced as she tried to align his fingers.

"I'm sorry," she said. "It is natural to have pain with the swelling." She began to wind a roll of adhesive tape around his hand, using her left arm to steady his. Her touch made him shiver. "This won't take long," she went on. "Try to relax."

"You have a reassuring voice, Ingrid. But I do not recognize the accent."

"I am Danish. Came to America with my parents when I was twenty, not long after the Great War. Met my husband the next year."

"I see. I am sorry for your loss."

She shrugged. "He was a hard worker. And a hard drinker."

Not knowing what to say to that, he nodded in polite sympathy. Just then he heard a noise which sounded like someone calling out from close by. He looked up at Ingrid's broad forehead, her kind eyes.

Sighing, she slowly lowered his arm to the tabletop. "Don't move," she instructed him. Without another word, she rose and left the room. He could hear her clogs clicking on the hallway floor and thereafter faint voices. In less than five minutes she returned. He looked up at her inquiringly.

"Most of the patients are not like you, Tom Stone."

"Not like me?"

"The ward, such as it is, has ten beds. Nine are filled right now, but only one is an accident like yours. A leg injury that got infected."

"I don't follow."

"The others are maladies of the mind. It does no one any good to be in this place."

This was not encouraging to hear, Tom thought.

"Anyway, I realize that you are likely the Tom that builds things. That is healthy. To be helpful to others."

"Maybe," he said. "Like you, if for different reasons, I try to stay busy. And that is what I trained to do in life: build things."

"Then you will be fine. Plus, I reckon you are not a Nazi."

He wasn't sure if she were trying to be amusing. She did not seem to have that key. "Actually, I doubt that any who are here are Nazis,

Ingrid, though some of them still think of Germany as their homeland."

"I believe we are in—what does one call it?—synchronicity," she said, pronouncing every syllable of the last word. With that, she rose to unlock a glass cabinet, and took out a tiny tin of aspirin.

"We are running low, only eight tablets inside. You will take two now, and one every four hours until Monday morning. Come early, around 7:00. Dr. Katz will be here."

"And you? I mean, to explain to him what happened to me. Will you be here?"

Rolling her eyes, Ingrid gave him the classic look to say that all men are alike when it comes to women.

"God willing, I go off-duty at 7:30. And remember. Sleep on your back and don't turn onto your left side. It will wake you up!"

As instructed, Tom showed up at the clinic at 7 sharp on Monday morning, having used up all but two of the aspirin. He handed the tin with the two pills back to Ingrid.

"They helped," he said. "But I didn't need them all."

"A good sign," she replied. "Dr. Katz will patch you up good and proper."

Within a half hour, Tom was fitted with a proper splint and a sling, which he was instructed to wear for a couple of weeks. And desist from heavy lifting or undue exertion.

"Nurse Ingrid already told me you head up the construction team. If you want to keep doing that, mind what I say," Dr. Katz, a kindly sort with a twinkle in his eye, admonished him.

"Will do, doctor."

On his way out, he spotted Ingrid struggling to start her old car. He tried to pop the hood, but it was stuck. Besides, he had only one good arm. "Come have breakfast over at the commissary. I have friends who'll know what to do."

Reluctantly, Ingrid went along, and over oatmeal, fell into conversation with Dieter. Apparently impressed with the fact she drove a rare model 1936 Studebaker, he was more than happy to take a look. It took half an hour for him to fix the nurse's car, but somehow the two remained in conversation for another hour. Animated conversation at that.

"I ain't never heard Dieter say so many words since we met him," Gunther said to Tom as they watched the two head off to the clinic.

"Or with so much enthusiasm," Tom replied.

Not a month later, the odd couple had become a fixture around the camp. Dieter played songs for Ingrid on the upright; she brought him treats from home and lent him her birdwatchers guide.

"What do you reckon will happen when all this is over?" Gunther asked early in the new year. He and Tom were repairing a pipe in the cafeteria that burst during the week's hard freeze.

Tom straightened up, rubbing his bare hands together to warm them. He still favored the left one, to be on the safe side. "If you mean Ingrid and Dieter, they'll likely find a way to stay together. As they should. If you mean the rest of us, I have no idea."

Chapter Twenty-Nine
EYES SHUT WIDE

B y Myra's count, German POWs were on the cusp of outnumbering American soldiers still training or recuperating from wounds at Camp Claiborne. She had been sending memos to the new commander as well as hounding Major Benson that it would do well to have the prisoners assigned to work crews, and not mope around all day, letting their grievances fester.

When Doris Mackie invited her along to the officers' club to hear the new camp head address the issues of the day, she jumped at the chance.

"Don't overplay your hand with Commander Tuckey, Myra. But dispatching some prisoners to the sugar cane fields and others to the bridge building project does makes a lot of sense."

"I would be grateful if *you* were to second my proposals, Doris. Your opinion carries weight. Now that Roosevelt has finally seen the light and made you officially a sergeant."

Her friend chuckled. "The president issued the proclamation, and it trickled down from there. A number of us WACs got a stripe or two. Great for morale, and hopefully for future assignments. When all this winds down."

The two women spotted Major Benson across the way, having a drink with several other officers. The truculent corporal who replaced Stephen Hill soon moseyed over.

"Did not expect to see you two here, but the more the merrier," Evans said, something disdainful in his voice. The two women ignored him.

The commander's speech was upbeat enough, hailing recent victories in Italy and in France, and extolling the contributions of soldiers who had passed through the camp itself. Whether sincere or not, he insisted that he was open to suggestions or complaints at any time. Any recruit was welcome to drop a note inside a box outside his office, "with no fear of reprisal."

"That'll be the day," Doris mumbled.

But Myra took him up on it and was unafraid to put her name on it. She suggested the prisoners make themselves useful by working in the sugar cane fields or building bridges. To her surprise, her plan was put into motion.

Her other ideas did not resonate as widely. Griping by black soldiers, she argued in another memo, had become "palpable." In particular, they were incensed that German officers under arrest were treated with more deference and provided more amenities than they themselves were.

"Who be fighting this war," she had heard one of the Negroes complain to his fellow recruits. "Us or them Krauts?" She mentioned the exchange word for word in her complaint.

As Doris had warned her, she'd not likely hear back, whether they looked into the issue or not. "You're a civilian. That gives you some privileges but excludes you from others."

Months went by but nothing was done about the black soldiers' quarters. Instead, Myra heard catcalls directed her way. It began to bother her enough to take action. If anybody had a handle on how recruits were behaving, it would be Ruby Tate. Myra had not run into her in months, and then only in passing, and always with a male in tow.

On a day when she had time to spare, she checked the camp directory and headed over to Bldg. F. Entering, she heard female laughter from down the hall. She waited for silence before knocking on a door marked *Supplies*.

"Long time no see, Myra. You're looking much the same." Alone in the room, Ruby was standing in front of a mirror, applying powder.

"And you, Ruby."

After a few perfunctory pleasantries, the two took a walk so that Ruby could deliver a ledger to an office across camp. "Knowing you, there's something on your mind, right?"

Myra did not waste any time, inquiring as to Ruby's opinion of the recruits she had recently come into contact with. There had been multiple reports of rowdy behavior, on and off the camp.

She gave Myra an amused look. "What's there to know? They're young, they're men, and yeah, they're on the make. I make a point of having one or another as my current date. Makes things easier."

"Easier?"

"Meaning I don't have to fend them all off if I'm tethered to one of them."

"I see," Myra said, trying not to estimate how many such men Ruby might have been tethered to over the course of two-and-a-half years. No wonder her engagement to Frederick was doomed.

"You probably think ill of me," Ruby soon declared. Myra made a face to suggest that such a sentiment was irrelevant, if true. "We are different. You have opinions—even *causes*, as Eleanor Roosevelt would put it. I, on the other hand, want to have fun, and eventually, find the right man to settle down with. One with a lot of stripes or a lot of money—ideally both."

Myra lingered in front of the supply storage unit while Ruby went in to update the ledger. She heard more laughter, and a young man's voice. Within a few minutes, her old high school classmate re-emerged.

"I'm done for the day, but meeting my friend Scott back at Bldg. 6, in fifteen minutes."

"Fine. I'll walk you back."

For a few minutes, neither woman spoke. Several clusters of men in uniform passed them by. A couple of them called out to Ruby by name. Another gave her a pathetic dog stare, which Myra imagined might indicate he was one of the suitors she had previously discarded.

Then, to Myra's surprise, her friend blurted out the unexpected. "Actually, I'm glad you stopped by. I want you to know I'm sorry about Frederick. It would never have worked out between us. I should have known."

"No need to apologize to me, Ruby. I guess we all three have moved on."

"Well, I don't shop at Bauer's anymore. His mother glared at me something fierce."

Myra stifled a smile at the thought. "But you have followed how he's doing overseas, right?"

"Not really. The war doesn't interest me. Anyway, he only ever wrote to me once, at the beginning. 'Somewhere in North Africa' it began. I couldn't think what to respond." Ruby shrugged, as though that was all there was to it.

"In case you don't yet know, he's up for a medal for heroism—at a battle in Italy. Monte Cassino. It was in the local paper."

"Huh," Ruby exhaled in reaction.

Myra rolled her eyes, waiting for a more considered response. None came. "His mother and aunt come over to see my parents occasionally and read aloud his letters. They're full of interesting details none of us would have expected."

"That so," Ruby managed, her eyes darting around in search presumably of her date. She checked her watch, then fiddled with stray strands of her hairdo. "So windy today," she complained.

Myra could barely contain her irritation. "Remember how good Frederick was in English class? He has a gift. It probably brings him solace over there to put pen to paper."

Ruby stamped her foot impatiently. "Damn it," she murmured. "Where could he be?" she fumed. Suddenly, out of the shadows, a young man materialized.

Myra counted two stripes on his uniform and a pin she didn't recognize.

Her friend brightened. "This, Scott, is my old school chum, Myra. She works liaison with the mayor's office in Alexandria." The young man briefly touched his cap.

Then the couple hastened off, arm-in-arm toward whatever awaited them.

For a minute or two, Myra stood benumbed in the dying light. It occurred to her that Frederick had escaped a bullet. She shook her head to throw off the image of Ruby Tate in her indifference.

"Why ever did I bother?" she asked herself as she walked back to her own office—and then drove slowly home.

That same night, Myra rang Claire. They talked for an hour, catching up on family news, progress from the front, the movies, and whatever else popped into their heads.

"Okay, you have to come down here. Soonest. So much I can't say on the phone," Claire said.

"If you only knew. There are things I can't say either or I'd be fired, if speaking from work, or thrown out of the house, if from here."

Both were only half-joking.

Neither wanted to talk on the phone about the letters home from loved ones. Those would have to wait.

Not a month later, Myra found herself overseeing the installation of new plumbing fixtures ordered from a firm in Baton Rouge for Bldg. N, which housed the remainder of black soldiers yet to ship out to northern France.

To his credit, Commander Tuckey had read her memo and called her in. "If you can access the requisite materials and keep within budget, it's your project to implement, Miss Kaminsky."

"I'll get to it soonest."

A no-nonsense Great War veteran, the commander puckered his lips, eyeing her closely. She stood at attention, expectant. "Never thought I'd be lobbied by a southerner to do something for these poor sons of bitches," he said. "But black or white, war's going to require every last one of us."

On her Saturday off, Myra drove down to the capital, found and paid for the fixtures before the commander could change his mind. She put in extra hours over at the black barracks to make sure the work was done expeditiously.

Doris came over at one point and approved. Major Benson nodded his assent, murmuring once again that she never ceased to amaze him. Corporal Evans made disparaging remarks behind her back.

It was comments like his that ignited the violence.

Not to get behind with her other duties, including a call to the mayor to sign off on a musical celebration in town, Myra stayed at her desk later than usual. Around 9 p.m., she walked some invitations over to the officers' club where she hoped the efficient receptionist, a WAC named Priscilla, would dispatch them in a timely manner. No one was about when Myra entered, so she left the packet, with a note, behind the counter.

On her way back to Major Benson's office, she sensed footsteps behind her, but she had things on her mind. Like, what her aunt would perform at the celebration, (Myra having already hinted that a medley of show tunes might go over better than Liszt).

As she rehearsed what she would say to Lena upon their next conversation, a voice broke in. "Isn't she that colored-lover?" A couple of sniggers followed.

"Sure looks like her. Jewish whore," another voice rejoined.

Then some filthy chortle, and comments she couldn't make out. Myra sped up, breathing hard.

Out of nowhere, she felt a wrenching pain. Her arm had been jerked. She wheeled around only to be grabbed from behind. She struggled to wrest free, kicking someone's shin, It felt hard as a rock. Someone slapped her cheek. She groaned.

"Get her over here. In those bushes," one of them ordered.

She tried to scream, but a huge hand clamped itself across half her face, fingernails digging into flesh. From behind, someone kneed her so that she crumbled to the ground, face down. Trying to assume a fetal position, she became dizzy, unable to tell up from down. Damp earth clogged her nostrils. She was being dragged through dirt and dry leaves. Warm blood trickled down her face.

Then it was all hands, turning her back over, ripping off buttons on her blouse and yanking her skirt off. She squirmed but was punched in the ribs.

One hand squeezed a breast, another pulled at her panties.

"Damn it. Let me at her first. See how much she likes it," one voice snarled.

"Shit. Go ahead. But we ain't got all night."

Myra froze as she was violated. Everything went blank. It was as though she had vacated her own body. For a time, she drifted in and out of consciousness.

At some point, she tried to torque to the side to dislodge the first soldier, but he kept pumping. Where were her arms, she wondered. A sharp pain across her chest told her. Another man had gripped both of them over her head.

"Fuck it, man. Time to give over," the one squatting at her head said. He dropped her arms, but it was too painful to move them. Of a sudden, he was atop her. Before she could react, he penetrated her with such force she gasped.

"You hear that? She's calling for you to let her have it," the first voice called out. Gleeful. He had put his boot on her limp right arm.

Then, somehow, over this second assailant's grunts, Myra detected the faint sound of machines, an odor of chemicals.

They must be near the laundromat. Someone would be there. She tried to gather her energy to call out. But nothing came forth.

"Come on. You're done now," the third man growled. He sounded older than the other two. He was standing apart, as though disgusted, or weary of the whole thing.

Myra pried open an eye. Looking up, in the dimmest of moonlight, she could make out a sash with MP on it.

Almost as abruptly as the assault began, it ended. The two soldiers brushed themselves off, kicked leaves to disguise the drag marks, and left their victim lying there.

"Fucking bitch," she heard one of them mutter as they slithered away.

Myra lay still, trying to grasp what had happened. Her face was smeared with blood and dirt and whatever else they may have wiped across her cheeks. Slowly, she turned onto her side, trying to prop herself up. Her first effort failed. She waited a few minutes. A light suddenly passed over. Footsteps approached.

"Is someone out here?" a female voice asked, shining a flashlight hither and yon. "Damn raccoons," she mumbled.

"I'm over here," Myra managed, her voice the faintest of whispers.

The Kaminskys' family doctor shook his head as he came out of Myra's bedroom. Over the decades, Dr. Hofmeier had become something of a friend, a well-meaning one. He was also a reliable physician, but of the old school, reticent to probe too deeply into the mysterious afflictions of his female patients.

"What do you think, Ezra? What could ail our daughter other than her working so hard?" Konrad asked.

"Burning the candle at both ends," Ilona hastened to add. "But that can't be all there is to it."

"Not like our Myra at all," Konrad went on. "All she says is she's exhausted, stressed out, or fell down and bumped her head. Can't seem to keep things straight."

To collect his thoughts and place them in the right order, the doctor began his descent down the stairs. He relied on his oldest patients, those to whom he made house calls, to offer a little bourbon and maybe, if they were like Ilona Kaminsky, provide some delicacy as well. Myra's parents followed behind him, still going on about their daughter's loss of appetite, her insomnia, her withdrawal from daily life.

After a few swallows of alcohol, and a slice of Ilona's fruit cobbler —how could anyone turn down this woman's cooking? he, a lifelong bachelor, asked himself—he put down his dessert plate. He cleared his throat.

"Let me first reassure you. Your daughter does not have a fever or a viral infection. She has lost weight, and her skin is sallow, but that is consistent with having a nervous—he paused—disorder. Of one kind or another."

"A breakdown. Is that it?"

"Not necessarily. I believe with time and proper care, she'll come around." Both parents looked dubious. The grandfather clock in the corner ticked over to 7 p.m.

"What, pray tell, do you mean by proper care?" Konrad asked more forcefully, "beyond checking in on her every few hours, making her fresh soup every day, and trying to cheer her up with good news from the front. Or visits from well-wishers?"

"Ah, that's exactly it. Having her own friends, or a special friend, come over would likely do her wonders. Someone she can confide in—"

"She can confide in us, Ezra," Konrad cut him off to claim. "She always has." His tone had an edge.

"Of course. But she is a young woman, unmarried, yet out in the world." He gestured with his hand, hoping that a fair description of things that might befall a young woman on her own would come to mind.

Konrad turned toward his wife. "You should contact her friend Claire. See if she can travel up to spend the weekend."

On a Friday evening, Claire left work early. No one seemed to mind as everyone on the top floor was celebrating the news from Leyte. Above all the booze and music, Commander Lassiter had stood on a stool to read from the latest telex that the island had, finally, been taken. Which meant, he went on to say over the cheers, that the Japanese Navy had been decisively crippled. More cheers. Toasts to MacArthur were raised. Having given a hug to Bernice, she headed out around 5 p.m.

Driving Addison's car at a clip, Claire wondered if her brother, on whatever flattop he was now stationed, had been involved in that particular battle in the Philippine Sea. She also wondered if Richard had found himself in the thick of it. No doubt the Carrolltons would eventually receive word, though they had stopped reading aloud from their son's letters. Albeit they were redacted, he had managed in recent accounts to convey the horror of these assault landings: "*boots flaking off in the insect-infested mud*" and "*the incessant strafing from the air.*"

They were not the kind of letters with which to regale friends on a Sunday afternoon.

Closer to Alexandria, Claire focused her mind on what could possibly ail Myra. Her friend had taken a leave from Camp Claiborne and was suffering some kind of malaise.

When she arrived around 8 p.m., Mrs. Kaminsky filled her in. "I've made you a soup—Myra's already eaten, a little anyway—so please, sit with us a few minutes before going up to see her. The guest room awaits you thereafter."

Although she had been forewarned, Claire was shocked to see not only how thin her friend was but how on edge.

As was their custom, the two talked around things for a spell.

Claire filled Myra in on her suspicions about the young lieutenant who might have trailed Tom and fingered him to Naval Intelligence. And beyond that, how her suspicions grew to the point in which she told the officer off. "I waited until I got the clearance to transfer upstairs—and for a better salary—and then I accused him of a lack of military decorum. Hopefully, that did the trick."

Since Myra volunteered nothing, Claire continued, shifting direction. "The only sad thing is how stilted and infrequent letters now are between Tom and me. He keeps hinting that my life needs to go on without him, as his must." Myra nodded, distractedly. "Do you think he has found someone else, way up there in North Dakota?"

To this, Myra did reply. "I would find that hard to envision. First of all, there aren't many young single women running around in detention camps, and second..." Claire looked expectant. "Sorry. I have not spoken this many words in weeks. My brain still feels muddled."

Claire waited a few minutes. She looked around the room, her eyes coming to light on the nightstand, where a bottle of Homocebrin stood, alongside a tin of aspirin and a half-drunk glass of water. She took her friend's hand in hers. "Let's do like the old days," Claire said. Myra shook her head sideways. "I'm going downstairs to make up a wine, cheese, and fruit plate. You're going to tell me what has happened. That way we can both get through it and move on."

Myra did not object. When the tray arrived, she nibbled on cheese, Greek olives, slices of apple, and sipped a little wine. Color returned to her cheeks.

The two friends then arranged themselves in bed together, Myra's head cushioned against the headboard, Claire cross-legged at the foot.

The awful story spilled out.

From what Claire could ascertain, the worst thing for Myra was not the rape itself, as violent and degrading as it was, but the reaction of the Army, specifically Major Benson's.

In the immediate aftermath of the attack, Myra had been helped back to Bldg. D by a woman who had heard noises and come outside to check. In the office, she had sponged Myra off in the major's private bathroom, and then rushed back to the laundromat to bring her a fresh skirt and a woman's blouse.

"I insisted the young woman leave me, which eventually she did. Her name was Annie, 'like the comic strip,' she told me. I woke in the morning, got myself to the bathroom, vomited, cleaned up, and then Doris—she's a WAC sergeant—walked in. She had become a friend, an unlikely one, but steadfast. She's about to head off to France."

"What did Doris do?"

"Checked me out. Being a WAC includes nursing skills. She said nothing seemed amiss or broken. Just a nasty scratch on my cheek, which she put ointment on and powdered over, and a swollen ribcage where I had been kicked."

"The men who did this to you?"

"She told me to recount everything I could remember about them, since memory fades after trauma." Claire nodded. "I told her what I could. She scribbled it all down."

"And then what?"

"She made me lie down on the couch in the major's office and put her notes in an envelope on his desk. She left me, shut the door, and I fell asleep until voices woke me. I sat up, and within a minute or two, the major walked into his office. He glimpsed me and shut the door."

At this point, Myra lost her thread. Wayward tears trickled down her face.

Claire made her drink a little water. "Is that enough for tonight?"

"No. I want to tell you why I left the camp."

To fortify herself, Claire took another sip of wine.

"The first thing Major Benson said was, 'You look upset, Miss Kaminsky. What can I do for you?'" Myra rolled her eyes and continued, "When I told him that I had been raped—obviously by soldiers —not far from the officers' club, he looked away. Then he scrunched his face, as though I had said something outlandish, and asked, 'Are you certain, Myra? I'm not sure I understand what you're going on about.'"

Claire sensed heat rising in her own chest. "Please, go on."

"I repeated what had happened as calmly as I could. I mentioned that one of the men appeared to be military police. The major then rooted around in his drawer for something. I don't know what. Out of nowhere, he declared, 'Our men are trained not to do things like that.' His tone—I can still hear it—was dismissive. In short, he did not believe me."

"Or pretended not to believe you," Claire rejoined. Ruefully.

"While I struggled to compose myself, he tore up that envelope with Doris's notes and tossed the pieces in the trash. At that point, I rather lost it."

Claire shook her head in dismay.

"Not five minutes later, the major picked up the phone and called over to medical services for a car. Before long, two orderlies showed up to accompany me, not to the infirmary, but home, to Alexandria. The major's words to them were that I had suffered a spell and needed time to recover. He would be requesting a month's leave from my duties."

"He was trying to squash what had happened to you."

"The last thing he said as I was escorted out was 'Remember, Myra. The Army takes care of its own.'"

Claire's eyebrows went up as she tried to parse those words. "Are we thinking along the same lines here?"

"Yes. The major was threatening me. Nothing could be worse in his eyes than besmirching the Army. Especially in a time of war."

Chapter Thirty

THE SUN GOING DOWN

A month after her assault and another weekend visit from Claire, Myra felt strong enough to take walks and to go into town. Coming as a relief to her parents were also a few telephone calls, including three—increasingly, more urgent—to drop by the mayor's office. In the most nonchalant of tones, the Kaminskys passed the messages along to Myra, careful not to pressure her.

She stopped by city hall on a brisk afternoon in late February.

The mayor's chief assistant, a middle-aged spinster named Suzanne, surprised her with a cake and punch to welcome her.

"We were worried about you, but thrilled to think you might work here in the office," she said, smiling broadly. "You have all the necessary contacts at local businesses as well as at Camp Claiborne, if and when we need them. But truth be told, we're now spearheading the event," Suzanne continued, looking pleased as, well, punch.

"We're trying not to jump the gun, but doubtless you've heard the latest intelligence, Miss Kaminsky," the mayor joined in. "It may be only a matter of months—at least in Europe. Great news what our boys have done."

"Yes, we're on the brink, hard-fought though it has been," she pointed out.

"Well said, well said," the mayor concurred, being one who made a point of agreeing whenever possible.

His assistant picked up where he left off. "We'll want your advice on several fronts, Miss Kaminsky. For one, the paper wants to run a photomontage of our local heroes—the ones coming home as well as the fallen. We need to gather biographical information."

Myra nodded, thinking of poor Lech Murkowski. His grandmother had not been the same since the news of his death on Omaha Beach.

"Oh, I forgot. A letter for you arrived the other day. Addressed here. We held it, in hopes you would be in soon," Suzanne said, holding out the envelope. It was clearly V-mail.

Myra read it on a park bench during her walk home. It was from Doris Mackie, now a major in the WACs. Written "from somewhere in France."

Dear Myra,

You have been in my thoughts ever since I shipped out—the very day after the attack you suffered at the camp. I have kept a copy of the particulars you put them together in case you ever wish to pursue the matter. I say this because these are very disturbing accusations and because this is the U.S. Army. Things that are difficult enough in civilian life are even more challenging in the military. Until you advise otherwise, all this remains between us. I have admired from close-up your conscientiousness but also your conscience. First and foremost, you must do what is best for your own well-being.

As for things over here, they have been bloody, but they are mercifully coming to a close. As you know, I had wanted to be in the midst for some time. With no pleasure do I find that my skills as a registered nurse are invaluable. In our studies at the war college, we learned that the enemy is most ferocious when he is cornered. And that appears the case as the Allies march, inexorably, toward victory over the Axis. But never doubt that we women have contributed mightily to this effort. God willing, I plan to return to St. Louis and take up a role at the veterans hospital there. I trust you too will find a calling in life that takes advantage of your talents, not the least of which, your defense of justice.

Yours in peace, Doris

When she finished, Myra fished out a handkerchief. Several tears had spilled onto the paper, smearing the ink, though not enough to obscure the words. Out of the blue, she heard a voice at her elbow.

"Are you okay, miss?" A little girl, not more than six or seven, was holding a balloon on a string in one hand and a candy cane in the other. Another child, of the same age, popped up next to her. "Did you get hurt?"

Dabbing at her eyes, Myra shook her head. "No, no. I'm fine. Reading a letter. From a friend."

"Is your friend sick?" the first little girl asked.

"She's fine too," Myra replied, looking closely at the two, wondering if they were old enough. "She's helping the soldiers in the war. She's a nurse."

For an instant, the two little girls looked confused but then they nodded. Myra thought they understood.

"It's my birthday," the second child soon piped up to say.

"Well then, happy birthday to you. Go join your friends. I'm really okay. But thank you."

The two scampered away, calling to others over near the monkey bars.

Myra folded the letter in half, slipped it back in her bag, and walked the rest of the way home, less heavy of heart.

As he watched the relationship between Dieter and Ingrid blossom within the confines of Fort Lincoln, Tom had to grapple with the likelihood that his own affair with Claire had fizzled.

And why wouldn't it? He was thousands of miles away and essentially in prison, whereas she was a beautiful young woman, full of life. Surely, any soldier or sailor would jump at the chance to be her friend, or, more pertinently, to be her lover. He tried not to think of the days and nights that they lay locked together. Not just physically, he wanted to believe, but spiritually. Surely, that counted for something, though with the passage of time and so much distance between them, would likely not endure.

If he took any solace at all, it was from the books of poetry that he borrowed from the rudimentary library they had set up (mainly at his behest), and to which Ingrid, and others from town, had donated tomes from their own bookshelves.

It was Shakespeare's sonnets that gave Tom hope that their love affair might somehow be rekindled, if and when this damn war ever ended. One of them, called "When in Disgrace with Fortune and Men's Eyes," he often repeated to himself as he walked across the camp or lay sleepless in bed.

The last letter he had received from Claire served as a Christmas greeting. Had she forgotten he was Jewish? In particular, she went on about the Higgins boats—how they figured in the amphibious landings on the beaches of Normandy and equally on those at Leyte in the Philippines Sea. Did she not remember that he himself had been involved in the building of those vessels?

Too long ago, too far away.

In Tom's mind now, those eighteen months or so were the happiest time of his life. He had made a concrete contribution to the war effort and at the same time conducted a passionate love affair with the only girl he had cared for since Katrin. Although he occasionally took up his pen over the following weeks, he ended by abandoning the effort. His better angels told him to desist, leaving everything up to Claire—if ever. He would no longer check his box in the mailroom.

However, one afternoon in early March while crossing the frozen ground in front of Bldg. A on his way to repair a heating unit, someone called out from the porch.

"Hey, Tom Stone, there's a letter in your cubbyhole. Been there for days."

He took the steps two at a time on his way in. On his way out, he slowed down. Confused. The letter had British stamps on it and a return address in Oxfordshire.

Dear Tomas,

Stunned I was to receive communication from you after so many years, it having arrived after passage through multiple hands in multiple places. It was thanks to contacts in the book world and in synagogues that it wound up with me here in England where I am safe but in disbelief as to what has happened to the Germany we cherished.

To bring you up to date: during the time of Kristallnacht, *I was studying in London. My parents were rounded up, herded to Poland, and eliminated along with 200,000 others. That, even before the invasion proper and the setting up of veritable extermination camps. As for your parents, (my uncle and aunt), they were eventually sent to that old brick factory called Neuengamme, not far from Lübeck, and subsequently, according to others, your father was sent on to nearby Sachsenhausen. Not to give you false hope, but prisoners healthy enough and possessed of useful skills, were put to work.*

As for our childhood friends, Hans and Katrin, I followed the saga of the St Louis *too. I do not believe Katrin ended up in England, because most of those arrivals stayed in touch, and I queried a few. As for Hans, you'll recall he admired the military. He wrote to me early in the war to say he had become a U-boat officer. Well, we know how dangerous that job is!*

Sorry I can't be of more help. Still, you and I both know one impressive thing about Germans: they keep records. Sooner or later, we shall learn who did what to whom in this tragic war. And I augur that you and I shall meet up again in a happier time and place.

Your forever cousin, Jonas Steinberg

P.S. I am now a consultant on German literature at Blackwell's of Oxford, one of the foremost bookstores in England and the most reliable place to contact me.

Tom could have been knocked over with a feather. Wisely, he had sat himself down on the steps of the building, oblivious to the snow falling all around him. He re-read the letter to make sure he wasn't dreaming, pocketed it, wiped snowflakes off his face, and hurried over to the schoolhouse.

Certain evenings when Claire let her mind wander, it would come to rest on thoughts of Tom, and how time and distance had, some days, made her heart grow fonder, and on others, stiffened her resolve to move on.

In short, she did not know what to make of his chatty letters, which centered on building projects, or the movies they were allowed to see, or the handful of friends he had cultivated at Fort Lincoln. The word *detention* he had stopped using, because, she suspected, it suggested that he had done something to merit what had happened to him.

Not that her letters to him, less frequent, more impersonal, were likely any more satisfying than his were to her. She had told him that she had moved back home to be "a better daughter," and not because the tiny guest house reminded her so vividly of their time together there.

She had overdone it with the references to Higgins boats, especially since Tom too would have seen newsreels of the battles in the

Pacific and the landings on D-Day to know how important a role they were playing. She knew he was proud of his contribution to that effort, but she did not know her insistence on the boats' contribution only heightened his frustration with no longer being part of the war effort.

That must be galling to him, she now realized.

If Claire had been completely forthcoming, she would have told her former lover that those eighteen months with him had been the happiest of her life. Despite her ever-stronger bond with Myra and her growing friendship with Bernice, the only men in her life now were—as for countless other young women—those caught up in the war. In her case, both her brother and her childhood friend. The Pacific, as she well knew from her perch at Naval Intelligence, was not for the faint of heart.

Addison's calls to the Endicott home were rare and discombobulating, picked apart at the dinner table for every plausible nuance. Over a typical crackly line, he described the weather, how the cobalt blue skies gave way to dazzling light shows and unearthly downpours. From there, how seagulls heralded the approach to some speck of land afloat in the vastness of the ocean, or how the hum of planes taking off from the carrier signaled the beginning of an assault on the enemy hundreds of miles away.

They would listen to his recitation and await their turn. Was he eating well, getting enough sleep, enjoying shore leave, making new friends? his mother would rush to ask. Then, his father, veteran that he was, would demand different answers over her shoulder. How seaworthy was his ship? Had intelligence predicted attacks well enough in advance? Had he and Richard managed to make contact?

By that time, the line might have gone dead but, if not, Addison would have provided the most generic, reassuring of answers, as officers of the Navy had been instructed when communicating with family members.

Claire did not point this out at the dinner table. She seconded

301

the opinion that her brother sounded good and that his ship was certainly one of the best the Navy had deployed.

Addison never asked after Myra, and Claire never volunteered an update.

Then one afternoon at work, she was alerted to a letter that had arrived, assuming that somehow Tom had decided it was now okay to write to her there. But the return address read, "from a cruiser in the Philippine Sea." That led the officer who handed it to her to quip, "Your sailor sounds like he does not want to be found." She did not smile at his bad joke.

She waited to open the envelope until she got home, and to her own bedroom.

Dear Claire,

We are finally coming up for air over here, having worked our way north over three years of slogging through rain-drenched islands full of coconut trees, which aren't too bad when you're dying of thirst, but also full of enemy soldiers, which are always bad. We came out here to meet the enemy, but we know as little about them now as we did before.

The only thing that never changes is that the Japanese are determined not to surrender, which means this thing continues to drag on, one ferocious battle after another. They only get more dug-in and more desperate; we get more brazen and brutal. As for Iwo Jima it has been secured. At heavy loss, including mates of mine.

The good news, which you may already know from my parents, is that Addison and I are at long last in contact, and in our different capacities, headed now in the same direction. You're in Intelligence: you'll know where that leads.

Keep us in your prayers. Richard

Taking a deep breath, Claire walked across her room, raised the window to the balcony and stepped out into the bracing air. It was depressing to think that this man—like millions of others—had been put through such a ferocious ordeal, and that many likely would be scarred for life by the experience. If they survived at all.

Richard Carrollton, of all people, to volunteer for the Marines. "Be a man," his father had cajoled him in the wake of Pearl Harbor. Not one to disobey, he submitted. She shook her head at the memory.

While she had often ripped from the telex machine at work the casualty figures from major battles, Claire had tried to regard the numbers as an abstract thing, with no personal import. Her childhood friend was not a poet, but in this letter, one of the few he had penned specifically to her, his anguish was evident. On that very balcony, the three of them had played games, read books, watched the world go by, told one another secrets. He was the fragile, generous spirited one of the three; she more frivolous; Addison, the more deliberate.

And for the last three years, while she sat behind a desk on Carondelet, and Addison studied charts aboard the safest of Navy vessels, Richard was firing a howitzer and hurling grenades. Or worse.

She felt ashamed for not having held him in the forefront of her mind. The next day, she determined to study the map in Commander Lassiter's office in hopes of pinpointing where the next major battle was likely to unfold.

Through tears, she looked out over the balcony at the near-deserted street. A woman was shouldering a wicker basket with a loaf of French bread sticking out. An elderly man was walking a scroungy-looking dog. Shivering as the wind picked up, she turned to go back inside.

Before going downstairs for dinner, she read the letter one more time, then consigned it to her desk drawer. Up on her bookshelves, she spotted a slim volume with an ox-blood cover. It was from that course years ago on the poets of the Great War. The professor had been so moved by a particular verse that she could not get through the reading of it. All the students, she and Myra included, were seated there, preoccupied with their own girlish thoughts.

Without taking if off the shelf, Claire now could conjure a few lines:

Age shall not weary them, nor the years condemn.
    At the going down of the sun and in the morning
    We will remember them.

Chapter Thirty-One

THINGS TO CELEBRATE

Determined not to bury her head under a pillow, Myra redoubled her efforts to go out and about, running the household errands, taking her parents to the movies to see pictures about the home front. All three enjoyed *Since You Went Away* and *The White Cliffs of Dover*, though none of the three wished to talk about the unspoken sadness of having so many men away, possibly missing, or worse, dead.

On days when her father was not feeling well, Myra manned the music store, dropping into the mayor's office at lunch time. She had volunteered to work on the bios of the fallen from around the area. Given the families' relationships, she started with the portrait of Lech Murkowski.

"You may have a hard time coaxing Myrtle to speak about her grandson at all, though if anyone can entice her, it will be you," Ilona said, pleased that her daughter had gotten her equilibrium back. She had decided not to inquire too deeply as to what had precipitated Myra's condition. She was not a person who believed in dwelling.

Once prodded and a little hard cider sipped, Mrs. Murkowski supplied Myra with a few details about Lech, enough to make her feel that she had unfairly dismissed the youngster for being, well, just ordinary. For one thing, he worked tirelessly after school at the Jewish cemetery, caring for the plots and cleaning the stones, the old woman explained, dabbing at her eyes in the telling.

"Lech was orphaned at eight. Been my mainstay all these years since." For another thing, she went on, brightening at the memory, he had an artistic bent, "like his father, like me in my youth, come to think of it. He was enamored of medieval cathedrals, stone bridges, and royal palaces. So excited about seeing Europe, getting to sketch some of those monuments."

Myra scribbled in her notebook. She needed the final particulars. "I have to ask, Mrs. Murkowski. What happened to him on D-Day?"

"What happened?" The old woman's wrinkled face turned crimson with rage. "He only just arrived abroad. He comes off a packed landing vessel onto that beach, along with thousands of others. Like sardines they were." Here, she paused to catch her breath. "Before he can take three steps, the Germans mow him down."

Myra patted her arm and poured them both more cider. Before she left, she passed on her parents' invitation to join them for dinner the following week. "Mother said your presence has been sorely missed. Plus, the Bauer sisters have another letter from Frederick. In addition, he sent pictures."

The guests for Ilona Kaminsky's dinner the following Friday night included not only Mrs. Murkowski but the Wallensteins and the Edelmanns, as well as Flora and Fannie Bauer. The mood was less lugubrious than it had been in some time, what with Allied advances up the boot of Italy and across France, the Germans ever relentless, but in retreat.

Myra had rung Claire, hoping she too would drive up, and perhaps bring news of Addison, or even of Tom, but she declined.

"A party on the top floor at Intelligence—finally, we have things to celebrate—so being a relative newcomer up there, it behooves me."

"Understood. Hopefully, soon. There or here."

Everyone ate heartily. Ilona figured the time had come to use up all her ration cards for the best cuts of beef she could cajole the butcher to part with. With Myra's help, she concocted a richly seasoned beef stroganoff accompanied by vegetables from her victory garden. Not to be outshone, Konrad brought out a vintage bottle of French Bordeaux and proposed a toast to the valiant partisans helping to drive the Nazis out of France. He was unusually ebullient.

Afterwards, and with a second, equally potent bottle of Italian Chianti, they all re-assembled in the parlor. Flora did the honors, reading Frederick's latest letter, while Fannie passed along the dozen photographs he had included, some of which he took, others presumably snapped by fellow soldiers.

Dear Mother and Aunt Fannie,

It is hard to contain our exuberance over here as, barring a surprise turn of events, we are racking up one victory after another—and now have the Germans on the run. And, like a hare, Mussolini has gone to ground and is being hunted down by Italian partisans.

We're now counting on our cohorts in France to finish their push north so that the enemy finally gets the message: drop your guns and raise your hands!

Pictures are worth a thousand words, so please enjoy and share these shots taken as we trudged up the Boot, in the rain, in the mud, up mountains, down valleys, every snap of a twig a possible danger signal.

But I cannot tell you the elation we felt draping the American flag from the Leaning Tower of Pisa or crossing the Arno River for a glimpse of the cupolas of Florence. These were followed more recently by our taking of Ravenna, Arezzo and countless villages dotting the Po Valley. Yes, ravages there are, everywhere, but also ravishing beauty. Both the country and its people. Despite all the hardships, I have grown fond of both, as you may judge from the pictures.

As usual, after the recitation of Frederick's letters, silence fell over the guests. In this instance, Myra thought his words opened themselves up to several interpretations. She did not know if this was intentional.

Soon, Fannie stood up to speak. "The photos have brief explanations on the back. I'll hand each of you one, and then everyone can pass theirs along, to your left. Otherwise, they'll be a free-for-all." Several people chuckled.

"He does look very thin," Mrs. Wallenstein said, about a shot taken in the town called Arezzo. "You'll have to fatten him up, Flora, when he gets back."

"I've got one with several soldiers overlooking the river. You can see a cathedral in the background," Mrs. Edelmann called out.

"And somehow—look at this one, everybody—they found time to play football. Frederick probably shot it. Never saw him pick up a ball in his life," Konrad said. Still ebullient.

What Myra keyed on, but no one else commented on, were two photos from Naples. In one, Frederick and another soldier were standing outside the San Carlo opera house. On the poster behind them, she made out the word *Tosca*. Flipping it over, the description read: *Naples, October 1943.*

In the other photo, Frederick is in a group, seemingly an entire family of eight or ten, unmistakably Italian. A young woman, with long dark hair and matching eyes, is positioned next to him, grasping his arm. They're all smiling, to one degree or another. On the back, the inscription read: *Napoli, the Ferrante family, February 1945.*

She compared the two shots until Mrs. Wallenstein held out her hand, passing her a picture of soldiers admiring a stained-glass window in Ravenna. Myra handed her two off in the other direction.

Might Frederick have received a three-day pass and decided to head back south to visit Naples? More than a year after he helped liberate the city...She did not dare ask, not wanting to signal her own curiosity.

"Oh, I nearly forgot," Flora suddenly piped up. "There's a postscript on another page. She picked up the letter and flipped to the third page. "Our hosts will certainly appreciate this," she added, nodding in the direction of Ilona and Konrad.

P.S. I do not wish to belabor my own exploits with regards to Monte Cassino, but I wanted the Kaminskys to know some news that may not have surfaced there in Alexandria. In the end, it was our brave Polish comrades who, after months of heavy fighting, took that hill and planted their flag atop. The Polish government-in-exile in London is having—and despite how hard-bitten we've all had to become, this has made everyone proud—precisely 48,498 Commemorative Crosses struck to honor each and every one of those soldiers.

"Hear, hear," Mr. Edelmann piped up. "What do you say, Konrad. Cigars, don't you think?"

Myra rose to retrieve her father's prized cigar box. There were just enough Monte Cristos from Havana to go around.

Down in New Orleans a few weeks later, Myra met her aunt for coffee on campus and apprised her of the mayor's plans back in Alexandria. Like most musicians, Lena rarely turned down an opportunity to perform, especially if her native Poland was being honored.

"I imagine a rousing polonaise will be in order," she said. "I shall be there, as the English expression goes, with bells on my toes."

"Precisely what we are all hoping," Myra replied without betraying her bemusement.

Later, she jumped on a streetcar to Canal Street to meet Claire at the Monteleone Hotel. To speak more freely, Claire suggested they sit at a corner table, away from the famous Carousel bar itself.

Myra eyed her friend closely. "Something's on your mind. What happened?"

"I've debated confiding this because of what you went through, but the more I thought about it, the more it seems like the right thing."

They both ordered champagne and toasted the latest Allied victories.

"Here's how it happened," Claire began, as usual *in media res*. "We were all in the midst of an office celebration, on the top floor where I now work." Myra looked bewildered. "You know, the victory at Iwo Jima, where they planted the flag that's in all the papers."

"And?"

"Only a few women work up there. I had to go down to the fifth to use the ladies' room. When I came out, he grabbed me from behind, dragging me into the nearby supply room. It's where we store all the old telex machines, mimeograph copiers, dictaphones."

Myra turned ashen. "Who on earth are you talking about, Claire?"

"I've mentioned him before. That junior lieutenant, obnoxious since day one. And no, I never led him on. I simply tried to be polite. You know as well as I do: the military is all about hierarchy."

"Okay...and what did he do? Please tell me he didn't—" Myra's hand began to tremble.

"He was huffing and puffing, and there was light from a small window. I could make out his eyes. Red, like they were on fire. He was calling me names, all the while maneuvering me up against a metal filing cabinet. His hands were all over me. You'll remember: my dark green taffeta dress, which I haven't had occasion to wear since our graduation lunch."

"Surely, that's not the point of this," Myra managed.

"Of course not. You know me. I digress when I'm embarrassed."

"Did you fight back, scream for help?"

"Yes, I think so, but it's hard to remember every detail. Anyway, when Forster put his hand up my leg—I do remember that—I freaked. I tried to push him off me, but when I couldn't, I reached up behind me. There was something on top of that cabinet. Cold to the touch. I grasped it and banged him over the head. Like so," she wound up, raising her arm, and making a motion as though wielding an ax.

Astonished, Myra put her hand to her open mouth. She glanced around, though no one was paying them any attention.

"Was he hurt?"

"He crumpled to the floor, bleeding from the side of his head, still cursing me. I sidestepped him and took the stairs back up."

Myra's eyes widened. "To the party? With all those people around..."

"Yes. I had the chance to do what you couldn't in your circumstances."

"What do you mean?"

"I no longer cared about my torn taffeta dress or my smeared lipstick or my mussed-up hair. I walked in, cut through all these people I work with, to the *sancta sanctorum* at the back. That's where Commander Lassiter was. My colleague Bernice was standing nearby and rushed to get me some water."

"What did the commander do?"

"He heard me out—and dispatched two officers to bring Forster back up. His head was still bleeding, but Bernice doctored it with the first aid kit attached to the wall."

"And you?"

"I felt disembodied, like looking down on myself. Yet strangely proud."

"Amazing. I don't know what to say. But I'm beginning to understand."

"I knew you would." Claire reached over and touched Myra's hand. "When the commander asked me for an official statement, he motioned for one of the stenographers to take it down. So I said, as calmly as I could, that the lieutenant had been verbally abusive in the past, but this incident was a physical assault. I defended myself by reaching for a weapon. I also apologized for breaking the Navy's trophy in the process."

Myra briefly closed her eyes and smiled.

"Several people chuckled over the trophy—some softball tournament they won back in '41."

"And what did the lieutenant have to say?"

"He would wait for legal representation from Annapolis or something. But after he regained his composure, he turned to me and suggested he had been 'overly forward,' having imbibed too much champagne."

"Already practicing his defense, as it were," Myra mused, shaking her head.

"Perhaps. Anyway, the amazing thing was when Bernice escorted me out."

"How so?"

"The women who were at the party, still a dozen or so at that point, all applauded. Some of the men joined in."

Chapter Thirty-Two

EVERYTHING EVERYWHERE

Victory in Europe did come within a few hectic months, Roosevelt sadly not living long enough to see the final surrender. Thereafter, in lightning quick succession in early May, Mussolini was strung up by his own countrymen and Hitler took his own life in his underground bunker.

It had taken well-nigh four years of brutal combat to get to this point. U.S. and British troops had finally dislodged the Germans from Italy; simultaneously, they and other Allies had driven them definitively out of France; the Russians did their part from the East, arriving at the gates of Berlin as Hitler did himself in. However begrudged, piecemeal and spottily accepted, unconditional German surrender finally came on May 7, 1945, the terms accepted by Allied commanders in Reims, France.

At Fort Lincoln, spring had sprung by then, the flower boxes that many detainees determinedly cultivated were full of color, a symbol of the hope that so many now felt might be attainable. If they did not celebrate as deliriously as their fellow Americans who were not incarcerated did, they nonetheless breathed a sigh of relief. Most all raised a glass or two or three to hail the end to hostilities and augur new beginnings—for themselves as well as for the country.

A festive dinner and a dance were soon organized; practitioners of polkas and the waltz as well as swing dancers took to the gymnasium floor that night. In the following days, phone privileges for every man were extended, and free-of charge, though, for security's sake, no trunk calls to Europe were allowed.

Dieter was one of the first in line. He called his ex-wife, who was surprisingly pleasant, and from her got the phone number of his estranged son. "We've bonded. He's already back from France with nary a scratch. We're going to meet up again—once Ingrid and I tie the knot." Tom gave him a slap on the back. "What about you, Tom? You getting in line?"

In the moment, he could think of no one to call. Mr. Caxton? Lena Walenska? Lady Monceau? None of them made sense in the circumstances. As much as he longed to hear Claire's voice, it was clear to him he had less to offer her now than he did eighteen months ago. His only solace was to think she and Myra might have had fun spending the money he left them and have spared a thought for him in doing so.

He went through his thin wallet and pulled out a short list of names.

Once the line for long distance calls petered out, he got his turn in the booth. He rang Bennie.

"Bowled over, I is bowled over, Mr. Tom. Wherever is you at?"

The warmth of the black man's voice made Tom tear up. Bennie had continued to work in the shipyard and was now a foreman. "We is still churning out those damn boats, Mr. Tom. Tanks, too. They still battlin' Japs over there. Every month a new island we is takin' over. We soon be in Okinawa. Gettin' close, gettin' close."

As for what he termed their "mutual friends," Bennie brought him up to date. Marie Monceau had passed away back in the winter, her only daughter having taken up residence at the main house. "Miss Claire done returned to her parents. Still working for the Navy.

She took only a few things, carrying that chess set in her arms, whiles I put all them books and records in the back of her car."

Tom could hear children's voices in the background and the faint sound of a trumpet playing. Of a sudden he was overcome. As much as he wanted to ask more about Claire and the people in her life, he desisted. "I will see you soon, Bennie. Likely within a month. Beer and po-boys on me."

"I is always ready for that. A sight for sore eyes you will be."

For Tom, the end of the war in Europe was bittersweet. He had followed the battles as closely as he could, and he imagined that things would never be quite the same for the men who had fought them. He also knew that his own kind had largely been decimated by the Nazis, while many around him and in the world at large had stuck their heads in the sand.

He happened to be with his friends Dieter and Ingrid at a movie screening in the gym when the first horrific pictures began to surface of the liberation of Mauthausen in Austria by the U.S. Army and of Auschwitz in Poland by Russian troops. The couple exchanged a worried glance. Then Dieter leaned over to his friend. "They will be punished, those that did this. Never fear on that count, mate."

What Tom hadn't confided to them, or to Gunther, was that his own parents, for all he knew, might have been among those interred at one or another of the camps in northern Germany. "*Neuengamme*," he whispered to himself, determined to find out more about the fate of those prisoners, even if it meant returning to Germany himself.

It did not take long for more disturbing news to make its way across the Atlantic.

Some citizens from in town soon brought batches of recent newspapers and magazines to the camp so that detainees might gain a better understanding of how things had wrapped up. As soon as he got wind of that, Tom re-arranged his work schedule.

Scattered across the table in the library were copies of the *New York Times*, the *Boston Globe*, the *Washington Post*, and several magazines which featured pictures from the various military ceremonies. He read the entirety of the front pages and scanned the inside ones. He missed lunch. He read on, catching details of Hitler's final day in his bunker, and disagreements among the Allies regarding the future of Berlin. Three hours had passed.

On the point of rising to leave, his eyes snagged on a headline that included the words *Lübeck Bay*. He sat back down. Soon his mouth gaped open. He looked around. One other person sat at the other end of the table, thumbing through *Life* magazines. Every now and then, the man quietly whistled, as if in disbelief.

Tom lowered his gaze. Not ten days earlier, he learned, some 10,000 concentration camp survivors, mainly from *Neuengamme*, had been conveyed to Lübeck itself and then, clueless of their eventual destination, were marched to the shores of the Baltic and herded onto ships. The paper referred to them as "floating concentration camps."

Where they were to end up was still conjecture, the paper said. What happened next was not in dispute. Mistaking the barely seaworthy vessels for German transports carrying Nazis on the run, Royal Air Force pilots bombed the ships. Untold casualties resulted. An investigation by the British government as to what went wrong was immediately undertaken.

In shock, Tom shuffled back through the other papers, finding one dated a couple of days later. Inside, he spotted a photo of a burning ship, identified as the *Arcona*, with a caption that estimated 6,000 former camp prisoners perished in the ensuing fire or drowned as the ship sank.

He exhaled in horror, and, his hand shaking, picked up his glass of water.

The man at the other end of the table looked up. "You okay? Mr. Stone, right?" Still dazed, Tom stared vacantly at the man. "Reading all this takes a toll. It ain't ever going to be the same in this world."

"*Ja, ja,*" Tom burbled back, then gulped from his glass.

Reading further, Tom soon discovered that the same fiery end befell the hapless passengers on the other two commandeered ships, the *Deutschland* and the *Thielbek*.

Rarely had he felt so emptied out. For several minutes, he tried to steady his pulse. And make sense of what he had come across.

What, he asked himself, *had his cousin Jonas intimated in that letter from Oxford?* What had Lena Walenska mentioned early on as to what likely happened to local Lübeckers when the Gestapo came knocking? If a citizen had even a drop of Jewish blood or was otherwise deemed undesirable, he or she would have ended up in *Neuengamme*. Including his own parents.

And now this *dénouement*? More tragically ironic than the ending of a Wagner opera. The papers referred to it as "a terrible incidence of friendly fire."

Tom pulled out a handkerchief to wipe off his face. Looking down, he noticed another photo from the scene, less dramatic, at the end of the article. It appeared to be of a smaller vessel, larger than a tugboat but smaller than a cruise liner. The caption read: "Anchored at the port, the *Athen*, which was ferrying another thousand camp survivors, was not damaged by the bombing in Baltic Bay."

So gobsmacked he was, Tom would have given anything for someone with whom to go over all this. As kind as some of them at Fort Lincoln were, he now desperately wanted to be with people in New Orleans—and to get back, by hook or by crook, to Germany.

Lists, he murmured to himself. Whatever else they have done to us Jews, they keep lists of them.

A few days later, as Tom and Gunther put away their chess pieces, they decided to walk over in the sunshine to check their mailboxes in Bldg. A.

On the bulletin board inside, they noticed that many detainees had received a precise date for their so-called exit interviews.

"I guess this means they're going to be letting us out soon," Gunther said, scanning to see if his name yet had an assignment day. "If not, we're going to break out of here. What do you say, Tom: had enough of this place?"

He laughed. "A little more patience. I doubt they want us around anymore than we want to be here."

Next to Gunther's name, *pending* was written in red ink. There was a blank next to Tom's name.

Neither made a comment.

Over at the mail dispatch station, Gunther pulled a letter out of his cubbyhole, with a smear of lipstick on the back of the envelope. "It's from my erstwhile girlfriend back in Hoboken," he said, feigning disinterest.

"Looks like she's still interested," Tom commented drily.

Gunther deflected. "And what's this you got? Looks official."

Anxious, Tom opened it on the spot, read the typed request and took a deep breath. "It's the Immigration Service. Looks like my naturalization papers are coming through. And seems my exit interview will be contingent on the State Department, whatever that means," he said.

"Don't worry. They never had nothing on you. As for me, I'm going to miss our chess games."

"Me too, Gunther. Teach your girlfriend. I played the game with mine, back in New Orleans."

"Did she ever checkmate you?"

Tilting his head in that considered way he had, Tom replied. "Yeah, she did. In more ways than one."

A month or two later, camp director Dirksen sent a runner to summon Tom. He was found on his haunches repairing loose siding to the camp cafeteria. "You've got visitors—from the U.S. government." Tom blanched. "You might want to shower first. They're wearing suits and ties."

In fifteen minutes and out of breath from running, he presented himself to the director at Bldg. B.

"Seems the government is looking for people like you," Dirksen said. Now that the war in Europe was over, his more genial side had taken over.

"What do you mean, sir, *like me*?"

"You acquitted yourself well here, son. They got wind of it." Dirksen winked, conspiratorial. "I suspect there's going to be lots to do back in your home country."

The director was not wrong.

For a couple of hours, Tom met with two officials from the Truman administration on a recruitment mission. They both had on dark blue suits and red ties with American flags pinned to their lapels. It occurred to Tom that he did not at this point in his life own a single tie, let alone an actual suit. He stood at attention.

"Relax, Mr. Stone—or Mr. Steinberg. No need for alarm," the first one said. "By the way, I'm Conway and he's Davis." He snapped open a briefcase and pulled out a flip binder.

"We've studied your file, Mr. Stone, and you fit the bill," Davis said. He paused to light a cigarette. "If you're interested in returning to Germany and serving our—now your—government, we're prepared to make an offer. A year-long contract to begin with."

"But what would you need me for?"

"You're a German native, right, and you *sprechen sie Deutsch*, right?" Tom nodded his head. "In addition, we understand you have an architectural degree, which you obtained in Berlin, and worked on amphibious landing vessels in New Orleans. How long was that for, Mr. Stone?"

"About eighteen months, sir. Until I was—" He failed to find the right word.

Conway looked at their notes. "Until you were nabbed by the FBI and ended up here, correct?"

"That sums it up."

"That's the past, Mr. Stone. What about now? Any family here? A girlfriend waiting for you somewhere?"

"No, sir. Not anymore."

Davis snorted. "How about back in Germany?"

Flustered, Tom hesitated. His left leg began to shake. He did his best to quiet it. "I'm Jewish, sir. It's unclear if my parents are alive."

Neither official spoke for a minute. Davis brought another cigarette out of his pack, lit it, and held it out. To be polite, Tom took it.

"Pretty horrific stuff over there," Conway muttered.

To avoid becoming emotional, Tom shifted gears. "What specifically are you looking for from civilians like me?"

"Liaising with the population, gaining their trust and cooperation, translating the essentials," Conway tossed out. "And in your particular case, lending your expertise to reconstruction projects in and around the city."

"Keep in mind, Berlin is to be divvied up between the four victorious powers. This is going to be a tricky dance. We need folks who can help with the steps," Davis chimed in.

At that point, director Dirksen poked his head in to say their other prospective candidate was waiting outside. Tom put out his cigarette.

"Well, Mr. Stone, if you're interested, we'll leave this packet with you. However, things are moving fast. The President, as well as the Department, wants folks on the ground ASAP," Conway said.

"You do know what that means, right?"

"I do indeed, sir. How long would I have before leaving here?"

Davis consulted another folder on the table. "You would be cleared to leave here within a couple of weeks and then would have another couple to do whatever—wrap up your affairs, say your good-byes. You'd be shipped out from New York come the beginning of August."

Although he tossed and turned for three nights, weighing the pros and cons of uprooting himself and returning to his ravaged homeland, Tom knew in his heart what he had to do. His parents had sacrificed for him, and as long as there was a glimmer of hope that one or both might have survived, he would do what he could to find out.

Nor did he dislike the opportunity of doing something worthwhile for both his new country as well as for the old—and be paid for it.

He walked over to the director's office on July 4th, a day he thought appropriate for such a decision, and asked Dirksen to place the call to the number Conway and Davis had provided.

"Well done, son. I'm sure you'll be an asset to the country. Remember, one thing is winning the war; the other is winning the peace."

From what the Carrolltons had gleaned from the increasingly downbeat letters from their son, and what the Endicotts had pieced together from disjointed calls with Addison, the two childhood friends remained in the thick of things in the Pacific. Not that they were unusual in that regard. It would have been hard for any young man to sugarcoat how bloody the battles to liberate the Solomon Islands or those like Saipan and Leyte in the Philippines Sea had been.

From the little Claire could intuit from her brother's calls or letters, the occasional failures of intelligence-gathering, which might mislead troops or leave them in harm's way, had taken a mental toll on him. Worse, the ceaseless brutality, not to mention hunger, thirst, lice, and land crabs that the Marines on the ground endured, had likely shaken Richard to the core.

In any case, neither of the two men wrote frequently now, and when they did, they kept their letters brisk. The seagulls they had once waxed lyrical about had long taken wing.

Neither family had heard more than a peep from their respective sons since the hard-fought victory on Iwo Jima, which had been plastered all over the newspapers, and described in triumphalist tones. Claire found that tone off-putting. She relied on more sober assessments, like the ones she heard at work. Often, she noticed Commander Lassiter shaking his head or muttering about miscues and mishaps during one skirmish or another.

A cryptic note from Richard arrived a few weeks after Iwo Jima.

"After mud, maggots and mayhem to last a lifetime, we've passed the baton to the B-29 fliers. We done our bit. Those guys can have at it!"

Which was opened and read aloud by his mother at the Sunday dinner table where the Carrolltons now routinely gathered with the Endicotts.

No one spoke for a minute or two, unsure what to make of the letter's tone.

Edward volunteered a strictly military assessment. "I guess our bombers can now reach Japan proper without refueling, which is a good thing."

Claire nodded her head; her father was right.

Shortly thereafter, Harold felt the urge to opine. "I've done calculations. The boy has been in almost every major battle since Guadalcanal. You'd think by now he'd be up for a medal, right, Helen?"

His wife turned pale. Embarrassed, the Endicotts stared at their plates.

Too irate to speak, Claire got up from the table, slapped her linen napkin down next to her plate, and left the room. Had there been a door to slam, she would have done so.

The next day at work, Claire sought out Bernice. "Much to say. My treat."

Over lunch in the warehouse district, they talked briefly about the incident with Forster.

"I cannot speak for the men in the office, Claire, but the women are all in awe. None of us know what we'll be doing when this is all over—I mean, who's going to hire Teresa to rivet when there are no more tanks to build?" she asked, not at all facetiously. "My point is, the women admire that you came forward. That you are not afraid of these men, or hopefully any men, whatever we all end up doing in this afterlife."

Claire blushed. "Tell you the truth, my reflexes took over. But, in retrospect, I credit Myra for what I did." Bernice looked puzzled. "She found herself in a much worse situation at Camp Claiborne. Sadly, she had no way to identify the culprits, or to be believed that such a thing happened. It took a toll."

"I see, or at least I think I do. You seized the chance, and you've put it in the rear-view mirror?"

"Exactly."

They ordered coffee and lemon cookies.

"What else is on your mind?"

"What comes next in the Pacific. My brother's there, as is our best friend from childhood."

"You know how tight-lipped Owen, Commander Lassiter, is. But, between us, Okinawa has been circled in red on the giant map."

"Soon?"

"Maneuvers already on neighboring islets. It's all they're talking about in the Monday strategy session," Bernice continued, keeping her voice low. "When to give the green light to the main assault."

After studying the island's relation to the mainland of Japan, Claire lingered late one weekday to catch the commander alone. When he looked up to find her in front of his desk, she started right in. Could he, she asked, indicate the specific aircraft carriers which would be in the vicinity of Okinawa in coming weeks.

"Is your brother likely on one of them, Miss Endicott?"

"Yes, sir. He doesn't tell us much."

"That's why he's in Intelligence," the Commander replied, enjoying the exchange. She managed a faint smile. "As you might

323

imagine, a number of flattops are involved—the *Bunker Hill*, the *Enterprise*, the *Wasp*. Sometimes, when there's damage to one or another, officers are moved around. I'll see what I can find out."

"Plus," she kept on, "my brother and I have a close friend, a Marine with the First, who's been everywhere, from Guadalcanal to Iwo Jima, another called Peleliu in-between those."

The commander's face clouded over. "Not our finest hour, that last one," he muttered.

Claire thought better than to inquire further.

"What is the lucky young man's name, Miss Endicott?"

Disconcerted though she was, Claire did not correct the officer. "It's Carrollton, Richard Carrollton. He is an NCO, unless things have changed."

The commander gave her a penetrating look. She stood there awkwardly, waiting for him to dismiss her. Instead, in a brisk tone, he said, "By the way, Robert Forster pleaded no contest, was stripped of his rank, and will serve six months in detention." After a beat, he added, "All because you did a brave thing."

"Thank you, sir. For everything."

Chapter Thirty-Three
ONE WAR DOWN, ANOTHER TO GO

With the war in Europe at an end, the country began to celebrate, especially as the first wave of soldiers and sailors began to return home.

Alexandria did not let itself be outdone. The town was festooned, bunting hung up and down Main Street, a fancy platform set up at city hall for the great and good to expound on "our victories." The date of the festivities was set for May 18.

Lena Walenska, who had remained a local celebrity, had graciously agreed to perform a military polonaise, courtesy of Chopin, to honor the Polish contribution to the Allied victory, while the town's local orchestra and vocalists would feature marches and patriotic songs. Myra was asked to read out the names of the local men among the fallen, and it shocked her to see that there were more than two hundred. Local restaurants were donating food but a dozen women, including Ilona Kaminsky and Winifred Wallenstein, had been volunteered, as it were, to provide their own specialties for the VIP buffet. A couple of swing bands were hired for the dancing.

Flora and Fannie Bauer had hoped that Frederick would have

been discharged by now, as they were looking forward to an announcement about his medal, but he had written to say he had been "delayed" in Italy for another few months.

Around the twelfth of May, Myra rang Claire to firm up the invitation to her and her parents. She had booked a room in a small hotel in the center of town for the latter two and expected Claire to spend the night with her, her aunt in the guest room.

Claire picked up, clearly preoccupied.

"Are you okay? I've booked a nice room for your parents if you don't mind staying with me."

"Sorry, Myra. I'm at sixes and sevens. Everyone's excited about Europe, but the fighting is brutal in the Pacific. The Japanese have bombed one of our carriers. The *Bunker Hill*. Lots of casualties. We don't know if Addison was onboard."

"Oh my. That's terrible." She swallowed hard. "How did you find out?"

"The sixth floor. Commander Lassiter is letting us know things as soon as word comes in."

"I see." Having tried to put Addison out of her own mind, despite his occasional note to her—carefully polite, bordering on impersonal—Myra had given up picturing a future with him. Still, her heart sank. "Have you heard anything directly?"

"Not in the last week or two. Not from Richard either. As you know, he's on the island. Okinawa, that is. The Japanese are holed up in underground bunkers. Civilians are caught in the crossfire, or forced to toss bombs themselves. Misery all round."

Claire's voice seemed to quaver. Myra thought she might be crying.

"I don't know what to say, except that things are going our way. All this will soon come to an end, and they'll be home."

"Yes, I believe it too." Claire paused a minute, then remembered the purpose of the call. "And yes, we'll do our best to be there on the eighteenth."

When she hung up, Myra realized she had forgotten to mention that Tom had rung her days before. It was the first time they had spoken since he had been handcuffed and led away at Camp Claiborne. He sounded well, his voice deeper, richer in tone. He was older, and free.

"How are you, Tom, and where are you?"

"Still in North Dakota, but not for long. I have an opportunity ahead of me."

"An opportunity?" she asked.

"From the State Department, to go abroad, back to Berlin to help rebuild."

Silence at the other end.

"That, that sounds amazing," she replied, her tone not fully convincing.

"There's a reason I'm telling you first, Myra. If you haven't already, you will soon begin to absorb what has happened to our people. But my own parents, they might still be alive. I have to know what I have to know. About my childhood friends as well."

"I understand. But what about Claire? Are you coming home first?"

"I am coming home, as you put it. Briefly. As for Claire, I'll have to see for myself."

After the conversation, Myra could have kicked herself. Was she or was she not authorized to say something to her best friend? Perhaps it were best not. Tom would be his own surprise. What she *would* do in the interim: have her father withdraw Tom's money from the bank. He could treat his new comrades in Berlin to a lot of beer with that. The thought made her smile.

Back on Carondelet, the atmosphere on the sixth floor of Naval Intelligence was more tense than anything Claire had felt when she worked on the lower floor. The pressure to get cables passed through, accurately and quickly, had intensified. So too the task of decoding the ever more challenging intercepts that fell on the desks of staffers.

Once the assault on Okinawa began in early April, few staffers dared to take lunch breaks. Po-boys and gumbo were brought in on a daily basis. The gatherings in Lassiter's office included top brass from other bases and folks Claire had only casually glimpsed from the other floors. The door was shut more often than not; voices were often raised from within.

When she did see the commander, either taking a coffee break or assigning a task, he did not linger to banter or, as had been his wont, admire the view of the city streets from the windows. Bernice imitated her boss, scurrying about with purpose, rarely stopping to chat.

What the military had hoped—that the battle to take Okinawa would be swift and that surrender would soon follow—appeared to be an inaccurate assessment. Everyone was trying to reassess, recalibrate, and save lives.

All in all, Claire thought, the moment was jarring. The country was in celebratory mode upon VE Day, though the news and the pictures from "the other war," as people referred to it, as though it were a distraction, were grim.

Around 5 p.m. every afternoon, Bernice usually entered what was called the Intel Annex to rip the wires and deliver the casualty figures from the front. Sometimes names were supplied, especially if high-ranking officers had been wounded or killed.

During the week of May 11, all hell broke loose on and around Okinawa. Kamikazes struck the carrier *Bunker Hill*, killing or wounding dozens and forcing officers to transfer to other vessels. Two days later, the *Enterprise* suffered even greater damage, a dozen sailors killed, many more injured.

Claire racked her brain to remember what Addison had said about his own movements, changing from one ship to another, depending on the task at hand. Where he was now was unknowable.

On her own one evening, she slipped into a movie theater for diversion, but before the feature began, she was bombarded with the most dramatic newsreel she had ever seen. Monsoon rains in the Sea of Japan had begun to turn the terrain on Okinawa into what the narrator called "a muddy morass of maggot-infested bodies." The latest skirmish was unfolding around a place dubbed Sugar Loaf Hill, where hand-to-hand combat had raged for days, each side claiming control two or three times in a single day.

By the time Claire got home that evening, she could not recall a single scene of the movie she had spent her ticket on.

On Friday, she worked late, hoping that she could cajole Bernice into joining her for coffee or a drink—anything to relieve the tension. Suddenly, her colleague appeared at her shoulder.

"The commander wants to see you if you can spare a minute," Bernice said without affect, turning away as soon as she delivered the message. Claire slipped her briefcase back in her desk drawer and walked into the *sancta sanctorum*. Lassiter stood up. Claire bit her lip.

"It appears, Miss Endicott, that your, your friend, Corporal Carrollton, is among the wounded in the ongoing assault," he began, his voice all business. He lowered his gaze to the folder in front of him. "At Sugar Loaf Hill. Still an ongoing operation there, but he and several others were stretchered out. They've been ferried to the *Comfort* and will be receiving the best care possible."

Feeling wobbly, Claire steadied herself against the front edge of the commander's outsized desk. Swallowing the acid in her throat, she made an effort to form a question. "Do you know, sir, if his parents have been alerted? Or, for that matter, my brother?"

The commander took a deep breath. "If his wounds are significant, and communications allow, yes, it's likely. More likely, your brother, who is *in situ*, has already been informed."

She nodded, too many scenarios now racing through her head. In a feeble voice, she said, "Thank you, commander, for letting me know."

"Not at all. Sorry for your—" he stopped himself. "for your

fiancé." Once again, she did not correct him. "We'll hope for the best," he added by way of dismissal.

Distracted on the streetcar home, Claire overshot her stop, making her arrival home later than usual. She berated herself for not pressing for more details of Richard's injuries.

All the lights in the front of the house were on as she fumbled with the front door key. She heard voices, strained, argumentative. The Carrolltons had come over. It was useless to try to sneak upstairs. The parlor was in the way.

"Ah, my dear, finally. We have something upsetting to tell you," Helen declared when she appeared.

"It regards Richard," Esther specified. "The Navy rang Helen and Harold a couple of hours ago. He has been wounded."

"I was informed as well," Claire said, "at work. But no details were available, other than he is aboard the hospital ship."

Ignoring the women, Harold, who was pacing the room, began to castigate Edward for not having a direct line to his own son. "Surely, Addison could be called upon to check this thing out and let us know what happened. How my son got himself into this mess."

Claire glanced at her father, seated, trying to smoke his pipe. He looked peeved. "It's not a Mardi Gras ball over there, Harold. At every step our boys take, there may be incoming," Edward shot back.

Harold muttered under his breath, something about Richard being a consummate bungler. Everyone ignored him. Dyspeptic though he was, he soon sat down and poured himself some of the Endicotts' cognac.

As soon as she could, Claire took her leave, telling her mother she would ring Myra to cancel their plans to attend the celebration in Alexandria. Mounting the stairs, she overheard Richard's mother say, "You'd think she'd be overcome by this, wouldn't you? Your daughter's become quite hard-nosed."

She did not linger to hear if anyone objected to the insult.

Not twelve hours after the dozen Marines trying to take back the steep hill on Okinawa got strafed, Addison was alerted that one of the seriously wounded—only dire cases were removed to the *Comfort* —had in his delirium called out, insistently, for "Addie, Addie, my love," to be at his side.

It took the medical team some time to figure to whom Corporal Carrollton was referring.

Having just deplaned after a quick tour of the airstrips secured so far on the island, Addison was whisked over to the *Comfort*. He found Richard sedated, a leg raised aloft by a pulley, an arm secured in a cast, his ribcage bandaged. Several cots down the row of wounded, sheets were being pulled over two other Marines.

"Corporal Carrollton had been calling for you, off and on for hours, sir. It took us a while to figure it out," the attending physician explained.

"We assumed he meant his girlfriend back home. No accounting for the effects of these meds," one of the nurses hastened to add.

Although disconcerted, Addison immediately peppered them with questions. Richard's diagnosis, they suggested, was not among the worst. "Shrapnel in the thigh, a few broken bones. Given the givens, he's a lucky man."

"I'll let his parents know," Addison replied. "And his girlfriend too."

He did so forthwith with one of the few letters addressed to Claire, not to his parents.

She received it in the days after Sugar Loaf Hill was taken and after radio reports that one of the Marines from Richard's division had planted the American flag over the most revered monument on the island. The war correspondent Ernie Pyle reported that the flag was the very same battered one that had been raised the year before on Peleliu.

In the Endicott parlor that evening, Harold had groused about that as well. "Could have been our son to do the honors if he hadn't gotten into such a jam."

Disgusted at hearing such a thing, as though getting wounded was Richard's own fault, Claire got up from her chair, the unopened letter from Addison in her hand. She bid them all good night and left the room.

"Aren't you going to share your brother's letter with us?" her father called out.

Pausing on the landing above, she called back. "I think not. It's addressed to me."

"My, my, aren't we..." she could not help but hear Helen declaim.

"What, Helen?" Claire heard her mother challenge her friend.

"Whatever. Headstrong will do."

Sighing, Claire went into her room, switched on a lamp, and sat at her desk.

Dear Sis,

Share this or not as you see fit. I have visited with Richard twice since he was wounded at Sugar Loaf. Assuming you have access to casualty figures yourself there on Carondelet, you will take solace in knowing how lucky he is. Amazingly so, given all the action he has seen over the past three years. But it is my feeling, from what I've noted of the Marines over here, unseen wounds are the trickiest, and likely to be the more challenging to treat. Do keep this in mind for when Richard is discharged and able to return home. We've known him all our lives. He will need you. And I have always admired your spunk. If anyone can straighten him out and set him on the right path, it is YOU. (Perhaps best you do not share this: the Carrolltons have never understood their son.)

Your loving brother, Addison

P.S. You will likely know of the jaw-dropping number of Japanese troops who have committed suicide and the civilians who have sliced

their throats on Okinawa rather than surrender. We still have our
work cut out for us. But never doubt. Hirohito will finally recognize the
futility of it all and we can all go home again.

Definitely not a communication that Claire thought wise to share. She turned out the light and willed herself to sleep.

Part Four

1945-1948

*Downtown spot for coffee
and conversation 1940*

Chapter Thirty-Four
UNTIL WE MEET AGAIN

New Orleans was sweltering as never before in early August, or so thought Tom after two interminable winters in North Dakota. His duffel bag slung over his shoulder, and looking like just another returning soldier, he made his way from the train station to downtown. Despite the heat, the city felt livelier than he remembered it.

The U.S. Army or the State Department—he wasn't sure which —had booked him into a modest but reputable enough hotel not far from Canal Street. Easily checked in, and saluted by the clerk, he showered, changed clothes, and, too keyed up to rest, headed into the Quarter. Soon the sound of music and laughter—a monkey grinder, black kids tap dancing for pennies, fancy women coming and going from fancy restaurants, vendors hawking voodoo dolls—lifted his spirits.

Having alerted no one of his arrival, Tom declined for the moment to look in on Philip Caxton and gave a wide berth to Mrs. Jennings' boarding house. By 6 p.m. his feet ached, and his stomach growled. Over a plate of fried oysters and a cold mug of beer at the Acme Bar, he considered what to do for the next three days. All he could come up with was pay a visit to the cabinetry workshop, the shipyard up at the lake, where he hoped to find Bennie, and drum up the courage to search out Claire.

He easily managed two out of three.

His visit to Caxton's brought tears to the old man's eyes.

"If you weren't headed back to Germany, I'd find a way to put you in charge," Philip Caxton said. Tom looked indulgently skeptical. "I ain't got the strength for this anymore, especially dealing with the ladies and their wobbly table legs. Mine are now worse than theirs!"

Found with a supervisor's cap up at the lake, Bennie would not take no for an answer when Tom showed up. The erstwhile handyman dragged him away from the construction site for a meal at his spiffed-up home in the ninth ward, more people than Tom could count crowding the buffet table.

"The war's been real bad for some folks, and real good for others," Bennie said over helpings of jambalaya. "I'm lucky to be among the latter," he added. "Like for you, Mr. Tom, building things keeps me on my toes, more than all them flowers in Lady Monceau's garden."

Tom nodded in agreement, but did not inquire about the guest house, or what the old lady's daughter planned to do with the place.

"I knows what you thinking, Mr. Tom. Miss Claire and what she be up to. War be winding down. Lots of young men coming home, lots of young men," he repeated, to make sure his friend got the point.

Tom did and didn't much like it.

One of Bennie's children, pigtails pinned up on her head, butted in. "My pop says you been in the big house all this time away. He right or what?" she asked.

"She mean the jailhouse, Mr. Tom. Is what we folks call it, seeing as we're in there so often," Bennie added.

Tom smiled. "Up there, Rosie, they called it a camp or a fort. I was 'interred,' because I am German. Or something like that."

"Well, you be out now, which is all that counts," Bennie said, raising his beer mug. Tom did the same.

That night, unused to a hotel, he slept fitfully. When awake, he rehearsed what he would say if he did manage to see Claire. If things were different, he reasoned, he might call her on the phone or show up unannounced at the Endicott home. But she might hang up on him or her father might come to the door. He decided not to risk either outcome.

Instead, after a cup of strong coffee the next morning, he rung the Kaminsky home in Alexandria. No one picked up. He could have used Myra's moral support. And more time.

Without either, Tom decided to do what he could to bolster his case, Bennie's refrain still playing in his head. *Lots of young men, lots of young men.* He marched over to Canal Street and took one of the Maison Blanche elevators to Men's Wear. Eventually, he settled on a beige linen suit, a couple of dress shirts and three ties, as well as a pair of dress shoes.

"Those loafers just came in," the clerk remarked. "Been a long wait for genuine leather. The war, you know."

Back at the hotel, the receptionist handed him an envelope along with his key. He looked flummoxed. Up in his room, he opened it.

A check fell out along with a short note.

Tom, I took the liberty of sending your money to the hotel. It has accrued while sitting in the Hibernia here in Alexandria. I trust it will come in handy abroad. You should have no trouble cashing it now with your government I.D. Myra

After a nap, a shower, and a shave, Tom ripped off the price tags and put on the first suit he had bought in years. The new shoes pinched but looked too good not to wear. He paced the room to break them in. Around 4 p.m., he grabbed up his straw hat and crossed over

Canal Street where he lingered around the various office buildings that faced onto Carondelet.

The war in the Pacific was still ongoing. No reason to think Claire would not be at her desk at Naval Intelligence. To steady his nerves, he pulled out a pack of Camels, lit one with the silver lighter Gunther had given him upon departure, and waited.

At 5 p.m., a clock above the entrance to the nearby American Bank chimed the hour. He stubbed out his cigarette and crossed the street. Soon, he spotted Claire making her exit. She was dressed in black, odd on such a summer day. She shook out her blond curls and turned her head back toward the ornate entrance. A tall man in uniform, presumably an officer, was holding the door for another young woman. They both stopped to speak to Claire. The man shook her hand and departed. The other woman walked arm-in-arm with Claire toward the streetcar stop. To avoid being seen, Tom slunk into the shadows, pulling his hat down on his forehead.

The two young women hugged at the streetcar stop. Only Claire hopped on. Tom hesitated, then bolted across the street to jump on the back. The car was crowded. He remained standing at the back exit, intent on looking out the window. The ride up St Charles Avenue seemed interminable. He could feel his heart pounding. He did not dare turn his gaze to the front of the car.

But he had come this far, he told himself, and could not go back. Not after the years the two had spent together. An image of pale flesh in the moonlight flitted across his mind.

Claire got off at the front entrance along with several other passengers at the corner of Henry Clay Street. At the last instant, Tom jumped off the back exit. Without looking back, Claire crossed the street. Then, abruptly, she turned and waited, a vaguely combative look on her face.

Game over, he thought. He approached, but slowly.

"If you are worried, my parents are out—at a church service. Where I should be as well."

Tom did not follow her words or recognize her tone. Before he could think what to respond, she turned toward the Endicott home. Refusing to give up, he caught up with her. They walked in silence, except for the clack of her high heels. They weren't that high, but they appeared to him as shiny as his own. He thought of the times he had unbuckled ones like those, removed them, and worked his hands up her slim legs.

He had to say something.

"I was hoping to see you before I left the country. But I fear I'm intruding. You are otherwise preoccupied."

Claire slowed her pace, and then halted altogether. The street was deserted except for a couple of kids on tricycles.

"I'm sorry. There's no way you would have known." Tom braced himself. His eyes downshifted to her left hand. There was nothing on it. "My brother Addison was killed. On Okinawa. Toward the end of hostilities. Needless to say..." She turned her head away, her eyes starting to fill up.

Without thinking, he reached out to embrace her. She did not resist. She let herself nestle into him for a moment, her limbs going limp.

Tom trembled from the touch of her. "I'm without words. I understood he was based on the carriers. Shielded from harm's way."

Wiping her cheek, she collected herself and stepped back. "They came to the front door to tell us. My mother answered. All she heard was something about a downed plane. And then fainted. My father did little better." Claire's voice cracked at the telling.

"And how are they now?"

"It's only been six weeks. They go through the motions. I have kept a few details from them, as they would make it worse."

"Like what?"

"The observation plane the four were flying on." Tom looked confused. "The Stinson Sentinel is a reliable aircraft," she said, as if by rote. "Apparently, this one had mechanical issues. It crashed while surveying the ruins of a place called Nahu, the old capital of

Okinawa. My parents believe the enemy fired at them." She shook her head again. "Not that it matters."

Tom took her hand. "I want to know how you are."

"Time passes."

"Yes, it does. In my case, apparently too much," he replied, pausing a beat. She said nothing. "Meaning, Claire, I still love you and want, somehow, to be with you."

His words washed over her. Her face remained expressionless. "I understood you are going back to Germany, to work for the U.S. government."

"It was the best way to get out of detention—and to find out if my parents are alive. There's a chance they may be."

"Reasons enough."

"But us? What will become of us, Claire?"

She started walking again. She pursed her lips as she often did when considering a move. As when, he recalled, deciding to take his bishop with her knight, or to sacrifice a pawn in order to check his king.

He did not press her to answer. Before he knew it, they were standing in front of her house. The once luxuriant potted ferns on the front porch looked stressed, he noticed. Perhaps in their grief, neither she nor her parents had the wherewithal to water them.

Claire started to ascend the steps, but suddenly hesitated. Instead, she took his hand. "To your question: there is no *us*, Tom. Not anymore. Not anyone's fault, certainly not yours."

"You must affirm that you do not love me, Claire. Otherwise, there is no getting past this." Tom tightened his jaw to keep from crying.

"There are things more important than our love. Like you, I have things I must do. In fact, the last thing my brother asked of me."

"What are you talking about?"

"I am going to marry our childhood friend. Richard was wounded at Okinawa. He needs me, more than anyone."

Struck dumb, Tom held his tongue, not knowing how to counter this declaration. His eyes, however, snagged on a couple maneuvering erratically along the sidewalk. The man used a cane, his free arm entwined with his companion's. From a few yards away, the man spoke.

"Is everything alright, Claire? This man bothering you?"

Her parents, it dawned on Tom. Both appeared to have shrunk. Sensing their disapproval, he automatically stepped away from Claire and faced them.

Claire spoke first. "It's fine, Father. You'll remember Tom Stone. He came by to extend his condolences."

Esther Endicott bobbled her head, a barely audible "thank you" escaping her lips. She clutched a small Bible against her chest.

No one budged. A child whizzed by on a tricycle. A car honked. A screen door banged shut down the street.

"Humph," Edward Endicott let out by way of finalizing the exchange. "Appreciate your stopping by, Mr., Mr.—"

"Stone, Father. Tom Stone. He's been away for a while."

"Very well," Edward concluded, having already lost the thread. His lifeless eyes seemed not to be focused on anything at all, Tom thought. Without another word, the older man tightened his hold on his wife's arm and jerked his body into motion. As a unit, they started up the steps to the front porch.

"We'll see you inside, dear," Esther said, tapping her daughter on the arm as she passed.

The two young people watched the older couple as they awkwardly ascended, Edward grasping the railing, his cane hooked around his left wrist. His other arm was still entwined with his wife's.

When the front door closed upon them, Tom turned back to Claire.

She closed her eyes briefly and shifted her head side to side. "You see what it is, don't you? Such grief."

"They lost a child. Nothing worse than that."

Claire nodded, distracted. She glanced at her watch.

Tom tried to temper his impatience. But he had so little time. "Unlike for them, Claire, there will be better days. We are young. We are—"

She smiled faintly, in no mood to argue. Tom wanted to shake her, but instead reached out to take her hands in his.

"The question is, with whom do you want to spend those future days, Claire?" His voice was firm, the look on his face ardent. "In my case, I know who that person is. She is standing in front of me."

Claire opened her mouth to speak but could not formulate a reasonable rejoinder. All she could muster was, "I can't..." and trailed off.

"We shall have to give ourselves time. That's all I can imagine for now," Tom said, leaning over to place a kiss on her forehead. She did not move. He dropped her hands and soon found himself walking away. How he had been able to break away he did not know.

That evening after a quiet supper with her parents—none of them brought up Tom Stone again, nor anything about Addison— the phone jangled. Esther rose to answer.

Helen Carrollton got straight to the point. Richard would arrive within a week from San Diego, his wounds healed sufficiently to travel unaided. "We'll expect to see all three of you at the train station. Our son will be thrilled."

By her silence, Esther confirmed their presence.

Later, while Edward sipped cognac and his wife, sherry, the phone rang again. Claire picked up. It was Myra, who called to say she was driving down in the morning to visit her aunt—and to see Tom off at the station.

"He told me he was no longer counting on you to be there. But no one should have to arrive or to leave alone." (An audible sigh at the other end.) "The Crescent City leaves at noon."

If Myra's tone was accusatory, Claire did not try to defend herself. Instead, she deflected. "I'm doing what they all want of me. What Addison wanted. Richard arrives on Sunday. I'll be there at the station that day, with Mother and Father."

All Tom heard at the bustling station that morning were the shouts of paper boys. "Extra, Extra, Read All About It." Louder than he had remembered it. He shelled out for a copy of the *Picayune* and rushed to find his carriage and compartment. He paused to hoist an elderly lady aboard, deposited his meager luggage and his newspaper, and jumped back off.

Just in case.

As the engine started to hiss and the wheels to crank, he spotted the two women. A broad smile crossed his face for the first time in ages.

"So glad we caught you," Myra said, out of breath. She was carrying a wicker basket covered by a checkered cloth.

"You have seen the papers, right, Tom?" Lena Walenska burst out in German. "Of course, you can read all about it on the train," she added, this time in English.

He looked flummoxed. "What is going on?" he asked.

"We dropped a bomb on the Japanese. An atomic bomb. A place called Hiroshima. The war will soon be over," Myra said.

Tom looked nonplussed, unsure what to make of this.

"Never mind for now," Lena said. "No one knows what this bodes, but everyone has to eat. My sister and my niece put together some Polish specialties for you. I added a bottle of Riesling. You won't starve en route."

"No, I suspect not. *Vielen Dank,* to all of you—for everything."

"Nonsense," Lena declared. "But in recompense, you must let us know how things are over there, *n'est-ce pas?*" she prompted him in her endearingly imperious way.

"Without fail. Although it won't all be good news."

"We'll trust some of it will be, for your sake," Myra interjected.

Tom swallowed hard. Departures were never easy. He remembered that French expression his parents used when they sent him abroad all those years ago. *Partir est un peu mourir.* He did not want to further upset himself by citing it. But it rang true: leaving *was* a little like dying.

His eyes darted about the platform even as the conductor called out, "All aboard."

Unavailing.

Tom embraced both women, took the basket, and hopped on the train as it began to chug off.

"*Auf Wiedersehen*," he called out from the window of his compartment. "Until we meet again."

The other three passengers glanced at him curiously. Ignoring them, he sat down and buried his head in the newspaper.

Chapter Thirty-Five

COMING HOME

A ragtag band met Frederick at the bus station in Alexandria on a cold starlit night at the end of 1945.

Family and close friends showed up to welcome their hero back, Mrs. Murkowski being the one who engaged the four musicians. Among them was a drummer whom Myra instantly recognized. It took the tired, dazed Frederick a little longer to place him: Skeezix, the gawky kid from the diner, recently upped to manager.

"Welcome home, Mr. Bauer. And congratulations on the medal," the kid, now noticeably older and less gawky, called out.

Ever polite, Frederick switched his duffel bag to his left shoulder and held out his hand. The band struck up a Sousa march.

Turning to his mother and aunt, he embraced each of them. They were too overcome to speak. Mrs. Murkowski too received a hug and a whispered condolence. "Lech did his duty. Take solace in that."

After shaking hands with the older Kaminskys, he turned to Myra. She smiled, and he took her hand. Eyes turned their way.

"I approve of the mustache," she said.

"And I, of the hair style. I've obviously missed a lot."

Weeks later, after Flora and Fannie stopped fussing over him, and the Kaminskys stopped going on about the lamp of Italian alabaster he had shipped back to them, Frederick invited Myra to lunch.

"It'll have to be the diner," she said, "or we'll never be forgiven."

By the time they were into the main course of shrimp creole—"I did dream about this, you know, all the way up to the Gothic Line," he quipped—Myra realized that the ground had irrevocably shifted.

Her childhood friend had not only survived the war, he had overcome it.

If she had heretofore pigeon-holed him as hopelessly provincial, if not small-minded, here he sat, expounding on the light in the piazzas of Palermo, the laughter at every angle in Naples, the ochre walls of Rome, the pealing of bells everywhere. His world had grown outward; and he had grown on her.

Then, he astounded her further.

"It may come as a shock, Myra." He leaned over to confide. "But I'm selling my share of the store and planning to move to New York City." Her eyes widened to saucers. "Anyone serious about writing needs to be there. And, if not now, when?"

She babbled something lame in response. He had bowled her over.

Their conversations continued for several more weeks, Frederick having intuited that the death of Claire's brother had hit Myra hard, and she having intuited that he'd had a dalliance with a Neapolitan girl, which had delayed his return.

One evening after the movies, he walked her home.

"We both went through a lot these past years, though different things changed each of us. I'm sure we'll get to all that eventually. We always have," Frederick said. Without thinking about it, Myra took his arm. "You know, despite everything, you have remained the most courageous, indeed the most entrancing, person in my life. Whatever you end up doing in life, I know I will support you in it."

No one, Myra thought, had ever spoken to her like that. She

arrived home thinking that what Frederick said was more important to her than anything she could imagine—even a marriage proposal.

A few weeks later, Lena came to visit, and quickly picked up on the mood in the Kaminsky house. Ilona and Konrad Kaminsky were flabbergasted that the young man they had set their sights on to marry their daughter had artistic pretensions.

"Literary ambitions," Lena corrected them. "You've read his letters. Frederick has talent. Why shouldn't he find out where those take him?"

Myra added nothing to these arguments. She was struggling with her own sense of uselessness. The war was over, and women were no longer needed to do much of anything. She and Claire had foreseen that outcome months, if not years, ago. So now what?

Her aunt took her aside.

"If I were you, Myra, and had your brains and your interests, I too would find a way to break away. It should not be only men who get to do this. Were you so inclined, I could help."

"I wouldn't think of it, Aunt Lena," Myra objected.

Her aunt sighed. "I did not, on that ship, stuff my bra with those Deutsch marks for no purpose."

By the middle of the year 1946, Myra left for New York City, having quietly applied (with the counsel of a few former professors) to the two most prominent law schools in Manhattan. She was accepted by both, on scholarship. She chose NYU Law School, situated on the south side of Washington Square.

Frederick, who, like many would-be writers, had rented a walk-up apartment in surrounding Greenwich Village, met her at Grand Central station, not with a band but a bouquet of roses.

They traipsed around together for the entire summer, taking in the sights, sounds, and smells of the city, arguing about this and that, but agreeing they were now inhabitants of the greatest city in the world.

One afternoon, they wandered into the Museum of Modern Art, hardly for the first time, and on the spur of the moment decided to take in whatever movie was screening that day. They had assumed a classic Charlie Chaplin or Harold Lloyd silent, but a museum official took the microphone to say simply: "This is not our ordinary fare, but we thought it important. You may judge for yourselves. Eventually, the country at large will do so. To invite you, as I usually do, to *enjoy*, would be inappropriate."

There was murmuring among the movie-goers. Someone nearby whispered that the footage they were about to see was shot by the Japanese. "Brace yourself," he advised.

Myra and Frederick looked at each other in puzzlement. And then the lights dimmed and a documentary, partially in color, came on.

"*Hiroshima 1945*" was graphic. And like everyone else in the audience, they were shocked to see it.

For the rest of the evening, they talked of other things, but they knew, however vaguely, that "the bomb" had changed the world forever.

Chapter Thirty-Six

THE WOUNDS OF WAR

Harold Carrollton knew how to strong-arm people. Including the unsuspecting society editor of the *Picayune*, to whom he dictated the details, unverifiable though they were, of the wedding announcement. The nuptials would take place between Christmas and the New Year of 1946.

Despite Richard's unceremonious return shortly after VJ Day, Harold made sure that the narrative surrounding his son's stint in the Navy emphasized bravery, rather than his breakdown during the campaign on Saipan. He did not disabuse anyone of a rumor that Richard might be up for a medal for his actions on Okinawa.

After a month or so, and without consulting his son, Harold appointed him to business manager of the Carrollton shipping company, in charge of an entire team of accountants. Admittedly, there were only three financial executives on the payroll, but none was pleased.

The marriage ceremony, which seemed to be a *fait accompli* despite no one having ever uttered a proposal or made any plan, would be a private affair, in the lovely home of the bride's parents. It was stated that the bride graduated Sophie Newcomb College on the eve of war and served for several years as a Naval Intelligence decoder.

The two childhood sweethearts would be setting up house in the Uptown area, not far from both sets of parents.

Helen Carrollton could do little but go along with this charade, though she would have liked to have her son feel able to talk about the battle that left him with shrapnel in his leg and ghastly scenes in his head. She often stood outside his door when nightmares assailed him, but never dared knock or enter.

"See what you can do for him, Claire. Naval Intelligence must stand for something," she told her prospective daughter-in-law.

Shortly after he got home, Claire called to invite Richard to meet up for a movie and then dinner, at Casamento's on Magazine Street, an old-time seafood place that, if she remembered rightly, promoted itself as unfussy.

Unfortunately, *Leave Her to Heaven* was a more upsetting than romantic movie. It seemingly left Richard troubled, and more taciturn than before. At the restaurant, Claire found herself in charge of the menu.

"How about soft-shelled crabs, something neither of us has had for a while? And some white wine."

Richard acquiesced. The food took a while. His eyes darted about constantly, as though the other diners were possible assailants.

Keep things on an even keel, Claire told herself. To fill the void, she rattled on about the renovations to the Saenger Theater, the concerts Lena Walenska had held to raise money for Europe, the opening of new stores downtown.

Nothing sparked a response.

The arrival of their plates was a relief, so too the bottle of Chablis. In her nervousness, Claire finished off a second glass before the main course was finished. And it did soon finish.

A waiter stumbled, a tray stacked with plates and saucers went flying. At the clatter, Richard jumped to his feet, upending his own chair, the ferocity of his expression silencing all nearby customers.

On the way home, Claire took his arm. She had vowed to try hard.

"I've read about this, Richard. It will get better with time."

He inclined his head. She pretended not to see the tears.

Things only got worse between the two, so much so that Claire had to walk on eggshells. Any inopportune word, any unexpected movement, any ambiguous expression could ignite her husband's ire or occasion his withdrawal. Sometimes both, within the space of minutes.

She felt unequipped to deal with either and no one to turn to for help. Instead, she prayed, to whatever deity might listen, that Richard's spells would attenuate, that his nightmares would fade, that his job would bring him satisfaction, that his interest in other people—indeed, in her—would eventually override everything else.

Sometimes, lying awake at night, in a solitary bed, she could hear the creak of springs as her husband thrashed about in the adjacent guest room, reconfigured from what had been a tiny study. Sometimes he screamed, more often she could hear muffled cries, and occasionally, she made out names—sergeant this, sergeant that, or simply "Addison, Addison."

Six months ticked by. By the summer, Claire had lost weight, lost her verve, and lost her way in the world. She relaxed only when Richard left the house to go to his office in the warehouse district.

"How was your day, sweetheart?" was not a question she could fathom herself blithely posing. In fact, though, she had no idea what he did at work until a Sunday dinner at the Carrolltons with her own parents there as well.

From the outset, the atmosphere was tense. Harold carved the roast with special vehemence, which made her flinch. Richard remained almost comatose. It was left to the elder Endicotts to spark conversation.

"So, Richard," Claire's father began, "we were wondering if business on the river has picked up. What's your sense of how the year will stack up?"

It took a long minute for the question to register. Claire squirmed in her chair but did not dare prompt her husband.

"About the same as before, I reckon," Richard stammered, his tone flat.

Of a sudden, Harold banged on the table. "Is that all you can come up with, young man?"

No response from Richard. Rather, he carefully speared a single green bean with his fork and raised it to his mouth. The gesture further infuriated his father.

"What else should I expect," Harold seethed. He fumbled in his waistcoat pocket, and, to general astonishment, pulled out a string of paperclips. He dangled the makeshift necklace in front of everyone. "That's what you spend your time doing, on my dime? Making daisy chains. Your desk drawer is full of them," he said, accusatory.

Richard's mouth began to twitch.

"Like some five-year-old sissy, that's what."

"That's enough, Harold," Helen admonished him, something the Endicotts had rarely heard her do. "Leave the boy alone."

Harold snorted but desisted. "Boy, my ass," he muttered under his breath.

Esther tried to catch her daughter's eye, but Claire's gaze was fixed on her plate. She had barely touched her food. For long minutes, the only sound at the table was of cutlery.

But then Claire rallied. "We are leaving, Richard," she announced, her tone brooking no dissent. She rose, pushing her chair back with force, it audibly scratching the parquet floor.

"Goodnight, Mother, Father," she added, more softly.

Stunned, Richard scrambled to his feet. The two left the dining room and searched about in the parlor for Claire's pocketbook and Richard's linen jacket. They both overheard the reactions from the other room.

"Quite a ruckus you've provoked," Helen rebuked her husband.

"It's her fault, in the end," Harold countered. "They're married, aren't they? She needs to have a baby."

As they headed to the front door, Claire could not detect her parents' response to all this, nor did she linger to find out.

In the coming days, she hoped the episode would encourage Richard to bond with her. But nothing changed.

A baby? Only by immaculate conception, she mused. Things had been so natural with Tom, including making love. (She forced herself not to dwell on that.) How is it, she wondered, that everything is now so impossibly hard?

With no one to confide in—Myra had blurted out, "You must be crazy," when the upcoming marriage was first bruited—Claire reached out to Bernice.

Unlike the other women at Naval Intelligence, she had been kept on by the command staff, albeit in a different capacity. Doing what, Claire had no idea.

They agreed to meet at the Sun Cafe the following Wednesday.

From her friend's disconcerted expression, Claire knew her marriage had taken a toll, even on her physical appearance.

By contrast, Bernice looked more self-possessed than ever, her suit impeccably styled, her heels more stylish than anything Claire wore. Her short bob accentuated her eyes, an almost violet color which had always been obscured by her glasses.

"It's been way too long," Bernice threw out. Claire nodded and gave her erstwhile colleague a faint smile.

"So, how is—" they both began, and then chuckled.

"Please," Claire said. "You, first."

"I was going to ask how married life was going. You look more haggard than I remember from the office."

Claire waited to respond until they placed their order. She took a deep breath. "It's not as easy as I imagined."

Bernice arched her eyebrows.

"Richard was in the Pacific, you may recall. From the outset. Wounded at Okinawa."

"That says a lot. Not many understand, but we do. Is he still shell-shocked?"

"If anything, he's worse. And it's more than that. My brother dying, and all that. He can't get past it."

Sensing she was being called upon for more than platitudes, Bernice rummaged in her handbag. "Mind if I smoke?"

Claire nodded distractedly.

"You do realize that I'm hardly the obvious marriage counselor, being of the other persuasion, as it were," Bernice pointed out. She took a long draw on her Lucky Strike to let that revelation sink in.

"Actually," Claire said, "your personal choices might make your advice more useful. Now that I think about it."

"It sounds like you need to get some mental distance from Richard and his condition. You can't lose yourself in his problems."

"I'm sure you're right. But our parents are a problem too. They think all I have to do is have a baby." She shook her head in dismay and then said, "And here's the rub. Even if I agreed with them, it would be impossible."

Bernice gave her a long, hard look. "You're implying it wasn't just the war that upended his—your—lives, right?"

Struggling not to tear up, Claire reached in her pocketbook and removed a crinkled piece of paper.

"Read this. The last letter my brother Addison wrote. Addressed to me."

Bernice stared at the letter for far longer than it took to read it. She made a reproving noise and refolded the letter along its crease. She took a sip of coffee and wiped her lips. "I gather there was a lot of love amongst you three, growing up. You are lucky to have had that."

Silent tears did stream down Claire's face, but Bernice ignored them. "All I can say is this, you cannot blame yourself for someone else's choices in these matters. Nor should you sacrifice your life on the altar of his."

"Problem is we went to the altar, literally," Claire responded drily.

"Marriage does not have to be a prison. If it is, find a way to break out of it."

Claire dried her eyes. She took a few sips of water. "I'm sorry. This has all made me a pitiable sight." Bernice shrugged. "I did not ask. How is Teresa? I've passed by the shipyard: no more riveting, at least no more women doing it."

"We've been lucky. Teresa is friendly with a sculptor around town. He works with metals, and she's adept with all these materials. She's helping him with a show he's mounting."

"That's impressive. And you, working with Commander Lassiter or what exactly?"

"The team is smaller, but he's still in charge. And something for you to mull. All the decoding. It continues. And from what I've picked up, the uses for these computing machines are expanding. Not just war. All kinds of businesses." Claire looked flummoxed. "They need people like you. No more torpedoes to worry about; more positive things to work on."

"Nothing like that had crossed my mind."

"Owen Lassiter says you had the best grasp of math in the whole unit. So, if and when…"

"Hard to imagine," Claire replied, immediately losing her train of thought.

Bernice cocked her head. "Wallowing in self-pity never helps," she said. "You should finish that master's degree you were studying for—and get back out into the world. Too many of us are disappearing back behind four walls. And that's not Richard's fault. It would be your own."

No one, with the exception of Myra, had ever spoken to Claire like that. It shook her. She had no retort. She bit her lip and nodded her head in assent.

And she did follow through, finishing up her advanced degree in the fall session with Dr. Penley's help. At the same time, she bumped into Lucille Truard, who excitedly announced that she and Lena Walenska were planning a trip to Paris the coming summer. Would it not be *superb,* she exclaimed in her Gallic enthusiasm, to have a young person, such as herself, join them for the voyage?

Claire smiled politely and continued on her way across campus. It helped to be home before Richard returned from wherever he was now spending his afternoons. Certainly, his complexion was less sallow, as though getting more fresh air.

Once Richard noticed that Claire had something to do besides be on tenterhooks around him, he too began to relax a little. She reckoned he felt less guilty seeing that she was ever so tentatively reclaiming space for herself or that his personal demons had been battered back, if not vanquished.

Things between them improved, minimally but nonetheless.

"You were always good with numbers, growing up, not to mention those chess games with your dad. A masters in math. That'll impress even my parents," he said over coffee one morning. She was floored by his praise but did her best not to show it.

Another day, he chatted about this and that news item in the papers without getting rattled. And then, an unexpected *non sequitur.*

"I've thrown out all the paper clips from my office," he announced. Claire was at a loss to respond. "I'm spending more time nowadays onboard the tugs."

"Oh, really?" she managed, again flabbergasted.

"The point is, I never had any aptitude for business. That was all my father's idea of what I should be doing. Even Addison had been skeptical at the time."

It was the first time she had heard Richard mention her brother in months, except inadvertently during his nightmares.

She tread lightly. "What is it you like about the tugboats?"

"Being on the water. Like the ocean during the war, the river calms me down. I'm jittery on land. Addison always said I was a different person when we went sailing."

She nodded in tacit agreement. This was all new territory for her; she did not want to trample on it.

After a bit, he added, offhandedly, "I'm fond of the captains. To a man, they're strong, silent types who know what they're about." He paused. "Kind of like Addison, I guess you could say."

It was arguably the longest conversation the couple had had since they were married. Claire thought of it as revealing, but she could not say revealing of what precisely. It would simply have to do as is.

Chapter Thirty-Seven
COMING TO TERMS

The first thing Tom noticed as the Army van crept through the pock-marked streets of Berlin was the oppressive color. In the first light of dawn on that mid-August morning, the buildings, the trees, and the faces of people all appeared dusted in gray.

It was the aftermath of war in the city that had been the epicenter of the evil unleashed on the world. And here he was, German by upbringing but American now in spirit, come all this way to help the victors put the place back to rights.

He felt outside himself.

The others who had traveled with him by uncomfortable cargo plane—two civil engineers, several WACs, and an Army major who had been on medical leave—were as dumbstruck by the desolation as he was.

No one spoke as they drove past the rubble of once proud symbols of imperial power toward the so-called American section, where "for the interim" Tom and the engineers would be lodged.

Not that he regretted having said yes to the opportunity. If, while in forced detention, he had not been able to do his part in the war, he could now do his part in the peace.

And, unlike most of the others in this endeavor, he was determined to reconnect with his past—conceivably with those nearest and dearest to him.

Among his documents, he had the latest letter from Jonas in England. His cousin explained that the compilation of lists of Nazi atrocities, including of victims and survivors at every now liberated concentration camp, had already begun. Not to mention, Jonas went on, ledgers of military materiel, troops, officers, battles, casualties, victories, even defeats which the *Wehrmacht* stored in its maniacally organized way.

Being now a naturalized American as well as a German native, Tom reckoned, should make it easier to obtain information regarding his parents as well as his childhood friends. All in due course, he cautioned himself.

Their caravan passed along the once magnificent *Kurfürstendamm*, dodging mostly old men on bicycles and G.I.s in Army jeeps. As a student in Berlin, he had often strutted along the boulevard— and like so many others, carefree, insouciant, oblivious to what was festering in the nearby corridors of power.

It was a dizzying time warp. The trees in the Tiergarten had been stripped for firewood, prostitutes loitered at street corners, and children thronged soldiers for candy, or cigarettes for their parents.

It took a couple of months for Tom to get his feet on the ground, but, as he had learned to do in America, he made himself useful, translating during official interrogations of suspected Nazis or helping dazed locals find safe lodging or food sources. Before long, he was assigned to work up repair plans for civic buildings that could be salvaged and blueprints for new housing in areas that had to be razed.

"We're playing catch-up here," one of the Army captains commented one day during a drive past the Brandenburg Gate. The officer jerked his head toward an outsized portrait of Stalin staring down upon the boulevard. First troops to liberate the city, the Russians had already muscled their way into control of crucial services and oversight of key municipal offices.

It didn't take Tom long to figure that cohesion among the victors in the war might not last. Still, he was a civilian and was there for purposes beyond support for the military occupation. He would start by trying to locate his childhood friend.

Because Hans Durst was a Naval officer, Tom reckoned he would come under scrutiny by the occupying powers. Nazis were being rounded up by the Allied forces on the ground in Berlin, at least those that hadn't already escaped or disappeared into the woodwork. He wasn't sure how career military officers like Hans might be treated, though rumor had it that the Russians had little patience with those they had collared.

Time, Tom figured, would be of the essence. He went to the commanding officer of the unit to which he had been assigned, a Major Thompson. The officer had served under Patton and looked like it: a no-nonsense, hard-bitten type.

"An officer aboard a U-Boat in the Atlantic? Do you know his port of call, his vessel number, or anything else useful, son?" the major asked.

"Only that he was loyal to the military, not to Nazism *per se*."

"That's what they all say now," the major deadpanned.

Tom looked crestfallen, not wanting to make life worse for his old friend by bringing up his case, but wanting to vouch for him, if useful for his defense.

"The good news, Mr. Stone, is that these Krauts kept accurate records, and that's praise I don't bestow often. I'll see what I can do."

As soon as he left the major's office, Tom figured he'd have to take a trip to erstwhile German Naval headquarters on the Baltic and dig through ship manifests. But within the week, an official-looking communication was left with the posted guard at the barracks where Tom was lodged.

He read the report in German twice and then sat down.

Re: Hans Durst (b 1912 in Lübeck, Deutschland)
    U-Boat 166, 10th Flotilla
    Second-in-command under Gunther Kühlmann

Said submarine torpedoed and sank U.S. passenger ship Robert E Lee in the Gulf of Mexico on July 30, 1942. Following which, U-Boat 166 was assaulted by the American ship's escort and itself was scuttled. All 49 officers and crew members were lost.
    The U-boat was not recovered.

A postscript in English read: *Mr. Stone, Hope this suffices. Major Thompson*

Tom felt stomach-punched. He lay on his metal cot for an hour, eyes closed, trying to empty his mind of everything except his fondest childhood memories. He failed.

Not wanting to be alone through the evening, he tagged along with several other civilian consultants to an impromptu outdoor concert amid the rubble of Alexanderplatz. Along with many others, including still shell-shocked Berliners, they sat on broken slabs of masonry to listen to Bach and Beethoven.

Some things Germans really did do well, Tom thought, like making sublime music, even more than meticulous lists.

Before Hans' inglorious end at the bottom of the gulf, his and other submarines had made quite an impact along the southern U.S. coast, taking out dozens of troop vessels headed for Europe, in particular around New Orleans. Claire, he recalled, had alluded to the tragedy of the *Robert E Lee* during that jittery time. Ironically or simply sadly, U-Boat 166 was, he had later read, the only German sub sunk in the gulf throughout the war.

In the throes of his first visceral reaction to Hans' fate, he intended to write to Claire and describe his feelings. But more months passed. And why should she care? The war was over; life was moving on.

His too. He was soon asked to weigh in on the plans to repair the *Reichstag*, the famed opera house, and various buildings along *Unter den Linden*.

Eventually, Tom secured a long weekend off and, with trepidation, took a train to Lübeck. His hometown too had been bombed, but only once, at the beginning of the war. From the train, he counted fewer of the spires he remembered in his youth. Several of the town's historic buildings, religious and civic, he found still damaged. As a child, he had gone to the main medieval synagogue—now gutted—and later, with his mother, to St Mary's cathedral, to admire the art and hear the organ.

Inside, on that Saturday, the church was nearly empty, the bells from the tower still lay half melted into the nave from the blast of British bombers five years before.

He slipped into a pew to re-arrange his thoughts and consult his map. The Red Cross, he had been advised, was tending to survivors from the region's camps, including those who ended up victims of the disaster in Lübeck Bay. He calculated that would mean mostly women who were fortunate enough to be on the *Athen*, the anchored ship that escaped the accidental bombing by the British.

He walked through the winding streets and out beyond the Trave River to what looked to be an old asylum. Elm trees dotted the lawn. Several old people in wheelchairs formed a half-circle in the shade. Someone somewhere was playing a Bach prelude on an out-of-tune piano.

Once inside the repurposed building, he filled out a form,

supplying his mother's and father's names and ages and last known whereabouts. And was ushered to a seat on a long wooden bench.

A few people, presumably patients, walked or hobbled past. He kept his eyes lowered. He could hear muffled conversations, a news bulletin from a radio, and no discernible laughter.

Eventually, an administrator with a badge that read Frau Biel led him into a small alcove. She wasted no time.

"We have three patients, or residents if you like, with that last name. Not an uncommon surname, Steinberg, so this is a long shot. Do keep in mind that their ordeals, for however long they endured them, have taken a toll."

Tom nodded.

Frau Biel paused to make sure he understood. "Not everyone here remembers things with clarity."

"I have long prepared myself for disappointment." He felt his stomach clenching. "Do any of these women appear to be of the right age?"

"One of them is, I believe, in her late fifties or thereabouts. But may I ask: did your mother sew?"

"Sew?"

"Was she a good seamstress?"

"I never thought about it. She was adept at so many things."

"Come with me. The lady in question made military uniforms in one of the *Neuengamme* sub-camps. In that way, she—"

"Saved herself?"

"Likely so. Now we have her making baby clothes. She seems to enjoy it." Tom could feel his heart racing. "Rather than upset our patients needlessly, you may peak through the window into the common room. Only a few there this afternoon. She'll be the one in the rocker."

Gobsmacked he soon was and braced himself against the glass. Sobs convulsed him. It took him minutes to regain control. When he did, the administrator had retrieved a glass of water from a nearby pantry.

"You are not the first one," Frau Biel said. "But are you sure it is she?"

"Absolutely."

Ruth Steinberg took a bit longer to comprehend that the young man standing in front of her was her only son, now returned from America.

"I came back, Mother, because I always believed you would find a way through all this." He found it hard to go on.

"One day at a time. It's what I told myself every day," she said.

Cautiously over the following weeks, mother and son took steps to get past the worst of what had happened to her. For a while, they did not mention the camps, though he did gently press her as to where his father might have ended up.

His mother shook her head in dismay. "When we were caught, we were separated. Likely, he remained at the main camp, and ended up herded onto that floating ship. From our vessel, we women heard the bombs. We saw the flames."

No more was said. And subsequently, Tom did not find a Steinberg among the names of the few rescued from the two ships sunk in the Lübeck harbor.

He went with what had been allotted him and felt blessed.

As his mother gained strength, he searched for a suitable ground-floor lodging for her in Lübeck proper, with a view of the canals, a spire or two, and in lively enough a neighborhood, with children's voices, the likelihood of laughter.

On the day he signed a year's lease for a sunny apartment on a street barely touched by the war, Tom walked around the nearby old town to see what buildings still needed repairs. Not as overwhelming a task as in Berlin, he noted, though arguably a years-long undertaking. Where all the money would come from, and from whom, he had no idea.

At dusk, he stopped in one of the restaurants that he remembered from his youth, ordered a beer, and scrolled through the menu.

At the table nearest his own sat two youngish men and a woman, one of the former with a fancy camera slung over the arm of his chair, the other with a notepad open next to his mug. At first, he figured they were tourists, but visitors were still rare eight months after the armistice. They were, however, speaking English with a British accent.

He listened.

Apparently, they were traveling across the continent to write about different cities as they came back to life, interviewing politicians and locals alike. They had been to Rome, they had been to Barcelona, and they had been to Lisbon.

It was this last destination that the three were going on about: the nightlife along the Atlantic port—guitar music everywhere, the free-flowing wine, the gentleness of the people.

"*A Taberna das Gaivotas*, the Seagull Tavern, right?" one of them mentioned.

"Your accent is atrocious, Colin. But yeah. That noisy one, always crowded, everybody talking at once."

"In a dozen languages," the woman at the table pointed out. "Flotsam and jetsam washed up on the shore—coming out of hiding, reinventing themselves."

"Exactly. That place was our best find. The owner, larger than life. Bustling about, regaling the customers. Like there had never been a war," the man named Colin said.

"Not to mention his wife, or whatever she was," the photographer added, supplying an approving whistle. "Definitely not Portuguese. Sounded Scandinavian or something."

"But surprising us all. At that old upright, remember? We were all soused."

"Yeah. Singing those old parlor tunes. A lovely voice—didn't carry far, but enough." The young woman hummed briefly, mouthing a few words. *"Flow gently, sweet Afton, among thy green braes."*

"You took a few pictures of her, right, Phil?"

"Naturally. They're back in the hotel."

Before long, the threesome called for their bill. Tom watched the journalists leave but did not stop them. It was enough to know that Katrin—Hans had always said she was inventive—was alive and well, in this newly hopeful world.

Chapter Thirty-Eight

WHERE YOU CAN JUST BE

Lena Walenska had developed a sizable following since coming to America. It wasn't only her vigorous attack of the keyboard. She had a well-honed stage presence, which included beaded gowns, sparkling jewelry, and a flair for the dramatic.

At the university, she became a well-liked as well as competent instructor, demanding but also encouraging. Plus, she made a point of emphasizing her Polish heritage, which stood her in good stead. Her countrymen, after all, had made major contributions to the Allied effort and were being celebrated far and wide for their exploits.

Including in Paris.

In short, although she had turned down occasional offers from afar to perform—the cowboys of San Antonio, Texas did not seem to her sufficiently civilized to appreciate classical music while Australia struck her as too remote to reach in her lifetime—she jumped at an invitation to appear in the City of Light.

The august Salle Pleyel would be honoring the Polish resistance, fighter pilots and soldiers alike, around the time of Bastille Day celebrations in mid-July 1947. She was invited to perform with a youth orchestra, where Polish and French composers would both be featured.

The invitation included lavish perks. Twelve days at the state's expense, two separate suites at the Hotel Verneuil to accommodate her and her "entourage."

"*Pourquoi pas?*" she asked herself, and immediately accepted.

Not only did she invite her bosom buddy, Lucille Truard, to come along, but she seized the chance to bestow something memorable upon her niece. Why shouldn't Myra take a break from her law school studies—it would be the middle of summer—and why shouldn't she bring along someone too?

I shall have Lucille; Myra should have Claire.

As for others who might wish to experience her performance, Lena sent her own invitations to everyone in her European black book, not knowing in some cases if they were even still alive. Some will be, she firmly believed. And, if they lived through the war, they deserved to be entertained.

It was Myra who suggested that it would be a thoughtful gesture to send out an invitation to Tom Stone in Berlin.

"Like both Claire and me," she said, "he may have never seen Paris." (Somehow, she failed to mention any of this exchange to Claire.)

Casting such a wide net for erstwhile friends and admirers appealed to Lena's sense of adventure. Moreover, she minded not a jot that traveling with other females (but *sans* males) might raise an eyebrow or two. She was her own person, and believed everyone in her orbit should be too.

Whatever anyone thought of this unlikely foursome traveling on their own, the quartet set sail on the France out of New York harbor at the beginning of July, arriving in Paris in time for sight-seeing before the concert on the twelfth.

It was after the standing ovation for Lena Walenska's interpretation of Chopin's Concerto in E Minor that the threesome seated in the audience headed to the foyer for refreshments.

With goblets of champagne in their hands, they milled about, admiring the French women who insistently dressed to the nines for such public entertainments.

Of a sudden, Lucille raised her voice.

"*Mon dieu*! We never expected to see you here, Tom. How *merveilleux*," she exclaimed. He raised her hand to his lips. In the French way. She beamed and turned her head to beckon the others.

Myra smiled, stepped forward, and pecked Tom on each cheek. Again, in the French way.

Claire remained rooted in place. The chandelier in the foyer began to dim. Without another word, Lucille and Myra hurried back inside the concert hall for Berlioz's *Symphonie Fantastique*.

As the room cleared out, Tom approached to take Claire's hand. "Come," he said softly, leading her out of the foyer and to the back of the darkened auditorium. "We can listen from here."

Discombobulated, Claire said not a word. Taller than she, he positioned himself behind her and pressed his body gently against her back.

They stood like that until the concert ended, the applause died down, and patrons began to file out.

"Tell me where you are staying," he asked before they went outside to meet the others.

"The Hotel Verneuil on the Left Bank. We had to because Professor Truard said it's where poets like Rimbaud congregated at one time." He smiled at the thought. "More to the point, Myra leaves tomorrow to fly back to New York. There's a launch party for a book Frederick wrote. I am here for another week."

"Then I am too," he said.

The others soon materialized. To everyone's surprise, Lena walked out arm-in-arm with a distinguished-looking gentleman she introduced as Stefan Schmidt, a violinist whom, if Myra and Claire remembered rightly, was the one she had referred to as her "special friend" all those years ago. While her companion held a bouquet of flowers thrown her way onstage, she obligingly signed a dozen autographs.

It turned out that, like Tom, Stefan had somehow received Lena's hand-written invitation. "She took the chance I might be still alive," he told them, clearly pleased with the outcome.

"How did you survive?" Myra asked. "I mean, during the war?"

"Thanks to the kindness of strangers, I fled one night by fishing boat to Sweden. Ended up in Uppsala, teaching music, performing now and again," he said, sounding almost lighthearted. Looking over at Lena, he added, "And now this miracle."

As for Lucille, she soon hailed a taxi so as to catch the overnight train to Brest. "My relatives will be stunned to see me, but if I don't do this now..."

"Go, go. We'll see you in Le Havre on the nineteenth," Lena called to her.

For the next six idyllic days, Tom and Claire took walks in the Bois de Boulogne in the morning and strolled the winding streets of the Left Bank in the afternoon. They sat at different cafes dotted around the Palais Royale, explored antiquities at the Louvre, and took in the views from the Eiffel Tower.

And they talked. Tom, about having recently had his contract extended another year to help Berlin rebuild and about having found his mother alive and gaining ground every month. Asked about his father, he shut his eyes and lowered his head.

"And your friends—Hans and Katrin?"

"That U-boat, Claire, the one that was sunk in the Gulf. Hans was on it. Second-in-command. On a happier note, I discovered, by sheer chance, that Katrin is alive and well and living in Lisbon."

It was harder for Claire to recount her recent past. To verbalize why her marriage was a failure she had not managed to do even to herself. But she intimated enough.

Tom was understanding, but it took all his willpower not to ask her to leave Richard and return with him to Germany. He hoped other things might make her change her mind, like their nights together when they left off talking, and slept only intermittently.

The Atlantic crossing went smoothly, and all three traveling companions were content to curl up with their respective books in French during the day and to dine together in the evening. Lena bought one of the few novels by Colette she had not read, Lucille tackled André Gide, which she would be teaching next term, and Claire, having heard speak of one Simone de Beauvoir, acquired her latest work.

Tom had accompanied Claire and Lena to Le Havre where they met up again with Lucille, pleasantly plump after a week of country cooking by her relatives. He lingered at the dock until the last moment, hugged the two elder ladies and, while they made their way onto the ship, embraced Claire.

"This is not for the last time. Tell me it is not," he said, releasing her and holding her at arm's length.

She was on the verge of crying, so he smiled at her. "Never mind for now. Write to me. Let me know all that you can. As will I."

Claire nodded and climbed aboard.

In New York, the three spent a day with Myra and Frederick, both in fine fettle. The first reviews of his debut novel, *Mud, Mules —and Me*, had come out, and were positive. "An affecting and keenly observed account of one soldier's journey up the Boot," one critic wrote. Myra had good news as well. She had aced the latest round of law school exams and would be clerking for a federal judge during the fall.

To Claire's eye, the two seemed happy together, their connection vibrant, while her own with Richard could at best be described as strained. She became agitated as the train drew closer to New Orleans.

"Is your husband meeting you at the station, my dear?" Lucille ventured. "If not, Tulane is sending a car for us two old ladies. We can drop you at your home."

Fortunately, there was no need for a lift. Claire's parents were waiting on the platform. On the way home, she described the delights of Paris. Those did not include Tom's visit. Nervous about what might lie ahead, she did not invite them in when they let her out.

"You may have forgotten, but the Carrolltons are celebrating their fortieth anniversary next weekend. At Antoine's. We'll expect to see you there. Both of you," her father declared, as he deposited her luggage at the front door.

She nodded in acknowledgment of the request.

Inside, she took a deep breath. The house had a musty smell. Richard was nowhere to be found, though it was almost dark on a Saturday afternoon.

To revive herself from the train trip, she showered, changed clothes, and checked the icebox. Milk, butter, and cheese aplenty, a few withered vegetables, and leftover soup in a serving bowl. But nothing enticing enough to tempt her.

In the parlor, she turned on a fan, scanned the newspaper, and dozed off. When she awoke, Richard had flicked on a lamp. The French clock on the sideboard said 8:50.

"I see you got back in one piece. The others, too, I presume."

"Everyone's fine."

She paused for him to ask the obvious, but he merely stood there, looking around, his eyes alighting on her things. Her luggage stood nearby unopened, her purse, her hat, and her book on the adjacent table.

"We all had a good time," she declared in response to the question he had not posed. He nodded distractedly. "Paris is, after all, Paris," she persevered. However inane the remark, it seemed to fit the situation in which she found herself mired.

"I'll put your bag in the bedroom," her husband soon remarked, and without waiting did just that. After which, in such a small house, she heard water running in the bathroom, then a squeaky faucet being turned off. Shortly, the guest room door opened and closed. A key turned.

How symbolic. I have been locked out of my own marriage, she whispered under her breath.

Too despondent to cry, Claire soon summoned the energy to gather up her things and go to bed herself, Tom's final words to her flitting through her dreams.

The celebration for the Carrolltons in the Quarter was crowded and noisy. Mercifully so. Claire and Richard duly arrived together but did not find each other again until after the elaborate sit-down dinner had wound down.

The only unfortunate incident took place during cocktail hour. Looking across the room, Claire noticed her mother chatting with Lucille Truard. The professor was waxing on vivaciously, likely describing the recent trip to Paris. And all its pleasures, which might have included the surprise appearance of Tom Stone.

A couple of months went by. Esther did not bring up the subject of Parisian encounters with her daughter, though occasionally she eyed her quizzically.

Soon, however, Claire needed someone to confide in who was not her mother. She thought of Bernice.

They met for coffee on one of the first cool afternoons in September.

"Paris must have suited you, Claire. You look radiant."

"Then I am in more ways than one," she returned. Bernice narrowed her eyes. "I think I'm pregnant."

"But I thought, from what you said—"

"Nothing has changed with Richard. But you might recall Tom Stone, the man you met at the movies."

"I do remember. Very personable."

"He is working in Berlin and, to my surprise at least, came to Paris. You can infer the rest."

"We might need something stronger than coffee," Bernice quipped. "What are you going to do?"

"Make sure my condition is as I suspect—and then have a heart-to-heart with Richard."

Bernice's eyebrows arched. "Are you certain that's a good idea?"

Claire let out a bitter laugh. "I can't go on living a lie. He'll have a choice: to leave me or to go along as though this were his child."

They sipped their coffee and tried the beignets. Claire ate all of hers. "You see. I'm hungry all the time now."

"But what about Tom?"

"I don't know as yet. A baby should make people happy, not throw their lives for a loop."

"Sometimes, the alternative is the better answer."

"Yes, for Myra, I believe it was. But not for me. Whatever else happens, I love Tom. I want to have his child."

"I do not envy you having to work through all this. But you will. Whatever I can do to help."

Wasting no time, Claire consulted her doctor, who estimated she was two months pregnant. She spent the rest of that day rehearsing how she would break the news to Richard.

The last thing she wanted to do was further alienate him. Since they lived as platonic friends—albeit even that description was a stretch—it was conceivable he might be amenable to the prospect of being a father. At least in the public eye.

More worrying thoughts soon intruded. All men, she reasoned, had egos. Richard might consider himself a spurned spouse, and her, a faithless wife. In his (however unjustifiable) jealousy, he might become agitated, even violent.

By 9 p.m. Richard had not come home, but his hours of late had become highly unpredictable. If Addison were alive, she reckoned, he might have talked sense into his friend. She shook her head over what war had wrought for them.

Two hours later she called it quits. The conversation would have to take place the next morning. She drank a cup of hot tea, nibbled at a piece of toast, and went to bed.

Loud knocks at the front door woke her. She stared at the night table. It was 6 a.m. Throwing on a bathrobe, she headed first to Richard's room—the bed was untouched—and then to the front door.

"Mrs. Carrollton? We're sorry to disturb you. May we come in?"

She looked around. Beyond them, Harold Carrollton was coming up the walkway. He looked apoplectic.

"Let me handle this," he barked to the officers.

They crowded into the foyer. "My parents. Are they alright?" Claire demanded, throwing off her sleep.

"An accident on the river," Harold said. "One of our tugs hit a barge. Richard and the captain went down with the vessel. They're both gone."

"Gone where? I don't understand."

"Why don't we sit down, Mrs. Carrollton, and we can go over this," one of the officers suggested.

Unsteady on her feet, Claire let them steer her into the parlor where she collapsed into a chair. The two cops sat upright on the nearby sofa. Harold remained on his feet.

"I'm going to have to look in on Helen, and then get back to the docks. There's a lot to clear up. I'll alert your parents so they can get over here as soon as possible."

Claire tried to wrap her head around what had been said.

"How could this happen, Harold? Richard knows the river; he knows the ocean. He's been in the war, for Christ's sake." She began to shake, enraged, apparently with everything.

Harold leaned over and patted her head, clumsily, muttering a few more details about river currents and boat speeds. She had no idea what he was on about. She turned her head toward the two cops. Her father-in-law thanked the officers and headed out.

"We can stay until your parents get here if you like, Mrs. Carrollton," one said.

"And we're sorry for your loss. Nasty business, this," the other one added.

Subsequent reports in the newspaper cleared up some, though not all, questions surrounding the tragedy. The Coast Guard, which had been involved in the recovery efforts, had its own theory about what transpired but found it hard to substantiate. The insurance company took issue with certain claims, given the unusual circumstances and the limits of its obligations.

Some people, including the Endicotts and Claire herself, suspected that Harold had a hand in keeping the final accident report as inconclusive as possible.

For one thing, it remained in dispute as to who was at the helm of the tugboat and why it was traveling at such speed. For another, the bodies were apparently intertwined when salvaged, which led to conjectures (unprintable by the *Picayune*) as to what the two were doing out on the river at that hour. As for the barge, it was plying its way upstream in its assigned lane when struck. It escaped unscathed, except for a couple of barrels which fell overboard.

In the end, adhering to the official line, the paper did not go out on flimsy limbs.

Rather, it wrote: "Richard Carrollton, thirty-three, the only son of Harold and Helen Carrollton, a war veteran, and a financial officer at the family-owned shipping business, died in a tugboat collision with a barge the evening of Sept. 27. He left behind his wife and childhood sweetheart, Claire Endicott. The tug's captain, Wayne Ferrell, thirty-nine, was an experienced sailor, who had worked for the Carrollton Co. for a decade. He had no known relatives."

Despite the sorry state of her marriage, Claire was distraught. Whatever his psychic wounds and character weaknesses, Richard had been a steadfast childhood companion. He did not deserve such a fate. She walked around the house like a zombie, oblivious to bouts of morning sickness, rarely venturing out.

It took Myra and Bernice, who both came to the funeral, to drag her out to dinner ten days later.

"You owe it to Richard—and to Tom too—to make this pregnancy a happy thing, Claire," Myra said.

"The baby is yours, Claire. The math makes it possible for people to think whatever makes them happy. You didn't get to tell Richard, but if I calculate rightly, the baby could in theory be his," Bernice added.

More brutally, the two friends pointed fingers at both sets of parents. "They got you into this and kept you from committing openly to Tom. Let them each take what they will from this."

Claire listened in silence.

In parting, Myra added, "Whatever else, you need to stop berating yourself. Concentrate on having a happy, healthy baby."

The clock ticked on. On October 20, she told her parents that she was three months pregnant.

"That settles that," her father blurted out, his meaning open to interpretation.

Momentarily dumbfounded, her mother soon broke into a smile. "That's wonderful news, my dear. Whatever we can do to facilitate, we shall do it with open arms."

The very next day, Claire steeled herself to go over to the Carrolltons' home. Heavy velvet drapes still blacked out the front windows. Taking a deep breath, she tapped the bell, twice in succession.

Once inside, she dispensed with niceties.

"I wanted you both to know, directly from me, that I am pregnant. Everything is fine in that regard."

For an instant there was stunned silence. Claire could make out faint music in the distance.

"You might have seen fit to do this much sooner," Harold sputtered. "Might have saved your husband from spiraling out of control."

"How dare you, Harold. Whatever else has befallen us, a baby is to be welcomed," Helen snapped back. Her face was contorted by anger.

Claire looked from one to the other, words for the moment beyond her.

"I, I misspoke, Claire. I'm sure you did what you could," Harold found a way to mumble, his voice a tremolo.

"Richard was a wonderful person in many ways. That will not be erased by anything said or done. By anyone," Claire replied, pointedly.

So chastised, Harold lowered his eyes, and held his tongue.

Helen walked Claire to the front door and out to the porch. "Never mind him, dear. You are not to blame. In fact, you deserve to retake your life."

Claire's eyes were now glassy. She had braced herself for the couple's coldness, even their suspicions, but not for Helen's sympathy. She gave her mother-in-law a spontaneous hug, something she had never done before.

"Now, now," the older woman said, caressing Claire's damp cheek. "Babies help move us beyond sorrow. Of all sorts. We shall look forward to that."

Chapter Thirty-Nine
TIMING IS ALL

They did find joy in new beginnings.

A baby girl was born to Claire in the spring of 1948, right as the azaleas, snapdragons and larkspur burst forth all over the city.

By all accounts, April Elizabeth Carrollton came into the world as a flower herself, with tiny sprigs of blond hair, emerald eyes, and the fairest of complexions.

If any of the grandparents peered closely into her cradle, they might have concluded that the infant did recall her father's mouth, or forehead, or cheek bones—or not. But no one felt inclined to voice an opinion one way or the other.

Claire decided to herald a fresh start, by giving her daughter such a spring-like first name, and to honor both her mother and mother-in-law by bestowing on her child the same middle name both grandmothers shared.

Born slightly ahead of schedule, on the fifteenth of April, the baby was kept in the hospital for a couple of extra days. But doctors were soon pleased enough, discharging her and her mother to much fanfare from the nurses and assorted well-wishers.

Bernice and Teresa came for a viewing soon after, as did Lucille Truard, Lena Walenska (along with newly transplanted Stefan Schmidt), and the elder Kaminskys.

In June, Myra and Frederick flew down from New York for the summer, he to work on his next novel and she to study for the Louisiana bar exam.

Would they be moving back to the state? It was still unclear.

The two old friends sat up late one night after April had fallen asleep to go over the one issue that remained.

"If we're going to wrestle with this, it may as well be with wine, cheese, and fresh fruit," Claire said. She went to the kitchen and soon brought out a tray of treats.

They toasted the baby, Frederick's latest achievements, and the good health and renewed spirits of all the parents and relatives involved.

"Just one thing left. But crucial."

Claire nodded, knowing what was to come.

"What are you going to tell Tom—and why haven't you already?" Myra asked.

Taking a deep breath, Claire did her best to explain.

"You can only imagine how much I've gone back and forth on this," she began, "but life keeps getting in the way."

"How so?" Myra asked, not letting her off the hook.

"I told Tom soon enough about Richard's accident, about which he was genuinely sorry. He did not in any way pressure me. And then, for so many months thereafter, I wasn't able to think or do much of anything. The pregnancy became my only delight."

"Still, Claire, he has a right to know the child is his."

"Indisputably. But, as it turned out, two things that have happened over there in Germany stymied me."

"What do you mean? I thought his contract with the Army was winding down. That the Marshall Plan was soon to kick in, bringing over its own people."

"Yes, but unfortunately, his mother's health began to deteriorate. If I've read him rightly, she hasn't much longer to live. I did not want to burden him." Claire paused and took a sip of wine.

"You said two things."

"Out of the blue, Tom let on that he had located the where-abouts of his long-lost love, Katrin, living apparently in Lisbon."

Myra's mouth fell open. "You're talking about the girl he went to meet off that ship in Havana. All those years ago?" Claire nodded her head in the affirmative. "But surely—"

"Nothing is surely so in this life, is it? I shall have to give this time. I do not want the child to be a pawn in this thing, turning it into a game."

"You're saying the next move is his, as it were?"

"You could put it that way. I'm here, he's there, and the baby is my main concern."

Myra hesitated but then plowed ahead. "But you will manage on other fronts, right? Between your parents and his parents. You are after all a widow."

"Obviously, I want them to have a relationship with April, and I suspect they'll be helpful when needed. Harold has hinted there may be a reasonable insurance settlement, but I am not counting on that."

Myra rolled her eyes, having picked up that Richard's father had not been a supportive figure either during his son's time in the Pacific or thereafter. As a soon-to-be lawyer, she wondered in whose pocket the insurance payout would end up. Likely not Claire's, she figured. She kept that thought to herself.

After a little more time, Claire returned to the subject.

"I know what you're thinking in that brainy head of yours, but things will work out. If all goes well with April, I may in the new year, go back, part-time, to Intelligence. Commander Lassiter has made me quite an offer. Much of the work, it seems, I can do from home. And it sounds interesting."

ELIZABETH GUIDER

"Excellent. One more reason for Fred and me to move back here. Actually, two reasons!" Myra said, swiveling her head toward the baby's room where all was peaceful.

Chapter Forty

THE VERY THOUGHT OF YOU

L ena Walenska surprised herself. She had never entertained the idea of marriage until the day Stefan carefully placed his violin on the Steinway in her music room. They had just rehearsed a Mozart piano and violin concerto for the umpteenth fundraiser for European war refugees. She was penciling in notes on the score when he cleared his throat.

"We can go over this later, my dear, but something has suddenly possessed me," Stefan announced.

Lena looked up. "*Avanti,*" she said, the two having for the thirty years of their intermittent collaboration, and ardent friendship, conversed in a mélange of languages. Whether that made for greater or lesser communication remained an open question.

"Now that the war is behind us, and we are entering a new era— hopefully one of peace and harmony, indeed, of music everywhere— I believe that we should join forces."

Stefan paused to keep from getting tangled up in his preamble.

Lena looked puzzled. "Out with it, Stefan. Does my playing lack lilt or what? You have rarely been satisfied with interpretations of Mozart, mine, arguably least of all."

Now he looked flustered. "*Pas du tout, ma chère.* I merely wanted to say that the hour has come."

She looked more befuddled. "Should I take it you want to ditch Mozart and start from scratch with Beethoven or, heaven forbid, Rachmaninoff?"

"You misconstrue my tone. I wish to place a ring upon your finger and make of you my wife." At this, Lena did look as though she could be knocked off her stool with a proverbial feather. "My request requires your assent."

Divested of this roundabout proposal, Stefan placed himself in the nearby armchair to await an answer.

Not normally flabbergasted, Lena paused to regain her composure and consider the options. If memory served, she had never fantasized about such a commitment—not since that brief gaudy hour in Warsaw when she thought she loved Konrad Kaminsky enough to forego her dream of becoming a concert pianist. But here she was now, in her fifties, and albeit surrounded by a trio of Kaminskys, a respectable number of friends and colleagues, and oodles of students, she often felt twinges of loneliness.

To delay an immediate response, she stared out the back window. The calico that Myra and Claire had given her was chasing a squirrel up the oak tree, the azaleas were popping out, and birds were chirping. The bench under the tree had been painted—(who precisely had done it she had no idea, but it was inviting enough now to sit two).

And thus, why not?

Stefan was more than a special friend, however casually she flung out the term. His love of music had seen him through the war, as presumably had his memories of her. As soon as bidden, he found his way to her in Paris, and then across the ocean to a wholly unexpected life in New Orleans.

"*Mais oui, mon amour. Pourquoi pas?*" she responded.

They set the date for a weekend in June, a small private affair at home.

And, as was her longtime practice, Lena sent out wedding invitations to all those in her address book who had not been determined to have died during or because of the war.

Once again, Myra suggested one should go out to Tom Stone in Berlin as well. At the bottom of the formal invitation, Lena wrote: "We trust you can come, Tom. You are much missed by all concerned."

"I recognize you from the photo. It is you, Tomas, right?" Katrin asked, the slightest of tremors in her voice. She had shown up at the work site on *Unter den Linden* in the heart of old Berlin. A couple of stately municipal buildings were finally being repaired.

Tom was bent over a table with an array of tools, jotting down specifications for the next phase of the project. The façade would never be the same after the bombing, but the team was doing its best to respect the lines, if not the ornamentation, of the originals.

He looked up into a face that for an instant threw him. A youngish woman, but her features were weathered, her hair wispy, her demeanor tentative. He put down the drawing pen he was holding and blinked into the morning sunshine.

"*Ya*, it's me, Katrin Kleindorf. I realized you were here from the newspaper. Working for the Americans, an architect now." She widened her eyes to suggest she was impressed, though whether because of his professional attainment or because he was alive was unclear.

"I thought you—"

Her face twitched. To recount the past was best done quickly, without dwelling. "No, no. I drew a lucky number when that ship docked, all things considered. Sent to Belgium, then I hid somewhere in France, then—it doesn't matter now—finally to Lisbon."

"Yes, it is what I hoped for you," Tomas responded. He refrained from mentioning the conversation he had overheard in Lübeck more than a year ago.

They stood there awkwardly, neither knowing what else needed to be verbalized. A few workmen approached the bench for further instructions, but settled for cigarettes since their American supervisor was otherwise occupied.

Katrin's eyes darted about, wary. Hardly unusual, Tom thought. Most female Berliners he had encountered over the past two years were similarly skittish. He suspected they had reason to be.

"You're busy. I am lodged in Charlottenburg for a spell." She dug into the pocket of her faded skirt and pulled out a piece of paper. "My address, if and when you'd like to talk. About whatever."

He took the slip of paper from her hand. It was thinner than he remembered. Blue veins were prominent. "I would like that. As soon as I can manage to get away."

At this point, Katrin hesitated, as though she had more to say. He looked at her inquiringly. Her eyes were still sky blue but the sparkle that had once warmed him was no longer there. A lot of things were duller now thanks to the war, he reckoned.

Smiling wanly, Katrin inclined her head, and walked away. Tom turned back to his worktable, too discombobulated to watch her steps recede.

For several days, Tom debated whether to follow up on the invitation. Their long-ago romance had vanished but, he reasoned, Katrin was still his childhood friend and deserved to know as much as he could impart about those dear to them both. Principally about Hans.

Thus, the two did meet for coffee a few weeks later not far from her lodgings. Rather than recount the particulars of the submarine disaster, Tom brought along the letter from Major Thompson that summed up what had befallen Hans and his U-boat. She blinked back tears as she read it, swallowed hard, then shook her head.

"Poor Hans. His love for me only went so far and could not get beyond the crucial hindrance. Being Jewish was a bridge too far."

"He did not deserve you, Katrin. That is indisputable."

"That thought will sustain me for many a year to come, Tomas," she replied, her voice touchingly wistful.

They turned to other things. He described how he had miraculously located his mother, and his enjoyment of her company until her death at the end of 1948. On a lighter note, he spoke of his serendipitous encounter with her long-ago piano teacher, a Madame Walenska, in New Orleans, his affair with a lovely young woman from that city, and the absurdity of ending up in a detention camp for enemy aliens in a place called North Dakota.

To make her smile, he exaggerated the high jinks during his internment and the good people he had bonded with there. To reciprocate, she told him of her escapes from the *Gestapo* and her eventual safe haven in Lisbon where—she blushed to reveal—she was "befriended" by a widower, a prosperous tavern owner in the city.

"He makes me laugh, Tomas, like we only ever laughed as children. You do remember such times, do you not?"

"Of course I do. Sounds like you should return to this man as soon as you can."

"And you too, Tomas. Surely, not even the U.S. Army should keep you here if such a lovely woman is waiting for you in New Orleans."

"*Touché*. I think we can each now do what we are destined to do."

Katrin cracked the slightly askew smile Tom remembered from their youth. He placed a gentle kiss on her forehead and took his leave.

His contract with the American forces at an end, and Lena Walenska's wedding invitation in his luggage, Tom left the land of his birth in better shape than he had found it. From what he could tell, the newly implemented Marshall Plan had a good chance of accelerating the recovery.

The U.S. Army flew him in a cargo plane back to Long Island, where he reveled in the sights and sounds of New York City for a few days. To cap things off, he took the ferry across the Hudson River to Hoboken, New Jersey.

His old friend, Gunther Gersh, now married to his girlfriend of yore and with a three-year-old son, was ecstatic to see him.

"Thanks to you, Tom, I did go back to college to finish that degree. Not only do I teach math at the high school here, but I'm working on a master's in the city. It's not Princeton but it'll do."

The two even managed a chess game, while Helga made dinner and tended to little Thomas Albert Gersh. "I'll introduce him to the queen's gambit as soon as he turns four—and we'll go from there. But that means you have to agree to teach him a few of your moves in years to come."

Touched by the request, Tom readily assented.

From Penn Station the next afternoon, Tom boarded a train west to St Louis where he spent a few days with Dieter and Ingrid Benz. They had built a home in one of the suburbs springing up around the city. Nowadays, Dieter alternated construction work with honky-tonk piano on Saturday nights and hymn-playing on Sunday morning. Tired of sitting at home, Ingrid had gone back to work at the veterans hospital. They dragged Tom along to a party to celebrate a number of staff promotions.

"You won't be bored," Dieter said. "I'm part of the swing band they hired. I saw you cut a rug, as they say, back at Fort Lincoln."

Tom did dance a few numbers, until, that is, his gaze alighted on an older woman at a table nearby. She had several medals pinned to her suit. Something about her...

During a break, he wandered over.

The seated woman looked up, squinting at the young man before it dawned on her.

"You're that unfortunate German! The one Myra befriended back in '43. How is it that you are here, in this city, in this place?" the usually phlegmatic head of hospital operations asked.

Equally as nonplussed, Tom came out with the first thing that crossed his mind. "Now I remember. The WAC that worked in Myra's office. If it weren't for that detention camp they sent me to, I would not have met Dieter or Ingrid, and would not be here."

"Doris Mackie."

"Tom Stone."

An hour went by as the two caught each other up on their lives since that fleeting encounter at Camp Claiborne. She had gone to France for the final months of the war, helping out in Berlin until the end of '45. He went from detainee in North Dakota to Army liaison in Berlin almost overnight.

Raising their beer mugs, they toasted their good fortune and their mutual friends.

When Doris learned he was headed back to Louisiana, she asked Tom to pass along her greetings to Myra.

"You'd be pleased. She's now married to a childhood friend. He's a successful writer. She's now a lawyer, much in demand."

"Exactly what I would have augured for her. Any children?"

"Not that I know of."

"And her good friend, Claire somebody or other. What became of her?"

"That, Major Mackie, is what I'm going there to find out."

On the train from St Louis to New Orleans, Tom newly puzzled over the last letter Claire had written him. It had arrived in Berlin shortly after Lena's wedding invitation. It simply read:

Come back to us.

The word "*us*" troubled him. Did Claire mean her circle of friends— Myra, Bernice, Lena, and Lucille, as well as her parents. Perhaps even that cat. Or was Claire signaling some sort of distance from him?

He had to know, once and for all.

Without advance notice, Tom showed up at Claire's front door on a late afternoon. A gold plate on the mailbox still read *The*

Carrolltons. It had been two years since his tryst with her in Paris, and almost that long since her husband Richard had drowned.

Tom swallowed hard and knocked.

After an interminable minute, the heavy front door opened. Claire stood there in front of him, more radiant than he remembered. She took his hands in hers. He drew her to him. Words could wait.

When they broke apart, Tom gazed deep into her eyes. Questioning her.

"Yes, it is as you suspected. I do have something to tell you. Or better, to show you. It can wait no longer."

Upstairs in her crib, April was waking up. One eye flicked open, then the other. They were sea-green, with a hint of gray mist. His own, identical, widened in astonishment.

"Why ever did you not tell me? I mean, as soon as you knew."

"Our lives had diverged, Tom. You had people and things to tend to over there, as I did here. Somehow, I knew the time would come."

"And her name?"

"April. She was born on the fifteenth of that month, precisely nine months after we parted Paris."

"And now, Claire? Might we finally—or rather, can I hope her last name, as well as yours, can soon be amended to include my own?"

"If that is what you still want, then it shall be so."

"It is what I have come home for. More than ever, it is what I want," Tom said.

Smiling, Claire reached into the crib and picked up the baby. Once April's eyes focused on her face, she spoke softly yet firmly, her voice rich with emotion. "Your father has come home, April, and we're all going to be together for a long, long time."

Epilogue

2001

April Stone stepped out into the blazing sun of the New York summer and headed straight to Central Park to eat her lunch and call her parents. A squib she had happened upon that morning in the *Times* had caught her eye—something both her mother and her father would want to know about.

She had another reason to call as well but planned to drop that in as casually as possible. The last thing she wanted either of her parents to do was stew over her love life. She was fifty-three, for God's sake, and did not need to be fretted over. Without ceremony, she unwrapped the crabmeat sandwich from her favorite deli on 57th St., not a block from her corner office in the gleaming IBM tower. After a bite or two, she snapped off the tab of her Ginger Ale.

In addition to other business-attired folk taking their midday break, joggers, dog-walkers, skaters, students, a couple of musicians, panhandlers, and countless tourists were all out and about.

And why not? It was another picture-perfect day in the greatest city in the world.

As ever, April basked in the energy of the place. And in her newfound happiness. Were her latest love affair to last, she would take the man in question to meet her parents—a math professor at Princeton, of German origin. "Like Einstein," he had told her self-deprecatingly. September in New Orleans would be an ideal time to introduce him.

First things first.

The *Times* had reported the discovery of that German submarine her mother had talked about all those years ago. It turned out the only one the U.S. Navy had managed to sink in the Gulf—and, of all things, it was the very one her father's childhood friend, Hans somebody, had commanded. Almost sixty years ago.

She had no idea how either of her parents would react to this news. The war had been a tumultuous thing for the two of them. So too their love for each other while apart and their lives together, and with her, thereafter.

Now her parents were old—very old. It was her turn in life to fret over them.

April pulled out her BlackBerry from her shoulder bag and hit the first number on her speed dial.

After three rings, her father picked up. He sounded chipper; she could relax.

"No, no. I'm fine, Dad. On my lunch break, sitting outside in the park. And you two?"

"Your mother went out for a hastily arranged lunch nearby with Bernice. Myra is joining them as well. Some breath-taking news going back to the war."

"I think I know why, Dad. In fact, it was in the paper here."

"I don't follow."

"That German submarine, U-boat 166. They found it by accident, on the bottom of the Gulf, not far from the *Robert E Lee*. You know, the passenger ship it had torpedoed."

Silence at the other end. She could make out the faint strains of violins in the background.

"*Verstehst du*, Dad?" April asked, reverting as she often did to his native language.

"Yes, I understand. But are you sure it's the one?"

"Number 166 is the one your friend Hans was on, right?"

"*Ja, ja.*" Tom's voice trailed off.

She sensed wistfulness, or regret, in his voice. For all the things that had happened to her father during the war, she imagined, and to which he and her mother now rarely alluded.

For an instant, April felt like a child again, sensitive to every minimal mood change in her parents. They were complicated people, and she loved them to distraction.

Tom and Claire Stone had been, as far as April could tell, inordinately committed to each other for the last fifty years. What the one would do without the other, she shuddered to think.

"So, sweetheart, did they say what would become of the wreckage? There were many men aboard. All of them..."

"It'll be designated a military grave site. Salvaging will be *verboten.*"

"As it should be," Tom replied.

Again, there was silence except for the music. It sounded like Bach.

"You said you had something else to tell us, April."

"I did, but it can wait. Until mother gets home. I think you'll both be pleased, as long as you don't go overboard."

"Ah, well, we'll look forward to that. And to your next visit. Soon, we hope."

"I will take a long weekend in early September. And bring someone. His name is Thomas. Quite accomplished, actually. Even plays chess."

"*Wunderbar.* Love you. Call us back this evening. We'll both want to hear all about him. And when you come, stay as long as you can."

Acknowledgments

I have many people to thank and myriad sources to recognize in putting this story of the home front during World War II together. To begin with are my parents, who were of the greatest generation as well as being great parents. Like so many, they did not dwell on their war-time experiences but rather on living their (blessedly) long lives thereafter. Still, once in a blue moon, my father referred to his four years spent at the European front. Also, he kept a journal during the Italian campaign which boasted specificity, humor and insight. As for my mother, she married my father three weeks after Pearl Harbor, then returned to her hometown of New Orleans and worked for Naval Intelligence. In her ninth decade, she occasionally spoke about that period. Snippets, but they stuck with me. In short, my parents' recollections were a springboard.

From there, I read some wartime fiction—including the entertaining and informative novels of Alan Furst and Joseph Kanon as well as recent bestsellers by Anthony Doerr, Kristen Hannah and Kelly Rimmer, among others. Also, I consulted nonfiction accounts including masterful ones by Alistair Cook (The American Home Front), Anthony Bevor (The Second World War), Robert Kee (1939: The World They Left Behind), Stephen Ambrose (Band of Brothers), Doris Kearns Goodwin (No Ordinary Time), Liza Mundy (Code Girls), William Klingaman (The Darkest Year), Mary Lou Widmer (New Orleans in the Forties), James Holland (The Battle for Italy), and Art Shaw and Robert Wise (82 Days on Okinawa).

In focusing on the home front, I also found much to orient and inspire me in Steven Spielberg's series on the war in the Pacific, Ken Burns' doc series "America and the Holocaust," Rachel Maddow's podcast "Déjà Vu" and bestseller, Prequel, the on-site exhibits and web resources of the World War II Museum in New Orleans, items of goings-on in New Orleans during that period published in the Times-Picayune 150th commemorative issue, and photos and commentary from the website, "New Orleans Uncovered."

Naturally, since this is a work of fiction, I dramatized, and took necessary liberties with, several real-life incidents Stateside and abroad that impacted my characters.

Regarding the tragedy of the Jewish refugees on the ill-fated ship, the St Louis, in 1939, I am indebted to a 1967 work by historian and broadcaster Arthur Morse called While Six Million Died, a recent BBC radio play about the tragedy by Tom Stoppard, and a number of newspaper reports of the time; for the Lee Street Riot in Alexandria, LA, in 1942, I was aided by a recent account by Matthew Teutasch on the online platform, Medium; for the sinking of the German U-Boat 166 in the Gulf of Mexico in summer 1942, I utilized several online resources, including from the Museum of the US Navy, and did similarly for the friendly-fire disaster of Lübeck Bay in 1945, along with a BBC doc called "Berlin 1945."

To get a sense of the detention camps for so-called enemy aliens interred by the U.S, government during the war, I turned to NationalArchives.gov and to WarHistoryOnline.org as well as to several YouTube videos of the actual facilities housing German-born immigrants and others suspected of Nazi collaboration.

I utilized excerpts from poems in the novel: WWI poet Laurence Binyon's "For the Fallen"; Rainer Maria Rilke's "Love Song"; and Shakespeare's sonnet "When in Disgrace with Fortune and Men's Eyes."

Regarding the photographs used to introduce each of the four parts of the novel, they are all part of Guider family memorabilia.

Finally, I am grateful for friends and colleagues who encouraged me with their advice, insights or research suggestions, including

Kenith G. Trodd, Sheri Schott, Linda T. Parker, Patricia Frith, Neil Gader, Dannie C. Weatherly, Judi Dickinson, Wendy Oberman, Virginia S. Miller, Giovanni Troianiello, Linda H. Guider, Fred Pajerski and Suzy Arthur.

Many thanks too for the expertise and patience of my publisher Laura Ranger, editor Andrew Burt, cover designer Dawné Dominique, marketing specialist Susan Pierce, and formatter Bella Roccaforte.

About the Author

Elizabeth Guider is a longtime journalist and more recently a novelist who has lived and worked in Rome, Paris and London as well as in New York and Los Angeles. Born in the American South, she holds a doctorate in Renaissance Studies from New York University.

During the late 1970s she was based in Rome where she taught English and America literature at the college level and where much of the action of her first fictional work, The Passionate Palazzo, takes place.

While in Europe she also worked as an editor for the International Daily News in Rome, a freelancer for several magazines and as an entertainment reporter for the show-business newspaper Variety.

Elizabeth also traveled widely, reporting on the politics and technological changes roiling media from Eastern Europe to Hong Kong as well as covering film festivals and media trade shows in Cannes, Monte Carlo, Venice, Milan, Berlin, Prague and Moscow. She served on various film juries, the International Emmys judging committee in New York, and the Peabody Board in Athens, GA. Over the years she has moderated numerous industry-sponsored panels with entertainment executives, both stateside and abroad, and won several media awards while working for the trade papers in Hollywood.

After moving back to the U.S. in the 1990s, she specialized in the burgeoning TV industry and eventually held top editor positions at Variety and latterly at The Hollywood Reporter, including executive editor at Variety and editor-in-chief at THR. More recently, she has freelanced for the magazine World Screen as senior contributing editor.

Elizabeth divides her time between Los Angeles where she freelances, and Vicksburg, Mississippi, where she grew up and where she focuses on her fiction. Her second novel, Milk and Honey on the Other Side, an inter-racial love story set in the post-WWI period, is set largely in Vicksburg. Her third novel, Connections, a family saga that spans fifty years, takes the reader from Atlanta to New York City and Hollywood, and eventually to South America. Her fourth, Our Long Love's Day, is an unflinching portrait of a divorce between two academics who struggle to pick up the pieces and find new meaning in their lives. Her fifth, The Casserole Courtship, written and set during the Covid pandemic, follows three women who pursue a recent widower on the California coast. This Nearly Was Ours is her sixth novel.

More from Foundations - The Courtship Caserole - A Shell Beach Novel

www.FoundationsBooks.net

Get it Here: https://www.amazon.com/Casserole-Courtship-Shell-Beach-Novel-ebook/dp/B0BKKT1Z8W

A recent widowed lawyer is pursued by three formidable but very different women.

Each has something tantalizing to offer him...

All of them can cook up a storm.

Casseroles become their calling cards. Since his own wife never bothered herself in the kitchen, the widower is needy enough to savor their dishes but wary about where their overtures might lead. Unintended miscues and mishaps ensue. For him, rejoining the circle of life becomes a dizzying, if much desired, prospect.

For the women, the pursuit becomes an unexpected journey to empowerment. This wry and wistful take on second chances is full of engaging characters who, in midlife, find themselves longing for new purpose - and more specifically, a lasting relationship.

From across the country, the widower's grown children cast a watchful eye on their father's entanglements but are eventually drawn westward into this enticing family of strangers. And, once the pandemic takes hold, twists and turns accelerate until, crisis resolved, the main characters find who or what most matters.

Set on the shores of California's Central Coast, crucial discoveries come to light. Including how little the widower knew about his deceased wife...

...and a mysterious musician that lives along the boardwalk.

Foundations Book Publishing

Our mission is to exceed the expectations of our authors and the reading community with an uncompromising commitment to quality, individualism and personal pride. We measure our success one book at a time.

You can find more great works in multiple genres including Romance, Literary Fictions, Thrillers, Suspense, Young Adult, and more!

Visit us at FoundationsBooks.net

Made in the USA
Monee, IL
30 December 2024

72537400R00243